THE MEDUSA COMPLEX

Also by Marvin H. Albert

The Gargoyle Conspiracy
The Dark Goddess
Hidden Lives

THE MEDUSA COMPLEX

A Novel by

Marvin H. Albert

ARBOR HOUSE
New York

 Published in the United States of America by Arbor House Publishing Company and in Canada by Fitzhenry & Whiteside, Ltd.

This book is printed on acid free paper. The paper in this book meets the guidelines for permanence and durability of the Committee on Production Guidelines for Book Longevity of the Council on Library Resources.

Library of Congress Catalog Card Number: 81-66972

ISBN: 0-87795-341-4

10 9 8 7 6 5 4 3 2 1

For my daughter Jan and my son David

Contents

I

THE MAN FROM THE MONASTERY

ONE

PRAGUE

COLONEL VASIL Kopacka awoke precisely two hours before he was due at the Monastery. He awoke still convinced that the conclusion he had submitted to his superiors was correct; the problem that was to be the subject of today's meeting could only be solved through the death of Senator Frank DeLucca, chairman of the United States Senate's Committee on Governmental Affairs.

Outside Kopacka's bedroom window Prague lay under a low shroud of early morning fog. He switched on lamps as he went to the bathroom to shower and shave. Returning to his bedroom he put on the dark gray suit he always wore to the Monastery, then entered the kitchen and made his usual breakfast of bacon and eggs, toast and tea. This morning he ate automatically, hardly tasting any of it, gripped by an increasing tension about the meeting now less than two hours ahead when he would finally learn Moscow's verdict on his report.

Vasil Kopacka was a tall, painfully thin man with the ravaged face of an insomniac and the concentrated energies of a compulsive worker. The perfect technocrat—he knew that he was what others considered him. Well, he took pride in it. In the modern world, communist or capitalist, no system could function without men like him.

There were those who regarded technocrats as no more than robots.

That was certainly not true of Colonel Vasil Kopacka. No computer brain could cope with the abrupt dangers and unexpected difficulties inherent in his job, especially when that job took him out into the West. It required an innovative, inventive mind, and a sharp sense of intuition.

He knew also that some people thought of him as a cold, lonely man. That was not true either. The reason he was always more fulfilled when he was outside in hostile territory was an emotional one . . . there could be no human relationship closer, deeper and more fulfilling than the kind which grew between a case officer and an agent he managed in the field.

It was this personal involvement, as well as professional conviction, that fueled his anxiety about the decision that would be delivered at the Monastery this day.

Colonel Kopacka lived in the heart of the Czechoslovakian capital, not far from Wenceslas Square. It was a small apartment, utilitarian, sufficient for his needs; he was, after all, away from Prague more than he was here. His daughter lived with a boyfriend in Warsaw, where she attended the best school of sculpture in the Soviet sphere, and he had not seen her in two years. His wife had left long ago.

The noise of early-morning traffic was just starting outside when Kopacka finished his solitary breakfast and put on his raincoat and hat. He picked up the framed photograph of his daughter and kissed it before going out. There was no picture of his wife. He could hardly remember what she'd looked like and he preferred it that way.

Leaving the building he strode through a muggy, misty drizzle, crossing the Charles Bridge and heading in the direction of the Monastery. He always followed the same route, taking the familiar crooked streets through the Old Town's historic jumble of romanesque, gothic, baroque and renaissance buildings.

The thick-walled building complex that Colonel Vasil Kopacka entered when he reached the destination of his early-morning hike was still referred to as the Monastery. Perhaps the old name clung because those who worked inside retained a number of monkish attributes: an unswerving secular faith to match any religion, absolute dedication to whatever tasks were assigned and an abhorrence of heretics. The Monastery was the headquarters of the First Section of the Czech Intelligence Directorate: the *Statui Tajna Bezpecnost*— usually shortened to the initials STB.

CZECHOSLOVAKIA IS A small country formed by the joining of Bohemia, Moravia and Slovakia, and has often had difficulty holding the three parts together. It has never been a major world power and never had an intelligence department worth the name until the task of creating one was given to a young infantry officer named Frantisek Moravec in 1929.

Considering his meager resources, Moravec decided to concentrate his efforts on the building up of a small espionage network of carefully selected agents strategically planted inside nations that might become his country's future enemies. His methods paid off. By the mid-1930s Moravec had risen to the rank of general and was receiving details of Nazi war plans from sources close to Hitler himself, plans which he passed on to the governments of France and England. They, in their wisdom, shrugged off his warnings and learned their mistake when Hitler struck—in exactly the fashion he had predicted.

When the Nazis took over his country General Moravec fled to London. Most of his small espionage network was still intact, and through the remainder of the war he used it to supply British Intelligence with some of its most accurate information. He also arranged the most spectacular resistance assassination of the war: the killing of the man Hitler had put in charge of Czechoslovakia, Reinhart Heydrich.

With the war's end General Moravec returned to Prague but when Russia took over he fled again—this time to Washington, where he worked as a Pentagon advisor until his death. His methods, however, continued to be followed by the STB under communist rule.

Nothing was planned inside the Monastery without the advice and consent of resident supervisors from Moscow's KGB. The much smaller STB, however, had earned a unique reputation of its own by concentrating—as General Moravec did—on placing well-chosen and carefully camouflaged agents in strategic positions abroad. The Czech success in this could not be matched by the KGB nor by the espionage networks of any of Russia's other satellites. . . .

VASIL KOPACKA HAD been a young neophyte courier for General Moravec in the last years of the war. He survived without a scratch the purges that decimated Czech Intelligence after Moravec fled to Washington, as he survived subsequent purges of the STB that came with each Czech political crisis. He survived and indeed thrived because he never became involved with internal power struggles and had absolutely no personal loyalty to any political leader, thereby not suffering when one of them was toppled by a charge of renegade revisionism.

This determined lack of involvement at home base was a counterpoint to the depth of his loyalty and concern for his field agents abroad. The importance of establishing these relationships was a lesson from his early days in espionage, learned from an agent who had been operating on his own in Bangkok for several years. The case officer who had been running that agent had become ill back home, and Kopacka had been sent out to take his place. He had first gone to the agent's secret letter-drop. The message he found inside addressed to his case officer turned out to be a suicide note . . . the agent had by then put the barrel of a shotgun in his mouth and blown his brains out.

Kopacka could still recall much of that message: "You constantly criticize the quality of my work. You claim to only be passing on the criticisms of our people back home but *you* are my only contact with them and you never provide me a word of praise, even when I have done a difficult job to the best of my ability. I live here in an alien land without a single friend. I live in a nightmare of danger and fear, and *you* are my only contact with reality, with sanity. Yet when I try to explain my dependence on you, you mock me. It leaves me with nothing to hold onto, *nothing at all . . .* "

Vasil Kopacka had absorbed that lesson and applied it when he had begun acquiring agents of his own, agents who came to know that they could depend on his understanding, judgment and concern; that he cared for each of them personally. In return they were willing to take risks for him that they would have hesitated about taking for anyone else. This mutual trust and loyalty played a major part in building Kopacka's reputation as the Monastery's best organizer of particularly difficult operations abroad—including those requiring "emergency eliminations."

Though he had occasionally been sent to the Orient to deal with especially threatening situations, most of his missions abroad had been to Europe and America. Many inside the Monastery knew this, but only two knew that these missions had finally narrowed down to operating as permanent field liaison for a single man.

This man—code-named "Gallia"—was the most important that the STB had ever managed to plant internationally. He had also become the most important person in Colonel Kopacka's life, emotionally as well as professionally. Only Kopacka was allowed personal contact with him.

In the West, where Gallia had established himself at the very highest level, his name was William Reinbold, but in the Monastery only Kopacka and the two who directed his work knew it. The files listed him only as Gallia. There was not even an indication of gender to go with the code name.

Gallia-Reinbold was, of course, not at all like the agent who had left the suicide note Kopacka had found so long ago. And Kopacka knew better than anyone how successful he had been and continued to be. But Gallia was still a human being with a normal need to have at least one other person who understood everything about him and admired what he knew. This Kopacka gave to him in full measure. Some might even have called it a kind of love.

The danger now threateing Gallia had been detailed in the report submitted by Colonel Kopacka five days earlier. The remedy he believed to be the only practical course of action at this stage had been laid out in equal detail. He now arrived at the Monastery with almost an hour to spare before he would learn if Moscow agreed with him.

Kopacka's office was part of a converted section of the main building formerly a complex of cells serving as living quarters for the monks. He settled down at his desk and methodically reread his report. It was divided into three parts. The first recapitulated the danger. It had actually begun in Washington, D.C., on the day that Senator Frank DeLucca's Committee on Governmental Affairs had turned to investigating possible contamination of American policies from two outside sources. But no one in the Monastery, not even Colonel Kopacka, had recognized the danger that far back. The direction of the committee hearings had been too generalized at first and there had seemed, at the start, to be nothing especially new about it. The initial hearings under the chairmanship of DeLucca had been concerned with the growing number of private business intelligence firms—staffed by agents who had previously been members of U.S. Intelligence and law-enforcement departments. Senator DeLucca called these agents and their private firms potential "Frankenstein Cells," created and trained by the government but no longer under its control.

DeLucca was not the first to cite the danger they posed. What became new about DeLucca's investigations as they developed was the two-pronged nature of his attack. The major employers of such private intelligence firms, the committee chairman pointed out, were powerful multinational business entities with tentacles reaching into every nation of the free world—including the United States.

Here again, though, DeLucca was not the first to be troubled by these global enterprises operating across frontiers with allegiance to no country and virtually independent of national controls, capable of toppling the governments of small countries and able to influence the stability and actions of even the largest. But Frank DeLucca had become the first to mount an effective, coordinated enquiry into both the multinational corporations and the private intelligence firms that worked for them.

Even then the Monastery had failed to foresee the dangerous direction the Senate committee might take. Vasil Kopacka blamed himself for that. The danger had finally struck home when the persistent DeLucca had decided to focus in on one such multinational corporation: Reinbold Enterprises—run by a financial manipulator of mysterious origins named William Reinbold. And at the same time, DeLucca's committee had also begun concentrating on one example of a potentially dangerous private intelligence firm—MARS Limited.

The initials stood for Management Analysts for Research and Security. Senator DeLucca redefined the words "research and security" as "business espionage and industrial sabotage." The firm had been incorporated in the Bahamas but it was directed by a former American intelligence operative named Paul Shevlin. And it was staffed by other ex-agents from various government branches—all with still-active connections within these branches.

DeLucca's investigators now suspected, though as yet they lacked sufficient hard evidence, that the main client of MARS Limited was Reinbold Enterprises. The senator had spoken of what this could mean during a television interview: "Take an outfit with the espionage know-how and government connections of Shevlin's MARS Limited. Put it together with an aggressive, shadowy, foreign-based international operator like Reinbold. What that adds up to is a synergism of a kind that we've *got* to find some way to control. Before *we* wind up being controlled by it . . . "

Of course Senator DeLucca had no way of knowing that William Reinbold was more than an overgrown business manipulator, that he was also the man known in the Czech Monastery as Gallia. And so DeLucca could not understand that his committee's investigation was getting too close to exposing a conspiracy with power and scope far greater than anything even he suspected.

The Monastery—and its masters in the Kremlin—understood too well, and had begun operations to halt or detour the direction of DeLucca's investigations some time before his speech.

The second section of Colonel Kopacka's report dealt with the failure of these attempts to block the threat to Gallia, the latest of which had still not been completed but this, too, Kopacka predicted, was certain to fail—because of the kind of man Frank DeLucca was.

The final section of the report derived from this prediction. It detailed Kopacka's projection for a final elimination of the threat, by eliminating its source: Senator DeLucca.

WHEN HE FINISHED the last page Vasil Kopacka glanced at his watch. It wasn't really necessary, his sense of time was uncanny. There were four minutes left before the scheduled meeting.

Replacing the report in its orange folder Kopacka carried it with him out of the office complex. In the Monastery's cloister the lean beech trees were dripping with rain. He circled under the shelter of the cloister's Baroque arcade and descended a Gothic stairway, its stone steps grooved by centuries of use. At the bottom a narrow, vaulted corridor led to a windowless room. It had been a crypt; now it had overhead neon lighting, an electric heater at either end and a conference table with straight-backed chairs set neatly around it.

The two men waiting for him were seated on one side of the table. Colonel Kopacka shut the door behind him, locked it and sat down at the other side facing them. He placed his report on the table. Each of the other two men had a copy of the same report in front of him. One was a barrel-chested Czech with a bald skull and careful expression:

General Rudolf Hájek, the head of the STB. The other man was a compact Russian with pockmarked cheeks, hard blue eyes and a protruding lower lip that gave him a look of pugnacious arrogance: Josef Petrov, the KGB supervisor who had taken Kopacka's report off to Moscow and had returned late the previous evening, presumably with the Kremlin's verdict.

Petrov gave Kopacka a smile that was meant to be reassuring—like a doctor, Kopacka thought, about to tell a patient he would be able to breathe just as well with a single lung—and opened his copy of the report. Kopacka saw that he had scribbled notes on the page margins. General Hájek opened his own copy. Kopacka left his closed. He knew it by heart now, almost line for line. It was Reinbold who had taught him how to do that. Reinbold, of course, was much better at it. He could commit twenty such reports to memory in any single day. But then, William Reinbold—Gallia—was, in his fashion, a genius.

Studying the first page of the report Petrov said quietly, "Colonel, Moscow is displeased by the lack of results from previous plans to halt the danger to Gallia. Your attempt to compromise Senator DeLucca's character with the voters did not work. And the most recent plan to discredit the direction of his investigation has not yet been developed to fruition . . . "

Kopacka held onto his temper—a problem that never came up in the field. These unnecessary preliminaries irritated him. "Only the first plan was mine," he said, "a low-risk attempt with a high-yield potential—"

"But which in fact yielded nothing."

"But we did not lose anything by trying. If Senator DeLucca had lost that election, our problem would no longer exist. Without him as its chairman the Senate Committee on Governmental Affairs would have turned to other matters and no longer presented a threat to Gallia. This is covered in my report. Page four."

General Hájek turned to that page, nodded. "Yes, it is." His tone was neutral, balancing loyalty to his own man with respect for Moscow's. The general was quite good at that.

Kopacka looked at Petrov. "The second plan is not mine. It was Moscow that decided to sacrifice one of your own KGB informants in Sweden in the hope of derailing Senator DeLucca's present line of investigation—"

"That sacrifice," Petrov told him, "is a small one. The Swede has outlived his usefulness to us, and has nothing to tell *about* us that will be of use to Western intelligence. And, may I remind you, we are sacrificing this Swedish spy in order to strengthen the position of your man, Shevlin."

"Paul Shevlin," Kopacka said, "is not *my* man. He has never met me, does not even know I exist. He is Gallia's man—the head of MARS—and has no reason to suspect Gallia has any connection with us."

Petrov nodded. "Your point is taken. But *my* point remains . . . Gallia informed Shevlin that the Swedish officer at NATO might be a spy for the Soviet Union—solely to reinforce Shevlin's credibility, so that Shevlin in helping to expose him will prove to the American public that he is being harrassed and persecuted by Senator DeLucca. If this has the effect we hope for, it may well discredit the senator's methods and intentions—bring his investigation to a halt before it can compromise Gallia."

The KGB man paused, then finished with: "What troubles us is that though this plan was begun, it has not been completed."

Petrov looked to General Hájek as he said this. The STB chief remained silent and expressionless. He had no intention of committing himself to either side in this exchange.

"The final move is in the hands of people we cannot control," Kopacka reminded the KGB man. "But if you will turn to page twelve of my report you will see why I believe that move can be expected soon."

Petrov turned to that page and checked his own handwritten notes next to Kopacka's typewritten paragraphs. His lower lip jutted out a bit further. "What is most disturbing here is the fact that though the final phase has not yet come, you already predict its failure."

"It *will* fail," Kopacka said. "It will accomplish nothing beyond embarrassing Senator DeLucca and creating difficulties for him with certain members of his committee. It will not *stop* him. The senator is not the sort of man who can be intimidated. Any further attempt to do so will merely stiffen his determination, and thereby *increase* the danger he poses to Gallia." Kopacka leaned back in his chair and looked Petrov into the eye. "As I have indicated, and you still seem unable to grasp, we have reached the stage where there is only one way left to stop DeLucca. To be explicit: by eliminating him."

Petrov did not like the tone Colonel Kopacka was using toward him, but he took it. Though he represented the greater power, all three men at the conference table knew his position was the most vulnerable. When higher-ups needed to push the blame for mistakes down the line, functionaries like Petrov—and even General Hájek—were expendable while a man with Kopacka's specialized skills and experience—and lack of political ambition—was hard to replace.

Petrov continued to hold his temper. "It *may* come to that," he said, "but only if our own less dangerous method fails to achieve its desired result."

Kopacka relaxed a bit. "Does Moscow agree that we should begin preparing for that eventuality now? In case?"

Petrov answered quietly. "Yes."

Kopacka resisted a smile.

General Hájek spoke again. "Which brings us to the final section of Colonel Kopacka's report. The operation which he now proposes. It's time to leave the past, I think, and turn to the future." The general turned the pages of the report in front of him.

Petrov seemed as relieved as the other two to be done with the preliminaries. Moscow, he told them, agreed with the basic premises of Colonel Kopacka's projected operation: Gallia was much too valuable to lose. Senator DeLucca represented a growing threat to Gallia. *If* DeLucca could not be stopped by other means there would be only one other way left to eliminate his threat. Eliminate him. "But this project would be a dangerous expedient. It would have to be prepared with great caution, one step at a time with each step evaluated before making the next. Above all, there must be *nothing* to be traced back to us—or to William Reinbold . . . Gallia."

"That is covered in my report," Kopacka told him. He was no longer irritated. Moscow had given the tentative go-ahead. The tension that existed among the three men at the start evaporated as they worked together for a common goal—the elimination of the threat to Gallia's cover and security, a threat even Senator DeLucca was unaware of.

The first step would be what Kopacka's report labeled a FEASIBILITY STUDY. It would be a two-pronged study. It had to pinpoint the how, where and when of the projected assassination. And a means had to be found to divert suspicion from the perpetrators and fasten the blame—believably—on someone else.

It was agreed that the feasibility study would be carried out by two people who knew Gallia only as William Reinbold, who had no idea that he was a link to anyone on this side of the Iron Curtain.

"Are you sure that neither of these two wonders where Gallia got his information about the Swede in NATO being a Soviet informant?" Petrov questioned Kopacka.

"They don't wonder," Kopacka told him, "because they assume they already know. Paul Shevlin has no reason to doubt what Gallia told him . . . that he learned about the possibility during a business discussion with a top Swedish banker who was becoming suspicious about the amounts being deposited by the informant in different accounts."

General Hájek added quietly, "A plausible explanation, considering Gallia's position in the financial world of the West."

Kopacka nodded. "Shevlin also has no reason to doubt that the man he works for—Gallia—is anything other than what he seems to everyone else in the West. No reason to imagine that there could be anyone higher than that for whom Gallia might be acting. And as for Shevlin's assistant in this matter—the Medusa—she has never even met Gallia. Her only contact to him has been through Shevlin, so she can only know what Shevlin tells her—"

Petrov cut in. "Why such an odd code name? Has it some particular significance?"

Kopacka shrugged. "Only a personal one, I believe, between Paul Shevlin and herself. Based on his interest in mythology, and something in his relationship with her that developed years before he hired her. Gallia told me that Shevlin also picked that code name to mislead anyone hearing it. Conjuring up, as it does, the image of a monster. When she is actually, I understand, an exceptionally good-looking young woman."

"I must tell you, colonel, that some in Moscow wonder about her. They are troubled that such enormous responsibility, in a matter so delicate, should be in the hands of . . . this strange, and rather frightening, girl."

Kopacka's reply: "She has never failed."

AS THEIR CONFERENCE neared its end, and the final details of the feasibility study were discussed, Josef Petrov drew another folder out from under his copy of Kopacka's report. "A new shopping list for Gallia," he explained, and handed it over to General Hájek.

The general looked at his watch before opening the folder, then went quickly through the pages of requests. Most were for data on scientific breakthroughs in Europe and the United States in microelectronics, fiber optical plasma physics and other advanced technologies. This information-wanted list had been compiled by the Soviet Union's State Committee for Science and Technology, chosen from targets suggested by such sources as the International Institute for Applied Systems Analysis in Vienna, a meeting place for scientists from different nations where each Soviet participant was a secret *gebist*—a KGB informant. Other sources included the U.S. National Technological Information Service—whose biweekly research reports revealed no scientific secrets but did contain clues about where these secrets might be. A smaller but more immediately important number of orders on the shopping list originated with the GRU, Russia's military intelligence. One order was for the latest advances in America's Manned Reusable Space Transportation System. Another was for the results of geophysical surveys carried out by Western oil companies mapping the seabeds around the North Sea and China Seas oil fields. Soviet battle plans for both outer space and under the seas had to be constantly updated. All in all, Petrov's shopping list was formidable. It was also a formidable tribute to the growing abilities of William Reinbold, the man known as Gallia.

The chief of the Czech STB glanced again at his watch. Five minutes left before his appointment with a man it would be unwise to keep waiting. General Hájek closed the folder, got to his feet and led the way out of the crypt. When they were up in the cloister he turned the shopping list over to Colonel Kopacka and told him not to leave the Monastery until they had a final talk. "I will call for you in about an hour."

Kopacka nodded and returned to his monk's cell to prepare for his trip into the West. The general shook hands with the KGB supervisor and walked off to his command suite, which took up all the Monastery's converted chapel. One end of his inner office was formed by the chapel's old stone wall. The other walls were of sound-proofed layers of metal painted the same off-white as his steel file-cabinets and desk. On one of the painted walls hung a framed portrait of Lenin. General Hájek made sure it was absolutely straight.

Two minutes later his secretary buzzed his intercom and announced that Comrade Mikhail Talgorny had arrived.

General Hájek positioned a hearty welcoming smile as he marched across the office and flung open his door. "Comrade Talgorny." He thrust out his hand. "This is indeed an honor."

Talgorny gestured for the two Russians who stood behind him in the reception room to stay there, advanced to shake the offered hand, briefly and without pressure. "Comrade General." His voice was neither warm nor cold. Neutral. He was said to order a new fur hat or a liquidation of political troublemakers in the same tone of voice. General Hájek had no difficulty in believing that. Mikhail Talgorny somehow managed to look nondescript and sinister at the same time. His clothes and manner were as drab as his voice, but the eyes behind his thick glasses seemed to hold perpetual suspicion. His tight little mouth spoke for itself.

If Petrov's shopping list was a tribute to the success of Gallia's deep penetration of the West's governments and industries, Talgorny's taking time from his two-day visit to Prague to come to the Monastery was a greater one. At fifty-six, he was the youngest member of the Kremlin's thirteen-man Politburo.

He permitted General Hájek to take his elbow and usher him into the inner office. When he sat down on the sofa against one wall he did so without leaning against its back. Talgorny had reached the top of the Soviet Union's power structure as a protégé of Suslov, the Party's chief ideologist. Like Suslov, he was an orthodox hard-liner in enforcing strict obedience within the Soviet bloc and a hawk in determining foreign policy. Talgorny was an old-fashioned ideologue—anything was permitted if it advanced the Party's purpose. General Hájek was no revisionist, but he feared this visitor from the Politburo . . . "Never feel safe around a fanatic," his father had warned him. He did not feel safe at this moment.

Talgorny was looking around the office. "Is there a listening device here?"

"Several. But I assure you they have all been turned off."

"I accept your assurance." And then: "You have just completed your meeting with Comrade Petrov, I believe."

General Hájek nodded. He was not startled that Talgorny knew of the meeting and its exact timing. Within the Politburo, Gallia was considered to be his responsibility. It was Talgorny who had pushed for acceptance of the Czech proposal for establishing Gallia at such a high level in the West. The decision Petrov had brought back with him from the Kremlin would have had to have been endorsed by him.

"Am I correct in assuming," Talgorny went on, "that you agree with Colonel Kopacka." It was a statement more than a question. "That you too believe the attempt to enhance the reputation of Gallia's man, Shevlin, and discredit Senator DeLucca through Shevlin's exposure of the Swedish informant, will fail. And that the only way to stop the senator, in the end, will be to terminate him."

"I believe," the general hedged, "that Kopacka would never suggest so drastic a solution unless he had solid reasons for such a conclusion—"

"I also assume that you concur with Kopacka on the point that the senator's removal can be carried out under the conditions we have stipulated."

Hájek said carefully, "If the feasibility study is carried out exactly as Colonel Kopacka has projected, it should succeed."

"It *must.*" Talgorny's voice was still colorless, even when emphatic. "The danger of DeLucca's Senate committee must be ended. Gallia must be freed from such close scrutiny." He looked at the general. "And as soon as he is, we wish him to conduct an extremely sensitive political-risk assessment for us . . . You will recall the Suez Crisis. How the combined forces of England, France and Israel nearly won control of the Canal and the entire area."

"Yes, indeed . . . until the Soviet Union persuaded the United States to force its allies to pull back."

"We were able to persuade the American president to do so by threatening to enter the conflict, with all the military forces at our command. The truth is that we were *not* in a position at that time to intervene. But we growled very loudly, and the American President *believed* we would go through with it. If the United States had had an equivalent of Gallia in the Soviet bloc at that time, the President would have been able to learn that we were *not* prepared to intervene . . . Now, let us reverse the situation. Purely as a theoretical exercise to determine how effective our Gallia really is. Let us say that the Soviet Union intends to establish a strong presence in Turkey, thereby finally winning for us what we have always dreamed of . . . full access to the

Mediterranean Sea, including the ability to send our atomic submarines down from the Black Sea to readiness positions at Turkish bases along the Mediterranean. I repeat, this is a purely hypothetical projection."

General Hájek's palms were perspiring. "I understand."

"If the Soviet Union were to move to achieve this," Talgorny went on, "the United States would certainly threaten us with war. We wish Gallia to assess how seriously we should take such a threat. We wish him to find out what the American contingency plans are, at this moment, for dealing with such an eventuality. In short, we must find out if the American President, who barks very loudly, would be prepared to use military force to stop our move and if the American Congress would support him in doing so. Or if they would, in the end, shy away from such a confrontation—even though it would give us the Mediterranean."

General Hájek understood that he had just heard a Politburo decision that few in the Kremlin itself knew about. A secret too great to be entrusted even to a KGB supervisor. Which was the reason for Talgorny coming here: to deliver the mission to him personally.

The general wiped his sweating palms against the sides of his trousers. "I will have Colonel Kopacka pass on your request to Gallia—"

"It is not a request, it is an order. But Gallia must not, of course, begin this mission until he is safe and can make his enquiries discreetly, without his every move under surveillance by that senatorial committee. And this means not until the matter of the committee's chairman has been disposed of."

"You may count on that, comrade."

"I do," Talgorny said, in that dreadful neutral voice.

THE BIG ANCIENT bell in the tower behind the Monastery chapel was tolling four in the afternoon when Colonel Vasil Kopacka left. A car with an STB driver took him back to his apartment and waited for him. He showered, unlocked one of his closets and selected the clothes he would wear in the West. He dressed in one set of this clothing and packed the rest in a single light suitcase. He relocked the closet, closed the window shutters and left the apartment carrying the suitcase and a briefcase he'd brought with him from the Monastery. The briefcase contained, among other things, three different passports.

The STB car took him to Ruznyě International Airport. Kopacka used his first passport, identifying him as a German, for a flight to Vienna—the first leg of his journey into the West. To Gallia.

In Vienna he switched to a French passport and a plane to Rome. It was past midnight when he checked into the room reserved for him at a comfortable little hotel two blocks from the foot of the Spanish Steps. Kopacka asked for an early wake-up call, slept soundly, but was up minutes before the porter rang his room. The porter brought him coffee and rolls and had a taxi waiting when Kopacka came down with his two pieces of luggage. The morning traffic outside was still meager when he got out at the central post office near the railroad station.

He made out two short identical telegrams: "YOUR LETTER OF THE SECOND RECEIVED MY REPLY ON WAY SIGNED IAN DIEHL."

Both were addressed to William Reinbold. Kopacka sent one to Monaco and the other to London. At one place or the other there was always someone who knew where Reinbold could be reached.

Colonel Kopacka now took another cab to the Leonardo Da Vinci Airport. He used a Dutch passport for a flight to the Côte d'Azur Airport in France.

By the time his plane was airborne, business hours had commenced in the City, London's financial center, and his telegram had been placed on the desk of a man named Phillip Martyn.

TWO

LONDON, TORONTO

THAT MORNING Martyn got off the Underground train at the Bank Station with the customary horde of men dressed, like himself, in black sobriety and carrying identical black umbrellas. Touches of flamboyance—a carnation in the lapel or *no* hat—were for those who came into the City in a Rolls. Martyn was a long way down the status ladder from that. But he was still young enough to quietly nourish hopes of upward mobility, an optimism encouraged by the extraordinary health of the City's monetary bloodstream.

On top of the Bank Station rested the full weight of the most powerful concentration of financial pumping-stations in the world. The fall of the British Empire and rise of British unemployment had not changed that. The City's banks, ship-charter market and insurance firms, all surrounding an heroic statue of Wellington astride his horse, were booming. Its Stock Exchange alone circulated more than $400 billion a year. The amount of foreign currency moved in and out of the City on an average day tallied 25 percent higher than Wall Street at its most active.

Eight exits rose up out of the Bank Station like the spokes of a wheel, with direction signs that explained part of the reason for this affluence: BANK OF ENGLAND. STOCK EXCHANGE. LLOYDS OF

LONDON. THE ROYAL EXCHANGE. THE BALTIC EXCHANGE. But equally important for the good health of the City were the many foreign banks operating there. The exit Phillip Martyn took brought him up into narrow King William Street, which contained four of them: The Banque Nationale de Paris; the Moscow Narodny Bank, Ltd., which advertised its services for the USSR's foreign trade and offered travelers checks in roubles; Italy's Banco d'Abruzzi; the Argentine Jalco Bank.

Major decisions by the boards of the latter two banks were subject to approval from William Reinbold, though he never visited either. His interests in both were handled by Sir Jerome Caslan, of Caslan, Ltd., who flew to Reinbold's headquarters in Monte Carlo once each month to present their reports and receive his orders. Sir Jerome was also currently acting as front man in Reinbold's take-over attempt of the London *Star,* a daily newspaper about to founder under accumulated debts. If the bid succeeded it would bring to nine the number of publications Reinbold Enterprises controlled in various national capitals. It would also bring to fourteen the number of companies nominally run by Caslan, Ltd.—which some years back had become a subsidiary of the Reinbold Enterprises conglomerate.

Phillip Martyn's job was to serve as liaison between Caslan and Reinbold. It was really not a very demanding job, consisting mostly of knowing where Reinbold could be located on any given day. People were always asking Martyn about the mysterious William Reinbold, but in fact he knew little more than anyone who read vague and contradictory stories about him in the popular press.

Caslan, Ltd., was housed near the rear of the Guild Church, whose posters advertised relaxation and mediation classes to teach City functionaries how to cope with stress. Martyn now entered the Caslan building and took the elevator to the top floor, where he shared an office with his secretary next to an unmarked office reserved for Reinbold, who seldom used it.

Reinbold's real headquarters was aboard a plane as he moved around the globe in one of his personal 747s—each with its paneled bedroom, office and conference room. Also a room with a solid gold bidet, for the use of obliging women on board to accommodate men Reinbold needed to impress or was pleased to impress.

On any given trip his entourage might include a former French minister, a former Malaysian general, and a former Vice-President of the United States. Or even former President. They never took part in his actual wheeling and dealing; they were along for decoration, to set the *tone* for the high-level government figures he needed to meet and influence in countries he intended to buy into or loot. . . .

As soon as Martyn stepped into his own office his secretary pointed to the desk. "Telegram for Himself. From Ian Diehl."

Neither of them had the faintest idea who Ian Diehl might be. They knew only that whenever any message arrived bearing that signature, Reinbold wished to be notified immediately. Martyn glanced at the telegram. Its wording was meaningless to him. He opened a drawer and took out his schedule of William Reinbold's movements. Some days Reinbold seemed to have vanished off the face of the earth. This was not one of them. It was right there on the schedule: Toronto, Canada.

Martyn sent a telex to the Toronto hotel listed for Reinbold, following Ian Diehl's telegram word for word, including the signature.

WILLIAM REINBOLD WAS not at his Toronto hotel when the telex arrived, having gone off during the night to Montreal. When he returned to Toronto early that morning he went directly from the airport to his scheduled meeting with the owner of the RAMDAX-Canadian Mining Company. He meant to acquire RAMDAX at a bargain-basement rate with inside data about the company's troubles obtained by various private means over the past weeks. The final piece of needed information had been acquired in Montreal the previous night from a mining engineer given a sizable bribe to tell the truth about the problems of the last job he'd done for RAMDAX.

The RAMDAX offices were in the Bank of Nova Scotia building, where Reinbold's Toronto representatives were waiting for him in the lobby. He took the elevator with them and entered the RAMDAX conference room, radiating the good will that was his usual opening move.

Actually William Reinbold was seldom in a bad mood. There was no reason for him to be. Life gave him so many fascinating toys to play with. He was a tall man in his early sixties with a rotund figure and chubby face. In the few pictures that had ever been taken of him, Reinbold looked somewhat like Hitler's blimpish Reich Marshal

Hermann Goering. Those who spent any time with him, however, eventually came to realize that he was a Goering at his most malevolent.

There was no flushed roundness to his cheeks. His flesh hung loosely, with the unhealthy, liverish gray of someone who never exercised and seldom let the rays of the sun touch him. His lips were thick, bloodless. Pale eyes peered between folds of fat. On occasion they could shine with an intense, near-feverish excitement. He did not think in terms of money. Only numbers. The calculation and manipulation of figures was his profession, his genius, his sole passion.

None of this, of course, showed in the photographs newspaper readers saw. In these Reinbold did not look like the mystery man the press compared to the late Sir Basil Zaharoff. Yet the comparison was based on certain realities . . . From 1890 through the First World War Zaharoff was an arms merchant on a scale unknown before him; sometimes fomenting wars to create an increased need for his products and manipulating governments to make sure it was his companies they bought them from. He ended with so much wealth and power that the British sovereign found it politic to bestow a knighthood on him. Yet Basil Zaharoff was not British. Exactly what country he came from, how he got his start, even his real name, were never discovered with certainty.

For William Reinbold military hardware was only one kind of product. Otherwise the similarities between the two men were remarkable . . . Reinbold's early days, like Zaharoff's, remained obscure in spite of determined digging by journalists and other investigators. He had first surfaced on the international business scene in the Middle East shortly after World War II, operating out of Beirut and Istanbul, just as Zaharoff had in the beginning. Again like Zaharoff, Reinbold preferred renting large suites or even entire floors in the better hotels to having his own home.

Reinbold claimed to be from East Germany and to have fled when the Russians took over. He did have what sounded like a Germanic accent when speaking English, French, Spanish or Italian, but other Germans detected a suggestion of some Balkan accent when he spoke what he claimed to be his native language.

He had already been operating with a respectable fortune at his disposal when the financial centers of the world began to be aware of him. One point investigation *had* established: his first fortune had been in gold, whose value he'd then hyped, rumor had it, by smuggling it to India, where it was fetching the highest price at that time. But no one could establish where he'd gotten that much gold in the first place. There was speculation that he'd looted it from Nazi hideouts at the war's end. That was one rumor which Reinbold never attempted to squelch. Much later, in 1980 when gold prices had soared astronomically in the West, Reinbold once more came up with an enormous quantity of it from an unknown source. He'd claimed it was from an unexpected strike at a mine in a remote part of Ecuador, but rival interests had sold him the mine precisely because it had run out of gold. And the government of Ecuador had no knowledge of his gold passing through the country and out of it. Where else could he have gotten it? There was one certainty: he'd gotten it cheap. The profits from his sale of it—legally, this time, on the open market—had been enough to finance a vast expansion of Reinbold Enterprises. Some mentioned one possible source: in 1979 a U.S. spy satellite had spotted indications of a huge gold strike in the Soviet Union, which already had a gold glut from other mines. But skeptics pointed out that Russia would hardly sell gold cheaply to a rampant symbol of freewheeling capitalism like Reinbold. There were other rumors about Reinbold's early days. One concerned military stores scattered around the West after the war, which Reinbold was said to have bought for a pittance and resold to Third World countries in the East. Another was that he'd increased his first fortune through bankrolling smuggling operations of morphine base from the Orient to Marseilles. There were strong indications that small banks which Reinbold had subsequently gotten his hands on—along Italy's borders with Austria, France and Switzerland—had been used by rich Italians for the illegal transfer of considerable portions of their wealth out of the country. Such funds deposited in Reinbold banks in other countries, where interest did not have to be paid to clandestine depositers, generated tremendous profits for Reinbold, who used them for his own investments.

In any case, Reinbold's origins were now far behind him. Few who mattered in the world's business centers were interested in digging up his distant past. They were too involved in trying to hitch a ride on his bandwagon, or in trying to avoid being run over by it.

The diversification of Reinbold interests continued inexorably. Currently he was in strategic metals, electronic components for military hardware, biotechnology, underseas exploration, agricultural chemicals, publishing, broadcasting, aircraft manufacture, banking, real estate, the microchip memory market, industrial diamonds, construction and mining equipment. Further appendates of Reinbold Enterprises included an investment consortium of Chinese Malaysians seeking a hedge in other countries; another of European doctors and lawyers in need of tax shelters; yet another of Iranians who'd brought their wealth out with them after the fall of the Shah. His successes with these funds, as a high-roll speculator on the New York Mercantile Exchange and London's new International Petroleum Exchange, were still making financial page headlines. The number of far-flung corporations in which Reinbold now had a stake had risen to more than two hundred, including more than sixty in which he owned the controlling shares.

About his social life, the press was also reduced to guesswork. The women he was seen with from time to time—jet-set heiresses, for the most part—tended to keep their private lives to themselves. There was speculation about why he was unmarried, about whether he was a good lover. There were rumors that when he was seen with women it was only window dressing, that he was no more interested in sex than in any other human relationship.

William Reinbold, indeed, loved what he did as he would never love a human being, or the material rewards of his success. He was like a chess master in a championship match, or an Arab trader haggling over price. The excitement was in the game itself—the reward in playing it better than any opponent.

His loyalty to those who had set him on this course could never be lost. He would always remain grateful to them . . .

He walked now into the Toronto conference room prepared to win another piece in the game, to add yet another company to his empire.

The founder and major shareholder in the RAMDAX-Canadian Mining Company, Horace Pierce, also started the meeting in a good mood, which he concealed rather well. Pierce wanted very much to rid himself of RAMDAX, for the best possible price. Since Reinbold had requested the meeting and flown halfway around the globe for it—and considering the lavishness with which Reinbold's representatives had entertained him beforehand—Pierce's expectation of getting a good offer was high.

When the meeting ended, less than one hour later, Pierce was a much older man.

In his aimiable fashion Reinbold went down the full list of everything that was wrong with RAMDAX, explaining points that not even Pierce had quite faced up to. The copper strike with which the company had started in Ontario's Algoma region had given out. The profits from that mine had been sunk into exploring other areas in an attempt to enter the booming strategic minerals market. RAMDAX stock had gone high, briefly, when it discovered titanium deposits south of Algoma at a site along Blind River. It had plunged again when it was realized that the find would take years to exploit and that the company didn't have the funds for such long-range investment. Reinbold startled Pierce by coming up with the exact amount of time and money required to exploit the Blind River site, figures obtained from the engineer in Montreal who had worked for RAMDAX until a month ago when the company had fired many of its skilled men as an economy measure.

In essence, Reinbold pointed out, RAMDAX was underfinanced and deeply in debt. It had struck lucky twice but was no longer in a position to make use of its second bit of luck. The company could only carry on if it received a massive shot of new investment. Nobody was willing to invest that much in RAMDAX under its present management, considering its past performance. These being the hard facts, Reinbold's offer for the company was so low that Pierce sat in shocked silence. Finally he mumbled that he would give the offer some thought. Reinbold said fine, and left.

What Pierce would actually do, he was certain, was to run to Consolidated Resources, Inc.—which had previously showed wary interest in buying out Pierce's controlling interest in RAMDAX. The price offered by Consolidated was low—but not as low as Reinbold's offer. Pierce would sell out to Consolidated now, at Consolidated's price.

But Reinbold Enterprises had acquired control of Consolidated two days earlier. The announcement was held up until after Pierce's panic sale of his company. Once he had RAMDAX, Reinbold would pump it up again. The Jalco Bank of Argentina and the Italian Banco d'Abruzzi would announce that they were prepared to extend development loans to RAMDAX, which action would send up its stock. Reinbold would sell out when the stock peaked—after having milked the company of all its genuine assets and sold them cheaply to another of his subsidiaries.

At which point the two banks would quietly withdraw their loan offers. . . .

Knowing nothing of this, Reinbold's Toronto representatives climbed into their limousine in a cloud of puzzled gloom. Reinbold rode off alone in the back seat of another. An armed guard from the Reinbold Enterprises security department sat up front with the driver. More were in cars that preceded and followed his limousine. Secure in his own armored bubble, Reinbold attended to other business during the ride to his hotel.

As always, he had two fat briefcases with him. Each was unlocked by a combination he changed daily. To open one of the cases in any other way would trigger a flash of light capable of blinding a man for several days and two seconds later emit a shriek that would paralyze the nervous system for hours. The cases contained concise monthly reports from the various firms he controlled, each in its own slim folder. Reinbold seldom bothered to attend time-consuming board meetings. These reports, and his dictated responses to them, were his substitute. He had taught the men who prepared them to reduce the reports to answers to thirty-eight questions. Like a good general, Reinbold chose competent men to whom he delegated full authority in directing the day-to-day tactics of their firms, but overall strategy was always his own. He read through each report swiftly but not superficially. At certain points he dictated a response or new concept to a recorder built into an elaborate console in front of him.

The limousine was approaching his hotel when he finished one of these reports, returned it to its briefcase and glanced at the console. There were ten small clockfaces set into it, each giving the time in a different zone around the globe. At seven PM the next day he was due in Tokyo, where he'd arranged for the American ambassador to Japan to set up an intimate dinner for the purpose of introducing him to the new head of that country's civil aviation.

When Reinbold entered the hotel, a secretary assigned to him by the Toronto office was waiting with the telex from London. He barely glanced at the message. Only the "Ian Diehl" signature had meaning.

He instructed the secretary to cancel his Tokyo appointment, to keep his hotel suite reserved for the next two months and arrange to send his traveling entourage home. He then returned to the limousine with his briefcases and drove to the airport. The crew of his 747 had everything ready to go when he arrived. Two of his bodyguards—the one from his limousine and one from a guard car—boarded with him.

The plane took off sixteen minutes later. Destination: Charles de Gaulle Airport at Roissy, outside Paris.

Halfway across the Atlantic, Reinbold told the copilot to radio ahead and have one of his smaller jets standing by to pick him up on arrival. Destination: southeast to the airport at Grenoble in the French Alps. Another message was sent to Grenoble, arranging for his transfer to one of his private helicopters which was always kept there.

The helicopter's destination was not given.

THREE

WASHINTON, D.C., MONTE CARLO, SORBIO

"HE'S A *MEAN* bastard," a Narc who'd worked with Paul Shevlin of MARS told George Ryan with a certain amount of grudging admiration. "He's tough and he's smart. With a lot of pride. He came up from pretty far down, and he came up hard. He likes to fight and he likes to win. Which to him means wrecking the other guy. But he's got talent, that boy. A lot of talent."

As director of Senator DeLucca's investigations in Washington, Ryan had done a full background research job on Shevlin, using his own old-boy network. He hadn't come up with much that was of use to the senate committee, but it never did any harm to understand one's adversary.

Another agent told him, "Shevlin's the kind who's always suspicious of other people's real motives. He told me he never met Santa Claus. Also that everybody wants something, usually the same thing you want, and only one of you can have it. According to Shevlin survival means somebody else doesn't."

Ryan was able to discover only three people who could be called true friends of Paul Shevlin: a Vietnam veteran and his wife and their young son. The veteran had been in combat with Shevlin and came home blinded and crippled. American hostility to men who'd fought in Vietnam had done him a final injury. He wouldn't talk about Shevlin to strangers, but he told a friend who was also a friend of Ryan's that he wasn't surprised when Shevlin quit the government. It was America's treatment of Nam vets, he thought, that had ended any respect Shevlin had for the government . . . "He just figured like me—screw the government, screw everybody. Give what you got—the short end of the stick."

When the veteran had sunk to the depths, a blind cripple feeling useless to himself and his family, it had been Paul Shevlin who had taken him out of the Vet Hospital. It had been Paul Shevlin who had bought him a gas station of his own down in Florida, where he now ran it with the help of his wife and young son. Shevlin sometimes dropped in on them when he was in the area—to share a beer and shoot the breeze. Not for repayment.

It was the only *human* item that Ryan was able to find in the entire background research job on Paul Shevlin.

Small wonder Reinbold had picked him as a right-hand man.

PAUL SHEVLIN'S VILLA was at the end of a curving lane flanked by palms and giant stands of cactus in the hills above Monte Carlo, surrounded by a small, neatly tended estate hidden inside high walls. Behind it flowering shrubbery screened the swimming pool: a long rectangle of blue water sunk into a curving patio of orange tiles. The dark green foilage of an ancient olive tree spread a lacework of morning shadows across Shevlin as he lay spread-eagled on his back across an inflated rubber mattress floating in the middle of the pool.

The years had treated Paul Shevlin with respect. There were flecks of white now in the thickness of his raven-black hair, and a trace of permanent puffiness above his prominent cheekbones, but these touches mostly added a note of distinction to his appearance, and his lanky body still had the look of hard power.

He seldom looked too long in mirrors, not liking what stared back at him. But women tended to find him fascinating from the first glance. Men's opinions varied . . . some considered him a pleasant acquaintance who listened more than he talked, easy to get along with. Others noted something else about him, that he was not the kind of man it would be wise to push.

His eyes were closed as he floated in his pool now, but he was not asleep. Angry tension pulled at the corners of his wide mouth. He was reviewing what would have to be done to counter the trouble he'd learned about in a phone conversation with Brussels late the previous night. Added to it other problems hanging fire while he marked time here, it made for a long list.

Lady Isabel Beaumont came out of the villa onto the patio. The sliding glass door made little sound when she shut it behind her to keep in the air conditioning, but it reached Shevlin and instantly brought him up on his elbows, his dark blue eyes snapping open. When he registered who it was, he once again let himself try to relax.

At twenty, Isabel was one of the better products of whatever was left of the British upper class: a perfect if somewhat too inbred English rose. Shevlin studied her, remembering what it had felt like, long ago, when touching Lady Isabel would have been the most impossible highlight of his greediest daydreams . . . Remembering the bedrock-poor Tennessee mountains his mother had taken him away from after his father got himself killed in a family squabble . . . Remembering the filthy squalor of the slum she'd taken him to on Detroit's east side between the Grand Trunk freight tracks and the Detroit Rendering Plant, a place where you had to fight for your right to walk the garbage-strewn, junk-littered blocks of partially demolished, half-abandoned houses. Where his mother had been reduced to two-buck whoring to support them. Where the putrid odors from the rendering plant clawed at his throat and turned his stomach, and he woke some nights to find the rats trying to eat him . . . Remembering the single-minded fury of his drive to get out of that sewer, to wrench open the invisible manhole cover above him and climb up into the *other* world . . .

Lady Isabel, aware only of his impassive scrutiny, took off her terry-cloth robe and let it fall to the orange tiles of the patio. Her figure was slim and elegantly turned, with a uniform golden tan. The hot Mediterranean sun made her pert breasts feel heavier. It probed the silky nest of her pubic hair, and her clitoris stirred in response.

She smiled at Shevlin, allowing his image to merge with the sensation in her vagina, then dove into the pool, making scarcely a splash.

He watched her swimming underwater toward him, a girl born to that world he'd reached for so hungrily, a world where clean and rich and self-respect were interchangeable. A world that didn't know the sewers under the manhole cover.

Isabel surfaced at the foot of his floating mattress. She pulled herself partway up, resting her dripping arms on it. She noted the dead-white scar tissue webbing the dark tan of his left shin—a memento from Vietnam, where his leg had almost been blown off. His body bore smaller scars, whose cause she didn't know but wondered about. For her, they gave him a deliciously scary aura of mystery.

She kissed the scar on his left leg and looked at what hung dormant at the juncture of his muscled thighs. She whispered, "Good morning, sir," and raised her head to meet his determinedly bland gaze.

The hard lines carved into his weathered face excited her. So did the cool intelligence lurking in the eyes, and the cruelty about his mouth.

Shevlin knew all this. It was one of the few things he'd heard as a kid that had turned out to be true: treat a lady like a whore. A certain disenchantment had come with that knowledge, along with the ability to use and discard them without undue sentiment.

When it came right down to it, there was only one woman he'd ever met who held his full respect. But then, that one was neither whore nor lady. Nor anything in between. No category at all.

The Medusa. She was something else, entirely. Something that was all her own. And he had given her the name . . .

Isabel didn't know where his mind was but she did sense him drifting away from her. She pulled herself up higher between his legs and took his penis in her slender fingers. Her nostrils flared as she began to lick delicately, with just the tip of her pointy tongue. He grabbed her hair and pulled her face up, looking at her closely. It *was* a lovely face, and still innocent. Innocent of evil and ugliness, anyway. What the hell, he decided, it wasn't *her* fault she hadn't had to come up the hard way.

His voice had a tinge of genuine fondness in it. "Hello, slut."

She liked that too. "Please, sir, may I have more?" It was all playacting for her, a different kind than for him.

He caught hold of her shoulders and rolled off the mattress, plunging them both into the sun-warmed water. They surfaced laughing and sputtering and raced each other to the end of the pool. Shevlin got there first, swung himself onto the patio and reached a hand down to hers, pulling her out with a single easy move. They sprawled across the multicolored patio cushions, and she kissed him with a fierce urgency, her slender arms and legs locking around him, her nipples hard, digging into his chest. A wild cry shook her when his hands seized her small, firm buttocks and yanked her closer.

The sound he made when he took her might have been laughter . . . he could still be hit by the wonder of it, even now. Paul Shevlin screwing a gorgeous English aristocrat beside his own swimming pool on the posh goddamn French Riviera. A long, long way from backwoods Tennessee and back-alley Detroit . . .

But afterward, when they lay on the cushions with their slippery-wet bodies drying in the hot sunlight, he found himself thinking of the Medusa again. Right now she'd be doing her own variation of what he was doing . . . marking time. Thinking about it made him edgy. Leaving the Lady sprawled half-asleep on the cushions, Shevlin went inside, lit a good Havana cigar and fixed himself a stiff Scotch and soda.

It was too early for either of them. All he'd had for breakfast was some black coffee—and Lady Isabel. Nerves—he was letting them dictate to him, they had him smoking, drinking and fucking on an empty stomach.

Nerves. He was getting old, letting them rag him like this. A weekend holiday down here was fine, but now it had stretched past five days. While a work load of other business piled up for him at the office, he was stuck down here playing with toys like Isabel—waiting for William Reinbold's decision.

Lady Isabel strolled inside from the patio, dangling the terrycloth robe in one hand, her face still childishly sleepy. She nodded at the glass in his hand. "Is *that* the glass that once belonged to Napoleon?"

"One of them. I have five more." Shevlin gestured at the ornate chandelier over the bar. "And that number belonged to Queen Victoria."

"You're joking."

"No."

"You *are* an eccentric."

"What you mean is I'm trying to cover up a low-class background with a new-rich bankroll and don't have the good taste to see how tasteless it is. Well, I just *like* it, buying things that belonged to famous people."

"Well, I belong to a famous father. And since you haven't bought me, as yet, it's time I was getting back to him. Will we see each other again, tonight?"

"I'll call you. Take a bath before you get dressed. The tub was Marilyn Monroe's."

"Truth?"

"Truth."

"My God. I think I'll try it."

Shevlin watched her go up the curved stairway with her cute little buttocks doing an exaggerated Marilyn Monroe wiggle. He went into the downstairs dressing room and put on the Sulka robe that had set him back $2,300. The Gucci sandals he slipped on his feet had cost more than two hundred bucks apiece. He had an unashamed pleasure in being able to put down that kind of money for the best. Reinbold had spotted it in him before he'd realized it himself. This villa was his latest acquisition, making it three houses he now owned. The first was outside Munich, the second in Virginia.

His yen for such things was not as simple as a hunger for rich trappings. Pride came from being able to pay for what he liked. Pay he earned because he was very damned good at what he did, maybe the best there was. Maybe. He'd be able to say that with assurance, if he lasted at it for another decade . . .

Shevlin returned to the bar and poured more Scotch in Napoleon Bonaparte's glass, bought at an antique auction down in Monte Carlo where he'd outbid an Arabian prince. He knew damn well he'd bid too high but the pleasure was worth it.

That sense of pleasure faded as the angry impatience rose in him again. He took a swallow of Scotch, relit his cigar. The bar was to one side of a media room he'd had built into the villa, complete with hi-fi stereo system, an extensive library of records and tapes, a videocassette player with projection onto a movie-sized screen and shelves stocked with over three hundred videocassettes: favorite films, pro football games, and a backlog of TV series from the States. But right now he was too irritable to sit still for any of it.

There was a piano on the other side of the media room. He'd learned to play back in the days when he'd thought he might use it to pay for a college education, but then the GI Bill had taken care of that. When he'd started playing again it had been only for relaxation. He knew he was good, good enough to have earned a living at it, but nobody ever made a fortune playing jazz piano.

Nowadays it just provided relaxation, a means of centering himself. But this morning he was in no mood even for that. What he needed was to get into operation again.

He wondered briefly if the waiting was getting to the Medusa like it was to him, and then knew it wouldn't be. She had her own ways of sweating out the tension. Shevlin took a long swallow from his glass and dragged more cigar smoke into his lungs. If Reinbold didn't make up his mind soon . . .

On the bar beside him, the phone rang.

AN HOUR LATER Shevlin drove a gleaming white Rolls Royce Corniche convertible into the high Monte Carlo district of Monaco. He wore faded jeans and an open-necked army shirt, a fisherman's cap and rope-soled canvas shoes. Dark wraparound sunglasses cut across his face like a mask, mirroring passing palm trees and ornate building facades as he swung around the Place du Casino. He turned the Rolls into the Grand Prix route and followed it down to the lower part of Monaco, where the office building containing the main headquarters of Reinbold Enterprises was located. Parking alongside the building, Shevlin went up to the RE communications center to pick up the short code message that had come in by radio from William Reinbold.

The RE headquarters took up only three floors of the building. Most of it consisted of what high-tech designers called knowledge cells, sophisticated interlinked complexes of high-speed, major-capacity computers, information processors and telecommunications systems. These compact centers digested a constant electronic inflow from all over the world, reassembled it in category breakdowns: markets, contracts, resources, technology, production and delivery capabilities, recent moves by competing corporations and currency fluctuations.

The RE headquarters staff was also compact, consisting mostly of accountants, experts on international business law and managerial specialists selected from top schools such as California's Stanford and France's ENA. There were no decision makers. At this level only William Reinbold made decisions.

The job of the headquarters staff was restricted to making a further breakdown of output from the knowledge shells into concise informational and operational reports. These were regularly updated for Reinbold's perusal in Monaco, or electronically encoded and forwarded to him abroad.

Reinbold had chosen Monaco for more reasons than the fact that resident businesses there were tax-exempt. It was a very small principality with a large and experienced police force and a quiet ever-present para-security group run by a man known to most only by a first name—André. It worked for the Société des Bains de Mer, which owned the casino and almost everything else that went on in the Monte Carlo district. Between them the principality cops and André's shadow-force knew every resident and regular visitor, spotting undesirables with a promptness that discouraged both crime and industrial espionage. Robberies were rare, terrorist activity unheard of, private bodyguards an indulgence. Interlopers trying to tail or bug resident businessmen were quickly escorted out of Monaco. Even top Mafia figures had been known to be turned back at one of Monaco's few entrance roads; or discovered and sent packing minutes after entering one of the principality's hotels or restaurants.

Nevertheless, after Shevlin left the RE headquarters he took extra measures to insure that no one was tailing him. The investigation by Senator DeLucca's committee—coming on top of the normal inquisitiveness of journalists and espionage attempts by RE competitors—made such precautions necessary, he felt.

He drove down to the marina complex recently completed below the palace of Monaco and doubled back into the old one-lane tunnel that cut under the palace hill. Halfway through, the tunnel forked—the right fork led to Monaco's old harbor, the left curled back toward the road to Nice. Shevlin turned left and pulled off into the short maintenance lay-by just after the fork.

Traffic was sparse in this tunnel, which was too low for large trucks or buses. Shevlin waited a few minutes, allowing several cars to turn into the left fork and go on past him, then backed the Rolls into the right fork, drove onto the old harbor and swung up and around, back to the new marina.

At the far end of the marina the helicopter that Shevlin had phoned for was on its pad, ready to go.

The little outfit that ran the two choppers based in Monaco did most of its business ferrying passengers to and from the airport outside Nice. But that was not where Shevlin told the pilot to take him.

BEHIND THE FRENCH Riviera's long curve of glamor hotels and glittering casinos, of topless beaches, noisy discotheques and yacht-filled marinas was another region seldom visited by the vacationers and jet-setters. A region of terraced farms and little stone villages perched on hilltops. Only the permanent citizens of the Riviera went there: shopkeepers and croupiers and restaurant owners seeking a day away from the heat and crowds of the coast.

Further inland, higher into the first surges of the Alpine ranges, lay yet another region little known to even the people of the hill villages below, a region where harsh mountain masses thrust up in disjointed plateaus, isolated from each other by chalky ridges and deep-cut ravines, by vast tangles of thorny scrub and dense spreads of pine forest. Certain areas here were virtually uninhabited and seldom visited. They were difficult of access and contain little to sustain or draw anyone. Except the isolation.

This was the region of the Vale of Tears, where a mad nobleman starved a succession of wives to death in a dungeon of his remote castle. It was the region of Frenchman's Leap, where troops trying to locate escaped convicts in the last century were ambushed and hurled from a high cliff.

In the heart of this region the stone ruins of Sorbio clung to an arid crest of eroded rock formations on top of a rugged slope of pine and scrub. Sorbio had been a Saracen chief who had plundered the coast and built a stronghold for his band here. In a later century the people who had cannibalized much of the fortress to build a village around it had kept the name, but in the early years of the present century Sorbio had been destroyed by an earthquake and partially buried under a landslide fallen from a higher slope just behind it.

For miles around it there was no village, farm or road. There had been a dirt road leading to it, winding its way around a mountainside, but that had collapsed with much of the mountainside during the same earthquake. With the only road cut, it was difficult to reach Sorbio even on foot. None of the earthquake survivors had returned. For decades Sorbio had remained abandoned.

But there were distant airfields, off to the north, south and west from which it *could* be reached by helicopter. And not all of it was entirely destroyed. Some of the stone houses remained standing among the ruins, though most of their roofs had caved in. Of the original fortress at the top, two squat square towers remained intact.

The interior of one had been renovated, complete with a two-way radio for contacting the coast, and was now used by Colonel Vasil Kopacka as a base of operations in this part of the West.

The other tower had been fixed up to house the two guards who always watched over the place, fugitives from Cambodia: former special-combat troops who had managed to escape the Khymer Rouge. Neither knew who or what Kopacka was. They knew only that he had found them starving in a Thai village, had employed them, and that they were no longer starving and that when their agreed-on two years here were finished they would be returned to the Far East with enough money to start small businesses of their own.

Another thing they knew nothing about was the identity of the fat man who often met with their employer here at Sorbio. Nor about the lanky, hard-faced man who sometimes came, and whose helicopter they now stood watching for.

Kopacka had bought the entire ruined village and a good amount of the mountainous land around it quite cheaply. For this purchase he had posed as a Yugoslav businessman interested in building a winter resort on the Sorbio site. The small firm through which he had made the transaction had no ties to Reinbold Enterprises.

While they waited for Shevlin's arrival inside the large main room of Kopacka's tower the STB colonel finished bringing Reinbold up to date on the Kremlin's acceptance of the feasibility study. With that cleared away he handed over a microfilm of the shopping list that had been submitted by KGB supervisor Josef Petrov.

Kopacka said that of the items on the list the one he believed to be of most immediate importance concerned the results of the oil company seabed mapping of the North Sea and China Seas areas. Obtaining this data would undoubtedly be easier for William Reinbold now than it would have been a year earlier. Reinbold Enterprises had acquired a stake in two marine engineering companies. One specialized in major repair and maintenance work on deep-sea production platforms and their wellheads. The other manufactured jack-up drilling rigs and semisubmersible production platforms. Both firms had contracts with the oil companies that had carried out the surveys.

Reinbold in turn handed over a microfilm of his answers to questions from previous shopping lists. Two of the items, he told Kopacka, would be of especial interest to Russia's Science and Technology Committee. One was a highly sophisticated innovation for the Linatron 3000, developed by Varian AG of Switzerland for the detection of flaws in steel castings and weld sections through the use of high-energy X-rays. The other was the formula developed by Du Pont for a new heat-resistant fiber, lighter than silk and stronger than steel.

Vasil Kopacka slipped this microfilm into his pocket. Later it would be passed on to the third secretary at the Czech embassy in Paris and carried back to General Hájek at the Monastery by an embassy courier with diplomatic immunity against search.

Kopacka then introduced the subject he had saved for last, the most important and the most dangerous: the order from Mikhail Talgorny himself for the political-risk assessment to be carried out by Gallia-Reinbold.

William Reinbold's success with the KGB shopping lists came partly from a judicious use of Shevlin's MARS Limited. The rest was due to the fact that companies in which Reinbold Enterprises had a stake were by now involved in so many facets of the West's military-industrial complexes that he had access to its latest technological and scientific advances. But far more important was Reinbold's increasing ability to gather the most vital information of all: *intentions* . . . directions that Western nations would take, ahead of time. How far they could be pushed without hitting back too violently. Whether an enemy's hard-line stance was real or a bluff from which it could be forced to back off. When a surprise move by the West was only a feint, when it presaged a new policy.

Again part of this came from the work of MARS Limited. But the highest level of knowledge in this area came from the kind of men retained by Reinbold's various corporations to act as goodwill ambassadors for them, men who received yearly fees in six figures and even higher expense accounts and bonuses. They did not have to learn much about the industries that retained them. The sole qualification for each was that he have a special relationship with highly placed figures in government, science or the military. One of these goodwill ambassadors for Reinbold Enterprises played golf on a regular basis with the President of the United States. Another was a retired chairman of the Joint Chiefs of Staff and continued to be consulted by the present Chiefs of Staff at weekly luncheons inside the Pentagon.

But Reinbold himself was becoming the best asset for political-risk assessments. A growing number of top-level government and military figures were eager to meet with him in a friendly, relaxed atmosphere. Usually they were courting him for favors and so were not inclined to be tight-mouthed about what they had accomplished and intended to accomplish . . .

Kopacka was now emphasizing the point Talgorny had made—that Reinbold was *not* to begin his new risk assessment until the trouble with Senator DeLucca was ended—when they heard the distant approach of Shevlin's helicopter.

They went to the tower window and saw it coming in from the direction of the Vésubie Gorge, flying low through air shimmering with heat haze reflecting off the sun-scorched rocks below. Inside the shaded tower room, where the air was stirred by mountain breezes, it was a good deal cooler than outside. They watched the helicopter thunder directly over the Sorbio ruins and swing around to hover over the only level patch anywhere in sight, an area of flat stone at the eastern end of the crest. As it set down and its engines were cut, Kopacka put a hand on Reinbold's shoulder. "Time for me to go upstairs."

Reinbold nodded. The room above this one had a listening device inserted through its flooring. Easy to find, if Shevlin were to search for it. But Shevlin had no reason to. He didn't guess that Kopacka, or anyone like him, existed. Shevlin had every reason to believe that William Reinbold was the top of the ladder, that every opinion and decision originated with him.

Outside in the hot sunlight Shevlin climbed from the chopper after telling the pilot to wait for him. If Reinbold had wanted him to send the chopper away, as on other occasions, a specific word would have been included in the code message phoned on by the Monte Carlo office.

One of the Cambodian guards watched the chopper from just inside the ruins to make sure its pilot did not wander far from it. He wore a pistol and held an automatic rifle with seeming carelessness. The other guard followed Shevlin through Sorbio to Kopacka's tower. He too wore a pistol, and carried a pump-action shotgun.

Both Cambodians had no connection with the security branch of Reinbold Enterprises; Shevlin had quietly checked that out. According to Reinbold they belonged to the same unexplained friend who let him use this ruined fortress. Shevlin had never tried to discover who that friend was. This was not out of blind loyalty to his main client; Shevlin gave that to nobody. But as long as the association with Reinbold continued to give what he wanted to get out of it, he was not about to jeopardize it by poking into areas that didn't concern his own business or welfare.

The guard who'd accompanied him stayed outside when Shevlin entered the squat tower. Shevlin removed the sunglasses and wiped sweat from around his eyes as he climbed a short flight of seemingly new wooden steps, relieved to be out of the area's harsh sunlight. Reinbold was waiting for him in the big room at the top of the steps.

Everything in the room—including the battery-operated two-way radio on a plain wooden side table—had had to be flown in. Reinbold did not offer to shake hands. Turning from Shevlin, he went around a small desk and settled his bulk into the wooden armchair behind it.

On the desk was a pitcher of water and two glasses. Shevlin filled one glass and drank all of it before sitting down on the other side of the desk. The water was from a spring that fed into an ancient cistern under the ruined part of the fortress, and was still cool. He put down the empty glass. The impatience that had ragged at his nerves was gone. The decision had been made or he would not have been summoned here.

But Reinbold still did not speak. His pale eyes were narrowed, almost invisible between the folds of flab. To Shevlin he appeared uncomfortable, hesitant about getting down to the subject at hand. Shevlin had never seen him like this before.

He had never liked Reinbold. The fat man lacked normal juices, impulses. Business and finance were his sex life. But Shevlin did respect the man. The scope of the operation Reinbold had put together was awesome. So was the brain that could accomplish it. Even if he were not working for him, Shevlin would never have agreed with Senator DeLucca's fear of that kind of power: that multinationals threatened the free-enterprise countries of the world and were becoming artificial nations of their own. Hell . . . every nation was an artificial creation, its borders made by rivers, mountains, oceans, or wars. Multinationals were a *new* kind of nation. People joined them out of self-interest. That was true free enterprise. And Reinbold Enterprises could be the biggest of them all. You had to respect a man with that kind of drive, nerve and smarts. Still . . . he was nervous now about Senator DeLucca and Shevlin could not quite put his finger on the cause of it. He knew that Reinbold didn't dislike people—he had no feelings at all about them. So his worry about eliminating Senator DeLucca was an oddity.

It was Shevlin who approached the subject, obliquely . . . "I'm losing a lot of business, Mr. Reinbold. All this publicity about your being my main client. It's making other companies shy away from MARS Limited. I've had our New York office hire a PR firm to offset DeLucca's charges. But that's costing too."

Reinbold's thick, bloodless lips finally moved. "Have your accountant put together a tight estimate of what all of it is costing you. Warn him not to pad it. Reinbold Enterprises will make good the losses."

"We may be about to lose more. I got another piece of bad news last night. DeLucca's investigator in Europe, Klaus Bauer, has begun sniffing around Brussels. If he penetrates the cover of my setup there I'll have to close it down. Permanently, if this goes on much longer."

"It is not going to." Reinbold's tone was now firm, the last trace of hesitancy gone.

Shevlin said quietly, "You've made up your mind to go ahead with it?"

Reinbold inclined his head slightly. "But one step at a time. Only the first step, as of now . . . the feasibility study we discussed the last time we met. I want that prepared and the results submitted to me, ready to put into operation if the gambit with the Swedish NATO spy fails to achieve its objective—"

"It will fail," Shevlin assured him, unknowingly echoing what Colonel Kopacka had told KGB supervisor Petrov.

"In that case we will have run out of alternatives. DeLucca's committee can't be allowed to continue along its present course. It could end in destroying the value of MARS Limited . . . for both of us."

Shevlin permitted himself a small smile. "And Reinbold Enterprises could wind up restricted in its scope of operations. At the least."

"Exactly." Reinbold did not add what this would do to his own value to those behind him, like the man listening in the room above. "Without DeLucca, with DeLucca neutralized, the committee would come under a new chairman, a man who, unlike DeLucca, could be influenced to steer the committee into safer channels."

That the senator who would take DeLucca's place was vulnerable to pressure was not news to Shevlin. It was the MARS office in Washington that had dug up the facts that made Senator Harding vulnerable, facts obtained through its memberships in two old-boy networks—the Society of Former Special Agents of the FBI and the International Association of Chiefs of Police—plus purchased access to data banks in Harding's home state: one belonging to the biggest credit investigation company in the U.S., the other to that state's police intelligence squads. Separately each of these facts was relatively harmless. Knitted together by Shevlin and MARS Limited's top analyst, they could destroy Senator Harding's career.

"If there is no other practical solution," Reinbold continued, "DeLucca will have to be removed."

Shevlin's own tone was matter-of-fact. "His ass or ours. Down to that."

Except, Shevlin thought, it would take some pretty devastating revelations from the senate committee about William Reinbold's business dealings to really hurt him . . . his company was so large and diversified. Still, if serious and persistent enough, the revelations could severely restrict Reinbold's activities, lose him huge amounts of money and reputation for being near-invulnerable. Yes, Reinbold Enterprises would probably survive even DeLucca's worst, but at what price? Obviously Reinbold had decided he didn't intend, after all this time, to pay that price . . .

And as for Paul Shevlin, exposure of certain things he'd done for Reinbold would absolutely mean the destruction of everything he'd created for himself. Even if he escaped prison, his usefulness to Reinbold, and all that it brought him, would be finished. MARS Limited would surely be forced out of business, and he seriously doubted that he'd be able—or have the stomach—to start another. For him it was, literally, a matter of survival. DeLucca was out to wreck him. His response was as uncomplicated as it would have been to a killer coming at him through a dark alley with a knife, or to a Cong sniper stalking him in a jungle . . .

Looking at Shevlin, Reinbold reflected again on how well he had chosen this man . . . The choice had been made after considerable research and analysis. The U.S. Army had sent Shevlin to Viet Nam in the early days of that war. He'd been moved up to combat sergeant when it developed that he was a man other men would follow into enemy fire. Finally he had been shifted to Special Forces operations for military intelligence. Invalided out with multiple wounds and a number of medals, he'd used the GI Bill to add a university education to his other assets. But when the CIA recruiters had come around before he'd gotten his law degree, Shevlin had been ready for them. He had never lost his war mentality . . . he'd had it long before Viet Nam.

Reinbold knew others who had worked so long in intelligence that they had trouble telling the difference between what was necessary in war and permissible in peace. Shevlin had no such difficulty. For him it was always wartime, and an adversary or obstacle was always the enemy. That Shevlin's first loyalty was to himself and to needs that came from his background, Reinbold considered a plus. To climb out of that background Shevlin first had had to break through the hard defenses society erected against such predators. It had taught him lessons he never forgot about the value of such vital weapons as distrust and cold-bloodedness. As long as their needs continued to coincide, Reinbold felt, he could depend on Shevlin to use these weapons on behalf of their association. That was the bottom line of the balance sheet, all that mattered.

"Very well," Reinbold told him, "we agree that the risks of permitting Senator DeLucca to continue are not acceptable. But there also are risks in stopping him. These must be minimized." As though reading Shevlin's thoughts, Reinbold added: "You will have to bear with me if I repeat the obvious. In something like this you are the professional, not I. That's why I pay you what I do. However, I do find it necessary to emphasize certain essentials. So let's break what worries me down to its fundamentals . . . "

They spent the next half hour reviewing them. One requirement ran through everything about the preparation of the feasibility study: there must not be a shred of evidence that subsequent investigations could follow to the source of the strike. If Senator DeLucca was killed, the first to be suspected would be the senator's present targets: MARS Limited and Reinbold Enterprises. *Unless* there was convincing, conclusive evidence that it had been committed by someone else—with an equally strong, or even stronger motive.

Shevlin decided to concentrate on that, pinpointing that "someone else" on whom the frame would stick. Working out the logistics of the operation would be the Medusa's job.

Reinbold nodded. Though he had never met the Medusa, he knew what he needed to about her. Enough to rely on her, in this matter, as completely as he did on Shevlin. He fixed his pale eyes on Shevlin for a moment, without a word, before ending their meeting. When he spoke again, his tone was hard: "One fundamental to be stressed. Again. There must be no one involved in this who could ever, later, point a finger in your direction. Which, of course, also means in mine. You must not, for example, make use of anyone else from your firm."

"I don't intend to," Shevlin told him.

The Medusa had never been associated with MARS Limited. From the start Shevlin had kept her separate, to be utilized only on very special jobs. He remained the only one in contact with her.

He thought about her again as he walked out into the scorching sunlight, returning to the waiting helicopter.

Remembering how he'd found her.

And why he'd given her the name.

II

THE BIRTH OF THE MEDUSA

FOUR

ISTANBUL

THE OLD man had been using the name Arakel since he'd settled down in Turkey two decades earlier. His right foot was missing, and a pair of crutches leaned against the chair in which he sat while he studied the face of Paul Shevlin. The night was hot and the air in the small room was stifling. Arakel had unbuttoned his muslin shirt. A small white stone with a hole in it hung by a leather thong on his scrawny brown chest. An ordinary, irregular stone such as one might find on any beach, it could have signified membership in some secret sect. Shevlin didn't recognize it, but it would fit what he did know about the old man.

Arakel was one of the last of a dying breed, a Serbian anarchist who'd started as a clandestine bomb manufacturer between the world wars, a hunted exile in many lands. Now he had his own profitable little import-export business in Istanbul's oldest market district on the Asiatic side of the Bosphorus. But he still detested any kind of government. From time to time he lent a helping hand to various revolutionary movements. "If you intend to betray me," Arakel told Shevlin softly, "you will not outlive me by long. Wherever you would go afterwards, I have friends."

"I'd have the house surrounded by cops if that's what I came for. By now that kid you sent out, the one who was supposed to get us tea, should have checked and found out it isn't."

"You are a man of quick understanding, I see. But I would not trust such an important task to a little boy. He has passed it on to someone more experienced in such things. Be patient, Mr. Shevlin. When I am certain, then we can speak a bit of this matter in which you are interested."

Shevlin wiped sweat from the back of his neck and shifted his position on the couch. The room was above Arakel's business premises overlooking the tea tables clustered around Beyazit Square under the Tree of Idleness. Through the window beside the old man Shevlin could see the roofs of the Covered Bazaar and the distant minarets of Yeni Cami rising into a star-filled sky above the Golden Horn at the Stamboul end of the Galata Bridge. Shevlin's gaze shifted from the view framed by the window to what hung on the wall next to it—a heavy, rusty chain with a broken iron manacle.

The old man saw him looking at the chain, reached out a hand and touched it almost caressingly. "A souvenir from my youth. I spent two months in a Syrian jail, fastened to the wall by it. Friends broke in to free me. They couldn't find a key so they hammered the other end out of the wall and dragged it out with me. The manacle had become embedded into my ankle and gangrene had set in. The only way to save my life was to amputate."

Arakel dropped his hand from the chain and looked at Shevlin again. "We couldn't risk going to a doctor with the problem so it was done with a carpenter's saw and an axe."

"You're a pretty tough old man."

"Old enough to let you know it."

There was a knock at the closed door. Arakel called, "Enter."

The door opened and a tall girl of eighteen with tawny hair and dark eyes stepped inside.

Which was how Shevlin first met the girl he would later name the Medusa.

His initial impression was only that she was exciting to look at. Not so much for the strong face and lithe figure as for the pure, natural youth of her and the relaxed, direct manner.

She was wearing a yellow scarf—long, made of heavy doubled silk.

He would learn that she always wore it, or another exactly the same. Sometimes as a sash around her waist, or as a head shawl. Now it was loosely fastened around her neck. Later, as the Medusa, it would end up around her victims' necks.

"He was not followed," she told Arakel. "And no one is watching this house."

"Thank you, Siri." The old man relaxed. "In that case I *would* like some mint tea. I'm sure Mr. Shevlin would also." He looked to Shevlin. "It is the best thing for one's system in this heat."

Before going out of the room the girl looked at Shevlin, a look of calculated appraisal that was nothing at all like the old man's. She didn't spend more than a moment on it but it stayed with Shevlin after she shut the door behind her. Coming from such a girl, it had caught him by surprise.

Shevlin knew all there was to know about that kind of look. Not unfriendly. He never was either when he sized up another man he might later have to go into combat with—or against.

He looked back to Arakel. "Is she the one who checked out the area for surveillance?"

"Yes. She is quite dependable in such matters."

Shevlin would have bet on it.

Arakel leaned back in his chair and rested his skinny hands on its arms. "Now then, Mr. Shevlin. You tell me you wish to supply arms to Kasra Hiwa's guerrillas in Kurdistan."

"No, I didn't tell you that. What I told you was that I want to meet him and check on how effective his group could be with the right hardware. *If* my report is favorable, then my client may pay me to smuggle some in to them."

"And who is this client?"

Shevlin got up and went to the window. He turned and sat on the ledge. If the girl had that good a counter-surveillance on the place he could trust his back to the slightly cooler night air for a while. His sports shirt was pasted to his skin from perspiring on the couch. "My client," he told Arakel, "is somebody who wants to be unnamed at this point."

"You wish me to trust you but do not give your trust in return. Come, now—what part of your government do you represent in trying to establish contact with Kasra?"

"None," Shevlin told him pleasantly. "I expect you'll check on me before making any decisions. I know how good your sources are. You're going to find out that I used to be with the Federal Drug Enforcement Administration. And before that with the Central Intelligence Agency. All that will tell you is that I'm not some bumbling amateur do-gooder, which means my client probably isn't either. But I'm not with any part of the government anymore. Just a private citizen, trying to start my own little business."

They smiled at each other, neither believing and the other not expecting him to.

But it was almost true . . .

It had been a year after Shevlin had made the switch to higher pay and authority with the strategic intelligence office of the drug enforcement agency in the Middle East, but it was his old CIA station chief, Ken Borg, who'd put the proposition to him in Nicosia: Shevlin's official resignation from goverment employ to enter the business world.

It wasn't the first time Shevlin had considered doing just that. He'd been thinking about it ever since a talk with a former air force intelligence officer who'd gone private doing "protective research" for the aircraft industry. As the ex-officer had put it, "Things being what they are these days, competitive business intelligence is *the* growth industry." Smart FBI men had shown the way, seldom staying with the bureau longer than they had to, to acquire salable tradecraft and contacts. And the bureau didn't mind, it got extra clout from having the security department of almost every big business in America run by one of its still loyal ex-members. The exchange of information between the FBI and its highly-placed ex-agents was mutual. Now men from the intelligence community were getting in on it. Most of them had gone private in a small way, for double or triple their government salaries. Which didn't attract Shevlin. What did interest him were the few who were making it big. Still, he was prepared to *start* small. By the time Borg had finished talking he'd known this could be a way to make that start.

Borg had approached it in a roundabout way: "Let's bring you up to date about our position on the Kurdish situation."

Shevlin already knew a good deal about it. He'd had to brief himself on the Kurds because many of them were active in the opium smuggling out of eastern Turkey to finance their rebellion in Iraq. The Kurds had always been a fighting people. Their mountainous home country of Kurdistan was spread over sections of what were now three different nations, but most of it was inside northern Iraq. So that was where the Kurdish battle for autonomy was centered—with the Iraqis using Soviet bombs and tanks against their villages, and the Kurds striking back from mountain caves with anything they could get their hands on.

America had quietly slipped them some aid, back when Iran was its ally, because Iran had a long-standing frontier dispute with Iraq and supported the Kurds. But that had ended with the signing of a pact between Iran and Iraq—followed by the loss of any U.S. influence in the area after the fall of the Shah.

"What we'd like to try doing now," Borg had told Shevlin, "is to reestablish some presence in that region. Through renewed aid to the Kurd guerrillas, and without getting caught at it. We've reason to think some new guerrilla bands in those mountains are building up pretty good. We'd like to make contact and have a look-in—without, I repeat, getting caught at it."

"Meaning you don't mind if *I* get caught at it, as long as the U.S. government doesn't."

"Right. We want you to resign from the government, Shevlin. Start your own business."

"Smuggling weapons to the Kurds."

"For starters."

"That'll take cash—along with the hardware. The government can't supply me without a record of it somewhere. So who does the supplying for you?"

"A legit industrial concern. My guess is that it's loosely connected to some big business friend of General Keegan."

Keegan was at that time deputy director of Defense Intelligence.

"I like your choice of words, Borg. *Loosely connected.* From Defense to CIA to Narcs to business friend to industrial concern to me. Detachable—like my neck if I get caught at it. You won't know me then, I take it."

"Oh, we'll know you, Shevlin. We'll just be surprised as hell to hear what you've been up to lately—out there on your own. Nobody'll believe that, naturally. But nobody'll be able to prove different."

Actually Shevlin liked it—with its built-in extra: the government would never officially be grateful for this service, but men like Borg wouldn't likely forget when he needed something in return.

"Any particular guerrilla outfit you want me to get cozy with for you?"

"Start by trying to make contact with a young Kurd leader who calls himself Kasra Hiwa. The first name may be real but the second isn't. In Kurdish, Hiwa means Hope. That's the name of his group. According to Israeli sources inside Iraq, Kasra and his Hiwa movement are giving the Iraqi army hell. Hit, run and vanish. Kasra's got his hideouts inside caves somewhere in the roughest mountain terrain in Kurdistan. The Iraqis haven't been able to find him in there, and neither have we."

"But you figure I can."

"You've built up a pretty impressive informant network inside the drug trade. Some of them are Kurds. One of them just might put you next to a contact with Kasra."

"If I do make contact, what are we offering and what do we want for it?"

"If he's worth a little investment, sound out whether he's likely to show some gratitude in exchange for a supply of hand-held antitank and ground-to-air launchers and missiles, plus some smaller stuff."

"You wouldn't happen to know who the businessman is, the one behind the company that's going to bankroll me."

"No idea."

It would be another year before Shevlin would learn it was William Reinbold . . . .

Arakel picked up the business card Shevlin had handed him when he'd presented himself:

MANAGEMENT ANALYSTS FOR RESEARCH AND SECURITY

Paul Shevlin, President

Shevlin had decided on that name for the firm as being just vague enough. The "Limited" wouldn't be added until a year later. At this point he was the whole staff of MARS except for a secretary who had nothing to do in the two small offices he'd rented outside Washington except answer the phone. The company funding his new firm was Miconfax, which turned out maintenance manuals for avionics engineers with military contracts. It was an affiliate of a large corporation, and Shevlin figured there was an even larger one behind that. On paper, the first job of his new firm was insuring that the Miconfax manuals didn't fall into the wrong hands.

Arakel looked at the address and phone number on the card, then stuck it in a pocket of his opened shirt. "Whoever your nameless client is, why does he—or they—wish to support the Kurds?"

"Why do you?"

"Because the governments of three different nations would like to see them crushed into servile obedience."

"If they win they'll form a government of their own. Then you'll have to do a turnabout and work against them. You only like losers."

"You are," Arakel observed without rancor, "an exceedingly cynical young man."

"Young enough to let you know it."

They were smiling at each other again when the girl came back into the room carrying a tray with a teapot and three small cups.

This time Shevlin saw it: a panther like quality in the way she moved and held herself. Something of the same prowling grace and power.

She knelt on a floor cushion beside the old man's chair and put the tray on a low table of hammered brass. Pouring tea into each of the cups, she handed one up to Arakel, giving him a look of deep tenderness, then picked up the other two cups, holding one out to Shevlin.

In the Middle East a female joining in with the men like this was in itself unusual. Shevlin took a cushion from the couch, dropped it to the floor near the girl and settled down on it. She gave him a smile as he took his cup from her. He smiled back, knowing she'd seen that he'd understood that special look she'd given him earlier. She wanted him to forget it, dismiss it as a mistaken impression and relax his guard.

Arakel gave him another surprise: he told the girl everything Shevlin had said to him, explained exactly what he wanted, then asked her, "Can we trust him, do you think?"

Shevlin said to the old man, "You ask a lot of your daughter."

Arakel caressed the girl's thick, tawny hair. "Siri is too young to be my daughter." He inclined his head toward the rusty chain hanging on the wall beside the window. "I lost more than my foot in Syria. Castration was one way they kept from getting bored in those jails."

The taut skin across Shevlin's cheekbones tightened even more. He said nothing.

The girl leaned her head against the old man's knee above the missing foot. "*You* are my real father. You took care of me, you sent me to be educated in Switzerland and England—"

"True . . . " There was great fondness in the way he looked down at her. "Even if I do not approve entirely of some of the education you chose for yourself while you were there."

Her eyes moved from Arakel to Shevlin. It seemed to take a moment for them to adjust. Then they focused, studying him gravely.

He stared back at her, looking for whatever lay behind the long dark eyes. Even then he knew she was different from other women he'd met, or was likely to meet. The surge of physical hunger he experienced, and its strength, was also different from the desire he normally felt for other women.

Without taking his eyes from his she finally gave her answer to the question Arakel had asked: "At this moment I believe it is possible to trust him—if your information indicates the same. But not for always. One would have to reevaluate him in the future, from time to time."

And I feel the same about you, Shevlin thought.

ARAKEL TOOK FOUR days to check on Shevlin's background. When they met again, in the same room and at night, the girl was not there.

"Siri has her own contacts to arrange," the old man said. "She will lead you to Kasra."

"You seem fond of her. This is pretty dangerous work you're throwing her into."

"The choice is not mine. I would turn her from it if I could, but she met Kasra when he was here one time and returned with him to Kurdistan as his lover. As it happens, why she is in Istanbul now coincides with your purpose . . . she's come seeking more arms for Kasra's band. I have some ability in that direction, but it does not compare to yours."

So the girl was Kasra's mistress . . . "She doesn't look Kurdish," Shevlin said.

"There might be some of it in her blood. Who knows? Her mother was Persian, according to her father. From simple, poor hill people who sold her to him. She died some days after Siri was born. Perhaps because the father delivered the child with his own hands. He told me the mother was very beautiful."

Shevlin was irritated with himself, wanting to get off the subject, but the itch to know more about her was stronger. "Is it just Siri? Does she have a last name?"

Arakel shrugged. "Her father had many names. Who knows which was the real one? He said he was Australian. But he might have been Canadian—or even American. A smuggler, of various goods. Drugs, guns, people. Even slaves, perhaps between Sudan and Arabia. A strange man. Like the daughter, in some ways. He left her with me when he went on one of his trips and died somewhere along the Persian Gulf. She has been a precious gift for my old age, but it has made me too vulnerable. I worry about the risks she takes."

"Out of conviction—or just for the man she loves?"

The old man considered for a bit. "Kasra is certainly in love with *her,* but I fear that Siri is more drawn to the intrigues and violence that surround him. Perhaps you can understand this."

Shevlin did; he had something of the same needs himself.

"It is one of the traits inherited from her father, I'm afraid, this taste for dangerous excitements. Strange to find it in a woman of the Middle East. We do not normally believe women capable of what men can do. But the Kurds are in a situation where they have learned to depend on anyone who proves himself—or herself. I know of two Kurdish girls who *command* small guerrilla groups. Siri is not only Kasra's mistress, she has become his second-in-command.

"Where do I rendezvous with her and when do we start?"

The old man told him . . .

FIVE

IRAQ

THE MEN hunting Siri and Shevlin were spaced well apart, following each other in single file down the steep slope. A heavily armed twenty-man patrol of seasoned Iraqi mountain troopers, each with an automatic carbine held at the ready in both hands, chest high. One at a time they crossed the limestone shelf jutting out of the cliffside.

Shevlin lay flat under it, less than four feet below the spiked soles of their climbing boots, his chin pressed to the ground. Inches separated his back from the underside of the shelf. Rock dust shaken loose from it by the heavy tred of the crossing troopers dribbled across the back of his neck. He didn't move. His hands held their grip on the rifle. His eyes continued to squint at the sunlit rocks outside their shelter, waiting. The girl lay stretched out against his left side.

The patrol had picked up their tracks and followed them. One after another the troopers came into sight, negotiated a right turn, and at that distance Shevlin could see their faces clearly, as well as the automatic weapons in their hands, Soviet AK-47 Kalashnikovs.

Siri's fingers slid across the trigger of her rifle. Her face was almost touching Shevlin's, and he could see her profile without turning his head. It had acquired a hardness. Her eyes were almost closed as she watched the patrol come on.

The last of it passed out of sight below. They stayed frozen in position. The narrowness of the canyon amplified the noise of the troopers' descent. Shevlin waited until the sounds died away, then dug in his elbows and carefully dragged himself forward, just enough to look down but with his head still in shadow. Siri inched up beside him.

In contrast to the stark rock walls of the canyon, the bright green of poplars and willows lined the gleaming thread of the stream at the bottom. The troopers were spreading out along one bank, studying the ground. A voice echoed thinly up the canyon, giving orders. Several of the troopers waded across the stream to search back and forth along the other bank.

Finding no tracks, the men who'd forded the stream crossed it again to rejoin the rest of the patrol. Minutes later they moved on toward the south, following one side of the stream running through the depths of the canyon.

Beside Shevlin, the girl let her breath out slowly. "That's the route we were going to take," she said.

Shevlin kept his voice as low as hers. "We risk running right into them if we take it now. Even if we give them a long head start."

Siri nodded, still watching the patrol below, then raised a long-fingered hand from her rifle and rubbed a knuckle across the strong bridge of her nose. "There's another way but longer. We wouldn't get there until almost nightfall."

"Better than not getting there at all."

Siri dropped her hand and nodded again, watching the patrol start around a sharp bend in the canyon. When the last trooper vanished Shevlin crawled out of the overhand's shadow and stood up. He reached a hand down to help the girl. She was already on one knee; his gesture causing her to pause, looking up at him for a moment. Then she took his offered hand and got to her feet beside him.

Slinging her rifle over one shoulder by its worn leather strap, she took the lead, heading back up through the rock formations of the canyon wall, climbing with incredible agility.

Shevlin followed. She knew this terrain, he didn't. He was the amateur here . . . .

Getting to this point, deep inside Iraq's Rowanduz region in the heart of the Kurdistan mountains, had taken some doing . . . Via Turkish Airline to the city of Van on the shore of the great lake of the same name, then picked up by a Kurdish cab driver arranged for by Arkel and south into the Hakkari Mountains to a Kurd village, where a man named Hamad waited to guide them across the border into Iraq and then take them by jeep to his own village, from which Shevlin and Siri hiked from the Rowanduz area to the Silik Pass, where a guide named Isa, who knew Kasara's whereabouts, was to meet them near a mountain hamlet that had been bombed out by Iraqi planes. They'd been within two hours' hike from the hamlet along the route Siri had chosen when the patrol had gotten on their trail and cut them off. As Siri had predicted, her alternate route was a rough one, taking them the rest of the day through ovenlike heat held in by the mountainside looming over them. It was dusk, with a blessedly cool night wind starting up, when they finally approached the rendezvous point . . . .

One dead vulture might not mean anything. But when they passed a second only minutes later, a creepy feeling started Shevlin's muscles quivering. He began scanning the shadowed terrain around them with extra care as he followed the girl out of the ravine and up a steep, man-made path between sharp ridges of granite. The old lever-action Winchester rifle he'd been dangling from one hand was brought up to rest in both hands, ready for a quick swing in any direction.

Siri stopped at the top of the path above him. Shevlin moved up beside her. The remains of a small village lay shrouded in dusk inside a pocket between wooded hillsides.

Another dead vulture lay in the dirt a few feet to Shevlin's left. He concentrated on what was left of the village. It had been some ten or twelve thatched, stone-and-mud houses grouped around a well. The Iraqi bombs had reduced most of it to mounds of rubble. Through the deepening pool of darkness down there he could not detect any movement. Or sound. But the wind was coming from that direction, and Shevlin didn't like the aroma it carried.

"Is that it?" he whispered.

The girl nodded, also studying the destroyed hamlet. "Isa should be there or nearby."

"We make sure he's the only one." He gestured to his right. "You take it from that side."

He watched her start down and take advantage of every shadow and bit of cover as she circled to approach the destroyed village from the right end. Someone had taught her well.

Shevlin circled down to the left, reached the edge of the village without trouble and entered what had been a narrow dirt lane now strewn with bomb-rubble. Still no sign of movement, no sound. Siri should be somewhere inside the village by now; he didn't hear her either.

Going in deeper, placing each step carefully to move as quietly as possible across the rubble, he came to a house that was still half-standing. It was empty, but his nostrils pinched as he again picked up the smell that stirred memories better forgotten. He moved out through a gaping hole in the wall into what had been the village square.

The well was still there. And at least a dozen dead vultures. Also three decaying human corpses. They had not been killed by bombs or bullets.

Siri emerged from dark shadows on the other side of the square. The man who followed her had the stocky build of the typical Kurd mountaineer and wore the traditional turban, baggy trousers and rope-soled shoes. His rough woolen coat was cinched at the waist by a cartridge belt and he carried an old Mauser carbine.

"This is Isa," Siri said when they reached Shevlin. She looked at the bodies around the well.

Isa said something Shevlin couldn't understand . . . he knew some Turkish and Arabic but not Kurdish. The girl explained tonelessly, "The Iraqis have a new trick. After they destroy a village they sometimes poison the well, in case some of the Kurds who fled come back. Kasra warned about this." She gestured at the bodies. "These three didn't listen to his warning."

And the vultures had died from eating their flesh.

That night they made camp under a high ridge, lighting no fire, eating their rations cold. Isa and Siri talked in Kurdish, Shevlin lay back against a rock watching the stars.

Siri turned to him and spoke in English: "Isa says he is happy America once more believes the Kurds will win their fight."

"I don't know about America's opinion. Personally, I don't think they have a hope in hell." Shevlin looked at her. "Do you?"

"If they don't, they'll keep on fighting. They'll never give up."

"That's what interests me. And how well they'll fight."

"Sometimes you sound like Arakel."

He let it pass . . . "I noticed he called you Zad. What's that mean?"

"Everyone in the Hiwa movement has a code name to protect their families from Iraqi reprisals. Kasra, Isa—those are not their real names. My code name is Zad." She said it casually but there was a hint of pride. "She was a legendary Kurdish princess who led the Kurds against other enemies long ago."

"And now she fights again, against the new enemies. Romantic. Do you believe in reincarnation?"

Siri leaned forward and rested her forearms on her raised knees. After a few moments she said, "I believe the Kurds' cause is just." She spoke with conviction but no passion. "The Iraqis treat the Kurds like beasts of burden, to be used only for menial labor. They get Russian planes with Russian pilots to destroy their villages—"

He cut in. "Listen, I'll give you a history lesson. Back around 1915 the Turks began a massacre of Christian Armenians in towns all over eastern Turkey. More than fifty thousand male Armenians up in Van alone. The women and kids were deported, forced to walk all the way south to Aleppo, across the desert and mountains. Along the way gangs of Kurdish tribesmen began jumping them, stripping them of whatever they had, including their clothes and food, raping the women. There was one deportation column that had twenty thousand women and kids when it started out. Less than two hundred made it to Aleppo. What the Turks had begun your Kurds finished."

If it bothered the girl she didn't show it. "That was long ago. History, as you said."

"Right. History's the best medicine I know against getting sentimental about just causes. Right now history is giving the Kurds a hard time. Tough. Don't ask me to bleed for them."

She smiled a little. "But you may have to bleed for them. Doing what you are now. Even die for them."

"Not for them, for me. For money in my pocket."

"That is not reason enough."

"Got a better one?"

"You do it for the reason people do most things. Because you *like* it."

Their eyes met, and Shevlin was startled by her again . . . by the sharpness of the contact between them. But all he said was, "It takes one to know one."

They took turns at lookout duty through the rest of the night. Siri woke the two men just before dawn. Shevlin was glad to leave the area, he could still smell decay from the bombed-out village even though it was more than a mile away . . .

Late that morning they were working their way up a shale slope between bulging rock buttresses when they heard the distant howl of jet engines somewhere on the other side of a high ridge ahead of them, followed by explosions.

"Those planes are firing rockets," Shevlin told the girl. "Is that where your boyfriend has his base?"

She turned to speak to Isa. Her face was somber when she turned back to Shevlin and nodded.

"Great. I get here just in time to turn around."

"You have a strange way of reacting to bad news."

"There's not much else to do when something falls apart on you."

The sounds of the exploding rockets finished some ten minutes later. Isa was speaking rapidly. Siri translated: "There are many caves on that side. The planes may have been firing their rockets into the area blindly. Not at the ones where Kasra and his men are hidden."

"So," Shevlin said, "let's get there and find out."

IT WAS LATE that afternoon when they walked into the Iraqi ambush.

SIX

KURDISTAN

SOME TEN miles off to the south the mountain of Handrin Dagh reared out of one of the endless ranges more than eight thousand feet into the sky. Twenty miles to the east the twelve-thousand-foot Algurd rose above all the other peaks. But the three on the ridge were giving all their attention to the steep, rocky slopes directly below them, searching for any warning of danger. Seeing none, they finally started down, Isa in the lead, Shevlin next, Siri as rear guard.

A burst of automatic rifle fire exploded from between boulders somewhere ahead of Isa, chopping showers of black rock dust out of a mound of debris to the left of his turbaned head.

Shevlin jerked to a stop, dropped to a low crouch. His finger was across the Winchester's trigger but there was nothing in sight to shoot at. A voice shouted an order in Arabic too rapid for Shevlin to understand. Ahead of him Isa twisted to run back. Another automatic weapon let go a burst from a different firing point, catching Isa across the head in mid-turn.

Shevlin spun around, still crouched, to sprint back toward Siri. She was no longer in sight, which meant her reflexes were quicker than his.

He ran past where she'd been and still couldn't spot her. He dodged to his right, staying low.

A submachine gun stuttered from above, off to the left. A blow like a hammer struck the back of Shevlin's head, and the ground came up and slammed against him.

HE HAD BEEN out for hours. The light in the sky was late afternoon, moving toward evening.

He was still in the basalt canyon, black boulders looming over him, lying on the ground with his arms bound behind him, his ankles lashed together. His head throbbed.

A man's voice, close, spoke slowly, having trouble with the English words. "Welcome back, Mr. Anson."

It was the name in the passport Shevlin had been given before the flight from Istanbul. The face of a youngish man wearing the shoulder insignia of a lieutenant in the Iraqi army looked down at him. "Is that your real name?" the lieutenant asked him. "According to your papers you are American. Is that true?"

Shevlin tried to answer. Only a dry, rasping sound came out.

The officer snapped an order in Arabic and a trooper came over and put a canteen into the lieutenant's outstretched hand. Shevlin made out at least fifteen more troopers gathered close and another standing sentry on top of a high pyramid of black stone.

The lieutenant unscrewed the cap from the canteen, slipped one hand under Shevlin's head and raised it a bit off the ground so Shevlin could drink.

"Yes," he said, "I'm an American."

"And your name *is* Harold Anson?"

"Yes. Why am I tied up like this? What's happened?"

"Please. I am not stupid. The man we killed was one of Kasra's guerrillas. Who is the man who got away?"

They hadn't even gotten a clear look at her. And they still hadn't found her. "Not a man," Shevlin said, "my wife. We came on vacation to hike in the mountains. What's happened to her?"

"Your passport, Mr. Anson—if that is your name—is stamped with permission to enter Turkey. *Turkey*—not Iraq."

"We hired a mountain guide . . . in Turkey. The man you shot. We don't know these mountains. If he took us into Iraq we didn't see any signs that would have told us that." Shevlin knew it wasn't going to work but he had to try.

"You *are* in Iraq, Mr. Anson. Much too far inside Iraq for even a fool to believe what you say. Your guide was taking you to Kasra. And the one who escaped was not your woman but your confederate. The truth is obvious. You are American spies, come to establish contact with Kasra. Why?"

"I never heard of any Kasra."

"You will tell me . . . your mission is finished anyway. There is no longer a Kasra for your country to make intrigues with. Our planes destroyed his headquarters this morning. Our troops entered his caves afterward. Kasra is dead, with most of his rebels. Only a few of his followers lived to slip away. We are one of many groups the army has spread around this area to catch those still trying to escape and those still trying to reach Kasra because they don't know yet of his death. Like you, and your confederate."

"You're making a mistake—"

"No, you are." He gave a series of orders.

Shevlin caught enough of the meaning to go rigid. A trooper brought a stake near Shevlin's feet and hammered it into the ground. When another came to untie his ankles so his boots could be dragged off, Shevlin kicked at him.

The lieutenant shook his head. "There is no way to prevent it except by telling me what I ask of you. Otherwise your feet will be bound to that stake and we will light a fire on them. And you will have accomplished nothing, except turning yourself into an ugly cripple."

Another order and a third trooper threw himself down across Shevlin's knees, pinning his legs in place so the other would be able to untie his ankles and remove the boots.

"*Wait,* I'll answer your damn questions."

"Truthfully."

"Yes."

The lieutenant raised a hand to his men, then to Shevlin: "Let us begin with simple questions. Is Harold Anson your true name?"

"No."

"What *is* your name?"

"Colfax. First name, Radley."

"And the name of your confederate. The man who got away."

It could be a trick, Shevlin couldn't be certain if they had seen her. He told the lieutenant, "It *was* a woman. Not my wife but a woman. I don't know her name. She's the one who got me over the border."

"You did come to contact Kasra."

"Yes."

"Who sent you—?"

A blast of rifles somewhere off to the left cut him short. The sentry on top of the pyramid did a slow turn, stepped out into empty air and came rolling limply down from his perch. Bullets slapped off the tops of boulders just above the lieutenant and his men, who flung themselves to the ground and unslung their weapons.

The hidden riflemen kept up their fire: single shots, not more than five or six rifles.

The Iraqi soldiers spread out to the left toward the source of fire, vanished among the boulders and rock piles, shooting short bursts from their Soviet AK-47s.

Two troopers remained behind. One crouched by Shevlin with his rifle set for full-automatic fire. The other knelt behind a low hump of black stone further to the right.

Shevlin braced himself on his bound arms. He'd caught a blur of movement down low between two close-spaced boulders beyond the Iraqis' temporary encampment . . . a fleeting impression. He watched but couldn't spot it again. Siri? He'd gotten an instant sense of her, but of course couldn't be sure. He did a swift calculation of the direction of the movement he'd spotted and the timing involved. He counted silently, then he began to talk, loud and fast. Gibberish, no meaning. It wouldn't carry over the roar of gunfire to the lieutenant and his men off among the boulders, but it did to the two near him.

The soldier crouched next to him looked puzzled. The other turned his head to stare in this direction.

Shevlin snapped, "Do it *now.*"

The one by the hump of stone turned fully to point his rifle at him in warning, and in the same instant Siri came up over the hump behind him in a single, smooth-flowing movement.

Stretched between her tight fists gripping the ends was the yellow scarf, which she looped over the trooper's head, then yanked it back into his throat. Judging, Shevlin thought, by how deep it sank in with that first tug, there had to be a wire inside it. An efficient garrote—cutting off his air and voice before he could begin a scream, arching him backward as her knees jerked up into the small of his back. With his mouth open wide, he clawed futilely at his throat, letting the rifle clatter to the ground.

It had happened so quickly the trooper alongside Shevlin was only just twisting out of his crouch when Shevlin kicked his ankles out from under him and he toppled to the dirt. Shevlin promptly rammed both bootheels into the back of his neck and the trooper's head hung at an unnatural angle, his arms and legs jerked several times, and then all movement ended.

Shevlin swung about to check on the other one. He was sprawled on the ground with Siri's weight on top of him . . . dead, with blood trickling from the cut across his throat where the garrote was imbedded.

Siri raised her head, and for a moment she and Shevlin stared at each other across the bodies of the two people they had just killed. Her face was rigid, her eyes held the cold dull shine of moonlight on passing clouds.

And then it was gone, as though warmth had suddenly swept back into her blood, and she was darting across the space between them, drawing a hunting knife from her belt. Shevlin sat up and bent forward. She dropped to one knee behind him and slashed apart the leather thongs binding his arms. He brought his arms around in front of him and she put the knife in his right hand. As he began cutting at the thongs holding his ankles together she went back to the man she'd killed, squatted beside him and pulled the scarf out of his throat. The silk had torn, and a thin strand of the wire showed through the rip. She swung the scarf back over her head. Drops of blood fell from it, running down one side of her face as she retied the scarf around her neck.

His legs freed, Shevlin stuck the knife in his belt and unbuckled the belt from the dead soldier beside him. He worked quickly. The firing among the boulders to the left was slackening. There wasn't much time. He buckled the other belt around his waist. It was heavy with the grenades, holstered pistol and ammo pouches.

Siri had dragged off the other trooper's belt, slung it over one shoulder and under her other arm, buckling it between her breasts. Picking up the automatic rifle that lay in the dirt she signaled Shevlin with an urgent swing of her free hand and sprinted away to the right around the hump of stone. Shevlin scooped up the other AK-47 and went after her.

She was heading for the far side of the canyon and kept shifting course to keep cover between them and any pursuit. Shevlin had trouble closing the gap between them. Each running step caused a jolt of pain in his head, running down the back of his neck and between his shoulders. But dusk was gathering, the gunfire behind them died out and they could slow down.

"Those planes did hit Kasra's base," Siri told him, then turned into a narrow defile cutting through the canyon wall.

THERE WAS STILL half an hour before nightfall when he saw the Iraqi patrol—not behind but ahead . . . coming in their direction through a wide notch in a long high ridge to the east. The lieutenant must have radioed ahead to the other Iraqi patrols spread around the area. There was no cover anywhere. They were following the edge of a long clifftop. On one side there was a gradual, undulating slope of bare stone. On the other the precipice dropped some three hundred feet to a narrow-bottomed ravine.

The Iraqi patrol was starting down a steep incline below the notch. Shevlin hurried after the girl.

"Is there a quick way off here?"

She nodded, studying the patrol, calculating distances, the difficulties of its descent. Then she glanced at the darkening sky. "I think we can make it in time." She moved swiftly across the rocks, around a sharp bend, and dropped onto a ledge below.

Bullets bounded off the cliff more than ten feet above their heads. Shevlin kept on after the girl without looking back. The ledge was too narrow here to look anywhere except just ahead of each step taken. The ledge led to another sharp bend in the ravine, cutting them off from the patrol's vision. Ahead a waterfall gushed through a notch far above and pounded down into the stream.

This was the stream's source. It was also where the ravine came to a dead end, with no way to climb out up the sheer, marble-veined cliffs. A gnarled shoulder of rock was blocking the way. Siri dragged herself onto this projection and from there to a higher ledge. Shevlin went up after her. The second ledge was wider and ended against the sheer wall beside the waterfall. Siri turned toward the falling water and vanished behind it.

Looking back again, Shevlin spotted through the deepening murk the first troopers coming into sight along the lower ledge. He turned in behind the waterfall after Siri.

Little light came through the curtain of water into the cave where he joined her. He could barely make her out beside him, fumbling with the belt she'd taken from the dead trooper. He unslung his rifle as Siri pulled a flat, square flashlight out of one of the belt pouches and snicked it on. The light showed more of the cave. According to Siri there was a way out of the back of it, clear through the womb of the mountain to the other side. He looked up at the roof of the narrow cave entrance, only inches above his head; the light revealed deep crannies between jagged projections of cracking rock.

His notion might work, and he signaled for her to cover him. She responded by placing the flashlight on a projection so that it shone up at the roof of the entrance, then turned to the waterfall and unslung her AK-47, setting it to full automatic. Shevlin leaned his against the wall, detached a grenade from the belt he'd taken, reached up and stuffed it into one of the deeper crannies above him, the pin hanging downward. He kept pushing until his hand was in to the wrist and the grenade was stuck fast inside.

He was taking a second grenade from the belt when the barrel of an assault rifle poked in behind the waterfall. The weapon in Siri's hands jumped as she triggered a short burst, and the assault rifle was yanked back out of sight.

Shevlin now quickly stuffed the second grenade deep inside a roof cranny and got a third as a barrage of gunfire from outside cut through the noise of the waterfall, through the water itself. Long bursts slashed into the cave entrance, slicing back and forth, tearing chunks of rock from the interior walls . . . and sending a bullet through Siri's shirt just under her armpit. She leaned against one side of the entrance, aimed the AK-47 in the direction from which the fire came . . . the only way in . . . squeezed the trigger and held it down, her body shuddering with the recoil of the weapon as she swung a long burst to the right and left. The enemy fire died abruptly.

By now Shevlin had the third grenade in place. Siri snatched up the flashlight and ran for the rear of the cave. Shevlin pulled all three pins, took up his rifle and went after her. They ran until they reached a bend. Swinging around it, they put their backs to the sharp-edged wall. A moment later it trembled with the force of the detonation at the entrance.

Shevlin directed the flashlight beam back toward the entrance, revealing that enough of the entrance roof had collapsed to block that way in completely.

A reprieve—for the moment . . .

SEVEN

IRAQ

It was the reverberating noise of a helicopter coming in low over the area that woke Shevlin late the next afternoon. He sat up under their shelter, a block of limestone tilting out of the foot of a rocky, densely wooded slope. His head still throbbed and his neck was stiff, but the pain had eased considerably.

Shevlin rolled over onto his knees to go out and have a look. Siri was still sleeping soundly, curled on her side. There was nothing left in her face of what he'd seen when she'd strangled the trooper. Sleep created the innocence of babes . . . untroubled.

He moved out from under the lip of their shelter and stood in the shade of a wild fig tree, squinting up through its foilage as the helicopter passed overhead . . . a CH-47 Chinook with enough capacity to airlift more than forty troopers with full field gear.

Like the other two . . . they'd seen the first by moonlight just after emerging from the cave system early the previous night. It had put down within striking distance of their exit point, keeping Shevlin and Siri on the move through the rest of the night. They'd put at least eleven miles behind them before dawn. The second had swung over them, going north as they crawled under the protection of the ledge. The Iraqis would not take this much trouble to catch two escaped guerrillas, Shevlin knew. It would be the lieutenant's radioed message that one of them was an American spy that was bringing this many troops into the hunt. He was the one they wanted. They were going to have to stay holed-up like this by day and travel by night.

Siri crawled out of their shelter now and stood up beside him, watching the Chinook swing low to the west and settle out of sight behind a ridge a few miles away. Much too close.

In the twenty-some hours since she'd literally saved him from the patrol there'd been little opportunity for talk. When they hadn't been on the run they'd been asleep. Now Shevlin asked her, "How did you persuade those five guerrillas to put their lives on the line to help me?"

"I told them you can supply us with better arms." She said it matter-of-factly.

"Well . . . it was Kasra my client wanted to supply." He hesitated. "And Kasra's dead—"

"Yes."

"You hide your grief well."

Her faint smile might have meant anything. "You want to see me cry?" She shook her head. "What's done is done. He is dead. Now *I* have to lead."

"Lead what? The Iraqis have destroyed your group."

"Many got away after Kasra was killed. They will have gone in hiding." She brought up her knees, crossed her arms on them. "I will have to gather them together again, and find others. When we are enough you will supply us. That is why we saved you."

"Always nice," Shevlin told her, "to know I'm loved for myself alone."

She did not smile as she stared into the shadows under the canopy of trees. "Someone betrayed us. Before anything else I will have to find out who. And make certain he never can again."

Shevlin leaned against a rock, watching her. There was still nothing of what she'd been when she had made her kill—except some flecks of dried blood on the torn scarf around her neck and the glimpse of wire inside it . . .

"Who taught you to use a garrote like that? Kasra?"

"No. My father."

"Your father had interesting ideas about the education of a young lady."

Without raising her chin from her arms, Siri turned her head to look at him briefly, then looked away to watch the shadows spreading through the woods with the turning of the sun. "My father did not agree that, as you say, a good offense is the best defense. He said that for man it is the *only* defense. We have no natural defenses: skin a fingernail can cut, bad hearing, poor sense of smell to warn of enemies, little speed, no sharp claws or hard hooves, no long teeth to use as weapons. That's why we had to invent weapons to survive. Man *must* strike first. My father said women were more vulnerable than men so they needed to be more expert at offense than men."

Shevlin touched the back of his head. She had cleaned out the wound with spring water before falling asleep at dawn and covered it with an improvised bandage torn from his shirt. "Your father had a point . . . he wasn't so crazy—"

"Yes, he was." She said it without sounding angry at his memory or sorry for herself because of it. "I was seven when he began teaching me about weapons and woodcraft. I enjoyed it, any child would. Sometimes he took me with him when he traveled on business. He made his living by smuggling in many parts of the world."

"So Arakel told me."

"We were in Malaya when I was nine. He took me out into the jungle and left me, just went off and didn't come back for me. I went looking for him. He wasn't anywhere around and he hadn't left a trail for me to follow. Then I understood. It was like throwing a child into deep water—sink or swim. He had left me a .22 rifle, and what he had taught me over two years." She looked at him, and he thought he saw the hint of a smile. "I made it back," she said.

"So I see."

"Sometimes you remind me of him."

"A couple of days ago you said I reminded you of Arakel. Your father doesn't sound much like Arakel."

"No, but there is something of both of them in you." She smiled suddenly. "Anyway, now you know about me, why I am the way I am. And do what I do."

"And I'd say you seem to like it."

She quoted what he'd said to her some days earlier. "It takes one to know one."

Shevlin smiled, but neither was joking, and they knew it. "For me it's part of my job."

"And for me, the same."

THE DEEP CLEFT cut between towering walls that bulged overhead, creating a sense of crushing weight pressing down against the motionless air trapped beneath. In places the ponderous overhangs from either side almost met, allowing little of the moonlight to filter into the depths. Springs oozed down the bulging cliffs and dripped on uprearing masses of sharp-edged rocks that choked the bottom.

Two nights on the trail and they were still too far from the Turkish border. But not so far from the village of Hamad, the Kurd who had taken them to it with his jeep after guiding them into Iraq. Hamad would know the safest way to get out again, as well as information for Siri about where the survivors of the attack on Kasra's base might be hiding.

Their problem was the same: reaching Hamad's village without being caught by the Iraqi army along the way. Siri took them toward it by diverging routes unlikely to be used by the enemy patrols, and this was one of them. The cleft was impassable for vehicles or mules, and too difficult for foot soldiers burdened with heavy equipment. Even without carrying equipment Siri and Shevlin found it tough, dangerous passage, scrambling over one high mass of rocks after another.

They were halfway through the dark cleft when Siri slipped on loose pebbles scattered across the rounded top of a smooth rock slick with moisture dripping from the springs. She twisted to regain her footing but slipped again and lost her balance, going over backward.

Shevlin, just behind and below her, lunged to catch her but only managed to get a finger-grip on the back of her jacket, which ripped out of his hand as she toppled awkwardly past him. He saw her strike heavily against a sharp tooth of rock and bounce off, rolling down a stone slope into a wedge at the bottom.

She was sitting up when he reached her, holding her right leg. She spoke through clenched teeth but her voice was steady. "It's broken."

Shevlin hunched down beside her, pulled her hands away and probed her thigh with his fingertips. She winced but her face was set against the pain.

"Goddamn . . . " he whispered and sat back against the side of the wedge, looking at her.

"If I give you directions, you should be able to find Hamad's village on your own. He can come back with help—"

"You said we still have another day and night between here and that village. Another twenty-four hours for them to come back here. If rain starts coming down anytime in the next two days you'll have a river pouring through here. You'd be drowned before they got to you."

"That's possible," she said.

"Give me your rifle."

She unslung it and handed it over. He dismantled it swiftly. Using the barrel, leather sling and belt, he fastened it against her broken thigh for a makeshift splint. She held perfectly still, making no sound while he tightened the splint.

She said, "I made a mistake bringing us in here. You can't carry me out of this."

Shevlin got up. "I once carried one of my men all the way out of Laos and he was heavier than you are. Come on, cooperate."

He helped her to stand up on one foot, then bent his knees until he was in a half-squat. When her weight was settled across his shoulders he straightened.

It was even harder-going than he'd anticipated. She was heavier than he'd thought, or he wasn't as young and in condition as he'd once been. There were places where it was impossible to carry her, where he had to lower her from his shoulders and let her lean against him while he helped her inch ahead on one leg.

The first gray light of the coming sunrise was showing on the horizon before they made it out of the cleft, but the clouds had grown heavier and the rain had begun. He came to a pocket in the side of a steep slope, lowered her into its shelter. Slumping down beside her, he dragged air into his lungs, breathing deep and slow.

"I won't drown here," Siri told him. "Tonight you can leave me and go on alone. You'll reach Hamad's village much sooner."

Shevlin didn't raise his head from the ground. "Sure, and if a patrol comes along you'll be stuck here, easy pickings."

She eyed him, then said, "I saved your life, so now you save mine. So you don't owe me anything. Do I have that right?"

"Something like that," he said, closed his eyes, and let sleep take him over.

THEY DIDN'T REACH the village until three nights later. With Shevlin at the ragged end of his strength, Hamad gave orders to feed them before going off to fetch a woman skilled at setting bones. Siri was in no condition to eat. She'd been lapsing into semiconsciousness and fighting her way out of it over the last few hours, her broken leg agonized by Shevlin's increasingly heavy and awkward steps. Finally she allowed herself to pass out completely once she was stretched out on a couch . . . .

Two days later Hamad was prepared to slip him north across the frontier. Siri was fully conscious when Shevlin came to her couch to say good-bye, but her eyes were feverish and her hand felt hot when it reached out to take hold of his, gripping it tightly. There was no dependence in her grasp, nor in the way she looked at him while her hand held onto his. It was more like a declaration of possession . . . "Always let Arakel know where I can find you," she told him. "I *will* form a new group and you will supply us with the arms when we are ready for them."

"Sure," he said.

But it was more than a year before he saw her again.

And by then he had met William Reinbold.

EIGHT

MUNICH

TWICE DURING that following year Shevlin's work took him through Istanbul, and when it did he dropped in to see Arakel. The first time the old man told him that Siri *had* managed to pull together a new guerrilla group in Iraq but she was entangled in trouble from an unexpected source, not from the Iraqis but from the leader of another force of rebel Kurds that wanted to absorb her group into his.

On his second visit Shevlin found that Arakel had died. A clerk who had worked in his import-export company told Shevlin they suspected that the old man had been poisoned by Siri's Kurdish rival. Siri herself had disappeared somewhere inside Kurdistan after a series of clashes between the guerrillas in which both groups had been decimated and her rival killed. Shevlin left an envelope with the clerk containing the address of his fledgling MARS firm in Washington.

Funds for MARS continued to come from the Miconfax company, whose ultimate head Shevlin still didn't know, and for a while the work he did was confined to jobbed-out assignments from the U.S. intelligence community. None of them took him back to Kurdistan . . . the U.S. had done a policy about-face—the Kurds were no longer considered a sound investment.

In the second half of that year, Shevlin had a long talk with his Miconfax contact. After that he began phasing out the government work and turning MARS into a genuine private business, and his funding was increased to handle a new line of work—espionage against business competitors of Miconfax's parent corporation, with a couple of sabotage jobs thrown in—so-called burn-and-blow missions.

After Shevlin had carried out a number of these he was summoned to a private meeting with William Reinbold. He didn't have to be briefed about the man who went with the name. Anyone who read the financial pages knew it. Reinbold Enterprises already had its own effective security and intelligence-gathering branches. What Reinbold wanted was a separate organization to carry out more clandestine services for him—much as Shevlin had originally done for the government.

"I'm prepared," Reinbold told Shevlin, "to finance an expansion of your firm to fill this capacity. I have, as you now realize, been testing you for some time, Mr. Shevlin. You have the qualities."

It would, Reinbold made clear, suit him if Shevlin took on enough staff to work for other clients as well, so long as this resulted in his gaining added insight into their plans. "In addition," Reinbold said, "there will be matters of an even more confidential nature I may ask you to attend to personally. Without your staff. Or at least without allowing them to be aware of the true nature and purpose of what they are doing."

The funding Reinbold offered for a start staggered Shevlin. With yearly increases if the arrangement continued to achieve its objectives, he would become a very wealthy man.

Shevlin incorporated MARS Limited in the Bahamas, its original financing paid out by the Grange Bank of Nassau. Funds from Reinbold Enterprises continued to be funneled through a series of interlocking corporations in different countries before reaching MARS Limited. Shevlin added two new headquarters to the one he expanded in Washington. Learning from William Reinbold's operation, he kept personnel at all three offices compact. Most of the specialized tradecraft and contacts needed for any specific job could be hired on a free-lance basis, by the day or week, or through yearly retainers. In every nation there were professionals already employed in the police forces, in the intelligence services, in the telephone companies, in the security departments and data banks of credit and insurance businesses who were eager to moonlight for a fast buck, undeclared and untaxable.

The two new staffers with the best connections Shevlin made almost-equal partners in MARS Limited—Nat Hallberg, an attorney whose employment by naval intelligence and various law-enforcement agencies had culminated in nine years with the Attorney General's Office, took over the firm's Washington headquarters; Elliot Judd, a financial expert who had worked for the FBI and then the IRS as a director of investigations, opened a new MARS office in New York. Shevlin made Munich his base of operations, his partners jokingly referring to him as "Director in Charge of Old Europe, the New-Rich Middle East, Reinbold Personally—and Real Trouble." In addition to Reinbold Enterprises, the first clients picked up by the firm included a number of companies specializing in "advance piracy." One of these pirate firms, a pharmaceutical firm based in Hong Kong, was in fact a secret subsidiary of Reinbold Enterprises. Less than one month after MARS Limited was incorporated, William Reinbold handed Shevlin his first special assignment . . .

One of the largest drug companies in America, Columbia Laboratories, was preparing to market a new sleeping pill. Columbia had invested over ten million dollars in developing the product and would spend more in marketing it. Shevlin's assignment was to steal the formula for the new pill, along with advance data on the vital Four Ps: production schedule, promotion plans, packaging design, and price. He did his job so well that Columbia Laboratories was unaware of the piracy when it brought out its product six months later. Two weeks after launch—a time sufficient for cashing in on Columbia's advertising and publicity—the Hong Kong firm hit the same market with an almost identical pill, using a similar name and packaging and at a lower price since it hadn't needed to sink any development money into the product.

William Reinbold rewarded Paul Shevlin with an unexpected bonus —an old farmhouse outside the town of Grafing, just north of Munich. It was fully paid for and beautifully restored, and, as Reinbold knew, it was the first house that Shevlin had ever owned.

LESS THAN A WEEK after he had moved from his rented Munich apartment into his new home Shevlin awoke early of a Sunday morning with a rare free day ahead of him. Leaving the master bedroom, he went into the big old-fashioned kitchen to make himself a leisurely breakfast. Taking a first sip of coffee, he carried the cup and a plate of eggs and bacon into the dining alcove.

He found a square of paper on the table that had not been there when he'd gone to bed the previous night.

On it was written: "Good morning."

It was signed: "Zad."

The legendary Kurdish princess.

He went out of the alcove, through the kitchen into the pine-paneled hallway behind it. The back door had been locked when he'd gone to bed. He checked the doors and windows because the alarm system had not yet been installed. The lock was not broken, but the door stood partly open. He looked out through the opening.

Siri was crouched . . . yes, that was the right word . . . in the garden between the rear of the house and its small private lake, her back to him, weeding a patch of mixed flowering plants bordering the water. She plucked the weeds out neatly, roots and all.

Shevlin opened the door wider and stepped out, crossing the grass behind her without a sound.

"You are giving too much water to the tulips," she said without turning her head.

"I don't water them. A gardener is paid to take care of things like that."

"He is not doing a good job." She got to her feet, slapping the dirt from her hands and nodding toward a rose trellis. "Part of that vine has a fungus. The leaves with the brownish spots. It should be snipped away before the disease spreads."

"I wouldn't have guessed that gardening was one of your specialities."

"I love it. Arakel had a garden behind his house. I learned by tending it. Doing this makes me feel a kind of peace inside myself."

She turned to him, and they smiled at each other. She was wearing stained jeans and an old wrinkled shirt. The yellow sash around her waist was a new one.

"Maybe," Shevlin said, "I should hire you on as my gardener."

"I would enjoy that." She almost seemed to mean it.

She had gotten thinner. Her face had the gaunt look of someone who had gone a long time without enough to eat and was just beginning to recover from it.

"I'm making breakfast," he said. "Ready for some?"

"Yes." She followed him back inside the house. They hadn't even shaken hands. But their silent appraisals of each other probed deeper than any touch could.

He made more bacon and eggs, along with a rack of buttered toast. She ate every crumb and he made her seconds. Sitting across from her, drinking his second cup of coffee, Shevlin asked how she'd found him.

"Arakel left a little money in a bank for me. I used some of it to fly to Washington and went to the address you gave Arakel's clerk. A janitor told me where you had your new Washington office, but your people there wouldn't tell me where to find you." She finished the last of her food. "So I followed one of your men when he left work and went into a bar. After a time he let me know where to find you."

"What was his name?"

She told him. He made a mental note to fire him.

"If you've come to get those arms for the Kurds—"

She shook her head. "No, for me that is finished. Arakel was right. No government deserves loyalty in the end. Not even small rebel governments. It came down to different leaders fighting over which would be the biggest and become the ruler."

She sipped her coffee and leaned back in her chair. "And I think you were right about not believing in any cause over the long view." There was no perceptible regret in the way she said it. She paused, looking at Shevlin. "You don't seem to be working for either any longer . . . neither a government nor a cause."

"Just for myself." He told her then something of the functions of private intelligence firms, and less about the operation of his own. It would not be until sometime later that he would tell her about William Reinbold.

"It seems you are doing very well."

"For a start. I'll do better in time."

It appeared that she intended to say something about that but instead she looked down at what she was wearing. "I didn't bring my suitcase and I'm filthy from traveling. Do you have something here that would fit me?"

"If you mean do I keep a wardrobe for visiting girl friends, no. But there's a clotheswasher and drier in the basement. And a guest bedroom with its own bath. Plus a spare robe."

There was no trace of a limp as she went with him up the stairs and into the guestroom. Apparently her broken leg had mended well. Shevlin gave her a bathrobe from the closet and went back down to a room with a bar next to the living room. He made himself a Bloody Mary, sampled it, then with Siri very much in his mind went up to the master bedroom, then to the bathroom connecting to his bedroom and took a shower.

He was toweling himself when Siri came in. She was not wearing the robe he'd given her. Her skin shone from her hot bath. Her thick, tawny hair hung in still damp ringlets around her face and across her wide shoulders. Her nipples were small, a pale shade of pink, their points hardening as she looked at his body. She smiled as she watched him react to her. There was desire in the smile; but more, a kind of complicity. She took a step closer, and let herself fall forward, still smiling. He caught her in his arms, stopping her fall, feeling her suppleness against him, the taut smoothness of her skin under his hands. When he picked her up and carried her into the bedroom, she wrapped her bare arms around his neck. They fell on the bed and attacked each other with a driving impatience . . .

She made love with all her body, without a trace of inhibition. At times it became a crazy kind of competition to see which could excite the other more, draw the greater feeling out of the other. They went on making love for a long time, and with an increasing patience and cunning as they came to learn each other's responses.

When they finally lay exhausted, sated, propped against the pillows, Shevlin took his Bloody Mary from the bedside table and shared it with her. She drank thirstily, her face beaded with perspiration in its frame of tangled ringlets.

He examined her nakedness again, stroked one of her breasts. "This is still perfect, but the rest of you has gotten too skinny."

"Yes. The Turkish police turned against the Kurd rebels too. I was arrested in Ankara. They didn't feed prisoners much. In addition to other unpleasantness."

She had recited it the way another woman might describe a day's shopping at a department store.

"We'll fatten you up." Shevlin led the way to the kitchen to fix a late lunch. They carried it back to the master bedroom and ate sitting cross-legged on the thick, shaggy carpet. When they were finished Siri reached for him and they made love again, this time on the floor . . .

DURING THE NEXT ten days Shevlin was away much of the time. Siri spent most of each day outside weeding, transplanting, watering, trimming back shrubs and trees, adding stones to a terrace retaining wall that was coming apart, and digging a shallow irrigation trench. When the gardener showed up, she discussed what still needed doing with an enthusiasm he found contagious. She spent one day in Munich shopping for new clothes. Her food shopping was done in the nearby town of Grafing. With her appetite and the good food she filled out and her face soon began to lose its gaunt appearance.

Each time Shevlin came home they spent hours making love, taking each other with an increasing savagery. Yet at the same time, by subtle degrees, the elemental passion of it was already beginning its metamorphosis into something else. Something to link them even more strongly.

IT WAS ON a Saturday afternoon that she joined him in Munich for a lunch in the plush restaurant of the Four Seasons Hotel. Afterward he took her to the double-towered cathedral known as the Frauenkirche, showed her the strange imprint in the stone floor of its entrance, and told her the legend of "The Devil's Footprint" . . . The Devil once came to see the Frauenkirche's interior but took only one step inside, sinking this single footstep into the stone. He went no further because the candlelight of God inside frightened him so that he turned back and ran off, ran so fast that the winds which always accompanied him were left behind. Which explained the strong winds that so often swirled in front of the cathedral . . .

Siri examined the Devil's Footprint, then placed her own foot in it. She shook her head. "No, my feet are not that big."

Shevlin gave her a short smile, and stepped into the Devil's Footprint.

Siri nodded at him. "A perfect fit."

"I know. I'm never sure if that worries or pleases me."

They strolled to the Hofgarten, and through it into the park of the English Garden. From time to time she glanced at him, noting that he seemed to be thinking out some problem. Finally she said, "I think you should hire me to do more than your gardening."

"What do you have in mind?" He already knew. It had been on his mind too.

"I could be of use to you, in the sort of work you do."

"Doing what?"

She shrugged. "You know that much about me."

It was enough of an answer for both of them. He knew very well how he could use her. Just as he knew what she needed—that adrenalin rush that came with special kinds of risk, of challenge that after a time got to be an addiction.

Only four days earlier Shevlin had had a private meeting with William Reinbold, and been given an especially confidential assignment, one of those for which it would be inadvisable to use any of the MARS Limited staff.

Strange, he thought . . . he'd grown up in places where you judged another man by whether you could count on him to stand back-to-back with you in a fight against odds. And now he'd come to the point where the only one he'd really trust at his back was this girl.

Partly it was her combination of attitude and strength. Not that she had more strength than other healthy, well-conditioned young women. It was her ability to center all of her strength on just the right point, and just when it was needed. But there was more to her . . . and only someone who'd gone around some rough corners with her could really know and appreciate them.

He gave her his answer as they drove out of Munich to the farmhouse in his new Mercedes. "We'll have to give you a different cryptonym . . . "

She frowned. "I don't know that word."

"Code name"—the CIA jargon stuck to a man—"Zad is no good

anymore, too many people knew you by it."

"All right, you pick one."

And Shevlin had a sudden, vivid image of what he'd seen in her face when she'd finished strangling the Iraqi trooper with her wired scarf. He said: "Medusa."

Siri made a face. "The witch who looked so horrible that just seeing her turned people to stone? I don't look that bad."

"No, and that's the point in its favor." (As he was later to tell Reinbold, who, of course, told his superior, Kopacka.) "It'll make people think of an old hag with snakes for hair and a drop-dead stare."

He turned the Mercedes into the graveled drive and stopped beside his house. "But that's a later legend. Originally Medusa was one of the three Gorgons, the priestesses of the Greek moon goddess. They were said to be ugly because they wore terrifying masks during their cult rituals to scare off anybody trying to discover the secrets of their goddess. Under the masks, though, all three were beautiful. One was named Euryale, the Seeker or, as they said, far-traveling one. The second was Stheno, the Strong One."

"And the Medusa?"

"It means the Cunning One. Feminine."

Siri gazed through the windshield at the lake. Cloud reflections drifted across its placid surface. Finally she nodded and said, "All right. *Medusa.*"

NOT LONG AFTER that they stopped making love. It had become a fierce contest that neither could win. They both came to understand that without a word being spoken, they were too alike, too evenly matched. It left them with a sense of something that had not quite been settled between them, that perhaps remained to be settled. Someday, somewhere . . .

SEVEN YEARS LATER—when Shevlin left William Reinbold at the ruined village of Sorbio and flew off to meet the Medusa and conduct the feasibility study for the elimination of Senator DeLucca—he still felt the same way about that.

III

THE FEASIBILITY STUDY

NINE

WASHINGTON, D.C.

She got out of the cab below the east facade of the Capitol. A warm spring wind molded the green skirt to her long thighs and whipped the ends of the yellow silk scarf fastened at her throat. She caught at the fluttering material and held it still.

For a time she stood looking up at the long white bulk of the Capitol, her expression an alert, solemn appraisal.

She was in her mid-twenties, and according to the documents in her shoulder bag her name was Sabina Remsberg. Siri was all but forgotten. And of course Medusa was for most private communications.

Above the Capitol's high white dome the sun shot out of a cloud scudding across the Washington sky, striking glints in the thick, tawny hair she'd coiled into a neat chignon that went with the businesslike green suit. Narrowing her dark eyes against the sunglare, she climbed the wide stone steps.

There was strength in the way she moved . . . a coupling of dancer's balance and animal energy.

Inside the Rotunda her glance swept past milling tourists and uniformed guards to pick out two men who were not in uniform but had the stance of security agents the world over. They didn't bother her. She identified them, noted their positions out of habit, but nobody in this city would know her . . . which was why she had been dispatched here by Shevlin.

One of the Capitol policemen gave her directions, and she moved off to the right and turned into the ornate marble corridor leading toward the Senate Chamber. Passing the Grand Staircase, she took an elevator down to the well-lighted passageway beneath the Capitol building, where a guard like the one in the Rotunda took the time to give her exact instructions. People generally liked to be helpful to her.

The Medusa boarded the open subway car the guard had indicated and it sped through the long tunnel that ran under Constitution Avenue to the basement of the Senate Office Building on the other side. Her destination: the office of Senator Frank DeLucca.

FOR ALMOST THIRTY years Frank DeLucca's home state had been re-electing him to the Senate regular as clockwork. The seniority thereby acquired had given him substantial political clout, the privilege of speaking his mind to press and presidents, and chairmanship of the powerful Committee on Governmental Affairs. It had also given him one of the more spacious suites in the Senate Office Building.

Much of his suite was partitioned into a warren of cubbyholes to accommodate Senator DeLucca's still growing staff. These days at least two staffers were crammed into each cubbyhole, sometimes sharing a single desk in their struggle to cope with an increasing flood of paperwork.

The Medusa's press credentials allowed her to pass through this cluttered warren to the office of Ruth McCormick, the senator's personal secretary. The credentials, she felt confident, would hold up if checked. In the books of the Vita Bureau, a smallish news agency based in Hamburg, Sabina Remsberg was listed as a roving stringer. She had never met anybody at Vita, but the agency did sell the occasional articles she sent in, mostly to one of the big-three German feature magazines: *Stern, Quick* or *Bunte.* Payment, after deduction of the agency commission, was mailed to an address she kept in London. Vita, of course, was funded by Reinbold through MARS.

Ruth McCormick's office was not only slightly larger than the cubbyholes outside, she had it to herself. A single window framed the Capitol dome across the street. On the walls were memorabilia of

Senator DeLucca's past political battles, along with black-framed photographs of the man with presidents and other heads of state. One picture of him shaking hands with General de Gaulle made Frank DeLucca appear almost ridiculously short and squat. Which he was: a fat little man with powerful shoulders and a cocky brawler's face that nonetheless exuded considerable charm. Plus something more rare in a politician: genuine humor.

"The man you should talk to is Jeff Berman," Ruth McCormick was saying. Ruth was an attractive dark-haired woman in her thirties with a deceptive look of fragility—nobody genuinely fragile could have survived nine years with a hot-tempered dynamo like DeLucca. "Jeff," she explained, "handles the senator's public relations. He won't be in today but I could arrange—"

"I'm really not interested in a publicity release. I would like to interview Senator DeLucca himself." Her sudden smile made it impossible to take offense at her determined attitude.

And Ruth McCormick found herself smiling back, approving the modest, relaxed self-assurance of the young woman seated across the desk from her. DeLucca's secretary was experienced at reading people, and what she thought she read in that face was a thoughtful competence. All in all, a capable, serious girl . . . maybe a bit too serious. But that smile, when it came, was a pleasure. She wasn't exactly *pretty*, Ruth McCormick decided, it was more the sense of vitality stored behind that smile. One could, she thought, recharge one's own batteries on that amount of energy.

"Your English is very good," she told the girl. "I can't place your accent. It doesn't sound German."

"You are right, it's not. I'm part Dutch and part Finnish"—this time the smile was rueful—"but I am afraid my English can't be so good if you still hear the accent. I had hoped I'd finally conquered that."

"Well, almost."

"You are very kind . . . could you be even kinder and help me to obtain this interview with Senator DeLucca? I am sure that *Stern* magazine would feature it prominently. The senator's committee investigations have begun to generate considerable interest in Europe."

There was something else about her, Ruth realized, a quiet authority, that was somehow disconcerting in someone her age. The kind women looked for in men and seldom found. With genuine regret Ruth indicated the appointment book on her desk. "I'm afraid it's just impossible. The senator's schedule is too full, for months to come." Then, still responsive to the special quality in the other one's unwavering gaze, she opened the book and flipped through a few pages. "But the senator does have a press conference scheduled for . . . here it is, the twentieth. In two weeks. I can speak to Jeff Berman for you. Try to get him to squeeze you onto the invitation list."

"Unfortunately I won't be in Washington that long . . . well, it was just a chance. I thought I might as well try."

DeLucca's secretary closed the appointment book. "I'm sorry."

"I am sorry too," the Medusa said. But she wasn't. She hadn't expected to get an interview with Senator DeLucca. Nor did she want one. She had already accomplished what she had come for.

Getting to her feet, she extended a hand across the desk. "Thank you, anyway. You have been very nice, to a complete stranger. Senator DeLucca is lucky to have someone like you. It speaks well of him."

Ruth found the girl's handclasp like her manner—firm and warm. It was, she thought, held just a tinge longer than mere politeness would have dictated. After she left, Ruth stared at the door that had closed behind her, and experienced a dull stirring of an old loneliness.

Outside in the second-floor corridor the Medusa punched the elevator button. She had learned some of the things she'd wanted to know . . . and others which she might need.

And she had met Ruth McCormick.

THE MEDUSA WAITED three days before the follow-up. She did not contact Paul Shevlin during this time. He was in movement between Miami and New York, working out his own part of the feasibility study, trying to determine who could be convincingly framed if the operation was carried to completion. Each morning she went to a Maryland tennis club just outside the District of Columbia and paid its pro for a grueling three-hour session of clay-court dueling. With most clients the pro tried to sharpen their play without making them look too bad. But the Medusa's instructions were for him to keep her on the run, which was what he did, slamming the ball from one corner of the baseline to the other. She wasn't at all bad—swift, agile and relentless, with superb concentration, a powerful precision forehand and a bludgeoning double-handed backhand.

She could have been better with an improved serve and more trickiness in her play, but she wasn't interested; all she wanted were sprinting volleys that pushed her to the limit and left her dripping perspiration. Tennis for her was merely one of the methods she used to burn off excess energy that threatened to explode inside her.

Each noon she returned to Washington for lunch in the dining room of her hotel, the Hay-Adams, which had upper rooms looking directly across Lafayette Square to the White House. The location attracted big-name guests; an interesting young woman waiting at the bar for a free table didn't have to work at it to meet some of them.

On the second afternoon the stout Arab who flirted with her turned out to be Hamid al Ruassad, a Lebanese who had begun as a truck driver and wound up as a major middleman between the Persian Gulf emirates and the oil-thirsty West. After lunch she interviewed Ruassad in his suite, taping it on her miniature Pearlcorder. If he was very disappointed that a handshake was his only thanks, he was careful not to show it. She gave the cassette to a typist supplied by the hotel, edited the results, had it retyped and airmailed it to the Vita Bureau in Hamburg. Ruassad hadn't told her anything earthshaking, but his wealth and flamboyant lifestyle had made him notorious enough so the interview should sell on just his name value. Especially with some stock photos appended of Ruassad entertaining Riviera skin-maidens *sans* bikini tops aboard his yacht off Cannes and St. Tropez.

And, more to the point, it kept her cover active.

Her evenings and nights were spent differently: following Senator DeLucca's secretary after she left the office.

Ruth McCormick took the same route home each time, stopping on the way to buy food for herself. She took no one home with her, and nobody was waiting there for her. Home was a two-floor house of orange brick with black trim which had been left to her by her parents. It was in Foggy Bottom, on I Street just off New Hampshire, two blocks from the Kennedy Center and even closer to the Watergate.

Ruth McCormick had been born into Washington politics. Her father had been a respected Washington attorney, his clients including a number of political figures as well as corporations doing business with the government. Ruth had been his secretary in the last years of his life. She'd also married one of his junior partners. The marriage hadn't lasted long. Ruth no longer blamed her ex-husband for that. He'd tried to be patient, but she had discovered she just wasn't cut out for marriage. After the divorce she'd spent almost a year taking care of her ill mother in her I-Street house. Senator DeLucca had come to her mother's funeral, and had offered Ruth a job shortly thereafter.

In time he had become almost a second father to her. She'd come to love Frank DeLucca for the innate decency and generosity of spirit under his rough exterior, as much as she admired him for the toughness and savvy of his political moves. Working for a man who inspired so much loyalty filled most of her life. Most of it . . .

Each evening after an early dinner she fixed for herself, Ruth opened the briefcase she invariably brought home and got down to things left unfinished from the hectic day at the office. On the first night that the Medusa followed her, Ruth left home at eight-thirty and went to a movie at DuPont Circle. The next night she went to another at Embassy Circle. Each time she resumed the paperwork when she returned-home, keeping at it until weary enough to sleep without taking pills.

She was by no means one to indulge in self-pity. There were many others, she knew, who had lonelier lives, and most of those were married. Sometimes she did sample Washington's social activities but seldom enjoyed it. Most people she met at such functions were just too shallow and opportunistic. Also, she didn't want to take chances—on herself. Political Washington was a small town, with gossip its main currency.

On the third night Ruth went to a theater in Georgetown that sometimes showed foreign films. This night it was the old French classic, *Children of Paradise.* She had seen it several times but never got tired of those passionate closeups of Arletty—her huge, poignant eyes gazing from the screen, lit from within by infinite experience and understanding.

When the film ended, Ruth took several moments before getting up to leave. There hadn't been many in the audience that night. One of them, near the last row, was the young woman she had recently met as Sabina Remsberg.

The girl was dabbing at her eyes with a small handkerchief. She looked very different now. Jeans and shirt, with a yellow sash around her supple waist, emphasizing her youth. Her hair was unbound, coiling around her face and cascading over her wide shoulders, creating a frame that softened her exotic, strong features.

Ruth felt a tingling impulse to sink her fingers into that thick, tawny mane. It startled—and frightened—her, and she would have hurried on past if the Medusa had not looked up at that moment and recognized her.

"Hello!" The Medusa glanced at the damp handkerchief in her hand, then laughed softly as she stood up. "This film always overstimulates my sentimental streak." Which was true enough. When she chose to indulge it, sentiment served as a means of giving her habitual tension a rest. It could also be a useful tool.

The impulse that had unnerved Ruth faded. She even relaxed. "Yes . . . best tearjerker I ever saw. This is the fourth time it's done it to me."

"In that case, let me buy us a drink and we'll drown our sorrows."

Ruth's hesitation was brief. "Okay, you buy me one and I'll buy you one. There's a bar I know that usually isn't too crowded."

They took a taxi there and settled into a comfortable corner booth. The place offered a sense of quiet privacy. Ruth explained that it was this quality that made it the only bar in town she really liked . . . "Plus the fact that it's just around the corner from my house. Where are you staying, by the way?"

"The Hay-Adams."

"Expensive. You must be doing well for yourself."

"As a journalist, you mean? Not yet. I'm still only a beginner. But I have some money of my own. From my parents." Her look grew somber. "They were killed in an automobile accident two years ago."

Ruth touched her hand. "I'm sorry. I know what that feels like." She changed the subject and began talking about the investigation being carried out by Frank DeLucca's committee. She spoke with pride about what the senator was trying to accomplish by searching out the links between multinational companies and private intelligence firms. The Medusa listened with polite interest. Actually she heard nothing that hadn't already been given extensive coverage by the press. Ruth did not reveal any secrets—and the Medusa did not try to get any from her. That was not her assignment.

Ruth noted the lack of prying and put it down to a delicacy, a discretion rarely found in Washington; certainly not among journalists. She had half-expected Miss Remsberg to use their chance meeting to pump her. That she didn't might be due to her being new to the profession, but it made Ruth warm to her even more. She let go of the wariness she'd kept in reserve . . . "I'm still sorry I wasn't able to help you get an interview with the senator. I hope you've been able to get enough others to make coming to Washington worthwile for you."

The Medusa mentioned the interview with Ruassad, as though it were only one example.

Over a second round of drinks their conversation eased into more personal channels. They discovered a number of thoughts and feelings they shared. Including a sense each had of the basic Washington loneliness when one was outside one's immediate work circle. And a common passion for moviegoing. They made a date to see one together the following night.

Outside the bar, the Medusa kissed Ruth lightly before they parted. She felt the woman stiffen, glancing around nervously to see if they were noticed.

"Ruth, don't be silly. Why lose that Arletty mood? In France you always kiss someone you like. A lovely custom." The Medusa's strong hand took hold of Ruth's chin, forcing it up. She looked into Ruth's eyes, her own expression becoming serious. Then she kissed her again.

Two nights later, Ruth took the Medusa home with her.

TEN

WASHINGTON, D.C.

RUTH WAS sleeping deeply when the Medusa slipped out of the bed and stood next to it, her breathing slow and shallow, looking down at the woman. Nothing but a loud noise or violent shaking would waken Ruth for some hours to come. The Medusa had done her work well, but seducing the senator's secretary had required all her concentrated powers.

It had turned out to be Ruth's first such experience since she'd been a teen-ager, and she'd been shaken by it: overwhelmed by both shame and relief.

The Medusa found that she liked her, and was pleased with her work. It had been like retuning a fine but long-neglected musical instrument. And she was in charge . . . with men or women she liked to be the one who seduced: conquering, controlling. That was necessary, both personally and now professionally. She had never had an orgasm . . . it would have meant losing control. Too dangerous.

She left Ruth's bedroom, going past the bathroom and into the upstairs study. She shut the door quietly, turned on a lamp. She had left her shoulder bag on the floor beside the sofa, with the miniature camera inside it. But first she went to the thick briefcase which Senator DeLucca's secretary always brought home with her from the office. Its lock was a simple one, which the Medusa opened in less than two minutes. What she found inside the briefcase was disappointing—a few papers of some interest but not what she was after . . . the appointment book containing DeLucca's upcoming day-by-day schedule.

Putting the papers back in exactly the order in which she had found them, she relocked the briefcase. The feeling of disappointment was gone, replaced by a methodical consideration of the other means of obtaining what she needed.

If Ruth McCormick did not bring the senator's appointment book home with her, she might have left it for the night in a safe at the Senate Office Building. Or, more likely, it was given to DeLucca, or one of his close aides. But to pursue these possibilities would be to incur an increasing risk of a mischance that could tip them off. Which was to be avoided at all cost.

There was a simpler, safer way, based on something she had noted during her visit to Ruth's office. She had already worked out how it could be done.

Her nerves were quiet as she reviewed her next move. Relaxing totally so that her nerves went tight only when needed was something she had learned long ago. She thought again about Ruth McCormick, and went back to the bedroom to check on her. She was still deeply asleep.

Returning to the study, the Medusa sat down at the desk. She turned on Ruth's IBM Selectric and inserted a sheet of typing paper.

DAWN LIGHT FILTERED through the bedroom's venetian blinds, wakening Ruth McCormick. She drifted up out of a well, slowly and at first reluctantly. Then her eyes snapped open as the previous night came back to her in a rush, and she felt her face burn at the memory.

She was alone in the bed. Softly, almost fearfully, she called out. No answer. She climbed from the bed, quickly putting on her robe to cover her nakedness, fastening the sash in place around her waist before going to look for the girl.

The windows of her study had a view, between higher buildings and trees lining the other side of the Potomac, along the Virginia bank.

They also let in the early morning light, illuminating the sheet of paper in her typewriter. It was neither addressed nor signed:

> I did not want to spoil our night together by telling you it was my last night in Washington. I must catch an early plane this morning. Be sure I will call you whenever I return to America. You are lovely.

Ruth sank into a chair, staring at the treetops across the river, holding the note with both hands and crying silently.

AFTER HIS WIFE had died Frank DeLucca had considered selling the Washington house they had shared for so many years. But in the end practicality won over grief. He was too busy to spend time looking for another place to live, getting this one packed up, and making the move. And the house was both comfortable and convenient: on a quiet, tree-lined street, ten minutes from the Capitol and close to Georgetown University where he often taught special seminars.

The ground-floor game room was at the rear, jutting into a small garden. It was equipped with tables for the three games DeLucca liked—pool, ping-pong and poker. General Timothy Keegan stood by the pool table looking at the mementoes on the pine-paneled walls as he waited for Senator DeLucca to return. Some were new. He hadn't been in the house in almost a year—since the direction taken by the senator's committee had put the two men into opposing camps.

Tim Keegan would have looked exactly right as a cavalry officer of the last century: tall, slender and strikingly handsome, with silver hair and piercing black eyes. He did like horses, and rode whenever he had a free weekend, which lately was not too often. His current job as national security adviser to the President did not allow for much recreation. A long way up from World War II, into which Keegan had been seconded to the OSS as a nervous lieutenant fresh out of West Point.

He glanced again at the two old framed photographs of Frank DeLucca from the same war. One as a buck private; the other wearing his captain's uniform. Such battlefront promotions were rare, but a high mortality rate among low-ranking officers in that war and the extraordinary leadership flare revealed by DeLucca in combat had earned him two: the first, to lieutenant in North Africa; the second after he'd been badly wounded leading an attack on the enemy's Gothic Line in Italy. Shipped south to Naples for recuperation and eventual return to the States, DeLucca had gone AWOL from the hospital. It had taken the MPs some time to track him down and discover that young DeLucca had made his way back up to the front and rejoined his old unit.

In both of the old photos Frank DeLucca looked the same: a short, wiry kid with a tough smile and a street-smart stare. Anybody who'd known him then would have no trouble recognizing him today—in spite of his lost youth and added weight.

Keegan's attention returned to a more recent addition to the game room's walls—two front pages from a newspaper in DeLucca's state. Framed side by side, one was from before and the other after the senatorial elections three months earlier. The first had a photo of Senator DeLucca beside a swimming pool with his arm around the bare waist of his bikini-clad companion, a pretty and voluptuous young lady whom the newspaper had discovered to be a high-priced call girl. The pool was at the back of her rented house in the Washington area; and the newspaper had acquired proof that the senator had spent a number of nights sharing the single bedroom in that house with the girl.

At first the scandal of the senator and the call girl seemed certain to bring an end, or at least an interruption, to DeLucca's long political career. But then he had gone on television and told his side of the story with characteristic directness.

"I didn't know the girl was a professional. I've made a lot of enemies by the way I've served the people of this state, and of my country. It's pretty obvious that some of those enemies set this up, and arranged to leak it to the news media. That doesn't matter now. What does matter is that I've always done a job for you in Washington. I think you know I have, and I hope you want me to continue doing so. My personal life is my own. But it is not a secret, and I have never been secretive about it. I was married for a long time to the most lovely, loyal wife a man could have. Now I'm a widower. I will never marry again, because no woman could take the place in my heart that my wife still holds there. But I am still a man. A normal man with normal needs. I like women. *If* that's a weakness, I think it's one that the voters of my state can understand and will forgive. Anybody who would prefer to be represented by a eunuch or some such can vote for someone else."

That last lost DeLucca a number of votes. But it won him a good many more—including a number from some people who had been upset by his refusal to fire his public relation's director, after the man had been caught in a compromising situation during a police raid on a gay bar.

A picture on the second framed newspaper showed DeLucca just after the election results came in, arms spread high in triumph, wearing the same smile as in his old army photos.

DeLucca came back in now from the kitchen carrying their drinks, a beer for himself and a martini for Tim Keegan. "Bone dry, general —I guess you still like 'em that way."

"I do, senator. Thanks."

DeLucca gestured at the framed newspapers General Keegan had been studying. "You figured me to lose that one, didn't you? You'd be able to relax, without me to kick you around anymore."

"Let's say I *hoped* you'd finally lose one. I didn't really expect that you would. You're too good at winning, Frank."

"Damn right. Just don't you forget it."

DeLucca didn't like having to look up at a man he was talking to. With tall women he didn't mind; it somehow added a tang to the challenge. But with men it tended to make him over-aggressive. He carried his beer over to the poker table and took a seat. He had a basic so-called peasant build—the sturdy legs short but a long thickened torso. Keegan sat down too, and DeLucca felt better. He watched the general down half of his martini in one swallow, then look again at the poolside photo on the first of the framed newspapers.

"That is one pretty whore," General Keegan said. "Can't blame you for climbing into the sack with something that looks like that."

DeLucca eyed him, knowing this was a slow lead-up to something. "She's got more than looks, Timmy. Made me feel twenty years younger—and that after a long hard week with not much sleep."

"You don't sound very mad at her."

"Why should I be? She was working at her trade, and doing a damn good job of it. I just might be sore at the guy who pointed her at me and arranged to have a photographer with a telescopic lens in position to shoot that picture. Your ex-employee, Paul Shevlin. But I guess you know that."

General Keegan shook his head. "I don't know it. Neither do you. Or you'd have him in court by now."

"Too hard to prove. So far. But it *was* Shevlin. Just like that police raid that just happened to get sprung when my PR man was in that gay bar. Paul Shevlin at work again."

Keegan finished off his drink and said mildly, "Jeff Berman wasn't there by accident, Frank. Your PR *is* a homosexual and you know he is."

"So what? That's his business, as long as it doesn't interfere with his work. And it doesn't—any more than your thirst for bone-dry martinis interferes with yours. Speaking of which, can I fix you a refill?"

"Nope. Still got a full evening ahead." The general looked down at his empty glass for a moment, then back up at the senator. "You make a lot of charges you're not dead-certain of, Frank. It's about to get you in trouble. I want you to be prepared for that—for old times' sake."

DeLucca leaned back in his chair with a grin that seemed worry-free. "Old times' sake. That's a nice touch. The President must be pretty upset with me."

"The President did not—repeat, not—send me here to talk to you."

"Of course not. And the President didn't send Mort Dorson yesterday."

Dorson was the secretary of the interior. General Keegan looked puzzled. "What did Dorson want?"

"To warn me that I've been going after Shevlin's client, Reinbold Enterprises, too hard. And that, because of it, William Reinbold may cancel plans one of his companies had for the development of natural gas resources in Montana and Wyoming. Which may come as a relief to environmentalists but, according to Mort Dorson, would be a tragic loss to the country . . . and now you're here to warn me about something else."

"I'll say it again, Frank. The President didn't send me here. I've got enough reason of my own. Your committee is making too much trouble for our intelligence branches. Making us look bad to our allies. That interferes with our ability to do jobs that need doing. And, you're hurting agent morale."

"It's *ex*-agents the committee is interested in. The ones who've gone out into the business world selling their skills and connections on the open market. I know most are fairly decent men. But big money means big temptations. In some cases they wouldn't even know who they're really working for. The intelligence community doesn't have a monopoly on false-flag recruitment, as you people call it. Plus—there *are* some rotten apples among them."

"We know that. But shouting it to the world isn't the right way to correct that. And making blanket insinuations that reflect on all of us . . . you're doing an injury to the government of this country, Frank. Why can't you see that? A clandestine service that's exposed to open view isn't worth much. Let *us* take care of our problems. In our own way. Without the noise."

"I'm trying to get you the tools to do that properly, Tim. New laws to give you the right you don't have at present to exercise some control over ex-agents, to make them *accountable.* That's all the committee is after—"

"The hell you say. You're riding an obsession and you don't give a damn if it wrecks our whole intelligence capability. As long as it gets you publicity. All these charges about Frankenstein Cells—what's that supposed to be but a gimmick, a catchphrase to focus attention on yourself? Well, you've got trouble. And nobody to blame but yourself—"

"So get to the point," DeLucca said. "I'm not a little flower. I won't wilt."

Keegan drew a deep breath, getting his control back. "I wish you would," he grumbled. He got up and went to the latest addition to DeLucca's walls. Taking it down, he returned to the poker table and put it down between them.

It was a blowup of a long-distance photo—the entrance to a bar at Tyson Corners, Virginia, not far from CIA headquarters at Langley. The picture showed two men emerging from the place, deep in conversation, their expressions dead-serious. One was a high-ranking official of the CIA. The other was former agent Paul Shevlin, head of MARS, Limited. The picture had been taken by one of DeLucca's committee investigators.

"You got a lot of play in the media with this shot," General Keegan said. "The inference was that it's another indication that what you claim is true. CIA officer being pumped for inside government information by unscrupulous former agent now in the employ of big, bad tycoon."

"That's so wrong?"

"Very wrong. Three weeks ago, you may remember, SAPO—the secret police in Sweden—arrested a Swedish air force officer and charged him with selling NATO secrets to the Russians."

"I do remember." DeLucca put both hands on the table and linked their thick, stubby fingers together tightly, enforcing calm. He could guess what was coming.

"Tomorrow morning," Keegan told him, "we will give a release to the media explaining how the Swedes caught onto this spy in their military. *We* told them about him. And your pet villain, Paul Shevlin, is the one who told *us.*" He tapped the photograph. "That's what's really going on in this picture. Shevlin found out about this Swedish spy, made the appointment at Tyson Corners with our man and tipped him about it. So much for Shevlin's loyalty to the United States."

"I never charged him with being disloyal," DeLucca put in. "All I want is laws that enable the government to keep a check on him and other former agents—so that we'll know at all times who they work for and exactly what they're doing for their pay . . . for example, I wonder how Shevlin learned that this Swedish officer was a spy."

"I don't know, and I wouldn't expect him to tell. He's got to protect his source, who's probably someone in a very sensitive position. But that's not the point. The point is that most former agents are not a danger to America as you claim. They are often an invaluable help to us, passing on information they learn from working in the private sector. Sometimes vital information—as in this case."

"Bravo. Nothing the committee wants will interfere with their continuing to do so in the future."

"Your committee," General Keegan said, "is about to get itself a very black eye tomorrow. When we release this story about how completely you misinterpreted this photo you'll look ridiculous."

"That I will," Senator DeLucca agreed. "For a time."

"Frank," Keegan said in his most reasonable tone, "we can phrase this release tomorrow to make you look *very* bad—or not so bad."

"I confess I prefer not so bad."

"Then give me your word to pull back. Get your committee off our backs. If we do have a small problem with a few former agents who're out of control, let *us* deal with it."

"No."

"In that case, we're going to have to hit you as hard as we can."

AFTER GENERAL KEEGAN left, DeLucca went to his study and phoned Robert Pryor, chief counsel to the Committee on Governmental Affairs.

"Bob, like they say, the shit is about to hit the fan. Our shit, Paul Shevlin's fan." He explained and said, "Please get your ass over here. And bring Jeff with you."

Jeff Berman was the smartest public relations man DeLucca knew. If anybody could figure out means to soften the blow that would hit the committee the next day, Jeff would come up with it. But there was no way, DeLucca realized, to deflect the blow entirely. Considering that, he made two more calls. One was overseas to Hamburg to Klaus Bauer, a German journalist with his own score to settle with MARS Limited and Reinbold Enterprises, and whom DeLucca had put in charge of committee investigations abroad. The other was to George Ryan, who directed committee investigations in Washington. What he asked of each was to come up with methods of *intensifying* the committee investigations. Since there was no way to deflect the blow, there was only one recourse. Strike back.

Before hanging up, Ryan told DeLucca he had a man with him that he'd like the senator to meet. "Name's Simon Hunter. I know him from way back, when we were both in army intelligence. Now he's with the State Department's WGCT—the Working Group to Combat Terrorism. "Mostly he acts as senior adviser and liaison between different units, ours and those of other countries. Part of the job involves protection for our VIPs in Europe. *If* you ever make that trip over there, like Bauer's been wanting you to, Simon's the man I'd like to have handle your security. Right now I just want you to size him up, see how you feel about him."

"We've got a lot of touchy business ahead of us tonight, George. I can't spare more than a few minutes—"

"That'll be fine. We'll get right over there."

Ryan and Hunter arrived by taxi, well before Pryor and Berman. Hunter glanced up and down the tree-lined street. He registered a man standing in the shadows to one side of DeLucca's small front lawn—a bodyguard or "minder" as some in the trade now called them. Ryan nodded to him when they left the taxi waiting at the curb and went toward the house.

Senator DeLucca came out onto his front porch as they climbed the steps to it. Ryan introduced him to Simon Hunter. Hunter was a bear of a man with a heavy mop of thick gray hair and a look of relaxed competence about him. To DeLucca he seemed huge, even standing beside Ryan, who was a pretty big man himself. There was a great deal of experience tucked inside his easy stance and dark, quiet eyes. DeLucca judged him to be close to retirement age.

"I wish I could invite you inside for a drink," DeLucca told him, "but we've got a heavy night ahead of us."

"I don't have much time either, senator. Got to catch a plane to France."

"His wife," Ryan told DeLucca, "is about to have their first baby."

DeLucca congratulated Hunter. "Do you live in France?"

Hunter nodded. "I'm in Europe more than here. And my wife is French."

Tall men tended to hunch themselves a bit when they were with DeLucca so he wouldn't feel so short, but Hunter seemed unaware of the height difference between them. DeLucca sat down in one of the porch rockers and gestured Hunter to another. Hunter ignored the rocker, instead moved sideways and half sat on the rail of the porch banister. His big frame blocked DeLucca's view of much of the street, and vice versa, the senator realized. He guessed that protective moves had become habitual with this man. Tilting back in the rocker, he observed the way Hunter glanced over his shoulder at the street again.

"Your security here is pretty minimal," Hunter said quietly to Ryan, "if that guy on the lawn's all you've got around the house."

"Well, any time somebody's pulled an attack on a political figure in this town they've been caught. There's just too much heat available in Washington for any rational enemy to try anything against the senator here—"

"That still leaves the political fanatics."

"Sure, but you know there's just so much you can do about loonies that're willing to die in the attempt. We've got a round-the-clock team. One man is always here and checks out the house regularly. Plus the

Georgetown cops, who are damn conscientious about prowling these streets on the lookout at unpredictable intervals. Capitol Hill has its own pretty efficient security people. And between here and there the senator has a top-notch minder-driver who never uses the same route twice in succession."

DeLucca, who had been studying Hunter, now gave him his own feeling about it. "Anyway, I don't figure I *need* bodyguards hanging all over me—in addition to the fact that I have no intention of living my life that way, in an attitude of fear—"

"There's a difference," Hunter told him, "between an attitude of fear and one of caution."

DeLucca made a dismissing gesture. "George is worried about possible retaliation from MARS Limited and Reinbold Enterprises. I'm not—not about physical retaliation. I'm not doing either of them enough harm for that. Even if my hearings finally manage to come up with some really dirty tricks they've been getting away with, what's the worst we could do to them with such a revelation? At best slap some restrictions on their activities. People don't kill over business restrictions. They put their lobbyists and lawyers to work."

"I'm inclined to agree with you, senator. Nobody kills or kidnaps a political figure just because he's giving them some *business* problems. That leaves politically motivated groups. George tells me you got a threat from one of them a couple years back."

"One anonymous letter. The writers weren't discovered—and no attempt against me ever followed the threat. The fact is, there's not a single case on record of any chairman of a committee ever having been murdered or kidnapped as a result of his investigations. And I can think of several who deserved it. We're just not important enough."

George Ryan nodded. "Loonies want presidents or presidential candidates. In Europe it's different. There are too many well-organized terrorist groups ready to hit any public figure they can get at. And too many successful hits, where nobody ever gets caught."

DeLucca changed the subject. "I understand, Hunter, that you were in military intelligence in the past. You must still have friends there who hate my guts right now."

"I don't know many people in the spook trade that well, senator. Never was in that end of intelligence work myself. Always been strictly a cop. Investigations and security."

"Tell me, anyway . . . what do *you* think of what I'm trying to do?"

As Simon Hunter considered the question he realized he was rubbing the knuckles of one large hand with the palm of his other. People who didn't know much about him sometimes mistook that for a nervous mannerism. It wasn't. He'd grown up in a coal mining area of Pennsylvania. When he'd been sixteen a shaft he'd been working collapsed on him, breaking bones in both hands from his wrists to his fingers. It had taken his father and six other miners eighteen hours to reach the cave-in and dig him out, and two years more before he regained full use of his hands. That had been long ago, but the places where the breaks had mended still hurt in damp weather or any sharp temperature change.

Hunter glanced over his shoulder at the sky. Sure enough, some heavy banks of clouds were closing in. There'd be rain sometime tonight.

He looked back to DeLucca and gave him his answer. "I think you're letting in some light on the sort of operations that can only be carried out effectively in the dark." There was no hesitation or polite hedging in the way Hunter said it. "And if our intelligence people can't function effectively, this country will wind up without information it badly needs. I do think you've put your finger on a real problem intelligence has on its hands right now. But anything you've got that will help them deal with it ought to be slipped to them quietly and privately. Not in a glare of publicity."

"You sound like General Keegan."

A grin appeared on Hunter's strong face. "Good. Then I'm not stepping out of line." He didn't give DeLucca the impression of actually caring much about whether he was or not.

"Don't you think," DeLucca asked him, "that the intelligence community is likely to correct the problem more quickly with public opinion pushing for it?"

"Maybe. But your kind of cure could do more damage than the disease itself."

Ryan broke in uncomfortably, "Senator, I've already argued this out with Simon. I'm afraid you won't budge him on that point."

"Not trying to. He's entitled to his own opinions. Which I'm sure don't interfere with his work."

Hunter glanced at his watch and stood up. "Got to go, senator. Good meeting you."

They shook hands and DeLucca watched Hunter go down to the waiting taxi. He said to Ryan, "He's pretty old to be having his first child. Or is this his second marriage?"

Ryan nodded. "His first wife died of leukemia."

DeLucca's mouth thinned as the words touched a special nerve.

Ryan looked at him, troubled by the clash of opinion between the senator and Hunter. He'd been around Washington too long to hero-worship any politician—but the affection he'd come to feel toward DeLucca came close enough to it to surprise him. And Simon Hunter was an old friend, whom he greatly respected. "I guess," Ryan said, "that the two of you didn't get along as well as I'd expected."

The warmth of the smile DeLucca gave him would have startled men who only knew him on the political firing line. "We got along fine, George. A good man. He'll do, whenever I get around to that European jaunt."

As Hunter's taxi pulled away Bob Pryor drove up with Jeff Berman. They joined DeLucca and Ryan on the porch and went inside to get down to business.

EVERY YEAR AMERICAN taxpayers pay out almost two million dollars worth of special services to each member of the U.S. Congress. Some twenty-thousand specialists are required to supply these services to Capitol Hill. They range from manicurists and speechwriters to gourmet cooks and electronics experts.

George Dain was one of the experts. Dain was not as tall as he would have liked but he was well built with good features, curly hair and a roving eye. He had celebrated his thirtieth birthday three months before, almost four years since he'd left Fort Wayne to try his luck in Washington. He had reason to be pleased with how well he had done. His regular job, which included maintenance of equipment in the Senate recording and TV studio as well as various electronic installations throughout the Senate side of the Hill, paid quite well, with yearly increases. The extra income required for the lifestyle Dain enjoyed came from moonlighting.

Over most of the past year his moonlighting had been confined to improving the digital readout system for a new voice-stress lie detector that a small company had been trying to market. But the company had gone under two months back, which left Dain short of the kind of money he needed to pay the high rent on his flashy bachelor pad, continue his habit of buying a new sports car each year and maintain the 36-foot cabin cruiser he used for weekend fishing and entertaining some of Washington's better-looking office girls. . . .

At two o'clock that Saturday afternoon he anchored the cruiser in Chesapeake Bay between Taylors Island and Flag Harbor. Either shore was far enough away at that point to make it almost impossible for anyone to record what was said on the boat, if the offer was an attempt at entrapment. Dain had checked the Medusa's shoulder bag when she'd come aboard at the dock, making sure she wasn't carrying a recorder or remote mike. There was no place else for her to conceal such equipment. It was a hot day, and she'd showed up at the Plumb Point dock wearing only sandals, skimpy shorts, an open shirt tied high to expose a taut, smooth-skinned midriff, and a yellow bandana.

With the iced drinks he'd fixed in the cabin's wet bar they settled into canvas chairs under the blue awning shading his cruiser's stern deck. Dain allowed her to see that he openly admired her long thighs and the provocative pointiness of her nipples against the nylon of her shirt. It was also one way to avoid showing how much he liked her cash offer. He didn't have to fake the sexual excitement the girl generated in him, though he found it difficult to explain why. The girls he went for were more conventionally pretty, softer. This one's jaw was too strong, her shoulders too wide, the high-bridged nose too arrogant, the darkness in the eyes too hard to read. But she did turn him on.

"The money sounds good," he said finally, "but not when you consider what you're asking for it. A job like that'd take some doing. I'm not even sure, right now, *how* I could do it."

"Yes, you are," the Medusa said. She told him how he would do it, in detail.

Dain scowled at her. "You said you're an investigator for some private company. Now you sound like an MIT graduate."

"I did my homework. Enough to understand what I'm asking you for. That's part of my job."

"You didn't mention the name of this company you claim to work for."

"No," she agreed, "I didn't."

Dain eyed her. "This company wouldn't be located in DeLucca's state, would it?"

She appeared to hesitate, then said, "Don't try to be clever. Think instead about your debts. You are in arrears with all three of your credit cards, you are a month behind in your rent and your yearly dock fees for this boat come due in nine days. Two thousand dollars will clear up all of that. Half now, half when you deliver."

He scowled again. "You really check up on a guy before you contact him."

"Yes."

Dain was certain he'd been right about whom she was working for—some of Senator DeLucca's political rivals back home, trying to find out what he was up to so they could get something on him. Such skullduggery wasn't unusual in Washington; the ethics of it didn't interest him, just the payment. He wanted more, if he could goose her into it.

"It wasn't the technical part of doing the job I meant was a problem," he told her. "It's the risk of getting caught at it."

"The risk is almost nonexistent if you use common sense. You are in and out of those offices all the time as part of your normal work. Nobody will notice that you're doing anything unusual if you handle it exactly the way I've told you to."

"Don't act like there's *no* risk."

"What there is, is covered by the two thousand. Otherwise it would only be five hundred."

Dain drew a short breath. "Fifteen hundred up front. Another fifteen when I deliver."

The Medusa studied him for a moment. "No. My offer is fair, and it stands."

"Suppose I turn it down?"

She shrugged, her manner calm. "Then I'll have to get someone else. There are others in your department who can do it just as well."

"I could tip the authorities, and louse it up for you."

"I am not the only kind of employee in the firm I work for." She didn't sound angry, and there was no emotion in her expression. "There are others who have experience using hammers on a man's legs. Also kidneys. You'd piss blood for years."

Dain stared at her. "Hey . . . I was only kidding, for God's sake."

She smiled a little. "I know. And, of course, so was I."

He wiped drops of sweat from his forehead. "Christ, it's hot, even under this awning." He knew he was going to accept the offer. He drained the last of his drink and eyed her again. "Let's take a swim while I think it over."

"I didn't bring a bathing suit."

Dain's grin was back. "That's okay. I'll show you mine if you show me yours."

It could, she decided, make what would be necessary that much easier. "Next time. When you deliver. Deal?"

"Deal."

When he docked the boat she left him and drove off in the car she'd rented that morning. She spent the next hour driving slowly along the bay shore, stopping at disused piers. At one of them she found what she wanted. A rotting net that commercial fishermen had discarded.

She bundled it up and took it back with her to her room at the Hay-Adams.

ELEVEN

WASHINGTON, D.C.

THE VIDEO camera the Medusa had noted when she'd been in the Senate Office Building was close to the ceiling in a corner behind Ruth McCormick's desk. It was positioned to record visitors on the suite's own closed-circuit system. Dain knew the installation. He had serviced it in the past, a routine part of his job around Capitol Hill.

The camera had been in use for some years and was larger than more up-to-date models. Dain told Ruth when he came to her office late that Monday afternoon that a number of similar installations had begun giving trouble lately: dulled images caused by worn-out vidicons.

Ruth saw nothing unusual in his checking it out. She continued with her work while Dain fiddled with the intensity control, then had a look at the video recorder and cassette player installed in her supply closet.

"Sure enough," Dain announced after a couple minutes, "you're about to have the same problem here. I might as well take the camera down to my workshop and fix it before it goes out of whack."

He explained that with his present workload he might not be able to get it done immediately. He'd bring up a replacement camera that would do the same job in the meantime. Ruth found nothing unusual in this either.

Office hours were almost finished when Dain came back to her office. The replacement camera he carried was even older and larger than the one now in use but it functioned perfectly, he assured her. Apologizing for the inconvenience, Dain shut off the closed-circuit video system and got to work.

He was still at it when Ruth left for the day, along with most of the senator's office staff. Like most of the maintenance and clean-up crews, Dain had his own keys to the office suites, so as a routine precaution Ruth and the other staffers before leaving put sensitive material away in cabinets with combination locks.

Alone now in the office, Dain removed the camera that had been in use and rigged up the replacement in the same position. He had spent most of his Sunday working on it, taking apart the replacement camera and making the alterations the Medusa had asked for. Concealed inside its large housing there were now *two* cameras. Recent models using the latest microcomponent technology and integrated circuits, each very small, weighing less than two-and-a-half pounds. One operated through the normal lens and would do the normal job of recording visitors to the office. The second camera did not have a protruding lens. It focused through a small hole Dain had drilled in the bottom of the outside casing and was angled down at the surface of Ruth McCormick's desk.

Dain ran double wires from the replacement unit to the office supply closet, along the same base wall as the previous connection. Inside the closet he made a split-off behind the suite's video-cassette recorder, where no one would notice it. The normal camera fitted into the replacement housing now fed into the suite's VCR, as it was supposed to. Dain ran the lead from the second camera to a cable inside the back wall of the closet.

The smartass paying him for the job couldn't have guessed how easy this part of it was for him. He'd had to go into this wall before, like he had in many other offices. So much new electrical equipment had been installed since the building had been constructed that the wiring inside all these walls were tangled spaghetti. After a while you got tired of having to knock holes in the walls to get at the internal wiring, so when you made a hole in a place where it didn't show, you just left it —for the next time you or somebody else had to get at the spaghetti inside.

Like here, inside Ruth McCormick's supply closet, behind the video recorder . . . Dain probed the hole with his flashlight, found the cable strands he wanted, and made a quick, temporary splice. Next, he took care of the other assignment the girl had given him. The closet was also used for the temporary storage of videocassettes which had recorded visitors to the suite over the past few weeks. Each was packed in a cardboard container marked with its date. Dain removed two cassettes —one from the container bearing the date when the Medusa had come to the suite, and another from a different date. He put unused cassettes in their place.

These cassettes were rarely consulted, and every few weeks they were transfered to a catchall storage room in the basement. If anyone ever did check, the missing cassettes could be the result of carelessness in transfer. If someone became suspicious that it was more than carelessness, suspicion would concentrate on people who had appeared on *both* cassettes, not just on one. In any event, nobody would have access to the pictures taken of the Medusa.

On leaving Senator DeLucca's office, Dain locked the entrance door as he was supposed to and went down to the subbasement. Nobody knew all of the building's complex electrical wiring, but Dain knew more than most. Opening up one of the multitude of cables running through the subbasement, he located the cable strands he'd hooked into up at DeLucca's suite, ran another splice off it to a line leading up to his workshop in the basement above.

While he was at it two maintenance workers came through. Dain went on with what he was doing as they exchanged complaints about overtime. There was no reason for them to be puzzled about what he was up to. He was always messing with cables in the routine performance of his duties.

When the splice was finished, Dain went up a flight of steps and unlocked his workshop. Inside he made the final connection to his own VCR. And that did it for the day. For the rest of that week all he'd have to do was to come in here regularly to change the cassettes.

From now on anything placed on Ruth McCormick's desk would be picked up by the second concealed camera and fed directly to Dain's video recorder—and nowhere else.

SENATOR FRANK DELUCCA scheduled a war council of his basic team for two days later—first thing Wednesday morning in his office across from the Capitol.

He didn't sleep well Tuesday night. The fallout from the revelation about the committee's misinterpretation of the Tysons Corner photograph was still radioactive, also TV- and newsprint-active. Members of the media kept hitting him with the same questions, all variations of how could he have made such an embarrassing error of political and legal judgment?

DeLucca refused to eat crow. He stuck with the tone set in the first press conference immediately after General Keegan's press release dropped the bomb on him—a shrug and the truth: "I goofed."

That got him a laugh, generally sympathetic but followed by a jeering thrust: "What do you plan to do for an encore, senator?"

"I plan," DeLucca answered with a smile, "to try to figure out what hit me."

Another laugh.

But he knew what had hit him. He'd been booby-trapped again. As he had been with the call girl; and the time his public relation's man got caught in the gay bar.

Booby traps set by MARS Limited.

For Reinbold Enterprises.

An agent was expendable in the cause of compromising the enemy —DeLucca.

DeLucca had been invited to an upper-echelon Washington party on Tuesday evening. He accepted the invitation, just to show that he wasn't hurting. The truth was that he was hurting like hell. There were people there whom he liked a good deal, but he left early. There were two single women at the party who suggested he accompany them home for a late drink: one a girl just turned thirty and the other a good-looking widow who had been a friend of his wife. That was one thing about Washington . . . if you were a power in this town you were automatically attractive to women, no matter what your age or theirs.

Ordinarily DeLucca might have gone off with one of them. He never mixed emotions. Like he said, what he had felt for his late wife, and still felt, was one thing. Quite another was the fact that he was still a male with normal sexual drive, for whom feminine warmth was both natural and essential. But this evening he declined, for the same reason he left the party early—he was tired of smiling when he felt like snarling.

His wife, Eva, had been the only person with whom he'd never had to conceal his wounds. Not that he'd complained much around her; whining was not part of his nature. But Eva had always *known* when something was really bothering him and handled him on these occasions in exactly the right way—with a solid optimism that in no way meant that she failed to understand the seriousness of the problem.

He missed having someone like that with him. He missed Eva. Damn, how he missed her . . .

He went home that night and drank four bottles of beer while he shot pool by his solitary self. He didn't feel lonely. Like a wounded bear, he preferred to crawl into his cave alone to lick the wounds . . . and plan his revenge.

At midnight he switched off the lights in the game room and trudged upstairs, walked past the master bedroom on the second floor and into the bedroom that had belonged to his son Johnny when the boy had been growing up in this house. Johnny now taught chemistry at the University of California and lived near the campus with his pretty wife, a girl DeLucca thoroughly approved of. He visited them whenever he was out on the coast, and they always made him feel genuinely welcome, fixing up the sofa bed in their living room for him and feeding him his favorite meals.

DeLucca had begun sleeping in Johnny's room after Eva had died. It had begun when Johnny and his wife came east for Eva's funeral. He'd given them the master bedroom and shifted in here. When they'd left he'd tried returning to the master bedroom, but it had felt wrong, sleeping there without Eva. He had shifted back to Johnny's room and had used it ever since.

It was one o'clock on Wednesday morning when he fell asleep. It was still dark out when he found himself wide awake with his eyes burning, his throat dry and his brain churning with strategy for the battle ahead of him. The luminous dial of the clock beside Johnny's bed showed a few minutes past five A.M.

DeLucca took a long shower, put on his robe and went down to the kitchen to make himself breakfast: coffee, flapjacks with butter and maple syrup and a string of sausages. By the time he finished and downed a second cup of coffee it was getting light out and the weariness had drained away. He dressed for the day, poured himself a third cup of coffee, carried it up to the master bedroom. By day, it felt good to spend time there. Somehow it gave him a feeling of renewed sharing, instead of the sense of loss.

He settled now into the padded rocker next to the big bed, sipping his coffee and looking at an enlarged photograph on the dresser table that had been taken when he and Eva were on their honeymoon, hiking and camping out in the Rockies. The picture, taken by another camper who had come by, showed DeLucca squatting down to pick flowers for Eva while she stood close by, laughing delightedly.

Lord, she was pretty. Even shorter than he was, curvy with huge brown eyes and a mass of black curls. And she was smart. It hadn't taken long after their marriage to find out he was no good at all at managing what he earned. He'd opened his own small law office and a year later had been bankrupt. Which was ironic, considering how good he was to become later at figuring out other people's problems involving millions and even billions of dollars. But small amounts of his own had just slipped through his fingers: spent or lent, with him making out checks without first being sure there was enough in the account to cover them.

After the bankruptcy Eva had taken over handling the family finances—much to her husband's relief. She'd continued to do so as he had risen in the hierarchy of a large law firm, and when he'd gone on into politics. It was Eva who had made out their budgets and saw that they stuck to them; who figured out what they could buy and when; who paid the bills and made out the checks. DeLucca hadn't even had a checkbook of his own, and had been grateful to be relieved of that temptation. The cash he'd carried on him had been whatever she figured he'd need, and never more, as he'd acknowledge, than they could afford to have him blow.

When Johnny had gotten married Eva had startled him with the announcement that they had more than enough socked away in the bank to buy Johnny and his bride a house as a wedding present. And she'd left him with a bank balance that had surprised him even more: not really rich, but with more than enough to last out his lifetime.

Now an accountant handled the senator's finances, but he'd had to relearn how to make out his own checks, Eva had done it so long for him.

Eva . . .

He looked at her picture beside the bed they'd shared and said aloud, "Well, kiddo, I really got clobbered this time, gotta face it, that Shevlin's one hell of an alley fighter. Trapped me and stomped me. Got to do better . . ."

He sipped more coffee in silence, then grinned at her and nodded. "Right, kiddo. Only thing to do . . . go back into that alley and find him. And beat the shit out of him—him *and* his boss."

AT NINE-THIRTY that Wednesday morning they were all settled down in DeLucca's office across from the Capitol, reviewing the latest developments and planning their next moves accordingly. DeLucca presided behind his cluttered desk. The others sat in four chairs spread around the other side of it: the committee's chief counsel, Bob Pryor; the director of the senator's public relations staff, Jeff Berman; the committee's chief investigator at the Washington end, George Ryan; and the man running its overseas investigation, Klaus Bauer.

Ruth McCormick sat unobstrusively on the sofa behind them, jotting shorthand notes in her pad.

"The latest bad news," Pryor announced, "comes from the attornies for MARS Limited. They're threatening to file suit against you personally, and against the committee. Defamation of Shevlin's character, integrity and loyalty. Irreparable damage to his firm and its financial future."

"That's not bad news," DeLucca told his chief counsel. "I'd welcome such a suit. But they'll never go through with it. Last thing they want. It'd let me force Shevlin to come into court and explain his firm's operations. Including its connection with Reinbold. And that most interesting detail . . . just how in hell he managed to find out that the Russians had a Swedish spy planted in NATO. The threat's just a bluff. Unfortunately."

He turned to Ryan with questions about how their new plans for intensifying the Washington investigation were coming along.

"I'm running into problems with it, senator. Reluctance to cooperate from other committee members, Senators Diamond, Harding and O'Toole especially. But some others too. Administration minions have been wining and dining them since General Keegan's press release. So have Reinbold Enterprises' best lobbyists—*including* former Secretary of State Gunther. They've been doing a squeeze job on one committee member at a time. Warning each of political damage he's likely to suffer back in his own state if the committee hearings continue along the same line . . . injuring American intelligence capability, as they put it."

Ryan hesitated, then gave him the rest of it. "We're also getting unpleasant vibes from two other sources, senator—the Senate Intelligence Committee and the Congressional Subcommittee on Multinational Corporations are both repeating, loudly, their old complaints that you're stepping on *their* territories."

"I wouldn't have to if they were taking care of those territories the way they're supposed to and aren't." DeLucca looked at his PR. "Dust off *my* old statement to that effect, Jeff."

"I already have, and have gotten it out to everybody in the media who's still on your side."

Ryan spoke up again. "What worries me, senator, are the complaints inside your own committee. Diamond, Harding and O'Toole again. They're making some nasty noises about it maybe being advisable, under the circumstance, for you to step down as its chairman—"

"Let them *try* . . . don't worry, they'll change their tune as soon as we come up with new evidence. Only next time it better be evidence that *stands up.*"

Ryan flushed. "I take full responsibility for that goof. I should have checked deeper, but I got over-eager. It won't happen again, I promise you."

"See to it—and let me take care of the committee chickens. I'll whip them back into line, depend on it."

It was Jeff Berman's turn to deliver the next piece of bad news. "Just got in the results of that voter poll in your home state, senator. Your lowest rating in over ten years."

Senator DeLucca's face grew dark. He didn't speak for a time and nobody else tried to break into his silence. Finally, he said heavily, "Can't blame them. Natural reaction. But we have a number of years to go before the next elections roll around. They'll get over it by then. I hope."

"Not if the press doesn't let you off the hook," Berman said. He reminded DeLucca that the many companies in which Reinbold Enterprises had financial interest included a growing number of American TV stations and newspapers. "My guess is that Reinbold will be getting into more of them . . . in your state. He'll see to it they keep hammering away at you right up to and into the next election."

DeLucca got out a cigar, bit off the end, spat it into his wastebasket and lit the other end with a lighter crudely fashioned out of an old 20-millimeter shell that he kept on his desk. He took a deep drag at the cigar, then pursed his lips and slowly blew three perfect smoke rings. "Well then, we'll just have to pin Mr. Reinbold's hide to the wall. Before election time rolls around again." He looked to Klaus Bauer.

The German—as a journalist and a foreigner—was an unusual choice for a position of such responsibility with a senate committee. But overriding such liabilities was the fact that he knew more about William Reinbold and Reinbold Enterprises than anyone else. He'd been at it longer, beginning some years before DeLucca's committee got around to it. Other journalists had dug into the uncertainties surrounding Reinbold and found the job impossibly hard-going. Even where he originally came from was clouded by conflicting rumors and vanished witnesses to his rise from obscurity. So was the true source of the first fortune with which he had launched himself into the world of international finance. It also proved extremely difficult to determine the extent of the empire Reinbold had spread out across the western world. He was not, it seemed, the director of any single one of the many companies in which Reinbold Enterprises had financial interest. Even the amounts he had invested in these businesses through a labyrinth of holding companies could not be proved. Nor could the amount of control Reinbold exercised over them. The other journalists had tried, and given up. Klaus Bauer had been more persistent. He had been the first to discover that the newly created MARS Limited might actually be a Reinbold tool—used to sabotage his business rivals and "persuade" political enemies in various countries to cooperate with his designs.

It had seemed that Bauer had finally hit paydirt during hearings by Britain's Monopolies Commission on a bid to take over one of London's most influential financial journals. The group that wanted to buy out the journal was headed by the highly respected Sir Howe Darly. But Bauer obtained documents that proved that most of the money for the take-over bid had actually come from Reinbold Enterprises—and that Sir Howe was under Reinbold's control. Bauer's newspaper article about this, and the documents supporting it, created a sensation. Which was promptly countered by a lawsuit filed by Sir Howe against Bauer and the papers carrying the story. In the trial that resulted, the documents Bauer had been given turned out to be forgeries. Another expert sabotage job by MARS Limited. But this Bauer was unable to prove . . . the man who'd given him the documents disappeared and was never seen again. Bauer, discredited, had trouble getting further assignments. Understandably he burned for vengeance, which was why Frank DeLucca had chosen him.

Klaus Bauer chose his words with care now. Though fluent in English, when translating his thoughts into a different language he felt it necessary to make certain his meaning was understood exactly as intended. He brought them up to date on his most recent progress in putting together the story of William Reinbold, his empire, his activities, and his use of MARS Limited . . . The first matter dealt with was Brussels, where Bauer had just spent some time following up a rumor that Paul Shevlin had recently begun a secret operation there. A newspaperman Bauer knew there, he told DeLucca, had finally tipped him that Shevlin's new setup might be concealed under the cover of a Brussels firm called Securpol. "With both NATO and the Common Market headquartered in Brussels," Bauer said, "whatever Shevlin is doing there for Reinbold *could* provide the sort of ammunition we've been looking for."

DeLucca's eyes narrowed. "It could indeed. What do you need to find out?"

"It would require my putting the best team of professional investigators we can afford to work in Brussels. It would be expensive—"

"Figure out an estimate of what you'd need to start with," DeLucca told him, and looked to Pryor. "I want you to help him with that, Bob."

"The committee budget is already spread pretty thin, senator."

"I *know* that. Cut the allotments in other areas and shift them to Brussels. Whatever he needs, at least until we find out if there's something there worth digging into."

Pryor nodded. Behind him, Ruth McCormick continued to record all this down in her notepad.

Bauer went on to a matter he'd discussed with DeLucca before. There were, he had reason to believe, a number of men—important men, in different European financial centers—each of whom possessed some piece of Reinbold's story . . . A member of London's Committee on Invisible Exports—the City's currency market. A commissioner of antitrust documentation for the Common Market in Brussels. In Paris the director of the Finance Ministry's regulation of multinational corporations' activities. The chairman of the most important brokerage house operating at the Brosa Valori in Milan. A Zurich merchant banker whose attempt to compete with Reinbold Enterprises for control of a biotechnology company had been sabotaged by MARS Limited. A financier in Vienna who had been clobbered in a similar manner when he had tangled with Reinbold in a take-over bid for a hotel chain . . . "The piece of the Reinbold story that each of these men knows," Bauer said, "would probably mean little by itself, but if we could get each of these separate pieces and knit them together I believe that might give us a picture that would make Reinbold extremely uncomfortable. My problem now is that none of these men will tell his story to me or my assistants in detail. Two have even refused to talk with me at all. A journalist in Europe, as you know, does not have the prestige members of the press have in America. Also, of course, my damaged reputation is well known. The error that Reinbold's people tricked me into continues to hurt me—"

"You're not the only one," DeLucca said.

The others laughed. Bauer did not. He was still not accustomed to American humor in a serious situation. He went on in his measured tone: "Senator, it is not the same for you. You continued to be known in Europe as one of the most important figures on the American political scene. None of these men I have mentioned would refuse to see *you.* They would consider such a meeting an honor. What I am proposing, senator, is that you make a short trip to Europe, and speak to each of these men. Explain that I am in your employ and have your complete confidence. And that you would appreciate it if they would open up to me. I am sure that they then would."

The matter was discussed for some time, with each of the other three across the desk from DeLucca giving his opinion. It was finally agreed that Bauer's proposal was a necessary step. DeLucca consulted his secretary about his future appointments, then set his trip to Europe for seven weeks from that day.

With Ruth McCormick taking notes, DeLucca and Bauer worked out an exact schedule for the meetings in Europe. London, first, then Brussels, Paris, Milan . . .

DeLucca paused at this point. "While I'm in that area, there's something personal I've meant to get around to for a long time. My parents immigrated to America from a village not too far from Milan. Rocchetta. I've never been there. The day after Milan would be a good time for it."

George Ryan asked him, "Do you have any family still left there?"

"Nobody. All dead, disappeared or immigrated. I'd just like to have a look at where my parents came from. Visit the graves of my grandparents, if they're still there." DeLucca smiled, shrugged. "A sentimental journey." He looked at his secretary. "Schedule a free day for it after Milan, before I go on to these other appointments in Europe."

Ruth jotted down the date and the name of the Italian village.

Once the rest of the schedule was set, Berman discussed ways to get the right kind of news coverage in preparation for the trip. Ryan interrupted him. "I don't think it's a good idea to publicize this trip too far ahead. Why tip off Reinbold—and Shevlin—in advance?"

DeLucca looked enquiringly at Bauer, who nodded. "I don't believe they could stop any of these men from talking to you, senator, but I agree that we should give Reinbold's people as little time as possible to . . . do anything to cover their tracks."

Agreed. When the conference ended, Ruth McCormick went back to her own office. First she typed up a full transcript of everything she had recorded in shorthand—including the decision to conduct an all-out investigation into Shevlin's new operation in Brussels.

On the wall behind her, Dain's video installation performed its function, recording everything she typed.

Then she opened Senator DeLucca's appointment book and transferred into it the schedule for his trip to Europe.

The camera, of course, recorded this too.

LATE THAT FRIDAY afternoon Dain brought the original camera unit back to DeLucca's office suite and announced that he'd cleared up the problem with the faulty element. He reinstalled it, and took the replacement unit back down to his workshop after the workday had ended and most others had gone home for the weekend. He locked the door and dismantled the old housing, removing the two small cameras so there'd be no evidence of how he'd used them. He'd also removed any sign of the splice jobs up in the senator's suite and down in the subbasement.

Which left only the videotape to take care of. Every evening of that week he had edited the day's cassettes: cutting away tape that held nothing of interest and burning it. Now he spent two hours splicing together the tapes containing the sort of thing the Medusa had asked for. These made a single cassette. Dain pocketed it, carried it home to his apartment, and stretched out on the couch with a drink while he waited. The Medusa had given him no address or phone number.

She phoned him less than an hour later. "How is it?"

"Beautiful. Everything you wanted, nice and clear."

"We'll meet tomorrow," she told him. "Eleven in the morning. Your boat—but not at the dock. I don't want people seeing us together again. Anchor in the same place. I'll rent a motorboat and join you."

"Sure you can find me out there?"

"I'll find you."

"Just don't forget the rest of what you owe me."

"Believe me, I won't."

SHE ARRIVED TWO hours late, which gave him the time and a reason to have several drinks while wondering if he was being stood up. A few minutes before one Dain spotted her coming across the slightly choppy waters of the bay. She had a rubber dinghy with an outboard motor, and he noted the easy skill with which she handled it, swinging neatly alongside and cutting the motor before it bumped.

"What the hell happened to you?" he said as he caught the end of the rope she tossed up to him.

"My car developed a loose fan belt on the way."

There was no reason for him to question her explanation. He made the dinghy fast to the cruiser while she climbed aboard. This time she was wearing sandals with a simple wraparound white sports dress, closed at the waist by the yellow scarf. As he had the previous time,

Dain took her shoulder bag and checked it for electronic bugs. The only thing of interest in the bag was his second payment: ten one-hundred dollar bills.

Dain reached for the money but the Medusa shook her head. "After I see what you've got for me."

He shrugged and climbed down into her dinghy, checking it out as he had her bag. He pulled a rotting fishing net out from under the seat. "What's this crap?"

"I don't know. It must have been left by the person who rented it before me."

Dain climbed back aboard his cruiser and led her into the cabin. Near the wide double bunk was a television set adapted to take videocassettes. For female guests who needed a little soft-core porn entertainment to steam them up. Dan inserted his videocassette. While she watched the results on the TV screen he fixed her a drink and a fresh one for himself.

The Medusa did not bother to conceal her satisfaction when the tape was finished. Over the past week Ruth had had many occasions to turn the pages of Senator DeLucca's appointment book in the course of making changes and additions to his schedule. The video tape held a complete record of where DeLucca would be and what he would be doing over the next several months.

Next, Dain gave her the two dated cassettes he had removed from DeLucca's storage closet: the one from the day she had visited the senator's suite, and the other chosen at random to mystify, should anyone later check back through the stored tapes. She had Dain run the first one for her, just to make certain it was the one on which she appeared. They downed another drink while it ran. That was enough. She didn't need him drunk . . . just with enough alcohol in his system. Giving him the thousand dollars, she put all three videocassettes in her bag. Then she kicked off her sandals and undid the yellow sash, taking off her dress. Under it she wore a brief bikini.

The suddenness of it startled Dain. The Medusa smiled at him as she tossed the dress aside with its sash. "We did talk about taking a swim this time."

Dain looked her up and down as he pocketed the money, anticipation quickening in him. Her body was beautifully erotic. It didn't put him in a mood for wasting time with a swim.

The cruiser had begun to roll a bit, making them spread their feet for balance. He took his cue from that. "Why don't we just wrap ourselves around another drink and relax? Current's a little rough today, and it's deep out here. If you get sucked under—"

"Worry about yourself. I'm a good swimmer. And I can probably hold my breath under water longer than you can."

"Don't bet on it. I used to be a lifeguard."

He kept making it easier for her. She gave him a challenging smile. "All right, *let's* bet on it."

Her game was beginning to annoy him. "Bet on what?"

"Which one of us can stay under longer. I'll bet you a hundred dollars I can beat you at that."

This bitch, he decided, was really asking to be taught a lesson. "Okay, you're on."

While Dain changed into swimming trunks the Medusa climbed down into the dinghy, taking her wristwatch with her. She put it on the seat when he came out of the cabin and climbed down to join her. "The one who stays up here," she explained, "times the other's dive."

"We'll both time it," Dain told her, indicating the waterproof watch he wore. "That way nobody can cheat. Want me to go first?"

She shrugged a wide shoulder. "If you want."

Dain swung off the dinghy into the water. Treading water, he took several deep breaths, then held the last one and jackknifed below the surface.

As soon as he was under, the Medusa picked up the old fishing net, shaking it out a little. The water was clear enough for her to make out Dain's form several feet down. She stood with her legs braced apart, holding the net ready as she watched and waited.

Dain stayed under longer than she'd thought he could. Finally she saw him start to stroke his way up toward the surface. Before he could make it, she took a deep breath and jumped in on top of him, casting the net wide and holding onto two ends. The top of Dain's head broke the surface, but he never managed to get his nose and mouth out to gulp in the air he now desperately needed. The impact of her body landing on top of him drove him back under, made him gasp, swallowing water. The next instant the Medusa was twisting around him like an eel, entangling him in the rotted webbing of the net.

Dain fought to regain the surface. The Medusa battled to keep him under. With his arms and legs caught in the net he couldn't manage to counter her downward drag, and his strength was no longer a match for hers. He had used up the last of his oxygen before starting to surface, his brain was fogging from the need for more. The Medusa's lungs were still full of the fresh air she'd sucked in before jumping. His struggle grew weaker as she drove herself toward the bottom, dragging the net after her, with him trapped inside it.

She stayed down until his movements had become disoriented and feeble and her own lungs were bursting, then she rose toward the surface. This time she had no trouble in keeping Dain's head under when her own rose above it. Taking another deep breath, she dove for the bottom again, pulling him along with her. She stayed under for two full minutes. No more was necessary. Dain had become a limp, dragging weight. Stroking toward the surface, she let the current carry off his drowned figure, still entangled in the old net.

Climbing back aboard Dain's boat, the Medusa got into her dress and sandals. Sun and wind would dry her quickly enough on the way back. She took the money she'd given Dain from the jeans he'd tossed on the cabin bunk. It wouldn't do for anyone to wonder what he'd been doing with that kind of money on him. She put it back in her shoulder bag, next to the videocassettes.

Picking up the glass from which she'd been drinking, the Medusa washed it out in the galley, then made a thorough check of the boat to make certain there was no other evidence that Dain had been entertaining a guest that day—and that there was no hidden tape recorder which he might have been using to keep a record of their meeting.

Finally she climbed down into the dinghy and cast off. She started the outboard motor and steered for the western shore, leaving the empty cabin cruiser swinging at anchor in the middle of the bay.

The next morning she took a Concorde to London.

Her plane was landing at Heathrow Airport when, back in Chesapeake Bay, passing fishermen hailed Dain's cruiser and got no response. Boarding the boat and finding it empty, they used its radio to call the Coast Guard.

The search their report instigated had been abandoned for over a week before Dain's body was finally discovered, entangled in a rotting fish net that had gotten snagged on some grounded driftwood on the east shore of the Chesapeake below Taylors Island. The autopsy findings were that Dain's death had been caused by drowning and that he had consumed a good deal of alcohol before it happened. The logical assumption was that he had been drunk when he'd gone off his boat for a swim, had become snared in the abandoned fish net as it drifted by, and drowned while struggling to get free of it.

There was no reason to investigate the matter further.

An unfortunate accident.

Nothing more.

IT WAS THREE days after the Dain autopsy that KGB supervisor Josef Petrov returned from Moscow to Prague and met again with Colonel Kopacka and General Hájek in the crypt of the Monastery.

Moscow agreed, Petrov told them, that they had run out of alternative methods for stopping DeLucca. The purpose of the senator's scheduled trip to Europe—along with his decisions to begin an investigation of Shevlin's Brussels operation—made that all too clear.

The feasibility study which had been prepared by Shevlin and the Medusa was found to be sound. Moscow approved the people Shevlin had selected to pin the assassination on: a militant Cuban exile group that had been put out of action by a previous committee under Senator DeLucca, and indeed had threatened his life.

Also approved was the choice of time and place for the assassination. Italy, as pointed out in the feasibility study, had a record of the highest number of successful terrorist attacks and the lowest number of assailants identified or captured. DeLucca's free day after his appointment in Milan would be ideal . . .

Two days after this meeting at the Monastery, William Reinbold summoned Shevlin to Sorbio and gave the decision:

Shevlin was to close down his Brussels operation immediately until the danger was past.

Then he and the Medusa were to proceed with the final neutralization of Frank DeLucca.

IV
THE FRANKENSTEIN CELL

TWELVE

THE IRISH COAST, BRUSSELS

IT WAS the coldest June that most people living along the ragged western capes of the Irish coast could remember. A hard rain added to the wintry discomfort that day, slashing out of a low sky the color of old ashes. Down at the farthest southwest tip of the coast, winds approaching gale force were smashing the entire Atlantic Ocean against the cliffs of Mizen Head.

Inside the weather station built snugly into the top of one cliff, the radioman was doing a binocular scan of the black, wind-shredded seas around the end of the cape. Suddenly he froze, then adjusted his focus.

"He must be crazy!"

The other man in the station, a meteorologist, turned from his wall charts. "What is it?"

"Some maniac is out there alone in a small sailboat."

The meteorologist picked up another pair of binoculars to have a look. At first he couldn't see it. Then a dark mountain of frothing water collapsed and there it was—an open sloop no more than sixteen feet long beating its way around the cape, coming south from Dunmanus Bay.

A lone figure wearing a hooded green fisherman's jacket was braced on the stern seat, fighting to maintain control of the tiller as a surging crosscurrent caught at the boat's rudder. The strengthening wind tugged the hood, pulling it back from the sailor's face. Side gusts whipped long strands of tawny hair from under the hood.

The meteorologist sharpened the focus of his own binoculars. "It's a girl."

The radioman saw it at the same time. "That she is, and flat out of her mind, God save her."

A large breaker struck the boat's side and heeled it over, threatening to capsize it. The girl at the stern leaned way out over the port rail, at the same time jerking up a rubber-booted leg and shoving the tiller in the opposite direction with her foot. The simultaneous movements countered the roll of the boat, which righted itself but then wallowed down inside a pocket between high, white-topped swells, almost foundering as it lost headway at the bottom.

She slid back onto the stern seat, easing up on the single sail and grabbing the tiller with her other hand, dragging it in sharply against her side. The natural buoyancy of the little boat did the rest, and it forged ahead again, smoothly climbing the slope of a wave that rose before it—but the full force of the wind hit the sail when it topped the crest, filling it drum-taut and bending the slender mast nearly to its breaking point. In the same moment another breaker came in from behind, the stern rose with it and the boat shot forward with a speed that took some of the strain off the mast but came close to driving the bow under. She shortened sail, relieving more of the strain and bringing the bow up.

"She's not a bad sailor," the meteorologist said. "And at least she's had enough sense to pay that sea anchor out astern so she can run before the sea without getting swamped."

"Carrying too much sail. Shouldn't have any at all in this wind. And she's steering too close. If a hard gust catches her this near the rocks . . ." The radioman raised his voice. "Get off, *get out to sea!*"

But the Medusa didn't; instead she proceeded to try to bring her in, completing the turn, closing in on the most treacherous short stretch of coastline in Ireland. Her eyes were crusted and burning with salt. Her boat rolled and pitched its way through the turbulent waters. She had been out in this three hours. Her body was trembling with fatigue.

Her hands were getting numb. She knew she had to dock before she lost all feeling in her fingers.

The cliffs of Mizen Head loomed beyond the bow, the waves smashing against and climbing them to an unbelievable height, meeting waterfalls pouring down from the waves before.

Dead ahead. There was no drug that could give her as strong a high as supreme physical effort joined to ultimate risk, combining to pull her far past normal limits. She leaned the weight of her body out over the port rail again, this time pulling the tiller with her, yanking it hard against her hip. The boat responded sluggishly, reluctantly, but gradually its bow swung to starboard—just enough so that Mizen Head slipped past to her left, deadening her with the thunder of the seas against its cliffs.

She eased up on the tiller and sailed into the bay, steering in the direction of Crookhaven. The water grew calmer once the boat was inside the bay, and the wind began to slacken, cut off by the cliffs.

Shevlin would be furious if he'd known what she'd done . . . Once he had visited the house she kept near the little village of Goleen, and she'd taken him out around Mizen Head in her boat. Later he'd said to her, "What if you smash on those rocks and drown, just when I need you?" . . . It felt good to still have one person in the world who worried about her like that. It reminded her of Arakel. It was one reason she'd gone to Paul Shevlin after Arakel had died . . .

The port of Crookhaven was in sight ahead. She swung her boat away from it and sailed across the bay to Goleen, whose harbor with its narrow entrance and sharp bend inside was too small to take vessels much bigger than hers. Once she was into the shelter beyond the bend there was barely enough wind to take the boat to the tiny concrete docking slope. The Medusa used up the last of her strength hauling the boat out of the water, removing its mast and sail and turning it upside-down on the shore. She then trudged up a short hill to her house, a two-room cottage, ample for her needs.

When she came here during these periods of waiting it was to use the boat or ride the horse she kept at a farm on the other side of Goleen.

A telegram was stuck under her door. It was addressed to Sharon Horn, the name she used here. It was signed "G.A. NELS."

The exhaustion of her battle with the storm dropped from her as her nervous system honed in on that signature. The waiting time was over.

The cryptonyms used between Shevlin and the Medusa were always changed in their messages. The Medusa changed hers by moving its first letter to third position, making it E. D. MUSA. Shevlin altered his code name—ANGELS—in the opposite way, transferring the third letter to the front.

The telegram read: "REMEMBER ARNOLD HAS TWENTY-SIXTH BIRTHDAY ON FIFTH CAN YOU COME CALL TOMORROW."

That last meant that Paul Shevlin wanted her to meet him tomorrow. The time of day for their rendezvous was always at twenty minutes past noon unless the message contained a code notification of a different time. Where he expected her was in the numbers.

They each had a copy of an old pocket atlas. The Medusa got out hers. Page twenty-six was part of a listing of cities in Belgium. The fifth city down on that page was Brussels.

PAUL SHEVLIN SPENT the day before he was to meet the Medusa in closing down his entire Brussels operation. Reinbold Enterprises had its own company representatives in Brussels, the self-styled capital of Europe and site of the headquarters of NATO and the European Common Market, for its business dealings with the concentration of government, military and commercial activity there. But for ferreting out secret information circulating inside the closed circles of the city's diplomatic, military, business and technological enclaves, William Reinbold used Paul Shevlin's network.

Shevlin had built up the Brussels network quietly. Most of the people who worked for it were former members of European police and espionage services. All had long-standing relationships with their counterparts inside Belgium. No office in Brussels bore the name MARS Limited, nor was it listed in any Belgian phone book. Shevlin's setup functioned from offices inside the headquarters of a firm named Securpol, its owner a former security officer in the Belgian army. Security was what he was still supplying, to businessmen, their companies, and their families, everything from alarm systems and deep checks of employee honesty to bodyguards and attack-trained watchdogs. On Shevlin's network was part of Securpol. In fact, it functioned separately with complete autonomy. Only Securpol's owner knew its staff worked for Shevlin; even he did not really know what they did for him. The rest of the Securpol personnel knew nothing about this small group with its separate offices and assumed they were doing the same kind of work but in different areas.

Still, in spite of these precautions Senator DeLucca's investigators had managed to catch on to them and were preparing to develop their own surveillance of its activities.

Shevlin did not go near Securpol that day. He had chosen the thickly wooded Forest of Signes—out on the Watermaal edge of the city—for his rendezvous with the two men who ran the Brussels network for him. They arrived separately, turning their cars into the seldom-used dirt road where Shevlin had parked. Jacques Andrau was of chunky build, had neatly cut features, bright blue eyes and a lovely smile; he could have passed as a good-looking Irish cop in New York, until you heard the fruity French accent. He had been a top officer in the Service 7—a secret branch of French intelligence first created by General de Gaulle. Service 7 agents had become specialists in stealing documents from France's allies, blackmailing political opponents of the government, and in the kidnapping and assassination of people considered too dangerous for the welfare of their nation. Most of Service 7 had been disbanded after Mitterand took over as head of France, and Jacques Andrau, out of a job, had been hired by Shevlin. The other man was Harold Ferguson, tall, skinny, with a cheerful wrinkled face, ex-detective superintendent with the West End Central CID and for two years was Scotland Yard's man at Interpol. Shevlin had met him long ago when England had sent Ferguson to Washington to study U.S. police techniques at the State Department's International Police Academy. The CIA regularly attempted to recruit such foreign cops to operate for the agency on the side when they returned to their own countries. Those who went along with the idea were sent for extra training to "the farm," a special fenced-in section of the army's Camp Peary along the York River in Virginia. For a time Shevlin had served as an instructor at the farm. He and Ferguson had discovered they had much in common, and four years earlier when Ferguson had begun to feel his age and contemplate the meager retirement pay soon awaiting him, he had contacted Shevlin and become part of MARS Limited. It was Ferguson who had learned that Klaus Bauer, directing European investigations for Senator DeLucca, had discovered Shevlin's Brussel's *aparat* . . . "I heard Bauer was in town so naturally I put our best Belge wireman on the job of monitoring his telephone calls. The first bit my wireman gets is that Bauer's hiring people to set up electronic surveillance on *us.*"

Both men checked to make certain no vehicle had pulled in anywhere nearby and that no helicopter was hovering overhead; then along with Shevlin they took a long stroll through the pathways that twisted through the woods. Neither Andrau nor Ferguson were happy about what Shevlin told them. They had worked hard to give him everything he'd asked for, had established electronic surveillance on half of the big company headquarters in Brussels, sometimes with the help of the company's own security department. They had managed to acquire access to computers and copying machines operating all over the city. They had the whole damn Common Market skyscraper wired. They'd acquired payment-on-delivery sources ranging from shorthand typists working for NATO to senior translator-revisers at multinational companies and junior administrators of the EEC Commission. They had bugs in the homes of NATO officers, foreign diplomats, company executives and Common Market ministers. Harold Ferguson had just finished setting up an elegant call-girl and gigolo operation for the entrapment of VIPs and their wives. Jacques Andrau almost had a minister of the EEC Council by the balls—his daughter had fallen in love with a pretty boy picked by Andrau and run off to Venezuela with him. She was about to be arrested and thrown into a most unpleasant prison there, charged with associating with terrorists. The man being paid to arrest her was an officer of the DISIP (Venezuelan secret police). He could also have her released—if Andrau had a good reason to want the girl returned safely to papa.

"And now you tell us to wrap it all up and call it quits," Ferguson said. "Fire everybody, close down the whole network—"

"No," Shevlin cut in. "I wish you would listen to me more carefully, Harold. I didn't say close down the network. I said close down its *operations.* Keep all your most important people on full salary, but only doing ordinary jobs, all aboveboard, going through material available at the various documentation centers, taking notes at open EEC conferences, searching through those releases turned out by every organization in town—"

"What a waste of talent," Andrau put in.

"An *expensive* waste," Ferguson said. "That will give Hallberg something else to whine about tomorrow."

Shevlin gave him a dry smile. "Probably. But he'll get over it." Nat Hallberg was flying in early the next morning to express his displeasure as head of the MARS Washington office—and that of Elliot Judd at the New York office—about the business they were losing from other companies because of the publicity about the special connection between MARS and Reinbold Enterprises. "Look, this operational shutdown is a temporary measure," Shevlin told them. "Let Klaus Bauer hire all the people he can. The more the better. With our own people doing nothing to justify all his effort and expenses. I give Bauer two, three weeks at the outside. He'll get tired of paying that kind of money to come up with zero. He'll call it quits and we'll still be intact, ready to go back into operation."

"I commence," Andrau said, "to feel a little less angry."

Ferguson nodded. No American Senate committee had enough funds to field full surveillance teams in different parts of the world at the same time. Only companies like Reinbold Enterprises had that kind of money to spread around. If Klaus Bauer was concentrating so much of the committee's funds on Brussels, his investigation efforts would be very thin in other areas. That could only be justified by results, which would no longer be forthcoming here.

Andrau asked Shevlin, "And my operation in Venezuela? DISIP is scheduled to arrest our EEC minister's daughter sometime tonight."

"Cancel it, Jacques, but pay off your man at DISIP. In full. It's a good ploy and we'll want to use it—and him—sometime in the future. But not this time. Have the boyfriend disappear but keep in touch. If the little girls are that hot for him he's gold in the bank. Have DISIP kick the girl's ass out of Venezuela—gently but immediately. On a direct flight home to Brussels."

Ferguson was actually smiling by now. "And then we just play possum here for a while."

"But very *dead* possum," Shevlin said. "Don't leave Bauer *anything* to play with here. Go off on a vacation and let Bauer's people follow you around some of the plush resorts. You can take your boyfriend along with you. That'll give them *something* to tell Bauer."

Ferguson colored. "I don't enjoy your spying on my private life, Paul. I really don't."

But Shevlin had turned back to Andrau. "And why don't you go to that country house you've bought in Normandy—out of the extras you keep adding onto your expense accounts. Spend a little more time with your other wife and kid there."

Andrau opened his mouth, shut it, opened it again. "I'm not actually married to her, Paul. So it is not exactly a case of bigamy, the way you imply."

"Sure it is. Under French law a woman you've lived with longer than three years stops being just your concubine and gains the legal status of wife. And I'm not complaining about a good man lifting a bit more than he's entitled to out of company funds, so long as you keep it within reasonable bounds, as you have so far. Let's call it a bonus. But don't steal any more until Bauer's gone and we're back in business here."

Ferguson was still upset. "I hope you haven't discussed my personal life with your partners in America."

"You should have noticed by now that I don't generally tell either of them more than they need to know for operational purposes." Shevlin smiled. "Why would I want them to know as much as I do?"

As they turned back through the woods toward the cars Shevlin changed the subject. "I need some information about Milan. Complete architectural, building contractor and municipal utilities blueprints of all the top hotels and office buildings. Along with detailed layouts of the areas around them. And under them. Below-ground passages, sewers, heating conduits—the works, including old stuff no longer in use but still there."

Jacques Andrau smiled. "Planning to wire all of Milan, like we have Brussels?"

"Something like that." Senator DeLucca's trip to Europe—with his stopover in Milan—still had not been publicly revealed. It didn't matter if these two men knew later, that he'd been interested in Milan—because nothing was going to happen to DeLucca there. But certain preparations had to be worked out in Milan to make possible what would happen after the senator left there.

"There is a police inspector in Milan," Andrau said. "Francesco Nola. He knows every employee of the phone company who can be corrupted. This means all of them in Italy. What he could not get you from them, he will be able to remove from the city archives and planning commission. A useful friend. I have his home address in my office."

"Get it to me by this evening. With a note telling him he can rely on my discretion."

"And your money, more important. I will get it to you."

As they neared the cars Ferguson asked, "Can I at least keep the taps on Bauer . . . just to know what he's doing?"

"No. It doesn't matter. He won't be coming up with anything. Leave him alone."

That was another matter he was going to have to lay down the law about with Nat Hallberg tomorrow morning before he went to his meeting with the Medusa . . . A month earlier he had issued orders to everyone in his firm—no further actions against DeLucca, his committee or any of his investigators.

After the senator's removal, Shevlin didn't want the landscape littered with evidence that MARS Limited had been that interested in him.

As Ferguson was opening the door of his car he paused and said, "By the way, Paul, I had some news by phone from a friend at the Yard this morning. Daniel Moys has finally turned up, in Manchester."

Moys, an ex-officer of Britain's MI 6, had become part of Shevlin's Brussels network, had then gotten religion and quit. And disappeared—apparently worried about retaliation from MARS Limited. What Shevlin had worried about was the possibility of Moys deciding to make contact with one of DeLucca's investigators, or with some corporation that had reason to want revenge against MARS and Reinbold Enterprises.

"Seems he's committed suicide," Ferguson told him. "Blew his brains out with his own pistol."

"Did he?" Shevlin said. "Too bad." He did not seem surprised to hear it.

Nor did Jacques Andrau.

SHEVLIN'S SUITE IN the Westbury Hotel just off Brussel's Grand Place was on a top floor with a view of the Town Hall's beautiful medieval tower. He admired the view while he ate the dinner he'd had sent up, seated at a table before the windows in the suite's living room. Then he got down to work again. He intended to go to bed early so as to be fresh in the morning when Nat Hallberg showed up. Everything else had to be cleared out of the way before he met the Medusa shortly after noon.

Jacques Andrau had given him, along with the introduction to the police detective in Milan, a stack of transcripts containing information the network had collected just before closing down its operations that afternoon. Shevlin settled on the sofa and went through it, page by page. He found two items that would be useful to William Reinbold. One was a decision by the NATO defense ministers to adopt a newly improved synthetic aperture radar for its Airborne Warning and Control System. The other was a highly secret agreement reached between France's finance minister and England's chancellor of the Exchequer to urge other members of the Common Market to back certain changes in the world's foreign exchange system.

Another item of interest to Shevlin was in the papers from Andrau—a transcript of a phone call Klaus Bauer had made that morning to a man named Simon Hunter at the American Embassy in Paris.

BAUER: "Mr. Hunter, my name is Klaus Bauer. I work for Senator DeLucca . . ."

HUNTER: "George Ryan mentioned your name when I was in Washington."

BAUER: "I am in Brussels, but I am coming to Paris next week. On Saturday. I would like to discuss the senator's trip with you. The security aspect . . . will you be at the embassy?"

HUNTER: "Not on Saturday. My wife just had a baby. I'll be home."

BAUER: "My congratulations to both you and your wife. I am sorry, but this leaves me with a difficulty. I have only that one day in Paris. And it *is* important that we meet at this point."

HUNTER: "Why don't you come over to our apartment then? If the baby gets too noisy we can go to a local bistro."

BAUER: "Thank you. Would five o'clock that afternoon be convenient?"

HUNTER: "Fine. The address is 38 Rue Descartes. Apartment 19."

BAUER: "Thank you. Until next week."

Shevlin sat for a time holding the transcript in both hands. A man named Simon Hunter at the embassy in Paris who had something to do with DeLucca's security during the projected trip to Europe. A seat was already booked for Shevlin on a plane for Milan the day after next. But he didn't know anything about this man Simon Hunter. If Hunter was part of DeLucca's security planning Shevlin decided he *should* know about him.

He got up and went to the refrigerator in the corner of the hotel living room, got out one of the small bottles of Scotch and built himself a drink. He put the glass down without drinking. He did not want his own people checking on anything or anyone connected with DeLucca's trip, but there were good private investigators in any city that would handle a job without enquiring into the identity of their client. Shevlin called Brussels National Airport. On the first page of the papers Andrau had given him was a warning: Klaus Bauer's people already had his hotel phone tapped. Fine. Shevlin booked a seat on a flight from Brussels to London two days hence. Let Bauer's spooks crawl all over the Brussels airport, watching for him to show up while others were sent on ahead to tail him when he reached London. He had no intention of going anywhere near the Brussels airport. The reservation for Milan, booked under another name, was out of Amsterdam. He would switch that when he got to a safe phone. But not to London. To Paris. And from Paris to Milan, after he found out what he needed to know about this Simon Hunter.

THIRTEEN

BRUSSELS

SHEVLIN GLANCED at his watch. Eleven minutes before noon. Time to wrap up his conference with Nat Hallberg and go to his rendezvous with the Medusa. He and Hallberg were in another part of the woods where he'd had the talk with Ferguson and Andrau the day before. Hallberg was a hulking man with mean little eyes and a broken nose left over from his college football days. At the moment he was not looking happy about the way this conference had turned out. But he'd brought a piece of good news. Harrison & Gillis, the public relations outfit that Elliot Judd had hired in New York, was doing good work with all the money MARS Limited was paying out . . . an increasing number of editorials and articles in the press contained reminders of how often in the past committees of both houses of Congress had abused their powers; the vicious records of the Dies Committee and the McCarthy hearings were detailed along with instances in which innocent peoples' careers and lives had been destroyed by ambitious committee chairmen riding an obsession. The clear inference was that Senator Frank DeLucca's behavior was a vendetta, the latest example of the same abuse of congressional powers. Three prominent Americans had taken part in television panel discussions to make the same point. It was difficult to present a shadowy billionaire like William Reinbold as an unfortunate victim, so the publicity was concentrating on the harm DeLucca's investigation was doing to the managers and employees of MARS Limited. Men who, like Paul Shevlin, had served their country well in war and peace. Men who continued to serve it well, even while struggling to establish their own small businesses. As General Keegan had pointed out when he revealed that it was Shevlin who had unmasked the Swedish NATO officer as a spy for the Soviet Union . . .

"That's it then," Shevlin told Hallberg as they neared their parked cars. "Pass on the word to Elliot in New York. My orders stand. Do nothing against DeLucca or any of his people. *Nothing.* We confine our actions to our publicity campaign to make him look bad."

"Which is costing us a mint, just when we're losing money. It's one thing that Reinbold's ready to pay us back for other clients we've lost because of our connection with him. But what about all the *new* clients we're not getting because of it?"

Shevlin didn't blame him for grumbling. Employees of MARS Limited kept getting the same pay no matter what. But Hallberg and Elliot Judd were partners in the firm with a percentage of its profits—and those profits were going down. What Hallberg didn't know, of course, was that the problem would soon be ended. Shevlin had not needed Reinbold to tell him that to spread the real DeLucca plan beyond himself and the Medusa was much too dangerous. Suicidal, in fact.

When they reached the cars Shevlin took an envelope from his pocket and gave it to Hallberg. "This may help—along with the way the publicity campaign is hurting DeLucca."

"What is it?"

"A letter to Senator DeLucca. I want you to give it to him."

Leaning against the side of his car, Hallberg took the letter from the envelope and read it. It asked for a personal interview with the senator, during which, the letter stated, Shevlin would open his firm's books to DeLucca and offer him other evidence that MARS Limited was innocent of the insinuations leveled against it by the committee.

"Are you crazy? You show him all our records and we *will* be ruined."

"I don't think so. That's why I've asked for all that time before the interview—to assemble all our records in a presentable form."

Hallberg nodded. "You mean time to doctor them."

"You've got it." But of course Hallberg hadn't gotten it, not at all.

The date on which Shevlin's letter asked for the interview happened to be several days after DeLucca was scheduled to return from his still-unannounced European trip.

Which would serve to establish that Shevlin and his firm had no prior knowledge of what was going to happen *during* that trip.

THE MEDUSA GOT there early. Which gave her time for a leisurely stroll around the Grand Place, taking in each of the people at the outdoor tables in front of the cafes. She saw no familiar face, detected no one paying an unusual amount of attention to her and spotted none of the telltale signs of someone keeping the big square under general surveillance. That, of course, did not necessarily mean that nobody was. There were literally hundreds of windows surrounding and overlooking the Grand Place. One did what one could.

She took a seat at an outdoor table in front of the cafe nearest to the Town Hall. For this kind of rendezvous, the meeting place was always as close to the local city hall as she could wait without being conspicuous. The waiter came out to take her order. She asked for a waffle sprinkled with powdered sugar and a pot of hot chocolate. Brussels was not experiencing west Ireland's cold storms, but it was cool and damp with a cloudy sky. She was wearing a light raincoat of pale blue and a matching hat with a brim should it begin to drizzle.

When the waiter brought her order she paid him immediately before pouring the hot chocolate into her cup. She cut up her waffle and ate with a keen appetite. The chocolate was too hot. She sipped it carefully, giving it time to cool.

Paul Shevlin strolled into the Grand Place from the direction of the Westbury Hotel, blending into the groups of sightseers preceding and following him. The Medusa finished off the last portion of her sugared waffle as he strolled past her. Eight narrow streets fed into the Grand Place. Shevlin entered one of them and disappeared. The Medusa sat where she was, pouring the last of the hot chocolate from the pot into her cup and stirring it with her spoon. A minute later Shevlin strolled out of the street into which he'd gone and reentered the Grand Place.

Among the people coming out of that street behind him was a man the Medusa had seen behind him before . . . when Shevlin had originally entered the Grand Place from the direction of the hotel. She drank from her cup and watched Shevlin turn into another of the narrow streets. The man followed him into it. The chocolate was cool now. The Medusa put down her cup and stood up. Taking her time, she crossed the Grand Place and entered the same street.

It was crowded with tourists. She worked her way among them, not hurrying. A block ahead, Shevlin had stopped to look at a rack of picture postcards outside a bookshop. She could not see the man who had been tailing him. As she neared Shevlin she reached up a hand to the knot of the scarf tied loosely around her neck, touched it once, adjusting it slightly, then dropped her hand and walked on past him.

The tail was standing inside a doorway half a block further on. The Medusa passed him, glancing in shop windows as she continued her stroll. Now Shevlin knew he had a tail on him. One person. Possibly hired by Klaus Bauer, or somebody working for a rival firm.

Shevlin strolled back to his hotel. He bought a *Herald Tribune* at the lobby stand, taking his time getting the correct change from his pocket. A man who had entered the lobby after him went to the porter's desk and began looking at leaflets advertising tours of the city.

Shevlin crossed to the elevator. The man stepped into it after him just before the doors closed. Shevlin got off at the twenty-third floor and entered the small Penthouse Bar. He settled into a comfortable black leather chair at a small table beside the panorama window with its spectacular view over the city. A waiter in a red jacket came over and took his order for a Scotch and soda.

A moment later the tail strolled in and took a seat at one end of the bar, ordering a cognac from the barman. He did not speak loudly but the room was small and voices carried across it. As he ordered, the tail hitched his stool around slightly; which allowed him to keep an eye on Shevlin without appearing to.

Shevlin opened his *Herald Tribune* to the financial pages and got out a gold fountain pen. He began going down the listings of international bond prices. At several points he used his pen to make a small mark beside one of the items. He frowned at something in the lists, got a small notebook from his jacket pocket and tore a page from it. On it he wrote: "Financiere Credit Suisse—50."

When the waiter brought his drink Shevlin asked where he could find the men's room. He was told that it was to the right, at the end of the corridor outside the bar, which he already knew. He took a sip of his drink and put it down. He placed the square of notepaper with his notation on the folded newspaper and put his gold pen on top of that. He left them there when he got up and walked out of the bar, turning right down the corridor.

Which left the tail with a dilemma. There was every sign that Shevlin was going to the toilet and intended to return to the bar. If the man followed him out and then back in he'd be advertising the fact that he was tailing him.

Shevlin punched the elevator button as he passed it. He went on into the men's room, counted to twenty, went back out into the corridor. It was still empty. The tail had opted for staying put; just long enough, anyway. The elevator doors opened. Shevlin stepped in. The tail still had not emerged from the bar when the doors closed. He rode down to the lobby and left the hotel, walking quickly now.

He reentered the narrow street where the Medusa had signaled that he had a tail. Pushing swiftly through the crowds, he spotted her along the same street, studying dresses displayed in a shop window. He went on past her.

After a moment she turned to take in each of the people in the crowd behind him. He turned into a shopping arcade cutting through the area. She did not go after him; instead she resumed her leisurely stroll up the narrow street.

Shevlin reappeared just ahead of her, having done a fast circle of the small block. She examined the people who came out of it after him. When he passed her she made no sign that there was anyone following him. She turned into a side street, keeping to a leisurely stroll, stopping at times to look in other shop windows. She emerged from the street behind the squat, ugly building that housed the Brussels Bourse.

By now Shevlin had circled the block again and was already there, studying a menu displayed outside a seafood restaurant. The Medusa passed him and circled the Bourse. When she passed him a second time he made no sign. No one was tailing her. They were both in the clear.

The car she had rented at the Brussels airport was parked across from one side of the Bourse near a taxi rank. Her overnight bag was in the back seat. She climbed in front behind the wheel. Shevlin got into a taxi. The Medusa drove after it, keeping well behind. The taxi went five blocks along the wide Boulevard Anspach and stopped in front of one of the new department stores. The Medusa stopped half a block back. While Shevlin got out and paid the driver she checked the traffic flowing past. All of the vehicles that had been behind Shevlin's taxi kept on going. The Medusa drove up beside Shevlin. He got in quickly, giving her directions. She maneuvered through the heavy traffic and got onto the highway to the coast.

She glanced at Shevlin's face. "It's on, then?"

"Yes."

"Good." When they were well outside the city she turned off the highway and stopped the car beside a country road. She turned from the wheel and wrapped her arms around his neck, kissing him on the mouth.

He took her in his arms, pulled her to him, stroking the thick mane of hair at the back of her head. He kissed the tip of her nose, and she smiled into his eyes. She liked to be cuddled . . . like a little girl, safe in her father's arms. That was one of the inconsistencies in her. In some ways she was surprisingly sentimental. She needed affection—not *too* much and not from more than one person—but she had to know it would be there when she wanted it.

She leaned back from him, still smiling, relaxed. "Where are we going?"

"Let me drive, I know the way." Shevlin got out and went around to the driver's seat while she slid over to make room for him. He drove them out to the seaside resort town of Het Zoute close to the Dutch border. They checked into the best hotel, taking a bedroom suite. The Medusa left her overnight bag there and they went out to the beach.

It was a wide, flat sandy beach, stretching for a long way, and they strolled the length of it along the edge of the water as they worked out the logistics of the role each was going to have in what now lay ahead of them.

There was no need to worry about someone listening in. Even a long-distance parabolic sound-collector would not be able to pick their words out of the noise of the pounding surf. Besides, any eavesdropping device would have to be in a vehicle traveling along the road parallel to the shore to keep even with them as they walked—and *that* would be frustrated by the high dunes rising between the beach and the road.

The Medusa and Shevlin would need to handle separately and far apart all the preparations leading up to the final execution. Shevlin explained what he would be doing in Paris, and then in and around Milan. The Medusa's preparations, in and around New York, had already been initiated. What she would have to do now was to bring them to fruition.

They would meet each other only twice. Once in America, when she would need Shevlin to complete the convincing of the two men she was going to New York to find. Then in Italy, before the end.

"Who will we have as a backup?" she asked.

"Nobody. We put it all on the two fall guys you're going to recruit."

She turned her head and looked at him; but she was not entirely surprised. "Somebody, I would say, is very concerned about this one."

He nodded. "Me, for one."

"So it will be just you and me. And them."

"If we do it correctly, that will be enough."

She thought about it, reviewing the details as they had planned them. One last time. "You are right. We do not need anybody else."

THEY RETURNED TO the town in time to buy a suitcase and change of clothing for Shevlin before the shops closed for the night. Ferguson would pick up his things from the hotel in Brussels after Bauer's watchdogs had realized he was not going to be returning there.

They bathed in their suite before changing for dinner. Shevlin was ready first; he sat and watched her get dressed. He always felt pleasure from watching her. It was not only the beauty of her body. There was an equilibrium in everything she did, physical and mental. He was proud of her, which reminded him of Pygmalion. But of course he had not created the Medusa . . . he had only discovered, and named her.

They had an excellent meal in the hotel's restaurant, sitting together in a curved corner booth, not speaking much. Their business discussion was settled, and they had no small talk when they were together. No need for any. They could *feel* each other at moments like this. Each was attuned to the other's state of mind and feeling. Communicating without speech. At once on a primitive and infinitely sophisticated level.

After dinner they took another long walk along the beach before going back to their suite. When they were in bed she curled herself against him. "A little loving."

She did not mean making love. That had been over between them long ago. She only wanted him to hold her; indulging her for a while in an illusion of being childish and warmed and protected.

He had even gotten to like it. There were enough women who could give him the rest of it. What they couldn't give was what he got from her in moments like this . . . it was like holding a jungle tiger in his arms and turning her into a gently purring kitten. Power of a very special kind.

"Sleep soft, baby."

And she did.

THEY LEFT FOR Holland early the next morning and reached Schipol Airport outside Amsterdam shortly after ten. Shevlin got their tickets while she turned the car in to the Schipol office of the rental company. At five minutes past eleven she watched him board his plane for Paris.

Two hours later she took off on a KLM flight to New York.

FOURTEEN

NEW YORK

THE MEDUSA sat at the counter in the Chinese Ice Cream Parlor and finished a concoction of shaved ice flavored with Asiatic fruits and spices. The counter took up most of the width of the narrow shop. There was just room enough behind her for one Chinese patient at a time to squeeze past to the wizened old doctor from Hong Kong selling herbal remedies in the rear. She did not look out of place there. At ten o'clock at night the tourists outnumbered the inhabitants in Manhattan's Chinatown.

She glanced at her watch, paid her bill and left. Going through a covered shopping passage, she turned up Mott Street, crowded and ablaze with the neon of stores and restaurants. She paused outside a Chinese department store taking up the first floor and basement of a five-story building. The other four floors were apartments.

It was one of these, on the third floor, that was visited on certain evenings by Virgilio Suarez—head of VOR, the Cuban terrorist group which Senator DeLucca had crushed some years earlier.

Whenever Suarez came here he left that apartment at about this time. It was important to check the timing under similar traffic conditions. The Medusa looked at her watch again. Two minutes past ten. She walked briskly to the nearest subway station. Suarez would probably not be moving so quickly when he left, but she had to know the shortest time in which he could make the trip. An uptown train was pulling into the station as she started down the steps. She ran down the rest of the way and across the platform, getting into a subway car just as the doors were closing. New York was already suffering under a sticky hot summer that June, and down in the subways it was worse. She was drenched in perspiration when she got off at the Forty-Second Street station. Climbing out into the muggy night, she went to the mammoth Eighth Avenue Terminal which handled all bus traffic between midtown Manhattan and New Jersey in addition to long-distance hauls.

When she reached it the Medusa again checked her watch. Thirty-one minutes to get from the building in Chinatown to the bus station. At that time of night, just before the after-theater traffic crowded the area, she would be able to make the same distance by car with at least ten minutes to spare. Enough time for her to set the stage for the kind of contact she wanted with Virgilio Suarez before he got here.

Turning her back on the bus station, the Medusa looked at the Terminal Bar on the other side of Eighth Avenue, named for its location across from the bus terminal, but those who knew it could think of other reasons for the name. It was a place for meeting people not ordinarily encountered the near side of a nightmare. Tough Marines coming into New York on leave had been known to cross to the Terminal Bar and wind up unconscious in a nearby gutter, stripped of cash, boots, ID. The month before, a boy from Ohio had wandered in for a beer and died twenty minutes later, running naked across 42nd Street in front of a truck, chased by six men wielding knives and chains.

The Medusa waited until the Eighth Avenue traffic lights changed to red, then crossed the street and sauntered into the Terminal Bar.

FRIDAY EVENING WAS the time Virgilio Suarez usually left his place in Union City, New Jersey, to visit the apartment in Chinatown. At six-thirty that Friday the Medusa drove under the Hudson River via the Lincoln Tunnel, came up into the bright sunshine of New Jersey and turned right along Bergenline Avenue, the main shopping street running through a string of Hudson County towns following each other along the New Jersey shore of the Hudson. The three largest—Union

City, West New York and Weehawken—contained the heaviest concentration of exiles from Castro's Cuba in the United States after Miami's Little Havana. Union City, in particular, had become a site of violently anti-Castro militants belonging to so-called action groups: Alpha 66, the CNM (Cuban Nationalist Movement), FLNC (the National Front for the Liberation of Cuba), Omega 7, Commando Cero, the Mano Blanco, Accion Cubana and the 2506 Brigade (veterans of the Bay of Pigs invasion).

Virgilio Suarez was practically all that remained of the action group called VOR. Senator Frank DeLucca, when chairman of a previous committee, had called VOR the most dangerous of them all. He had charged it with extorting funds from Cuban exiles, murdering moderate exile leaders who spoke against the use of violence and violating American neutrality laws by bombing offices and apartments of members of the Cuban delegation to the United Nations. At the height of the Senate hearings C-4 explosives had been discovered hidden aboard an airliner about to carry over one hundred exiles back for a one-week visit to their relatives in Cuba under special dispensation from Castro. Prodded by DeLucca, the FBI had pinned the attempt to blow up the plane and passengers on VOR.

The initials that formed the group's name stood for the first names of its three founders: Virgilio, Orlando, and Raul. Orlando and Raul were now in prison, along with three lesser members of the group. The two imprisoned leaders had specifically blamed the length of their sentences on pressure applied by Senator DeLucca.

All that had happened two years earlier. Virgilio Suarez had been tried along with the others but freed when the prosecution failed to produce proof that he had prior knowledge of the bomb plot. Now what he continued to lead for all practical purposes had ceased to exist, except within his own bitter memories.

It had been shortly after the trial that a death threat had been sent to Senator DeLucca. The Medusa, through her investigations, had reason to be reasonably certain it had been sent by two young VOR true-believers who had vanished afterward. It was around these facts that she and Shevlin would construct the frame for the assassination of Frank DeLucca. Though she could not be sure that Virgilio Suarez could lead her to them, at this point he was her best chance.

She drove along Bergenline with the slow, thick flow of its vehicle traffic. The street was flanked solidly by storefronts painted in brilliant yellows, reds, greens and blues; by big signs in Spanish; by restaurants, most of which specialized in Cuban food. She turned off Bergenline into 52nd Street. Like most of Union City's short side-streets, it was lined with trees and ended on a view of Manhattan's skyscrapers on the other side of the river. Relatively new eight-floor apartment buildings alternated with three-floor clapboard and brick houses with old-fashioned porches and upstairs balconies.

She found curb-space just after crossing New York Avenue. Parking, she put on sunglasses and tucked her hair up inside her yellow headscarf before getting out of the car. She did not want Suarez to spot her —not here, not yet. Walking back the block to Bergenline, she turned along it in the direction of the VOR office. A block from where she was walking, the editor of a Cuban-exile newspaper that had attacked extremist, terrorist activities had stopped his car at a red light and had his head torn apart by a shotgun fired from another car that pulled up beside him. Three blocks in the other direction one person had been killed and three others badly injured in a bomb blast at a travel agency arranging visits by exiles to their families in Cuba . . . The Medusa paused at the intersection of another side street. The fourth building inside it to the left had a green clapboard front. The bottom floor contained the El Bambi Children's Wear store. The one above had a small balcony and a sign: "Havana Photos." The top floor was the headquarters of VOR; it was also the apartment of Virgilio Suarez, now that most of the office space was no longer needed. Its front windows were painted black, with the VOR emblem in white: a fist squeezing the letters CUBA. The windows were open to let in air, so Suarez was still there. The Medusa continued half a block along Bergenline to a bus stop with a blue bench on which was printed in yellow: "Operation Pride—Keep Our City Clean." She bought a newspaper from a candy store near the stop, crossed the street and went into a McDonald's, a favorite hangout for Cuban teen-agers—tough-looking boys and pretty girls wearing tight jeans and colorful blouses. None of the boys tried to make a pass at her. Flirting was confined to girls they knew from their own crowd. There were two lines to the counter, one for those who only spoke Spanish. The Medusa joined the other line, bought a Big Mac and a chocolate shake and carried them to a front table with a view of the bus stop across the street.

She finished her food and ice-cold drink, then opened her newspaper, occasionally turning a page while she kept an eye on the bus stop. Nobody thought what she was doing strange. Sitting for hours in a dining place, after one finished eating or having a coffee, was a time-honored custom the exiles had brought with them from Cuba. Also, no one was overly curious about her presence. They had seen her around here often enough to become accustomed to her. She had spent nine days in the area, interviewing leaders of the various action groups —Virgilio Suarez among them.

None of the leaders had resented her questioning, which was obviously sympathetic. And they were all accustomed to being interviewed by the press, welcoming it as an opportunity to talk about the resentments of the Cuban exiles. Not one bothered to ask for her credentials, accepting the false name she gave and her explanation that she represented a British news agency.

It was almost half-past seven when Suarez came around the corner from his side street to the bus stop. He was a mild-looking man with thinning blond hair and a pudgy, ruddy face on which black-rimmed glasses glinted in the sunlight. The suit he wore needed a pressing and gave a shapeless look to his overweight figure. Out of habit he glanced sharply up and down Bergenline. Across the street, the Medusa lowered her head over her newspaper. Not noticing her, he sat down heavily on the blue bench, feeling much older than his forty-seven years. It annoyed him that, with his automobile repossessed by the finance company, he had to ride a hot dirty bus into New York with the kind of people who could never afford a car of their own. His living standard had gone down considerably since the trial. The members who had raised funds for him were either in jail or fugitives or had joined other groups. Even the Cuban exiles who ordinarily gave to the action groups did not want to contribute to one that was no longer effective . . . But he was lucky, he reminded himself. Though the planting of the explosives aboard that plane had been his idea, he was the only one who had gotten off. And the depressed state of his fortunes would not last much longer. He was merely keeing a low profile until the authorities got tired of checking on what he was up to all the time. That would have ended by now if it hadn't been for what had happened after the trial . . . somebody had sent a hand-printed letter to the press, *on VOR stationery,* threatening Senator DeLucca's life. He'd been taken into custody again and forced to print the same letter so it could be compared with the original. The police experts had found that he *hadn't* done the original letter. In spite of that he'd been hauled around from one police station to another and third-degreed in each of them about who *had* sent the letter. It had been three weeks before they'd given up and let him go.

The truth was, at the time of his questioning he hadn't known who'd sent the letter. If he had, he would have given them to the law—just to get even with them. It was only later that he came to suspect Torriente and Lugo—two young men who hung around the fringes of VOR. He'd used them as errand boys and fund collectors. When he'd come out of police custody threatening to kill whomever had sent the letter, if he ever found out, those two had disappeared.

After that his suspicion had hardened into certainty. Writing that letter was exactly the sort of thing those people might have decided was a great idea one night while they were on guard duty at VOR headquarters and getting high on pot or whatever they did. Once more Suarez cursed their memory. He was almost sure he knew where to find them now. It was only his need to keep the low profile, along with his present lack of the kind of tough followers he'd once had, that kept him from having them killed. They'd made it necessary for him to keep his head down that much longer . . . But he would surface again, in spite of them. He would once again have what he'd had before . . . the power, the excitement, the women. Then the leaders of the other action groups, who now regarded him as a has-been, would have to think again about Virgilio Suarez.

His wife and girl friends had left him long before. Now it was humiliating to have to accept this kind of charity each Friday evening . . . a Chinese mobster, a Triad leader who seemed the only one left who remembered the former power of Virgilio Suarez, tossed him a bone in case he should ever become important again. Once a week, he was allowed a couple hours with that aging hooker in Chinatown. Each time put him deeper into debt to the Triad leader. But he was still a man, with a man's hunger, and no other way, at the moment, to feed it . . .

The Medusa raised her head as a bus pulled to a stop outside, blocking the view between her and the bench on the other side. It was a number seven for New York. When it pulled out Suarez was aboard it. The Medusa got up and left, walking back to the street where she'd left the car.

The lowering sun cast her shadow far down that street when she turned into it. The air held an orange-violet glow. She'd noted it before, the gorgeous colors of the sunsets over the Jersey shore, thanks to the pollution in the air from the oil refineries and chemical plants.

"Beauty out of filth," Shevlin had said when she'd pointed it out to him.

She smiled to herself, got into the car and drove back to Manhattan.

FIFTEEN

NEW YORK

VIRGILIO SUAREZ felt drained and disgusted with himself when he left the apartment in Chinatown shortly before ten this night. The prostitute had had a paying customer waiting, and she had hurried him.

Down on the pavement he loosened his tie and unbuttoned his collar.

From the passage down the street the Medusa watched him trudge off toward the subway station. She turned and went through the passage to her car. Sixteen minutes later she left it at a parking lot on 37th Street west of Seventh Avenue. She quickly walked the rest of the way toward the bus terminal and the Terminal Bar across from it.

When Suarez got to 42nd Street and Eighth Avenue after exiting the subway, he crossed to the bus terminal's side of the avenue, keeping away from the Terminal Bar. It was not that he was afraid of the dangerous types who hung out in front of the bar. He had never been afraid of physical violence, which was one reason he'd become what he was. But he was not looking for senseless trouble. He was about to turn into the bus terminal when he heard a woman's voice screaming his name. He turned toward the sound, automatically unbuttoning the front of his jacket. On the other side of the avenue a girl in a black dress with a yellow sash was struggling with two young punks, her thick tawny hair flying as she fought to hang onto the shoulder bag they were trying to rip from her hands.

Suarez recognized her just before she was thrown to the pavement—the young reporter from Europe. He ran across the street, dodging screeching cars. Both of the punks were on top of her now, one still yanking at her bag and the other ripping open the front of her dress. She was still fighting back, kicking one of them in the chest and pushing him away from her. He came back in a crouch, drawing a knife.

Suarez stepped onto the pavement, panting. "Stop it, get away from her."

For a second they just stared at him. The onlookers from the bar who'd been egging them on began to laugh. "Hey, the fat boy's *tough.*"

The one with the knife began to close in on Suarez while the other got to his feet, drawing his own knife. Suarez brought out the small automatic pistol he always carried inside his jacket. He held it close to his body so the two could see it, though anybody much farther away couldn't. "One step closer," he whispered, "and you're both dead."

The way he said it apparently stopped them. Also, they hadn't been expecting a gun. They'd done enough to earn what the girl had paid them for. They backed off, making threatening noises, then turned and walked away.

The Medusa sat up on the pavement. "My God . . . was I glad to see *you* . . ." Her voice was carefully shaky.

Suarez put the gun back out of sight and helped her to her feet, still clutching her bag in one hand. He had a glimpse of white flesh before she gathered the torn material of her bodice over her breasts with her free hand.

"What are you doing here?"

"I was trying to interview—"

"This is a dangerous place. Not a place to come alone."

"I know that—*now.* I'm shaking . . . listen, my car's near here, can you drive me home? I'll pay for a taxi to take you back to—"

"I don't take money from women." Suarez took her arm. "Where is your car?"

When they reached the building just off Central Park West where she had sublet an apartment, she invited him up for a drink. "I could use your company for a little longer."

There was nothing seductive in her invitation. She knew him too well to flirt with him, or even to respond if he made a pass at her. He would become instantly suspicious of any suggestion that she might find him attractive. He was a practical man who knew what he was. No longer young and never handsome. Without funds.

She was right . . . he also felt a woman such as this one didn't go for money. He knew he no longer had any of the kind of authority about him which did attract women like this one. That was going to change but at the moment, such was the sad situation . . .

The Medusa was careful to show nothing but appropriate gratitude for his rescuing her, and a feeling of security that he was with her. Nothing else.

Suarez accepted that, and her invitation. At least it would be a little change for him, a bit of something unexpected, different, to take his mind off his problems for a while.

They went up to her apartment. In the small living room she sat him in a cushioned wing chair and turned on the TV for him before going to the bedroom to change. He was watching the late news when she came back, wearing a T-shirt and jeans.

"What will you drink? I have Scotch, vodka, bourbon—"

"A beer, if you have one cold." He eyed the way her hard nipples stuck out against the T-shirt, watched her buttocks when she walked into the kitchen. Someday, he promised himself, he'd be able to have them like this one again. No more once-a-week charity hookers . . .

She came back with an opened bottle of beer and a glass, a Scotch on the rocks for herself. Sitting on a couch near Suarez, she gave him the bottle and glass. He poured some of the beer in his glass and thirstily drank it down. The Medusa curled her legs under her and watched him while she sipped her own drink. There was no way to ask him for the information she wanted; not even slipped in casually among other questions. There would be too great a risk of his remembering her curiosity about that point later. Nor was the risk worth it, when he might not even know the answer, or not all of it. There was only one safe way to find that out.

"Are you still working on your memoirs?" she asked him.

"They can hardly be called that. Merely some thoughts and facts about the history of my group. Perhaps as self-justification. But perhaps, also, to help Americans understand how badly we feel we have been treated." Suarez shrugged. "At least it gives me something to do."

The false modesty of his words and manner was obvious to her. The memoirs he'd told her about when she'd interviewed him were a kind of ego-insurance for him, to be released only in case of his death—or when his cause was victorious and he was back in Cuba in a new government. One way or another, he intended to become known again and remembered.

She knew more about Virgilio Suarez than he could imagine; and had before ever talking to him.

He was beginning to look sleepy. She watched him pour more of the beer into his glass while she chatted on about her attempt to explore New York's lower depths. He managed to finish off the beer and put the empty glass down carefully. His face was groggy when he turned his head to stare at the TV screen, having difficulty distinguishing the words being spoken by the commentator.

He was asleep when she got off the couch. She carried her glass into the kitchen and emptied it into the sink. Bringing it back to the living room, she put it down beside the couch, to make it seem she'd drunk all of it. He was slumped in the chair, head leaning against the cushioned back, his legs sprawled out. The drops she'd put in his beer would keep him under for at least four hours.

A slim chain was hooked to his belt and ran to a bulge inside one pocket of his trousers. She unhooked the chain and pulled out the batch of keys attached to it, then went through his other pockets. Deep inside his wallet was another key, flat and intricate. She took that too.

He was snoring faintly when she left the apartment, went back down to the car and drove to Union City.

AVOIDING BERGENLINE, THE Medusa drove in and out of a succession of residential back streets to the west end of the one where Virgilio Suarez had his office and living quarters. She got a heavy suitcase from the trunk of the car and carried it up the street.

Suarez was the only one who lived in the house. The children's clothing store on the ground floor and the photo studio on the second had closed hours ago. The front door was in a pool of darkness under the second-floor balcony. The Medusa got out the chain of keys. The second one did it. She relocked the front door from inside and felt her way up the darkened steps to the top floor. There she put down the suitcase and took out a pencil-flashlight. The door was of heavy metal, with VOR and its emblem painted on it. There were two locks. When she'd interviewed Suarez inside, she'd seen that the locking system shot steel bars into wall sockets. Without the keys even an expert couldn't get through quickly without leaving marks of a break-in. She found the two keys that opened the door. Inside the air was thick. The black-painted windows were shut but she did not turn on the lights. Closing the door, she played the thin beam of the flashlight around the office. There were bars across the insides of the windows. A Cuban flag and a pennant with the VOR emblem hung on one wall. On another was a big blowup of a photograph of Castro, and smaller photos of two young Cubans. Target circles had seen drawn on all three pictures, and a dart was stuck in the bull's-eye of each. The smaller pictures were newer: Ricardo Torriente and Hernan Lugo—the two boys who'd fled the wrath of Virgilio Suarez after issuing the death threat to Senator DeLucca on VOR stationery.

Suarez hadn't told her that in so many words. When she'd expressed curiosity about their photos he'd merely said, "They betrayed me and the cause. They finished my ruin." The rest she'd guessed, and confirmed from others. One even suggested that it was Lugo who had printed the letter, since Torriente was not very good at English.

The Medusa knew the faces of Torriente and Lugo very well. She'd studied other photos of them before coming to this office the first time. All of the members of VOR had been arrested and photographed by the police after the bomb attempt more than two years back. These two boys had been released with several other members, considered by the police to be of no consequence in the group.

Their pictures had been stuck away in a back file, after routinely being sent to the FBI photo library. Shevlin had secretly made copies from the FBI file while visiting an old FBI friend.

The Medusa looked at the darts that Suarez had stuck in the two tough young faces.

Now Torriente and Lugo were *her* targets.

She needed them. And she needed them in a cooperative frame of mind, convinced that what she and Shevlin were going to take them into would make them heroes to the whole Cuban movement. And that such conviction would make sense, be credible to the public later, after the assassination. Otherwise, the frame would neither fit nor stick.

To accomplish that, she first had to find at least one of them—and get him alone long enough to do a selling job on him—without anyone else becoming aware of the contact.

Of course, this entire part of the operation—the hunting down of the two young Cubans—could have been accomplished much more quickly and easily if Shevlin could have made open use of his contacts. Just a small payment to some Hudson County cops would have taken care of what she was doing, and without all the elaborate preparations. Suarez would have been taken in for questioning, his pockets emptied and the keys given to a cop who could have walked in here and gone through all the papers in the office. The whole thing would have taken an hour, start to finish. *But* that would have meant other people knowing about Shevlin's specific interest in the young fugitive pair. So this time it had to be done the hard way, and the long roundabout way. This time Shevlin and the Medusa had to be the entire investigation staff, as well as the final hit team. . . .

She got out the flat, intricate key she'd found inside the wallet. After trying several of the drawers, she fitted it to the heavy steel cabinet in one corner of the office. It worked. Inside was a cardboard box containing the "Memoirs of Virgilio Suarez."

The Medusa took the typewriter off the desk, put it on the floor. Opening the suitcase, she took out the newest model high-speed portable copying machine. She put it on the desk, plugged it into a wall socket, stacked the pages of the memoirs in the machine and flicked its switch. The machine did the rest, automatically and swiftly.

While it worked she searched the desk drawers and file-cabinets. Among the records of VOR she found basic data on Torriente and Lugo, but the last address listed for each was an old one that she already knew. They'd shared an apartment in Weehawken but hadn't been near it for almost two years.

She went through the living quarters behind the office without finding anything more recent on the two Cubans. If there was nothing in the memoirs, she was going to have to renew her search from an entirely different direction.

When she returned to the office the copier had finished its job. She put it back in the suitcase and slipped the copied pages of the Suarez memoirs into a plastic shopping bag. From a desk drawer she extracted several sheets of stationery with the VOR letterhead printed on them. Placing the typewriter back on the desk, she inserted one of these sheets and typed a message on it. This joined the copied pages in the plastic bag along with the other two VOR sheets of stationery.

When she left, everything was as she had found it.

Virgilio Suarez was still asleep in the wing chair when she got back to the apartment off Central Park West. She put the plastic bag in a locked briefcase inside the bedroom closet, locked the closet and took off her sneakers. Going back into the living room, she carefully returned the keys to Suarez's pocket and wallet. He stirred in his sleep but did not wake up. Stretching out on the couch, the Medusa willed herself to sleep within seconds. . . .

Some two hours later Suarez began to awaken. He straightened with a groan, the small of his back hurting. His glasses had slid down his nose. He pushed them back in place and looked around him, puzzled for a moment, then remembered where he was, and why. Glancing at his watch, he cursed softly. He *was* getting old, falling asleep like that in such an uncomfortable position. His head hurt from it, as well as his back.

Struggling to his feet, he stifled another groan and gazed down at the girl sprawled out asleep on the couch. At least he wasn't the only one, and she was young. Simple fatigue after a long day and a little excitement. He continued to stand there looking at the girl for a time. So young and fresh. His fingers itched when he studied the curves of her superb breasts. The temptation was strong to touch her or at least to stay and share breakfast with her in the morning. But either would only be embarrassing, he knew, for both of them.

Quietly, Virgilio Suarez let himself out of the apartment.

BEFORE NOON THE Medusa finished going through the pages of the Suarez memoirs. They were typed in Spanish, a language she did not know well enough to read, but each time she came across the names she wanted she marked the entire passage around them, then typed her own copies of the marked passages—substituting the names Sam and Joe for Ricardo Torriente and Hernan Lugo. She deleted references to VOR and Union City.

That afternoon she went to an address in Brooklyn that Shevlin had ven her. The elderly Spaniard who lived there was named Juan Domecq. He had fled Franco's regime in 1939 and gotten himself smuggled into the United States. Domecq had used forged papers to obtain work teaching high school Spanish until he reached retirement age. A teacher's retirement pay being what it was, his apartment was a single room with kitchenette, and a bathroom he shared with others down the hall.

"A friend of mine," she told him, "says you'll do verbal translations from Spanish and then forget you did them. He said you charge fifteen dollars an hour for this service."

Domecq smiled at her. "Your friend has obviously not availed himself of my services for quite some time. I now charge twenty dollars per hour. Inflation, you understand."

"Twenty dollars is fine." She gave him the passages she'd typed up.

The old Spaniard settled into a chair. There was only one passage he translated which was of interest to her. "The last I heard of Joe was that he is across the river, somewhere among the scum in the South Bronx, making his living now as a pusher of narcotics. About Sam I have heard nothing since he fled. But since they were always inseparable, I imagine that Sam is still with Joe and doing the same thing. I understand that Joe has adopted a new street name for himself: calling himself Gonzo—a fitting name for an irresponsible. And a fitting occupation for both of them."

It was a starting point. Hernan Lugo was in the South Bronx: a Cuban in an area where most Latins were Puerto Ricans. He was a dope pusher. Street name: Gonzo. Ricardo Torriente was probably with him.

The Medusa knew how to take it from there.

SIXTEEN

PARIS, MILAN, THE SOUTH BRONX

THE NEXT day, Saturday, when the Medusa switched her target area to the South Bronx, Klaus Bauer met with Simon Hunter in Paris.

It was not as hot in Paris as in New York, but enough to be uncomfortable for Bauer, who had to stop several times to catch his breath as he climbed the five flights to the Hunter apartment. Hunter lived at the top of an old building in which the poet Verlaine had died. The unpainted wooden steps had apparently not been changed since then, and were deeply worn by generations of climbers. Bauer waited at the top landing until his breathing was back to normal, then knocked at the door.

The pretty young woman who opened it had freckles and ginger-colored hair and a distinctly French style of feminine self-assurance. She stared at Bauer, somewhat startled by his appearance. He was used to that. It was his dead-white hair, forming a hippy-style halo around his deeply lined, moonlike face—still in defiance of his mother, who had been begging him to cut it to a respectable length since he was twenty.

"I am Klaus Bauer," he told her in cultured French. "Mr. Hunter is expecting me."

She recovered quickly from her initial surprise and gave him a charming smile. "Come in. I'm Odile, Simon's wife."

She was still quite round from her pregnancy, and much younger than the huge man in the living room behind her. Bauer gave her the small bouquet of flowers he'd bought for her on Rue Mouffetard, and Odile Hunter thanked him with another charming smile, closing the door as he stepped inside.

The apartment took up all of the building's top floor. What had been an attic had been converted into an open sleeping loft with a short spiral staircase leading up to it. The main room comprised most of the lower quarters. It was furnished in Scandinavian modern, softened by Moroccan cushions and rugs. One large window framed the distant porcelain whiteness of the church of Sacre Coeur, atop its hill way up on Montmartre.

Simon Hunter greeted Bauer and went on with what he was doing, not at all embarrassed to be caught changing his baby's diaper. The baby was crying, but that didn't seem to bother him either.

"Boy or girl?" Bauer asked him.

"Girl. Her name's Sivane. Looks like a pixie, doesn't she?" Hunter finished the diapering and picked up his squalling daughter. The baby looked unbelievably tiny in his big hands. It's crying changed to a sleepy murmuring as it was held against his shoulder and gently petted.

"You are a happy father," Bauer said.

"I'm still in shock at finding myself one, at my time of life."

Odile Hunter gestured Bauer to the sofa. "Please sit down, Monsieur Bauer. What will you have to drink?"

"Only a glass of water, I am sorry to say. I am taking the cure."

"Oh? Are you an alcoholic?"

Bauer smiled as he sat down. "I don't think so. I stop drinking often enough to persuade myself that I am not."

Hunter lowered his daughter into a wicker crib as his wife went into the kitchen. He offered his little finger to the baby, and her tiny hand gripped it as she fell asleep. He remained at the crib, looking down with pride. "Do you have children?" he asked Bauer.

"I have a son. Whom I seldom see, unfortunately. His mother and I are divorced and she has turned the boy against me." He sighed unhappily and took the glass of water Odile brought him. "Never get divorced, it is always so messy."

"You are a little too late with that advice," Odile told him. "I've already had a divorce—to marry Simon."

"Odile," Hunter complained fondly, "will you please stop giving people the impression I stole you from Jean-Pierre? The two of you were separated before I came along."

"Yes, but we *might* have gotten back together, if you had not come and forced me to fall madly in love with you."

Hunter smiled and gently extricated his finger from his daughter's grip. "Let's go for a walk," he said to Bauer.

Bauer put down his glass. "I am sorry to disturb your weekend this way," he said to Hunter's wife as he got to his feet.

"Odile is used to this sort of thing," Hunter told him. "She grew up with it. Her father was a cop too."

His wife turned on him. "A little more respect, please. My father is a retired *commissaire* of police."

Hunter grinned at her. "Still a cop. Like me."

Bauer knew that "cop" wasn't the usual term for what Hunter did. He knew of the man's reputation, first with army intelligence and then with the State Department. He had been told of Hunter's breaking up an assassination conspiracy aimed at the secretary of state and a foreign head of government. According to George Ryan, Hunter had stopped the assassination some hours after his State Department boss had officially fired him for stubbornly following the "wrong track."

As Hunter went to open the door his wife told him, "If this new job of yours takes you away from Paris for any length of time, I think I'll go down to Villefranche with Sivane and visit papa. The country air will be good for her."

"Let's first see how it develops."

Hunter kissed his wife and led Bauer down the steps. They went along the street to a corner bistro. Hunter ordered draft beer and Bauer asked for a glass of mineral water. They carried their glasses outside and settled at a sidewalk table in the shade of a big red-and-green umbrella. Bauer told him when Senator DeLucca was scheduled to begin his European jaunt. "Ryan can arrange to have the State Department assign you to supervise the senator's security during his trip—if you're still willing to take on the job, of course."

"How does the senator feel about it?"

"He never likes having too much security around him. So whatever you arrange would have to be kept to a minimum. But he liked you, if that's what you mean. I understand that you quarreled. Don't take that seriously."

"I don't." Hunter smiled. "I figured him for the kind that likes to fight with a man before he makes friends with him." He took a swig of beer. "Okay, we're on. I'll need his entire schedule."

Bauer took an envelope from his inside jacket pocket. "Here it is, Mr. Hunter. When he arrives, where he will go, how long he will stay in each place."

"If you call me Simon, I can call you Klaus. I prefer working with you on a first-name basis."

Bauer laughed. "Simon it is."

Hunter put the schedule in his pocket and looked at Bauer's glass of water. "Would one little glass of wine do you any harm?"

"I'm afraid so. Usually, I don't mind that. But I swore an oath to myself. Not until this job is finished. Then I will have a drink. I will, in fact, get terribly drunk. *After* I have . . . uh, nailed the skins of Mr. Shevlin and Mr. Reinbold to the senator's wall."

"I understand you got hurt pretty bad the last time you went up against that combination."

Bauer nodded. "I was hurt. My reputation as a journalist in Germany still suffers from it. But I come of an old family whose men did not accept such treatment without fighting back." He looked at Hunter with a small smile. "I am the black sheep of my family, but I am not such a weak fellow as I may look."

"What are you doing in Brussels?"

Bauer told him.

Hunter glanced up and down the narrow street. "Shevlin's people probably know you're in Brussels by now. They'll see to it you don't get much there."

"Probably. But I must try what I can with my limited resources." Bauer hesitated. "A man of your experience, and with all the relationships you have developed in Europe, could be of help to us."

Hunter shook his head. "I'm only in charge of the security for DeLucca's trip. Nothing else. I don't even agree with his methods—or yours. I'm only doing it because George Ryan's an old friend. And because I sort of like the little guy."

"Little guy?"

"The senator."

It was a few minutes past six-thirty when they shook hands outside the bistro and parted. Before returning to his wife and daughter, Hunter once more scanned the street. Nothing.

Paul Shevlin did not think it necessary at this stage. He had already known that Bauer would meet Hunter today. Now that he also knew who Hunter was, and what he did, it was not difficult to figure out the purpose of the meeting. Nor was it difficult to anticipate that sometime prior to DeLucca's visit to Milan Hunter would arrive there to arrange for the senator's security while in that area.

By eight o'clock that evening—while Simon Hunter was contentedly watching his wife breast-feed their daughter in their Paris apartment—Shevlin was completing his own preliminary arrangements in Milan.

THOUGH SECOND TO Rome in population, Milan is Italy's most important commercial city. The American Consulate there is assigned a permanent, high-level SY (chief security officer) with a staff as large as most U.S. embassies abroad. Shevlin had met him before. Over a social dinner that evening the SY made it clear again that he was eager to change to a higher-paying job in private industry. Shevlin in turn promised to recommend him for the next executive opening in the security department of Reinbold Enterprises.

By the end of their dinner Shevlin knew everything he needed about the security routine laid on by the consulate in Milan for visiting VIPs.

Shevlin had already made contact with Francesco Nola, the Milan police official Jacques Andrau had recommended. For a generous advance payment, Nola was prepared to produce the city and building blueprints Shevlin wanted without asking why they were wanted. He had also put Shevlin in touch with the best electronics surveillance specialists in the area, most of them employed by the state-controlled telephone system.

To one team of these specialists Shevlin gave the job of bugging the apartment of the consulate's SY and monitoring his telephone calls from there and his office, and of doing the same job on the SY's staff. He assigned another team to the offices near the Brosa Valori and house in the suburbs of Carlo Vizzini, the stockbroker whom Senator DeLucca would be coming to Milan to meet.

With all of these gears in motion, Shevlin drove out of Milan to reconnoiter the roads around a small village named Rocchetta, in the Nervia Valley near the Ligurian coast some two and a half hours away.

It was shortly after nine in the European time zone when he left Milan. In New York it was a few minutes past three in the afternoon.

AT EIGHT-THIRTY New York time that same evening the Medusa drove across the Harlem River from Manhattan into the South Bronx. She had marked her route with a black crayon on a detailed Hagstrom street map of the area. The map lay open on the front seat beside her, ready in case she needed a fast check on it. Day or night the South Bronx was not a healthy place to stop and ask directions in.

The streets she drove along cut through parts of the South Bronx that looked like pictures she had seen of bombed-out Berlin at the end of World War II. There were empty blocks littered with garbage and mounds of rubble, where all the buildings had been torn down to make room for new housing projects that never happened. There were other blocks where the demolition had begun and been canceled before completion. And there were blocks in which most of the tenements had been burned out by vandals.

The gangs that roamed these blocks were very young. The Medusa did not pass anybody walking the area alone. Nor did she see a policeman walking through it. The cops stuck to their heavily armed prowl cars, ignoring the gangs and ignored by them. Up here the roaming teen-agers went almost as heavily armed as the police; which made it a standoff.

In the heart of this devastated and decaying section was a neat little area where cheerful tranquility incongruously reigned. Five blocks long by four blocks wide, solidly Italian, much smaller than the famous Little Italy in downtown Manhattan, it was sometimes called Tiny Italy. Its shops and restaurants and food markets stayed open late and enjoyed a thriving business without paying for protection. Old people sunned themselves on the front stoops. Couples strolled the sidewalks unmolested. A lone girl closing a bakery at midnight could walk home without fear. People tended to leave their parked cars unlocked. A number of the families who lived in these blocks had nephews, uncles and cousins in the Mafia. The muggers, addicts, and gang warriors surrounding the fringes of Tiny Italy never dared set foot inside it.

The Medusa parked at the curb near its Arthur Street market. She walked across the street to an Italian restaurant that those who knew considered one of the best in all New York. It was filled with customers, spicy food smells and the din of voices. A perspiring young waiter found her a seat at one end of a long table crowded with three generations of a single family.

After she had ordered her dinner the Medusa picked up her shoulder bag and made her way to the rear of the restaurant. There were two toilets, neither marked women or men. She tried the door of the right-hand one and found it in use. Without trying the other, she waited.

When the one on the right became free she entered it and locked the door from inside. From her bag she took a sealed envelope and a roll of Scotch tape. She put down the toilet seat and climbed on top of it. The bowl of the light fixture bulged out of a fiberboard ceiling. When she pressed her hand against it, the bowl raised up a few inches. She inserted the envelope through the opening and taped it to the other side of the ceiling, then let the light fixture settle back in place and climbed down off the toilet.

Her meal and a half-bottle of wine were waiting when she returned to her seat. She enjoyed both, paid her bill, tipped generously. The restaurant's owner wished her a good-night as he held the door open for her. Crossing to her car, she drove out of Tiny Italy, through the dark and dangerous ruins of the South Bronx and back into Manhattan.

On the envelope she had left behind she had drawn a small identifying mark: three circles with a line through them. Inside the envelope were ten one-hundred dollar bills. It also contained a typed enquiry, unaddressed and unsigned: "There is a Cuban pusher in the South Bronx calling himself Gonzo. Real name is Hernan Lugo. Need to know where he lives or operates. If cannot provide this, will accept name and business location of his supplier."

Shevlin had given her the names of three police officers who added to their private retirement funds by furnishing answers to such questions—without any contact between themselves and the questioners. Each had his own secret letter box where he picked up enquiries and left answers and to which he would return nine-tenths of the payment if he could not supply an answer. Usually they had to split with others who obtained the answers for them. Each charged the same, one thousand dollars per question. At that price nobody used this service unless anonymity was essential. No one who knew of it would touch somebody else's envelope. That would disturb service, make it unusable in the future.

One of the three who ran the service was a detective-lieutenant who worked out of the 46th Precinct station in the Bronx just off the Grand Concourse. He always had dinner late each night at the restaurant where the Medusa had left the envelope.

The next night she went back to the restaurant for dinner. After ordering, she checked the same toilet. There was nothing there.

She tried again the night after that. There was an envelope, but it bore somebody else's mark on it: a crude drawing of a tree.

On the third night she found her own envelope, marked by the three circles and line. She waited until she was in her car before opening it. Inside was a single sheet of paper with the data typewritten on it:

> HERNAN LUGO: aka Gonzo.
> BUYS: From abandoned New York Central System pier on New Jersey side of Hudson River between Jersey City and Weehawken but closer Jersey City.
> DEALS: On 181st St. and Mapes Avenue in the Bronx.
> LIVES: In one of condemned buildings around Seabury Place facing empty lot.

The empty lot stretched across two square city blocks. All of the buildings which had once filled these blocks had been razed to the ground. The lot had become a semiofficial dumping ground with weeds and bushes growing up out of the garbage and junk. There were a number of fire-gutted, condemned apartment buildings around it near Seabury Place. Sheets of tin had been nailed across their doorways and lower windows. Most of these had since been ripped away, leaving black holes that blended into the general darkness of the night. People living illegally in two of these buildings had managed to reconnect their electric lines to a municipal source of current. The lights showing in the third building were dimmer, candles and oil lamps.

The Medusa used the darkest stretches of the lot as she moved across it. She was dressed entirely in black: jogging shoes, loose-fitting dungarees, a zippered nylon jacket with a hood. The hood shadowed her face, concealed her hair, which she had tied back in a ponytail using the yellow scarf. She could pass for a boy, but it was the darkness she depended on most; and the silence of her reconnaissance. She squatted in the middle of the lot, resting her forearms on her knees as she surveyed the buildings around this end. The answer to her enquiry gave her three places where she could make contact with Lugo: where he lived, where he peddled dope, where he bought it. The next step was to reconnoiter each in turn to determine which would be the most practical.

This was the first place to be tested—where Lugo lived. The most likely of the condemned buildings for Lugo to live in were those where lights showed. Across from these, at an angle to them, were a couple of attached buildings in much worse shape where all of the windows were dark. The Medusa started toward these.

Footsteps crunched across broken glass in the murk off to her left, coming in her direction. She backed against the bottom of an overturned truck that had been stripped of engine, seats and wheels, then remained still, watching the approach of shadowy figures.

She counted eleven of them as they passed her and went out of the lot up a street in the direction of Crotona Park. When they were gone she moved again, approached the gaping doorway of the most dilapidated of the dark attached buildings. Halting, she listened for noises inside. What she heard she identified as scurrying rats. After some thirty seconds she mounted the steps and went in.

Inside, she used her pencil-flashlight for a swift look around the interior—fire-scorched walls, hanging support beams, collapsed ceilings. Snapping off the flash, she felt her way to a staircase and went up to the second floor. Peering out into the night, she confirmed what she had suspected earlier. This was the wrong place. There were too many people using these buildings. She had to make the contact without others observing it. She shifted to her feet—and froze in position. Noises below. Heavy footsteps, loud voices. Her mouth tightened. They'd come into the building through some side entrance. The glow of flashlights came up through the hole in the floor. Silently she circled the hole and went out to the second-floor hallway. She estimated a minimum of seven voices down there. Hugging the wall, she went past the top of the stairway, heading for the dark doorways at the rear.

Someone was coming up the stairs, preceded by the beam of a flashlight. The Medusa turned into the first room she came to, feeling her way to a window. It was not until she had almost reached it that she saw the window had been sealed shut with a sheet of tin nailed in place over it. The flashlight's beam gleamed against the metal blocking her way out. She slid along the wall and stopped with her back pressed against the wall beside the doorway. A tall, skinny figure stepped through the doorway, flashlight in one hand, a bottle of wine dangling from his other. The Medusa lashed the side of her forearm across his throat. His mouth sprang wide open but the blow had made it impossible for any sound to come out.

She managed to catch the flashlight as it fell from his hand but missed her grab for the bottle, which exploded into fragments when it hit the floor.

A yell from below. Someone else started up the stairs. The Medusa spun out of the room into another. The broken window in this one was not blocked, but it opened on an enclosed airshaft. She turned back through the room, moving swiftly.

A burly figure reached the bend in the hallway just as she came out of the room. The flashlight he held illuminated a lead pipe and a sawed-off shotgun hanging from his studded belt. They saw each other in the same instant.

The Medusa closed the distance between them with two long steps, her right hand driving upward at his face, palm first, as he tugged the shotgun loose from his belt. The heel of her hand rammed against the base of his nose, driving the sharp cartilage above its bridge into his brain. He thudded to the floor, the truncated shotgun clattering against the base of the wall.

The others were rushing up the stairs now. No time for anything except getting out. She scooped up the fallen shotgun and sprinted into another room. Using the stock of the shotgun, she broke away the last shards of the smashed window pane, then dropped feet-first onto a pile of refuse, rolling down its slope, to come up on her feet again at the bottom and run off.

By the time members of the gang emerged from the condemned building, there was no way for them to figure out where she had gone. The darkness had swallowed her.

SEVENTEEN

NEW JERSEY, THE BRONX,
NEW JERSEY, MILAN

THE NEXT morning the Medusa drove to a boat basin on the upper Manhattan side of the Hudson River. It was time to check out the second possible contact site. She hired a man with a motor boat to take her on a cruise of the New Jersey side of the river.

He eyed her Nikon with a telephoto lens. "You a reporter?"

"Free-lance. I want to shoot pictures of the abandoned piers the Army Corps of Engineers keeps promising to clear away. The ones running from Jersey City towards Weehawken."

He gunned his boat across the river and swung along the New Jersey side. The boat slowed each time they came to a stretch of the old, long-unused piers. Disintegrating wooden derelicts from another era jutted out from the shore between the gleaming aluminum of the modern container ports that had taken over. For half an hour the Medusa snapped pictures of them. The best were sagging, splintered, weather-bleached hulks. The worst were down to the old oak pilings, now supporting only a few planks that were left from structures that had swept away, piece by piece, on the tides.

"Do you know where the old New York Central pier is?" she asked him.

He took her to it.

It was a rotting eyesore, slowly decaying into the industrial wastes forming a thick, oily coating on the sluggish river surface around it. It was swaybacked, and whole portions of timber had fallen away from its sides. The broken stern of an ancient ferryboat stuck out of a mudflat beside it. Debris bobbed in the stagnant water between the piles the pier squatted on.

But it was from inside this pier, according to her source, that Hernan Lugo bought his narcotics.

While the boat she had hired idled near it, the Medusa snapped pictures without paying attention to focus or light. What she did pay attention to was the close-up view the telephoto lens gave her to the pier. Its curved roof was still fairly intact; and there was a brand-new black Cadillac limousine parked on the dock behind it. Up on the heights above it, tall apartment buildings were in the process of construction, work cranes towering between them. She was able to make out only one road still leading down directly to the dock behind the pier, neglected but still usable.

After returning to the Manhattan side of the river she drove across the George Washington Bridge to New Jersey, to have a look at the pier from that end. Where the new apartment buildings were being erected she used the telephoto lens to study the areas the road passed through on its descent to the dock behind the pier below. Finally, she focused on the pier itself. Other than the limousine parked on the dock behind it, there was no sign of activity in or around the pier. That was to be expected. The dealing would be done by night.

This, she decided, was the most likely place to take Lugo. But first she would have to preset the conditions, to manipulate *when* he would decide to come here. The vital conditions for the contact with Lugo remained the same; she had to gain physical control over him quickly until he was won over by the version of the operation she and Shevlin had worked out. And—there must be no witnesses.

She drove back to her apartment and slept for eight more hours to insure that she would be operating at her peak that night.

IT HAD BEEN dark for less than an hour when the Medusa went up into the Bronx that night. She was wearing black again, but the effect was different than the previous night: low-cut tailored silk blouse and shiny hip-hugger slacks. Even the pageboy wig concealing her natural hair was black. There was a string of pearls around her neck, and the scarf was cinched around her waist. She wore oversized sunglasses.

She drove north of Crotona Park along Southern Boulevard, and turned into 181st Street. To her left, shadowy figures formed a circle around a fire in the middle of a lot surrounded by partially demolished factories. On her right there was a short block of three- and four-story houses in relatively fair condition.

At the corner of 181st and Mapes, where Hernan Lugo was supposed to deal, a Puerto Rican girl in a silver plastic jacket and skin-tight jeans leaned against the window of a small general store. The Medusa pulled to the curb in front of her. The girl looked at her with no expression, hands jammed inside her jacket. Her age might have been anything between ten and thirteen.

The Medusa spoke to her through the open window of her car. "I'm looking for Gonzo. I want to score."

The girl took a hand out of her jacket and made her a signal to wait. She rapped at the store window behind her. A kid of about six came out, and the girl whispered something. The kid sprinted off into Mapes Avenue, disappearing among its shadows.

As she waited the Medusa was briefly conscious of the weight of the shoulder bag on her lap, and of the slight pressure of the snub-nosed revolver between her thighs under it. It was unlikely that anyone would try to attack her . . . this was a pusher's corner, if a customer got hurt here the other customers would stop coming, and nobody wanted to louse up the neighborhood's biggest source of income.

A boy of not more than nine rode out of Mapes on a bike. He went past her car, looking into it, then turned his bike in a long circle, glancing up and down 181st before swinging back.

"Go around," he said as he rolled past her.

She did not understand at first. The boy made another long circle with his bike. "Go around, go around," he said when he passed her again. "Right on Prospect."

The Medusa pulled away from the curb and drove through the next short block to Prospect, turning to the right when she reached it. She took it slow. The watch force had made sure she was alone in the car and now they wanted to make sure no other car was following her. She turned right again at 182nd, and then once more into that end of Mapes. She caught a glimpse of something white shifting position on a dark porch up ahead to her left, then spotted a figure up on the roof of the house. The lookout system around Gonzo's location might be young but it was also efficient.

A stocky young man in a white shirt and dark jeans came down onto the sidewalk. The Medusa stopped at the curb and recognized the tough, muscular face of Hernan Lugo.

"Gonzo?"

"Yeah." He bent to study her through the open window. "You're new."

He had a small walkie-talkie on a shoulder strap. Whoever was up there on the roof would have one too. The Medusa made her accent strong, letting him hear it: "A man I met at a party today told me he buys Quaaludes from you. He knows other people who get marijuana from you, so he thought you might be able to supply other things. His name is Frederick Voss."

That was safe enough. Lugo would know most of his customers by sight but not by name. At the same time she was showing him she *thought* he would recognize the name, establishing herself as coming through a recommendation.

"Just tell me what kind and how much." Lugo's speech was soft and quick, the words clipped.

"Cocaine, you have it?"

He did, though not much. Mostly he dealt pills in small quantities —along with pot in five-dollar packets called nickle bags. He did keep some coke and heroin for the occasional customer, but people who wanted them usually went to those who specialized in that trade. C and H were big money; Hernan Lugo was not at that level.

"Snow goes for a hundred bucks a gram," he told her. "You got that much?"

The way she looked at him seemed nervous. "If anything should happen to me, Mr. Voss knows that I have come to you here."

Lugo gave her an exasperated look. "Hell, I ain't gonna mug you for the dough. I got a steady business here."

"I need," she told him, "two thousand dollars' worth."

Lugo's armpits began to sweat. A combination of greed and sudden suspicion. "You snort, shoot or freebase?"

She looked puzzled. "I'm sorry . . . I don't understand what you mean."

That was better. No undercover cop would show up acting too dumb to even know the common street names for stuff like that. Anyway, why would the cops want to bust a little small-time dealing? He paid them for the right . . . "Where you from?"

"Germany. Tomorrow I have to fly to Chicago to start a new job. I don't know anybody there. I *need* enough to last until I find someone who can supply me."

"All I got's two grams." Lugo was frustrated. Two thousand for just one score would have been so sweet.

"That's not enough! That won't last me . . . listen, can't you get more? Or perhaps you can direct me to somebody else who has it?"

That did it. This blizzard-maker was all *his.* Lugo was not about to give her away to anybody else. He thought about his supplier at the old pier. Two thousand was worth a fast trip to Jersey and back . . . "I can get it for you."

"Tonight? It has to be tonight. My plane for Chicago takes off tomorrow morning. I'm prepared to pay you a bonus if you will do this for me. An additional . . . one hundred dollars."

He had her on a hook. "*Two* hundred. I'll have to go to a lot of trouble, and that's what it'll cost you—"

"All right. Two hundred dollars. If I get it tonight."

"I'll have it by four A.M. You can come back then?"

"Yes."

"Beautiful. So let's take care of what I got to sell you now, before I go for the rest. Go around the block again. Do it slow, give me time to get my stash. Have the dough ready, two hundred for my two grams plus a hundred for my bonus in advance. We call that earnest money."

She started looking nervous again. Lugo flashed her a smile, a lot of even white teeth. "You got to start trusting me. Like I'm trusting you to come back for all that toot."

"All right." She pulled away from the curb, driving through the rest of Mapes Avenue. . . .

Lugo was inside the house before the car turned into 181st. The excitement was pounding in him like an electronic guitar. Two thousand and two hundred bucks with one shot! He'd never sold a whole ounce to a single client before. He pressed the talk button of his walkie-talkie and talked into it. "How's it look up there, Chino?"

"Cool. Nobody else moving in."

Lugo went to a corner of the room and crouched to pry up a floorboard. He got out his two-gram stash of coke. His head was already working on the problem ahead of him. His pier dealer charged exactly half of what pushers sold for on the street. That meant a 100 percent profit for Lugo. But this foreign girl wanted another eighteen hundred bucks' worth—and he didn't have nine hundred. He took what he did have out of his pocket and counted. Two hundred and thirty-five dollars plus change. Add the three bills she'd give him now. Five hundred and thirty-five. He'd have to get over to the all-night clinic on Jerome Avenue near the reservoir, see if he could borrow the other three sixty-five from his friend Ricardo Torriente, who worked there as a guard. If Ricardo couldn't come up with all of it, Lugo would just have to adulterate whatever he could buy with enough lactose and other shit to bring it up to the weight she'd be paying for.

His dealer already cut the snow he sold pretty thin. But he doubted the girl would know the difference if he stepped on it a little more. Dumb foreigner.

There was a temptation but he didn't seriously consider slugging her and grabbing all the cash she was carrying. He was not a mugger, or any other kind of criminal in his own eyes. What he did here was to supply goods that respectable people wanted to buy. No different than selling cameras or hot dogs. He was just getting by as best he could under rough circumstances . . . If VOR hadn't fallen apart, and if Virgilio Suarez hadn't marked him lousy to all the other action chiefs he'd still be working for The Cause. For that he would have done anything, given anything, risked anything. But none of them wanted him anymore. No one except his partner Torriente. It wasn't right. Everybody was entitled to one mistake, and a chance to make up for it—

His walkie-talkie squawked, Chino's voice came through. "She's coming around again, Gonzo. Everything's still cool."

Lugo went out onto the porch. When the car pulled to the curb he walked down to it and snapped his free hand at the girl through the window. "The dough."

She put it in his upturned palm—two hundred for what he was holding and a hundred in advance on his bonus. Lugo gave her the two grams of coke. "Be back at four A.M. Right here. On the dot."

"I will." She drove away, much more quickly now, the tires squealing as the car went around the corner.

Lugo walked rapidly in the other direction, got into his own car and headed over to Jerome Avenue to see what Ricardo Torriente could lend him.

IT WAS ALMOST one in the morning when Hernan Lugo drove along the highway on the heights above the New Jersey shore of the Hudson and reached the road that led down to the pier. He waited for the traffic light to change, then turned off the highway onto the unlighted road. Three minutes later he parked at the dock behind the pier. There were four cars belonging to other customers, in addition to the dealer's Cadillac.

When he got out of his car two men converged on him out of the shadows, frisked him expertly. Lugo wasn't carrying a piece. He wasn't stupid enough to bring one, he'd left his gun with Torriente.

Two pushers came out of the pier and went to their cars. The man on Lugo's left patted his shoulder. "You can go in now."

Lugo crossed the dock and went into the pier. There was a fetid odor inside from the decaying sewage trapped in the stagnant water just under the sagging boards of the floor.

Six minutes later he was outside again, getting back in his car with his buy. He had paid all he had for it. Seven hundred and ninety-two dollars. Plenty of time left to return to his place of business and add enough to bring it up to weight.

Leaving the pier behind, the car climbed the turns of the dark, potholed road. The traffic light was red when Lugo reached it. She stopped, waiting for it to change to green. The front door on the right-hand side of his car was yanked open and the Medusa slid into the seat beside him.

Without her black wig and glasses it took him several moments to recognize her. It did not take him that long to recognize the feel of the gun muzzle pressed against his ribs.

Long after they were gone, the traffic light continued to burn red for the river road and green for the highway. It was not until six in the morning that an emergency maintenance crew came to check out the problem. They found somebody had broken open the control box and jammed the switch inside.

Two days later the Medusa sent a cable to Shevlin.

PAUL SHEVLIN WAS still in Italy. He had spent several days driving and walking around the village of Rocchetta, working out his tactics in detail. From there he drove down to Rome, where he went to a small warehouse in one of the old, crooked streets behind the Castel Sant' Angelo. The place was run by an illegal armorer who supplied weapons to anyone willing to pay his prices, no questions asked. Shevlin had never met him before but knew his reputation—both his goods and his discretion were dependable.

Introducing himself with a false name, Shevlin placed his order for the items he needed. It took the armorer two days to fill the order. Shevlin checked each item before placing it in one of the burlap bags provided by the armorer. He put his purchases in the trunk of his car and returned to the Rocchetta area.

Several miles from the village, Shevlin pulled his car off a narrow mountain road into a heavily wooded section. Taking his purchases from the trunk, he hid them under a rockslide at the foot of a rugged slope overgrown with thorn bushes, then drove along the Ligurian coast to Genoa and switched onto the A7 highway leading back to Milan.

At any time of day the A7 between Genoa and Milan carried a heavy stream of traffic speeding in both directions. There was no reason for Shevlin to pay special attention to one of the cars that swept past going the other way. Nor did the man driving the other car notice Shevlin. The other driver was Simon Hunter, en route to carry out his own reconnaissance of the area around Rocchetta, the village from which the parents of Senator Frank DeLucca had immigrated to America.

On reaching Milan, Shevlin drove to a large commercial hotel across from the railroad station. He checked in using the name G. A. Nels —the anagram for the code name he used only with the Medusa. Leaving his suitcase in his room, he went out to collect the first results of the operation he had set in motion before leaving Milan.

Two hours later he was back in his hotel room, going through those results. One of the phone calls received by the consulate's SY at his office late the previous afternoon had been from Simon Hunter calling from the Milan airport. Hunter had asked the SY to meet him early that evening at a cafe in the Galleria. Calls which the SY had made later that evening from his apartment to several of his security personnel gave Shevlin the basic essentials of the arrangements Hunter had set up for Senator DeLucca's visit. There had also been an interesting phone conversation picked up by the wiremen Shevlin had assigned to Vizzini, the stockbroker. It had been from Klaus Bauer, confirming the date of Vizzini's appointment with DeLucca. During the call, Vizzini offered to let the senator stay in the guest room of his house in the suburbs if he was staying overnight in Milan. Bauer had thanked him for the invitation but said a reservation had already been made for DeLucca to stay at the four-star Hotel Colomba D'Oro just off the Corso Vittorio Emanuele near the Duomo.

Shevlin turned next to a suitcase filled with the builders', architects' and municipal planning blueprints that the police inspector Nola had lifted from the city archives. Discarding most of them, Shevlin settled down with the ones that now interested him most—the layouts of the Hotel Colomba D'Oro, of the blocks surrounding it, and of its below-ground area.

He had been studying these blueprints for almost an hour, using a strong magnifying glass, when there was a knock at the door of his room. It was a hotel porter with a cable that had been forwarded to Milan by the MARS office in Munich. Shevlin tipped the porter, closed and locked his door and opened the cable. It had been sent from New York and was addressed to "G. A. NELS":

BOTH PARTIES READY NEED YOU CLINCH DEAL.

It was signed, "E. D. MUSA."

EIGHTEEN

MILAN, PARIS, MILAN

ANY POTENTIAL victim of an assassination or kidnap attempt is most vulnerable in transit. Ninety percent of all such attacks are carried out while the target is using an automobile. To combat this an industry has sprung up in Europe and the United States: conversion of cars into rolling fortresses by installing armor plating, armored glass and accessory defensive and counterattack devices.

There are two schools of thought about the value of these fortresses on wheels, even among specialists in the field. Over the past few years Simon Hunter had argued the question in the course of his work with members of the world's top counterterrorist squads: Germany's GSG-9 (Grenzschutzgruppe-9), Israel's Saiyeret, England's SAS specialists, France's Gigene group and Italy's Squadra Anti-Commando, in addition to America's Secret Service and the Blue Light unit of the United States Army. One school holds that for full protection a passenger car should be armored as strongly as modern technology makes possible—against bullets, bombs or land mines. This will enable its occupants to survive the first ten seconds of an ambush situation, the short time span within which most assaults either succeed or fail. The other school points to three disadvantages in this method. One: the cost factor. A complete shell of overlapping tungsten steel plating fitted inside the passenger area can triple the car's initial cost. Transparent armored windows are also enormously expensive. Another seventy thousand dollars can be poured into adding a Radar GS Hostile Fire Indicator, plus a full CTVSS (Counterterrorist Vehicle Security System) to reveal any tampering with the auto. Two: the weight problem. Enough steel-plated armor to render a car relatively impregnable adds well over two thousand pounds to its normal weight, which makes it slow and clumsy, impossible to maneuver quickly out of an emergency situation. The weight problem can be compensated for somewhat by adding extra-strong gears, engine and suspension. But even with these an automobile so heavily burdened has to be taken in for overhauling after every few short trips. Three: no car can be made bulletproof, only bullet-resistant. Admittedly this is usually enough to turn away an attack with small arms, including submachine guns. But even the hardest interior protection shell is not impervious to armor-piercing shells, and certainly not to a large enough explosive charge. In Spain an army general's automobile was blown so high off the road that it wound up as crushed metal on top of a nearby roof.

This other school of thought opts for a normal, easy-handling car equipped with extra speed, strengthened brakes and a special gearbox —able to twist, spin and race out of any trap in split seconds. The target passenger is protected during this shortened escape period by properly armed security pros; and by having a hot driver trained in basic evasive action: the instant reverse out, the fast J-turn, the around-end swing and the bootlegger braking-spin.

The final security procedure aims at avoiding getting anywhere near a trap in the first place. Terrorists and other potential attackers plan their ambushes by observing a target's normal travel routine. The countermeasure is never to establish a routine—to take unpredictable routes and change them without notice to anybody not in the target's car.

In each of the countries on Senator's DeLucca's European schedule Simon Hunter had prearranged for a compromise between the two conflicting expert viewpoints. First place on the schedule was London. When the flight carrying DeLucca and Hunter from Washington's Dulles Airport landed at Britain's Heathrow, two cars came out onto the field to take them from the plane. One was a fast-handling Ford

Granada with a chauffeur-bodyguard and two more plainclothes guards in the back seat, all schooled in counterterrorist techniques. The Ford would be the watchdog car.

The second automobile, driven by another experienced security-chauffeur, was a Mercedes-Benz with medium-weight armor sufficient to withstand gunfire from hand-held weapons. It was enough, also, to divert the trajectory of anything that did pierce the protective shell, making accurate shooting at the target inside impossible. This would give its driver the vital seconds needed to maneuver out of an ambush while the watchdog car behind it established a position from which its men could dominate the attack site and riddle the assailants with heavy counterfire.

It would be difficult for the State Department to scatter enough armored vehicles around the world to handle all the VIPs passing through, but every major city had at least one private company that maintained them for rental at hourly or daily rates to customers with legitimate credentials. In each city Senator DeLucca would visit, Hunter had made prior arrangements with one of these firms, selecting the armored car he wanted.

These same firms would also supply trained drivers and guards, but on this trip these men would all be from embassy and consulate security staffs, men Hunter had worked with before and whose ability he knew well.

The security procedure Hunter had worked out began at Heathrow. First the three men from the watchdog car climbed out and spread apart to cover all approaches to the cars. Then Hunter emerged from the plane and made his own scan of the area before signaling DeLucca to follow him to the armored Mercedes. Its driver, who had remained inside the car, picked up a small metal box and pressed a button on it as they approached. The electronic locking system responded, the bolts of the rear doors snapping open. Hunter opened one of the rear doors, looking around again as DeLucca climbed inside. It was only when the door was open that one saw the thickness of its window's layers of transparent armor.

Hunter got in back with the senator and shut the door. The lock bolts shot into place when the driver pressed another button on the electronic control box. The Mercedes pulled away from the plane, angling for one of the airport exit ramps. The watchdog car followed, keeping far enough behind so that if the Mercedes rode into an ambush the Ford would not be caught in it too, leaving it free to take whatever action might be needed. All according to regulation in-transit procedure.

As the two cars left the airport Hunter continued to survey the sides of the road on both sides. He had been over every route he and the senator would travel and knew what should be there, what was new and what might pose a threat. Like DeLucca, he did not actually expect trouble, but on a security job like this he always acted as if he did.

The cars parked in the rental lot beside the airport exit were normal. So were the people getting into and out of them. There was nothing special about the black-haired girl with the sunglasses and yellow scarf to attract his attention. . . .

The Medusa finished pulling her bag out of the car trunk while she peered through the sunglasses at the Mercedes and Ford Granada going by, noting the number of men inside each. She closed the trunk and straightened, watching the two cars disappear in the direction of London. Making sure her wig fitted well, she carried her bag into the terminal and presented her reservation for the flight to Brussels—the next stop on Senator DeLucca's schedule.

After boarding the plane and taking her seat, the Medusa thought a moment about Paul Shevlin: up there in the Italian Alps above Aosta, training Lugo and Torriente in handling the weapons they would be using for the strike. She had watched for a bit before leaving them to make sure the senator held to his schedule.

The two Cubans were not bad at all—dedicated, eager to do their part in the operation correctly. Or to do what they *thought* was their part. As Lugo and Torriente understood it, the attack would be aimed at *kidnapping* DeLucca, then using him as a hostage to force the release of the imprisoned VOR leaders . . .

The Medusa dismissed them from her mind as the plane took off. She closed her eyes, leaned back and slept like a baby until the landing at Brussels National.

FOUR DAYS LATER she ordered lunch sent up to her room at Le Crillon, the hotel for diplomats and other upper-strata political figures in Paris. She hungrily ate all of it, seated on a satin-covered chair before a Louis

XV table. When she was finished she crossed the Persian rugs scattered on the parquet flooring, snapped off the air conditioning and opened the windows overlooking the Place de la Concorde.

The sluggish air that flowed in from the hot July sunlight was moist and heavy, but the Medusa did not like to sleep in a sealed room breathing refrigerated air. Besides, the thick heat was welcome. In two days, it would be essential.

Turning from the windows, she stripped, put her clothes away neatly, then stretched out on the bed to add a long nap to the nine hours sleep she had had the previous night.

There would not be much sleep the next two nights, which would be followed by a day in which she would need to function at peak awareness.

She awoke three hours later, sprawled on her stomach, the sheets soaked with perspiration. Sunrays slanting through the windows burned across the skin of her buttocks and thighs. She swung off the bed and took a long cold shower before phoning down for a pot of black coffee. . . .

It was after 6 P.M. when Senator DeLucca left his meeting at the Finance Ministry and returned to Le Crillon. The Medusa sat beside one of her windows and watched the senator's two-car entourage make a curving approach to the hotel around the large *place.* They were different cars than in London and Brussels, but their spacing and the placement of the men inside them remained the same.

The Medusa got up and packed her bag. DeLucca and Hunter would fly from Paris to Milan the following morning. Her plane would get her into Milan early this night—to join Paul Shevlin and complete the final phase of their prestrike preparations.

SIMON HUNTER'S BIG hands ached from the damp heat when he and DeLucca left the offices of Carlo Vizzini, the chairman of the best stockbroker firm in Milan. It was not any better once they were back inside the air conditioning of their armored car, heading through the city's muggy summer evening toward the Hotel Colomba D'Oro.

Frank DeLucca noticed the way Hunter was unconsciously kneading his hands with his fingertips. By now the senator knew all about the mine cave-in that still gave Hunter trouble with those hands in damp weather. He'd come to know a good deal about this big pro with his shaggy gray hair, and had grown increasingly fond of him. The only irritating thing about Hunter was that it was difficult to provoke him into any sustained argument. He kept blunting DeLucca's fiesty moods with soft answers. Yet one was always aware that Hunter was in charge when he had to be.

In a way Hunter reminded the senator of his son Johnny, who only revealed his stubborn streak when a dispute involved his profession—when he could get impossible to move. Hunter also reminded DeLucca of his father—an enormously strong construction worker who had always managed to rule family decisions without saying very much, and while allowing his wife to fulfill her role as titular head of the household.

Hunter glanced back through the rear window to make sure the watchdog car was the correct distance behind as they turned into the Corso Vittorio Emanuele. It was. No need to use the car radio to pass instructions back when they left the Corso and neared the hotel. Procedure for getting their man in or out of his car was standard, deriving from the rule that he never be allowed to stand out in the open waiting.

The first car pulled up to the entrance. Its electronic door locks stayed locked, DeLucca, Hunter and its driver remaining inside. The three security men from the other car got out and scanned the narrow street. Its driver stayed there and continued to watch. The other two went into the hotel and checked the lobby. One remained there while the other stepped out and nodded. The armored car's rear door locks snapped open and Hunter got out. DeLucca climbed out and entered the hotel with Hunter on one side of him and the bodyguard on the other. They got into the elevator and rode up to their rooms on the fourth floor.

Outside, the two drivers took the cars around the corner into a side street and down into the hotel's underground garage. The armored car's driver, Jim Early, left the garage and walked back to join the others in the hotel. The other, Joe Mayer, stayed with the cars. He would be relieved later, the security men taking turns guarding the cars until the garage was locked up for the night.

When Hunter opened the door to DeLucca's suite the man waiting inside its living room was already on his feet with a pistol in his hand. As soon as he saw Hunter and DeLucca he put the gun away and snapped off the TV set he had been watching. In each country on the senator's schedule the police had assigned one of their own men as liaison with the American security team. Sergeant Matteo Roselli was from the Italian Carabinieri. Hunter had checked him out with an old Carabinieri friend, Major Diego Bandini, and gotten an unqualified recommendation.

"All quiet here," Roselli told Hunter. "Not even a phone call."

"Good, you can go off now. Be back here at eight in the morning."

"Where do we go tomorrow?"

"Tell you tomorrow."

Roselli nodded, saluted Senator DeLucca and left. DeLucca frowned at Hunter. "You *are* exaggerating. Keeping it a secret, even from your own men."

Hunter smiled, shrugged. "You're probably right. But it keeps me in practice."

DeLucca grimaced. There was just no way to get into a fight with this man. He picked up the phone and ordered dinners to be sent up in an hour.

Hunter relocked the living room door from the inside and went to check out DeLucca's bedroom. Sergeant Roselli had been guarding the suite the whole time they'd been out of it but he would have spent most of the time in the living room. The bedroom had two doors, neither to the hotel corridor. The open one was to the living room, the locked one to Hunter's adjoining bedroom. Hunter unlocked the door and checked out his room too, then kicked off his shoes, took off his jacket and tie and tossed them on the bed. Unbuttoning his shirt, he placed a long-distance call to his father-in-law's home in France. . . .

The house was just below the Col de Villefranche, east of Nice, on a tree-filled slope blessed by breezes from the Mediterranean below and the mountains above. A good place for Odile and the baby to spend part of the summer while Hunter was away. Her father, Olivier Lamarck, had finished paying for it shortly before retiring from his position as commissioner of the Police Judiciaire. His wife had been killed in an auto accident in that same year, and Lamarck always welcomed company.

It was Odile who picked up the phone. Hunter asked her how her father was working out as a babysitter. Her laugh warmed him. "Papa only has to *look* at Sivane and he melts," she told him. "He has just taken her down to town with him. To show his granddaughter off to all his friends. The cops and the criminals."

Hunter grinned. "Especially the criminals." Lamarck had a running chess war going with a retired gangster who now ran a restaurant; that would be the first place he'd go.

"How is your trip going?" Odile asked. But she already knew from his tone that there'd been no problems. They chatted for nearly ten minutes. After the call Hunter took a shower, changed to fresh clothes and went back to the living room of DeLucca's suite.

The dinners had already arrived. The two bodyguards, Bronson and Leary, had returned from their own room and were eating with the senator. Hunter joined them. Leary had finished his dinner quickly and gone down to relieve Mayer, who'd had his sent to the garage.

When their dinners were finished Senator DeLucca had the table cleared and invited anyone who cared to lose money to join his nightly poker game. Hunter, Leary and Bronson sat down to it with him, and Mayer came in from his room and joined them later. DeLucca did usually wind up the winner, but tonight Hunter was ahead when Early came back up from the garage.

"Hotel's full up and they've locked the garage for the night," he told Hunter, and gave him a black bag—and a plastic card with a thin strip of metal foil laminated to it. "This is the only one. If the night clerk wants to open the garage before we get up in the morning he'll have to call you for it." The card's metal strip had a pattern of holes punched in it. The garage gate had an electronic lock that would only respond to that pattern, which was computer-changed every night. Hunter took the card and a small black bag from Early and went down to make his own final security check before turning in for the night. Behind him, Early took a seat in the poker game.

Leaving the hotel, Hunter walked around the corner into the side street. There was no way to the underground garage from inside the hotel. There was only the street-level, drive-in entrance, its steel gates now shut. Hunter inserted the card in the lock. Opening the gate, he stepped inside and turned on the garage lights before walking down the wide ramp.

First he did a tour of the entire garage, making certain there was no one in or under other cars. Then he checked out his own two.

This time the watchdog car was a souped-up Chevrolet Impala. The armored Cadillac Hunter had selected had the basic combination of protection and maneuverability he favored. The armored shell around the interior was tough but relatively light in weight: layers of hardened plastic laminated with tightly interwoven, bullet-resistant Kevlar synthetic fiber. The limousine's windshield, rear window and side windows were made of so-called transparent armor—bullet-resistant glass with a Polycarbonate lining. The thickness made it impossible to have side windows that could be opened. The air inside had to be supplied by the air-conditioning system. In this heat that was a necessity anyway.

Other security measures included heavy-duty shock absorbers and brake linings, and a fast-reverse gearbox. Plus a complete CTVSS installation that would register a warning if anyone tampered with the Cadillac while it was unguarded.

Hunter opened the black bag Early had given him. It contained several small electronic devices. He took out a remote starter that could turn on the Cadillac's engine and electrical systems from up to a block away. If explosives had been wired to the car's electricity, it would trigger the explosion before anyone came near. There had not been enough time since Early had left the garage for anyone to booby-trap the armored car, but Hunter pressed the switch to make sure the device worked. It did. Hunter switched the device off and put it back in the bag.

He took out the control that actuated the Cadillac's electronic locks. The doors, hood and trunk could not be opened or relocked without it. Hunter unlocked the doors and slid into the front seat. The most important item he checked was the CTVSS sensor indicator, a weld-sealed metal unit with a display dial built into the dashboard panel. There was no way the unit could be altered short of cutting it open with a hacksaw or blowtorch. It was wired to vibration and microwave sensors inside the Cadillac's hood and trunk and on both sides over the wheels. Any attempt to tamper with any part of the limousine would be detected by at least one of these sensors. The panel indicator dial would then flick on a number revealing which part of the car should be inspected for trouble. Hunter saw that the dial number was what it should be: zero. The black bag contained a unit that could switch the numbers back to zero if their own use of the car caused the indicator to register one of the other numbers.

Getting out, Hunter relocked the doors and made a brief inspection of the underside of the armored limousine. That would be done more thoroughly in the morning after the other checks had been gone through once again.

Hunter returned to the hotel. The poker game was still going in the living room of the senator's suite.

"Time to get some sleep," Hunter announced. "We've got an early start on the board tomorrow."

DeLucca gave him a mocking look. "You have to *try* to remember you're not an old-maid aunt in charge of some grade school nephews."

Hunter nodded amiably. "You're right, senator, I've got to watch that. But *I'm* getting old. If I don't get my eight hours I'll be foggy in the morning. Goodnight, all," and he waved and sauntered through DeLucca's bedroom to his own.

He did not have to hang around to know what would happen. The four security officers got up from the table. Early, Mayer and Leary said good-night to the senator and went off to their own rooms. Bronson locked the door behind them and prepared to settle down on the living room couch.

DeLucca sighed, patted Bronson on the shoulder and went to take his bath before going to bed.

As he dried himself and put on his bathrobe he thought about the pilgrimage he would be making tomorrow to the little village his father and mother had immigrated to America from. They had left for the most common reason . . . the village had been poor and his father hadn't been able to earn enough to raise a family properly. In spite of the village's poverty Frank DeLucca's parents had described it to him with increasing nostalgia as they'd grown old. He'd come close to seeing it during World War II, but the direction of the final battles in northern Italy had abruptly shifted and DeLucca's combat until had swung away from it off to the east, finally ending the war near Trieste.

Settling down in his hotel bed with the nightstand lamp on, sitting propped up against the pillows, DeLucca rested a notebook against his raised knees and began making notes about what he'd accomplished so far during this European swing. Each of the men he'd met to date had agreed to meet later with Klaus Bauer and give him a detailed rundown on what he knew about William Reinbold's dealings.

DeLucca often thought and spoke of Paul Shevlin as the personification of the antagonist with whom he was engaged in battle. Shevlin, after all, was the most visible weapon Reinbold used in that battle, but DeLucca was well aware that Reinbold himself was the more important enemy. To crush Shevlin and his MARS Limited would accomplish only half of DeLucca's purpose, the lesser half. William Reinbold could always find himself another Frankenstein Cell.

It was Reinbold himself who had to be broken—or at least clamped under tight restriction and observation wherever his operations affected American interests . . .

For the next hour DeLucca filled page after page of his notebook with ideas about how he could use the information Bauer would be gathering to expose Reinbold's manipulations and wring if not break his economic neck . . .

In the next bedroom Simon Hunter was also not yet asleep. He lay in bed with his aching hands under his head, staring up into the darkness and reviewing everything that the next day might hold.

It *should,* he told himself, be the most relaxed day of the entire trip. DeLucca simply wanted to visit the village his parents had come from, to get a feeling of what it was like and to look at the gravestones of his grandparents on both sides. He had no family left in Rocchetta and nobody there had any advance notice that he would be arriving.

The senator considered his visit to Rocchetta a deeply personal and private matter. It had not been announced to the press. According to Hunter's information *nobody* knew about it outside DeLucca's inner circle—George Ryan, Klaus Bauer, Jeff Berman, DeLucca's secretary and his committee's chief counsel, Robert Pryor. Even the consulate SY in Milan didn't know that Senator DeLucca intended to go to Rocchetta. Hunter had told him that DeLucca simply wanted a day off from his schedule of European meetings to take an aimless drive around the countryside. The four-man security team and Sergeant Roselli would not be told where they were going until they were on their way out of Milan. Once certain they were not being tailed, they should be in the clear—certainly from any kidnap attempt by terrorists after ransom, political extortion or publicity for their cause—including the Cuban VOR from which the threat two years back had possibly originated. Such attempts depended on prior observation of the target's routes, and/or prior knowledge of the target's destination. The same applied to any assassination attempt. But there Hunter was inclined to agree with DeLucca–nobody had ever tried to assassinate a senator or congressman because of his work as chairman of a committee. He also had to agree that Reinbold Enterprises had simpler ways to deal with any damaging business revelations turned up by the committee hearings. Reinbold had the best law firms in the world, capable of handling any problems DeLucca might cause . . . Hunter finally relaxed and allowed his eyes to close. The next day, he decided again, should be the easiest one.

The flaw, of course, in his thinking came from his ignorance of one vital piece of data: William Reinbold was not merely an unscrupulous and merciless business enemy. He was also the most important single source of information in the West for the Soviet Union and its bloc.

NINETEEN

MILAN

At one-twenty in the morning the Medusa drove a Fiat 238 van past the Hotel Colomba D'Oro. Paul Shevlin was not with her as he had been the previous night when they had gotten most of the heavy work done. He was back in the shepherd's hut six miles from Rocchetta, with Torriente and Lugo. It was not safe to leave them alone too long, and they could not be any part of what the Medusa was going to do tonight, having only a false version of what all of this was leading up to.

Three blocks from the hotel the Medusa turned into a very narrow street without sidewalks or lights. Halfway inside the block the street came to a dead end at the front of an auto repair shop. The shop had closed for the night hours ago. The Medusa stopped midway between it and the open end of the street. She cut the engine and lights, set the hand brake. There was not enough room on either side of the van for another vehicle to pass.

There were blind walls without windows above the auto repair shop and on both sides of the dead end. The van blocked the view of anyone who happened to pass the street's open end. Not many were likely to. Fear of terrorists had turned Milan into a late-night ghost town.

The Medusa got out and gave her eyes time to adjust to the darkness.

She was wearing coveralls with reinforced pads at the elbows and knees. Opening the back of the van, she climbed in and pulled on rubber hip-boots and heavy-duty canvas gauntlets. She put on a hard hat with a curved plastic visor, a battery lamp attached to the front of it. Picking up a waterproof sack, she hung it over one shoulder and climbed out of the van, closing and locking it.

She walked to a point between the van and the shop. Taking a sewer worker's pry bar from the sack, she used it to lift out a manhole cover sunk into the middle of the narrow street. She lowered herself into the hole, climbing partway down the metal rungs in the wall. When her head was just below street level she reached up and pulled the manhole cover back in place.

Now she was entombed in utter blackness. Snapping on her headlamp, she descended the rest of the way. At the bottom the sewer odor was already strong. It would get worse further on. She took an antiteargas mask from the sack and put it on under her raised visor.

Inspection tunnels went off in two directions. Shevlin's blueprint of this area of the sewer system was in her pocket but there was no need to consult it. The two of them had spent most of the previous night down here.

The tunnel she entered was only a bit more than five feet high, forcing her to walk bent over. Soon she began to perspire under the heavy outfit she wore. After two hundred yards the tunnel forked. She took the right-hand fork, going through the length of it until she reached an open manhole that led deeper into the bowels of the city. It was a long climb down. When she reached the bottom she was knee deep in flowing water, sewage and mud.

This was one of the main drainpipes of the Milan sewer system. It was made of reinforced concrete. Crouching, she waded through it, past openings from which sewer water issued on either side. After several turnings she climbed into one of these openings. The drainpipe she now followed branched twice, and each time she took the one leading leftward. Twenty yards into the second fork was the bottom of a vertical shaft. It was a fifty-feet climb to the top.

There she entered an older section of the drains, built in the middle of the past century as a runoff for rainwater. It was a maze of very low vaulted tunnels made of crumbling brick. The only way through this maze was on hands and knees, with her back almost touching the vaulting above. Milan had not had rain in over two weeks. The bottoms of the vaulted brick tunnels were covered with soft mud but only an occasional pool of shallow water, formed by drops falling slowly from wide holes above.

Deep inside the maze she entered the low tunnel that led to her goal. Several side openings she passed held canvas sacks filled with cement rubble that she and Shevlin had drilled and chiseled out the night before. Crawling past them, she came to a stop below an overhead opening. No water dripped from this one. On the wall beside her a large plastic-sealed rubber sack hung from a nail hammered into the mortar between the old bricks. Another item had been left from the night before: a light metal ladder, braced on the floor of the tunnel, leaned into the opening above.

She was now directly underneath the garage of the Hotel Colomba D'Oro.

Milan is subject at times to short but torrential rainfalls. When they occur the older parts of its drainage system fills and backs up into the streets, the overflow running into cellars and everything else below street level in these areas. Until eleven years ago there had been a metal grill in the stone floor of the hotel's underground garage which had covered an iron pipe almost three feet in diameter that lead down to the city's sewer system; after a heavy rain, the water in the garage had an outlet to drain off through. But after the hotel had made renovations that raised it to the status of a four-star establishment, some of its four-star guests began complaining . . . the sewer smell that rose from this opening into the garage sometimes even permeated to the lobby and lower rooms. The grill had been removed. Cement had been poured into the pipe below until it was fully packed. A block of paving stone, similar to the others in the garage floor, had been set into the place where the grill had been. Its sides had been sealed to the stones around it with more cement. After that there was no further smell from the sewers. In the years since, this paving stone had become indistinguishable from the others. Now when rains flooded the garage, the water was pumped out through a hose that was run from the bottom of the garage up to the street.

Shevlin and the Medusa had spent most of the previous night drilling and hammering out the blockage of hardened cement inside the old drainpipe. Only the final barrier was left—the stone cemented into the garage floor across the top of it.

Opening the plastic seal of the rubber sack hanging on the tunnel wall, the Medusa took out a battery-powered drill. Selecting a bit of the right size, she locked it into the drill, then climbed up the ladder, inside the pipe.

When she tilted her head back the hard hat lamp shone on the stone block over her. Pulling down the visor to protect her eyes, she turned on the battery power and set to work drilling out the cement that sealed the sides of the stone to the others around it.

It did not take long. When she had finished, the stone rested free on the top end of the pipe.

There had been the potential danger that someone might park a vehicle with a wheel on top of that block of stone. That had been solved. The night she had arrived in Milan she had checked into this hotel with a rented Land Rover. Another automobile had been taking up the garage space she wanted. But the next morning the car had been taken off and she had shifted the Land Rover before checking out of the hotel.

She had informed the management that she would be back in a few days and wanted to leave the Land Rover until then. The management had no objection since she paid for the garage space in advance. The Land Rover was now directly above her, with its wheels straddling the block of stone.

Going back down the ladder, she replaced the drill in the rubber sack. Next she removed her muck-covered boots and stuck the gauntlets in one of them. Picking up the waterproof sack she had taken from the van, she hung it over one shoulder and climbed into the pipe again. It took all her strength to raise the paving stone. The Land Rover had been chosen because there was enough space under it for the stone to be lifted completely free and shoved aside. She pulled herself out of the hole and rolled from under the vehicle.

As soon as she was on her feet she stripped off the hard hat and gas mask, breathed deeply, filling her lungs with air. Under her coveralls she was drenched in persiration, but she felt good, as she always did whenever she was working.

She took a square-shaped flashlight from her coveralls and snapped it on. Walking over to Senator DeLucca's armored Cadillac, she put the light on the floor with its beam shining on the limousine. She took the sack from her shoulder and placed it between the light and the armored car. Inside it were the specialized tools she needed, and three items that Shevlin had acquired more than two weeks in advance . . .

A businessman from Kuwait who worked closely with one of Reinbold's companies had arrived in Milan with his own bodyguard-chauffeur and selected this same Cadillac from the rental firm for a one-week trip through Italy. The Cadillac had been left for five days at a palazzo in the country outside Sienna. Five days had been sufficient for a subsidiary of Reinbold Enterprises to take the vehicle apart and furnish diagrams of its electricity systems, plus exact copies of two electronic control units which the rental firm supplied to those using the car. The Cadillac had then been put back together and returned to the rental firm . . .

Opening the sack, the Medusa took out the control for the limousine's locking system, pressed the buttons which opened the hood, trunk and all four doors. Taking up the tools and the electrical diagrams, she set to work.

The job took almost two hours, most of which time she used to get to the proper electric circuit, and then to carefully replace its coverings. When she was finished there was only one sign left that the armored limousine had been tampered with—the sensor indicator unit built into the dashboard panel had flicked to the number 8.

She took the second electronic control from the sack, activated it and turned its dial until the dashboard warning indicator flicked back to zero. Then she relocked the Cadillac and replaced everything in her sack. Returning to the Land Rover, she put on the mask and hard hat, slid under the car and lowered herself into the hole. When the paving stone was dragged back into place over her head, she descended the ladder to begin her return trip through the sewers.

It was almost dawn when she drove the Fiat van away from Milan, heading west. Three hours later she rejoined Shevlin and the two Cubans at the shepherd's hut six miles from Rocchetta.

AT SIX-THIRTY in the morning the phone beside Hunter's bed woke him. It was the desk. A guest whose car was in the garage wanted to leave early. Hunter phoned his two drivers before getting dressed and going down to unlock the garage. After the guest had driven out, Hunter stood at the opened gate on top of the ramp and activated the remote control that started the Cadillac. It purred smoothly to life. There was no explosion, as there would have been if a bomb had been wired to any of its circuits. Turning off the device, he went down to the Cadillac and opened all of its electronic locks.

Sliding into the front seat Hunter checked the CTVSS warning dial. It was still set at zero, indicating that no one had tampered with the car. He was removing the seat cushions when Jim Early and Joe Mayer, having eaten a hasty breakfast, came down into the garage. They joined him in carrying out a detailed visual and manual inspection: first the interior, then the trunk and under the hood. That completed, Early slid underneath the limousine with a flashlight and made a thorough check.

They found nothing.

Next they did the same with the watchdog Chevrolet that Mayer would be driving. It was clean. Mayer and Early remained on guard with the cars when Hunter returned to the hotel, joining DeLucca, Leary and Bronson for breakfast.

Sergeant Roselli arrived promptly at eight. He sat up in the front seat of the armored Cadillac beside Jim Early when the two cars rode away from the hotel and took the A7 Autostrada out of Milan. At the first exit they went off the A7. Pulling over to the side of the road they noted each car that came off after them. After a full minute and six cars went by, they circled back onto the Autostrada. From the back of the watchdog car Leary and Bronson checked whether any of the cars that had gone off after them followed them back on. None did.

The Cadillac and Chevrolet went out of the A7 again at the next exit, followed a parallel highway for some miles, then switched back onto the *autostrada.* All according to standard procedure—unpredictable routing.

There was only one stretch ahead that still troubled Hunter. Some two miles from the village of Rocchetta there was a town named Dolceacqua. There were two ways that Dolceacqua could be reached by road, but between Dolceacqua and Rocchetta there was only one way—a narrow, twisting hill road that came to a dead end at the edge of the Rocchetta village. It was for that short stretch that Hunter wanted Sergeant Roselli with them this day. When they neared the area he would have Roselli radio ahead to the Italian highway police, arranging for one of their cars to inspect that hill road, and Rocchetta itself, before Hunter's two cars got there. A needless precaution, perhaps, considering that no one outside DeLucca's inner circle knew this day's destination. But it made Hunter feel more at ease.

One hour outside Milan the air-conditioning system of the armored Cadillac failed.

JIM EARLY USED the Cadillac's two-way radio to inform the other car of the reason for swinging off the highway onto its wide gravel shoulder. The Chevy did the same ten yards back. Leary and Bronson jumped out and trotted up along the shoulder to take positions at the rear and front of the limousine. Not till they were set did Early open the electronic locks. By then the air inside the Cadillac was already stifling. The burning sunlight was magnified by the thick glass of its armored windows.

Hunter opened the rear door away from the highway and got out. He scanned the terrain as Senator DeLucca came out behind him.

Sergeant Roselli got out of the front seat and shook his head. "There we have the fallibility of engineering," he told the senator in Italian. "All that fancy equipment and it still develops the same problems as any ordinary automobile. Like modern medicine and the common cold."

DeLucca laughed. Hunter understood enough of it, but did not. Early was down under the dashboard. He climbed out wiping sweat from his face. "It's not the fuse." He opened the hood and fiddled with the wires leading to the shielded air condiditioner. "Nothing wrong with these either. Trouble's got to be inside this goddamn unit."

DeLucca said, "How long will it take you to fix the thing?"

Early shrugged. "Take maybe an hour to just get it all apart and see if I *can* fix it with what tools I have." He looked to Hunter. "Might be better to call Milan and get them to send out another armored car."

Hunter shook his head. "They don't have one free. The demand's too big here in Italy. You have to reserve at least a couple weeks in advance."

"Well," DeLucca said, "I certainly don't intend to suffocate the rest of the way to Rocchetta, with windows that can't open."

Hunter told Early to radio the rental firm in Milan. "Have them get a team out here to fix it, fast."

As Early got in to make the call DeLucca faced Hunter. "It will take more than an hour for them to get here. Say another hour to find the problem and repair it." He pointed to the other car. "We'll go on ahead in the Chevy. Early can join up with us after he gets this fortress repaired."

It made sense but Hunter hesitated. "There's no hurry, senator. Nobody's waiting for you in Rocchetta."

"I'm not going to hang around here for two-three hours, Simon. That's not caution, that's ridiculous. Either relax or I'm going to drop you after today." Without waiting for a response, DeLucca walked briskly to the other car.

Hunter grimaced, then nodded to himself. He told Early to keep in touch by radio and arrange to meet them when the air conditioner was fixed. Signaling the others to follow, he went back to the Chevy.

DeLucca was already in the backseat. Hunter got in on one side of him, Leary on the other. Bronson and Roselli got in front beside Joe Mayer.

As the Chevy pulled out around the Cadillac and sped toward the Ligurian coast, the senator leaned back with a satisfied smile. "At least this car has air conditioning that works."

Hunter looked at the closed windows. They weren't armored but they *were* tinted to keep out sunglare. That would make it just a bit less easy for a marksman to get a fast beat on the target inside. The Chevy also had some features that made it a formidable weapon on its own—dual reinforced ram bumpers front and rear; front and back lights that could be switched to ultra-intensity to blind attackers; a submachine gun clipped under the dash and a Remington shotgun under the rear seat, in addition to the weapons worn by Hunter and his security team.

DeLucca had turned his head to study Hunter's profile. "I'm *not* a President riding through the middle of Dallas in an advertised motorcade, Simon. You do worry too much, you know."

Hunter drew a slow breath. "It gets to be a habit," he said evenly. "Maybe it's a bad habit." He waited until Mayer switched onto the A10, above the coastline between Genoa and Savona, then instructed Sergeant Roselli to radio ahead to the highway police at Bordighera, their nearest headquarters to the village of Rocchetta. "Explain that we've got a very important and impatient American politician with a rotten temper and bad judgment on his way to Rocchetta." Hunter did not respond to DeLucca's laughter. "Ask them to check out that stretch of road between Dolceacqua and Rocchetta and make sure it's clean. Also to find out if any strangers have been seen around the village."

Roselli turned the radio to the highway police frequency and made the call. When he got an acknowledgement from the dispatcher, he identified himself and explained what was wanted. After several minutes there was an affirmative . . . a car was on its way and would make direct contact once it reached Rocchetta.

DeLucca smiled at Hunter. "Feel better?"

Hunter did not return the smile. He told himself he was jumpier than the circumstances seemed to warrant, but he had his educated instincts, and they went against reason. *That* was what was gnawing at him.

THE TWO-MAN police team that left Bordighera drove in the direction of Ventimiglia along the Via Aurelia, a road originally laid down two thousand years earlier by the legions of the Caesars as the main route between Rome and Paris. This stretch followed the Ligurian shore. The police car turned away from the coast at the entrance of the Nervia Valley and took a fairly straight two-lane road which rose with the valley into the mountains of the interior. Just after passing Dolceacqua, the car swung left into the much narrower road that curled around a series of hills on its way to Rocchetta.

The terrain on both sides of this hill road remained the same most of the way to the village. On its left were steeply rising, terraced slopes planted with olive and wine groves. On its right was a sheer drop of some fifteen feet from the road's edge down into a wide ravine. A shallow stream meandered through the bottom of the ravine. Between the stream and the road above the ravine cultivated patches of tomatoes, corn and potatoes alternated with groves of eucalyptus trees. On the other side of the stream densely wooded slopes climbed between low, broken cliffs. To prevent vehicles from going off one of the sharp bends at night and plunging into the ravine, a low stone wall had been built the length of the right-hand side of the road.

The police car took the bends slowly, with the pair inside giving most of their attention to the rising slopes on their left. On the other side there was no place where a marksman would have a view of the road —except from the cliffs across the stream, too far for pinpoint shooting at a moving target.

But at several points along the road there were narrow openings in the low wall on the right. Below them access steps lead down the sheer drop to the farm patches. The police driver stopped at each. His partner got out and inspected the ravine area around the bottom of the steps. Finding nothing out of the ordinary, he got back into the car.

When they reached the village both got out and talked to the old men playing cards in the square where the road ended. Since the road did not go anywhere beyond Rocchetta, the village got few visitors other than relatives of its inhabitants. No stranger could come there without being noticed. There had been none during the past few days.

The cops got back in their car and radioed Sergeant Roselli, who asked them to rendezvous with the senator's automobile at the town of Dolceacqua.

Both cops remained alert as they drove back along the hill road, but again they spotted nothing out of the ordinary.

Their car slowed as it reached the tightest bend in the route. On the steep slope above, the Medusa watched it make the turn almost directly beneath her. Even if she had been out in the open the police pair could not have seen her without craning their heads out the windows and looking straight up.

She sat in the shadow of an olive tree on an overgrown terrace halfway up the slope. That a police car might be called in was a possibility that had been taken into consideration. When it vanished around the other side of the bend she spoke into the small walkie-talkie that hung from a strap around her neck.

"It's on its way back. Probably to meet the target."

Shevlin's voice responded. "Means we don't have much longer. Get set."

"I am." She continued to hold the walkie-talkie, her thumb poised over the transmit button. A Mauser 66, one of the best sniper rifles in the world, lay ready on the ground beside her. Attached to her belt were two grenades. She watched the direction in which the police car had gone, and waited.

Down inside the ravine Shevlin led Torriente and Lugo away from the stream toward the drop below the road. Even if the police car had not come, his estimated time for the arrival of the target car began after the next five minutes. When they reached a set of steps leading up to one of the breaks in the road wall, Shevlin climbed first. He crouched when he reached the last steps, not showing his head above the top of the wall. An irrigation pipe ran along the bottom of this side of the wall. Balancing on it, still keeping low, he moved to his right until he reached a point where he had left a small chalk mark on the wall.

Whatever the disposition of the rest of the men in the target car, DeLucca was certain to be in the middle of the rear seat. When the car finished coming around the bend, from this precise point the senator would be in Shevlin's sights for at least a full second.

Lugo edged over along the pipe and stopped close to Shevlin. Torriente came next, taking his position on the other side of Lugo. He was taller and slimmer than Lugo, with almost girlish good looks. Each of the young Cubans gripped a FAMAS 5.56, the French-made assault rifle. Both had their weapons set for full automatic fire. Like Shevlin, they crouched low behind the ravine side of the low wall.

The top of the wall would be on a level with the car's windows, making their job simple. When they straightened, all they would have to do was to rest their weapons on the wall and blast away, swinging them back and forth in long bursts.

"Any minute," Shevlin told them.

They looked frightened and eager at the same time. They had been told that the first car around the bend would contain only the bodyguards. With them wiped out, their car would block the one behind it, the one carrying DeLucca and perhaps one guard. The woman, as they understood the plan, would hit this guard and the driver. Then Torriente and Lugo would converge with Shevlin to drag the senator out.

Shevlin's instructions were for them to start raking the first car the instant after he fired the first shots. By the time they realized the rest of it was not going as they'd been told, their part would be finished anyway.

Unslinging his own FAMAS 5.56, Shevlin set it at semiautomatic. Attached to his belt were two grenades—and a .38 revolver he had selected because it was the same make that Hunter and his team wore. That might not prove necessary, but it was an extra bit of insurance, in case.

He leaned against the wall and waited for the Medusa's signal on his own walkie-talkie. His lips were stretched so tight that his teeth were bared. It was not a smile.

THE CHEVROLET ENTERED Dolceacqua and found the police car waiting. Sergeant Roselli got out and joined the two cops to make sure they maintained the correct distance. That left Bronson alone in the front seat with Joe Mayer, and DeLucca in back between Hunter and Leary. Mayer drove out of Dolceacqua and turned into the road to Rocchetta. The police car kept well behind as it went in after the Chevy.

UP ON THE terraced slope the Medusa watched them come. When the lead car started around the bend she depressed the transmit button and gave the signal. *"Now."*

The Chevy was completing the tight turn when Hunter caught a flash of movement along the top of the wall just outside the car windows. He grabbed DeLucca to yank him to the floor—in the same instant that Shevlin triggered the first short burst at the senator. The side windows exploded. A bullet slashed Hunter's face with drops of blood and splinters of bone. He felt the senator sag under him before they hit the floor together.

Above them long bursts from Torriente and Lugo joined the staccato hammering of Shevlin's weapon. The car went out of control as a burst stitched across Mayer's chest. The Chevy sideswiped the wall and spun halfway around before jolting to a stop in the middle of the road.

Under Hunter, DeLucca lay limp with blood oozing from his broken skull. Above him, Leary was sprawled along the rear seat with most of his face caved in. There were no guns shooting from the front seat, which told him all he needed to know at this point about Mayer and Bronson. The three automatic weapons were still raking the front and side of the Chevy, making it impossible for Hunter to hear the spaced shots being fired at the police car from high up the slope.

He dragged the shotgun from under the rear seat and pumped a shell into the firing chamber. Kicking open the rear door on the slope side of the car, he slithered out and fell onto the road. He did a fast roll, came up on one knee at the back of the car and triggered a fast shotgun blast in the direction of the automatic fire.

Up on the slope the Medusa switched aim and fired a Mauser shot at Hunter. The bullet went into his shoulder blade and rocked him off his knee, battering his temple against the car's ram-bumper. The shotgun rolled from his nerveless fingers as he sank into darkness . . .

The Medusa turned the Mauser back on the police car. Her first shot had gotten the driver. The other two had jumped out when the car skidded to a halt and were firing up in her direction from behind it. She fired another shot at the hood of their car, to keep them pinned down there, where they couldn't interfere with Shevlin. Then she waited, well under cover, keeping tabs on the crucial points at either end of the tight bend and holding the Mauser at ready.

Behind the low wall Torriente had been flung backward by Hunter's shotgun blast. He lay sprawled in the ravine below. It was moments before Lugo suddenly realized Torriente was not beside him. He looked down and screamed his friend's name. Shevlin clubbed him in the head with the stock of his rifle, dropping him unconscious into the ravine.

There were no further shots from the target car. Shevlin let go of the wall and jumped. He landed beside the Cubans with his feet spread, his knees bending to absorb the impact.

Torriente needed nothing further from him—the top of his head was gone. Shevlin pulled the pin of a grenade, placed it under Lugo's cheek and sprinted away across the ravine. He counted as he ran, dropping flat to the ground just before the detonation of the grenade. Then he was on his feet again, running across the farmed patches toward the stream.

Up on the road Sergeant Roselli used the cover of the police car to crawl to the low wall. Holding his pistol ready in one hand, he braced the other on the wall and rose just enough to see the running figure in the ravine below. Roselli eased a bit higher to take aim with the pistol. The Mauser on the slope hammered out another shot. The bullet slanted down over the hood of the police car and smashed Roselli's hip, spilling him back across the road.

Behind the car the remaining cop fired twice at the source of the shot, one of his bullets ripping leaves from the olive tree ten inches above the Medusa's head. She looked again toward the ravine. Shevlin crossed the stream and disappeared into the woods on the other side. Returning her attention to the police car, she detached one of her grenades, pulled the pin, threw it.

The cop behind the car threw himself face down in the road when the grenade hit the hood and bounced high in the air. The explosion shook him, but he was untouched by the shrapnel striking the car, wall and road surface to his left. It was several moments before he regained the courage to rise again—just long enough.

The Medusa swung up from her position under the olive tree and made a rapid climb of the terraces above. The cop below began firing again as her swift-moving figure went over the top of the slope. None of the shots came near, and seconds later she was down the other side of the wooded ridge, jogging away toward the dirt lane where Shevlin had hidden the car.

Nine minutes later she stopped the car where the lane joined an asphalt road. Shevlin stepped from behind a tree and got in. She turned onto the road and sped away. By the time a police and military dragnet had been closed around the area they were well south of it. Their weapons lay at the bottom of a river behind them.

There was nothing to distinguish them from thousands of other American couples touring Italy that summer.

TWO HOURS LATER they were settled into their hotel room in Florence, watching the television news broadcast about the terrorist attack on the American, Senator Frank DeLucca.

The announcer was relieved to report that at least the terrorist group responsible for this latest outrage was not one of Italy's own. Though some of the assailants had escaped, two had died during the attack—one killed by counterfire and the other by a grenade that had apparently gone off before he could throw it.

The two dead terrorists had not yet been identified, but both were found to be carrying notes obviously intended to be left at the scene. One was typed and the other was handprinted. Each was on stationery bearing the letterhead of a militant Cuban group called VOR.

The essence of both messages was the same: Senator DeLucca was being taken as a political hostage. He would be released unharmed if the imprisoned leaders of their group were set free and flown to political refuge in France or Spain. The deadline was four days; if they were not released by then the senator would be executed.

Obviously the assault was a kidnap attempt that had gone wrong, an attempt by an organization well known to be an enemy of the senator.

It had not, of course, gone wrong so far as Shevlin and the Medusa were concerned. All had gone exactly according to the original plan.

Except—

Frank DeLucca was not yet dead.

Not yet . . .

V
THE DUEL

TWENTY

PRAGUE, LONDON, WASHINGTON, D.C.

PRAGUE SWELTERED under a muggy August heat, but it was relatively cool inside the crypt underneath the Monastery. A recently installed air conditioner labored noisily above the three men who sat around the STB conference table.

"Senator DeLucca is as good as dead," Colonel Vasil Kopacka pointed out. "The result is the same. He is no longer a threat to Gallia. That threat has been eliminated. Under its new chairman, Senator Harding, the committee has dropped the line of investigation which posed the threat. It has begun hearings, instead, into finding means to suppress all militant Cuban exile groups in the United States. The results of which hardly need concern us."

"Your choice of words is rather careless, Comrade Kopacka." Josef Petrov, the KGB supervisor, consulted notes he had spread before him. "Senator Harding has not officially replaced Senator DeLucca as head of the committee. He has been given a position as *temporary* chairman—until such time as DeLucca may recover sufficiently to resume his work. Also, the investigation which threatened Gallia has not been *dropped.* It has been *postponed*—again until Senator DeLucca is able to resume his position as the committee's chairman."

"I speak of facts, Comrade Petrov. You speak of official wording—

which is nothing but a sentimental gesture to indicate American hopes for Senator DeLucca's eventual recovery. Hopes which no one in the government has faith in. The facts are against any such faith. The senator remains in a coma in spite of the first operation performed on him. A splinter of the bullet and fragments of bone are too deeply imbedded in his brain to risk removal unless and until his physical condition improves. *If* the second operation becomes possible, the medical odds are strongly against its success . . ."

Kopacka paused deliberately, fastening his gaze on the KGB man across the table before continuing. "The three brain surgeons who performed the first operation—one American, the second Italian and the third English—would also carry out the next operation. They agree on certain points. First, none can predict how much longer Senator DeLucca will survive, with or without the second operation. Second, if he does survive there may be so much permanent brain damage that he will live only as a vegetable. Third, even if he does begin to recover it will be a year or two before it can be known whether he will ever regain all his mental capacities."

General Hájek shifted impatiently in his chair. "I am sure," he told Kopacka, "that our friends in the KGB have already obtained all of these details from sources of their own. The subject of this meeting is to decide how to proceed from this information."

The KGB supervisor gave the Czech Intelligence commander an acknowledging nod. "Precisely. As a matter of fact we probably have certain information which you do not have as yet. Senator DeLucca will shortly be flown by hospital plane to London. To a private clinic where they have special facilities for hastening his physical recovery, so that the second operation can be carried out." Petrov consulted his notes again. "Now—we agree that if Senator DeLucca does survive it is likely he will do so as little more than a vegetable. In that case it *is* the same as if he is dead—for us. Mission accomplished."

"And," General Hájek added, "the other basic stipulation of the feasibility study has been carried out." He ticked off points on his fingers. "The note discovered on the body of Torriente has been found to have been typed on the machine in the VOR office. The hand-printed note found on Lugo's body matches the printing on the threat sent to Senator DeLucca two years ago. Suarez, the remaining leader of their group, has been arrested. All investigations are concentrating on VOR and the other militant Cuban exile groups. As you say, mission accomplished." The general hesitated, then said what was apparent to all three of them. "Unless the senator should show marked signs of mental recovery."

"Yes." Petrov said it flatly, looked to Kopacka. "If that happens, we must be in a position to know about it immediately. To need to go through the same problem with DeLucca again—in a year or two from now—is not acceptable. A means *must* be established for keeping a close and constant check on his condition."

"That is already being attended to," Kopacka said evenly, and added, "in London. Paul Shevlin has the Medusa establishing preliminary contacts at the clinic to which Senator DeLucca will be moved. A thorough investigation of every member of its staff has begun, to determine which might be vulnerable should the need arise."

Petrov did not permit himself to show surprise. "Excellent. I am certain we are in agreement on one point. If the senator does begin to recover after the next operation, it would be unwise to wait until it is known whether his recovery will be a complete one. Action will have to be taken quickly, while it is still possible for his death to seem a natural one from medical causes."

"The means for accomplishing that," Kopacka informed the KGB man, "is also already under investigation."

IT WAS CLEAR and sunny in London with just a hint of cool breeze in the air when Paul Shevlin came up out of the Cannon Street underground station. He walked for half a block, then turned abruptly and walked back, observing the faces he passed. He bought another ticket, went swiftly down the station steps he had just come up by and waited on the platform, watching the people who joined him on it.

When the Circle Line train came through, Shevlin boarded it. He got off at the next stop. Monument. Climbing out of the station, he circled the tall marble pillar commemorating the spot where the Great Fire wiped out most of old London in 1666. There was the same sunlight and breeze as at Cannon Street, but none of the same faces.

Shevlin walked down the cobbles of Fish Hill Street, leading for one short block to the Billingsgate Market. Old, narrow brick buildings lined the street. Many of them were being torn down, but the one containing the Britannia Saloon Bar was still untouched. Shevlin went inside and looked over the few other customers.

He saw no one he had not seen there on previous visits. The rumbling vibration of steam hammers ripping apart one of the adjoining buildings made the Britannia too uncomfortable for any but diehard regulars. The same racket made it impossible for any method of electronic bugging to pick up conversations inside the place. Shevlin bought a half-pint of bitter and settled into the last booth at the end, where nobody could take a place directly behind him.

The Medusa came in six minutes later. Without looking at Shevlin she went to the bar and ordered a gin-and-lime. Shevlin watched the frosted glass doors. When she turned from the bar with her drink he nodded. She came over and swung into the booth beside him.

"How was your trip?" she asked.

"None of the investigations are going to come anywhere near us. But Simon Hunter's back on his feet. He's set up an appointment to fly to Washington and talk with his boss at State. I'll have to go there too, set up a system for keeping tabs on what he's up to. He just might take a different approach from the others. He's sore enough. At himself. He's also no dummy." Shevlin sipped his beer and added angrily, *"I know how he feels."*

The Medusa changed the subject. "I had lunch in the pub across from the clinic again. It was as crowded as usual. I shared a table with one of the clinic physicians. A friendly young man named Jacobs. We gossiped a bit, weather, fashions, patients."

"How is he?" There was no need for Shevlin to say whom he meant.

"Still in a coma. Still not ready for a second operation."

"And still not dead."

"No." She watched the way Shevlin gripped his beer glass with both hands. "It's not your fault," she told him. "That he is still alive with that kind of head wound is a freak. You did hit him."

"Not dead center."

"Hunter moved him faster than anyone could have anticipated. Unexpected in a man that big—"

"It was my job to make *sure.* To check. I was in a hurry to get away. I'm getting too old."

She shrugged. "Everybody gets older. Arakel was old. It did not interfere with his work."

"It interferes with mine, obviously. Maybe it's time for me to think about retiring."

"And do *what* with yourself?"

"I already have everything a man needs."

The humor left her dark eyes as she studied him. She shook her head. "No, you don't. You would bore yourself to death if you settled down with what you have. Like me."

His eyes met hers. "*You* would have checked. Gotten close and tossed a grenade in the car. And then looked to make sure."

"What happens when *I* get older? Do you shoot me like a horse with a broken leg?"

He smiled crookedly, then abruptly shoved his glass aside and snapped himself out of it. "Was this young Dr. Jacobs friendly enough to make a date with you?"

"He hinted around the subject. I let him understand that I would not accept."

Shevlin frowned at her.

"The security around DeLucca has tightened while you were away," she explained. "Now it includes checking out everybody that any of the clinic personnel has contact with. And they are under orders to report any new contacts. Jacobs was indignant about infringement of personal liberty, but he's an obedient type. He won't bother to report having shared a lunch table in a crowded pub with someone, but he will if I go out with him."

Shevlin nodded slowly. "That makes researching the clinic staff for weak spots that much tougher."

"Yes. But I have started and I'll get it done. It will just take longer." She took a drink from her glass and put it down on the table in front of her. "Did you get the drops from Reinbold's laboratories?"

Shevlin took a small medicine bottle from his pocket and slipped it under the table to her. She opened the handbag on her lap and put the bottle inside it.

"Not to be used," Shevlin told her, "unless necessary. If DeLucca doesn't show signs of recovery, it's not worth the risk. But if he does, we'll need somebody who can get to him with it."

"Don't worry," the Medusa said quietly, and closed the bag on her lap. "By then I will have someone ready in there."

HUNTER'S SUPERIOR OFFICER was Ben Chavez. Though Chavez was presently a deputy director of the State Department's WGCT, it was as a temporary, on loan from the Department of Defense. He retained his active rank of colonel in the United States Army and continued to operate out of his old office on the third floor of the Pentagon's E-Section.

Hunter sat stiffly across the desk from him now, his right shoulder and upper arm held rigid in a bulky cast. An ugly scar crossed his ear where it had been stitched back together. Little of the deep anger riding him showed through the habitual stolid calm. But Chavez felt it, and he didn't like the intent he detected behind it . . . "You're pissed off because you loused up this time." There was no kindness in the way Chavez said it, nor in the set of his dark Aztec face. "But that's not going to make anybody forget all the times you haven't loused up. You've got an impressive record. So now it's got a black mark on it. That's less than most of us have—"

"DeLucca will be relieved to hear that," Hunter said quietly. "If he ever revives sufficiently to hear anything. And I got three other men killed outright. Leary, Mayer and one of the Italian cops. Bronson alive is as much of a miracle as the senator. Three slugs in the chest and most of his left cheekbone gone."

"But he *is* recuperating, and the cheek can be reconstructed—"

"Fine, but right now he isn't feeling too good. Neither is Sergeant Roselli."

"Cut it out, Hunter. You took on a job. Take on enough of them and mistakes are bound to happen. It's a built-in percentage. You're taking it too personally."

"Uh-huh. That's what happens when you're handed responsibility for another man's life and drop it. You know that."

Chavez did know that. He looked at Hunter while he weighed conflicting impulses. Chavez was the son of Mexican wetbacks who had snuck across the border with him. He'd joined the army at seventeen as a way to get legal citizenship. One reason he had lasted, and moved up so far from that background, was that he was good at keeping his own ass from getting burned when there was trouble brewing. And he smelled trouble in the request Hunter had made within a minute of entering this office.

But Chavez had spent his entire adult life in the army; too long to shake off certain things it had ingrained in him. One was that a good officer took care of each of his men. Hunter was one of his men.

He looked at the tape recorder on the table next to his desk. It was not supposed to be turned off when he was using his office. He turned his swivel chair to look down through his window. His office was part of the Pentagon's inner A-ring, overlooking the vast courtyard surrounded by the five mammoth wedge-shaped sections that were joined together to form one of the biggest office complexes in existence. Most of the outdoor tables of the courtyard snack bar were unoccupied at this time of day.

Chavez got to his feet. He was a head shorter than Hunter and just as wide, and none of it was soft. "Let's go down for coffee."

There was a pot of coffee simmering on a hotplate on top of the small refrigerator in one corner of the office, but Hunter did not point that out. He put his left hand flat on the edge of the desk to help lift himself up out of the chair and followed Chavez out into Corridor 6. They took a series of escalators down to the ground floor and went outside to the snack bar. Chavez bought two cups of coffee and carried them to a white table under an elm tree. Neither touched his cup after they sat down.

"My sources," Chavez said, "inform me that you've already started an investigation on your own back in Italy. Conducted by Major Bandini, your old friend in the Direzione Generale di Pubblico Sicurezza."

Hunter nodded. "He's checking into a few things for me. Like where the two dead Cubans stayed in Italy before the hit. And who with and how they got there."

"You know you're not supposed to do something like that without authorization."

"That's why I'm here. I want your go-ahead. Italy is only a small part of it. Both Cubans were from the United States. I want to dig into their associations here, plus some other things—"

"Right now," Chavez said, "I can name you *six* full-scale investigations of the attack on Senator DeLucca that are already under way. In New York, New Jersey, the Cuban exile community around Miami—

and three right here in Washington. That's not counting the regular Italian police investigation and what Interpol has been doing to pull in information from other countries."

"I don't consider any of those real criminal investigations. Some are just looking into why DeLucca's security measures failed—and there they've got a ready-made fall guy. Me. The others are just putting pressure on all the Cuban exile groups, assuming from the start that it *was* a Cuban group that planned the hit."

"A reasonable assumption," Chavez pointed out. "Both of the dead Cuban kids have been identified through their fingerprints. Ricardo Torriente and Hernan Lugo—both members of VOR. Whoever printed the death threat to DeLucca after he helped send VOR members to prison also printed the note found on Lugo."

"Which ties it all up in one neat little bundle. Maybe too neat." Hunter shook his head. "Worst way to start any investigation is with a preconceived notion of who did it. Even I know that. And Suarez, the remaining chief of VOR, has been in custody for a while now. Has he cracked?"

"You know he hasn't. Not surprisingly, he still claims he tossed Lugo and Torriente out of VOR long ago and hasn't seen either of them since. He's also sticking to his story that somebody must have broken into his office to make use of his stationery and typewriter." Chavez picked up his cup, looked at the coffee in it, put the cup back down. "I admit some of the boys who've been interrogating him are inclined to believe him. But that doesn't rule out some other exiled terrorist gang planning the hit and using the two Cubans to frame it on VOR. The senator went after more than one—"

"*Anybody* could have done that," Hunter said. "Not just a Cuban group."

"So who do you have in mind?"

"I don't know. I just want your okay to do some digging in a different direction."

Chavez picked up his cup and finally drank from it. He made a face but then drank more, giving himself some time. There were certain practical aspects operating in Hunter's favor. Chavez was still taking pressure because his own men had been responsible for Senator DeLucca's security. It would help if it was also his own man who tagged the ones who had planned the hit. Plus, Hunter did deserve a chance to mitigate in some measure the black mark that would now become a permanent part of an otherwise distinguished military and civilian record . . . "I can give you some time, that's all I can give you. No funds outside of the normal expense account you can already draw from. No extra personnel—"

"That's okay. I've got people in the trade who owe me one for free. Here and in Europe."

"I guess you do. But watch it. I'll pull the string on you if you go too far with that."

"That I know, colonel."

What Hunter also knew was that there was another catch built into his authorization to proceed. He worked out what he was going to do about it as a taxi carried him up out of the Pentagon's underground mall via Army-Navy Drive, and headed back across the river into downtown Washington.

TWENTY-ONE

WASHINGTON, D.C.,
MOSCOW

SOME HOURS after Hunter had left, Paul Shevlin paid his own visit to the Pentagon.

Borg, the station chief who had originally talked Shevlin into leaving government employ and starting his own firm, had transferred out of the CIA several years back. Now he served as General Keegan's liaison with the regional directors of ISA, the Defense Department's Office for International Security Affairs.

It was a good job. Borg told Shevlin so while they sat in his office in the outer ring beside a window overlooking the Pentagon heliport. But with retirement looming, he explained, he wanted some assurance of future employment in the business world—with MARS Limited, for example.

Shevlin, in turn, explained what it was that *he* wanted.

It worked out to be a mutally satisfactory discussion.

Shevlin left the Pentagon by way of the River Entrance, picked up his car and drove around past the heliport to the parking lot of Arlington National Cemetery on the other side of the highway. The men in charge of the MARS offices in New York and Washington, Elliot Judd and Nat Hallberg, were waiting for him. They strolled together between long rows of gravestones inside the cemetery.

"Let's get one thing out of the way before you bring me up to date on other business," Shevlin told them. "I want both of you to keep on top of all the investigations into the attack on DeLucca. Let me know of any new developments."

Judd looked annoyed. "What for? DeLucca's finally off our backs—and we're in the clear on that, thank God. What more do you want?"

"It could turn out," Shevlin said, "that somewhere along the line *we'll* be able to come up with something that'll help. I might get a lead to the attackers that got away from the scene, for example. That would improve our public image considerably. Right?"

Hallberg liked it. "You've got a point there."

Judd nodded in agreement.

"There's a new investigation about to start," Shevlin told them. "Run by Simon Hunter." He filled them in on Borg, who had just given him this information. "Hunter's smart, and he just might come up with something of interest. If he does I'll want to know about it. With Borg in our camp there's an easy way. Hunter'll have to keep Chavez current on his progress. And Chavez will have to keep Defense informed, as well as State. Which makes it simple for Borg to keep tabs on Hunter."

"No problem then," Hallberg said. "I'll just check with Borg regularly. Every day, if that's what you want."

"That's what I want." Shevlin looked to Judd. "Hunter will be nosing around the New York area too. I want you to keep on top of that sector, Elliot. And I want both of you to keep *me* informed of what he's up to—daily."

THE NEXT DAY was Saturday. Klaus Bauer had flown in from Europe the previous evening and checked into Hunter's hotel. When they had breakfast together in the morning Bauer mentioned that Hunter looked tired.

Hunter gestured at the heavy cast on his right shoulder and arm. "I can't find a comfortable position to sleep in with this thing. Keep waking up. And walking around lopsided from it all day doesn't much help either."

They took a cab to Hertz to rent a car for the drive into Virginia to meet George Ryan. Hunter signed for it and grimaced at what his signature looked like. By now he'd had practice using his left hand for everything, but it was still awkward. Late the previous afternoon he had tried his left-handed marksmanship at a police pistol range and found his shooting as sloppy as his handwriting. He was still disgusted with himself for using up most of an overseas phone call complaining to Odile about it . . .

With Hunter giving directions, Bauer drove across the Potomac River into Virginia and took Route 66 out to the site of the Civil War battles known to the North as Bull Run and the South as Manassas.

Ryan and his family had a converted farmhouse between the stream of Bull Run and the town of Manassas, but by now they were all too jumpy about electronic surveillance to meet there. Ryan was waiting for them in the parking area of the battlefield's visitor center.

"I had a phone call an hour ago," Ryan told Hunter as the three men strolled around the battlefield, avoiding other groups. "There's one guy who's not gonna be able to answer any questions you had in mind for him. The head of VOR. Suarez killed himself in his cell some time last night. Poison."

Hunter slowed his pace, did not say anything. It was Bauer who said, "Suicide? How did he get the poison?"

"That's the question," Ryan agreed. "They'll start checking out all his past visitors today. But if it wasn't suicide—if the poison was slipped into his food, say—I'll lay odds there'll be no way to find out who did it."

Bauer spread his plump hands. "I could make a good guess."

"Somebody from MARS Limited?" Ryan shook his head. "I still don't buy that either Shevlin or Reinbold are behind the attack on DeLucca. I'd *like* to, but like the senator said, businessmen have attorneys and lobbyists. They don't have to rig assassinations to deal with business problems."

Hunter spoke, half to himself . . . "Maybe they had a reason none of us knows about."

"We do know that they're not some political fanatics, Simon. We were hurting them but only in the pocketbook—"

"According to Klaus they've both pulled some pretty dirty stuff. Could be the senator's committee was getting too close, without your realizing it, to something rough enough really to hurt them. Maybe even rough enough to make them start worrying about a prison term—"

"Shevlin? Maybe. But he wouldn't do anything like that without Reinbold's go-ahead. And if you're talking about Reinbold's being worried about prison, you know that's fairy-tale territory. Never happen. Not to people that high up there—"

"*Somebody,* goddamn it, had a reason to try to kill DeLucca," Hunter said. "Do *you* buy those Cubans from the VOR? Two kids with no good connections even among the Cuban exile militants. Nobody trusted their judgment anymore, nobody wanted them. Not as storm troopers, not as collectors, not even as errand boys. Yet look at what *somebody* gave them. They needed passports to get from America to Italy, and they wouldn't have used their own names so that means they must have used false passports. Getting those took money and connections. Somebody paid their airfare to Europe, somebody got them places to stay and transportation—"

"And guns and grenades," Bauer put in. "*After* they reached Europe. It would have been too dangerous to attempt to smuggle those aboard an airplane these days."

Hunter nodded. "And who did they know who could have gotten hold of the senator's schedule? How did two political hoods like Torriente and Lugo know the senator was going to Milan, and from there to a little village called Rocchetta? How did they know *when?* How did they know every detail of the security arrangements, and the ways to circumvent them? Who gave them all that? VOR? It's been broke a long time and its leader hated their guts."

"Well," Ryan began uneasily, "that's what we think we know. Anyway, maybe they *thought* they were doing it for VOR, or for the whole Cuban exile movement. Whoever planned the hit had to persuade them of that, and it wouldn't have been too tough."

"False flag recruiting," Hunter said. "That's still what the schools that trained people like Shevlin call it."

"So do the ones that trained *us,*" Ryan reminded him. In a way he was playing devil's advocate, but he still wasn't convinced of what Hunter was saying . . . "If you can just give me a reason why somebody like William Reinbold would have to resort to having his people kill a—"

"I can't," Hunter cut in harshly, "but somebody did try to kill DeLucca. Somebody did think there was a good enough reason for it.

Maybe we'll never find out what it was, but we can damn well try to find out *who.* Forget about the motive. If we rule out VOR, what does that leave us?"

"Too much, too many, Simon," Ryan said.

"Not so. It leaves us two points to go at. First, the movements of Torriente and Lugo before the attack. What were they doing? Who with? Somewhere in there they made contact with whoever set them up for the kill. Second, how did whoever planned it get DeLucca's exact schedule? They knew where he was going ahead of time, day by day. My information was that only six people knew he was going to that village on that day."

"That *was* all," Ryan said. "The three of us, Ruth McCormick, Dick Pryor, Jeff Berman—"

"And I am certain," Bauer added, "that we were all very careful—"

"Someone wasn't careful enough," Hunter said. He was getting tired again from tilting his body to compensate for the heavy cast. He turned and started up Henry Hill toward the mounted statue of General Jackson, the other two men climbing it with him.

Ryan chewed on what Hunter had said. "If you rule out the Cuban militants going in, before you've turned up any evidence to—"

"*Rule* them out," Hunter told him. "At least for now. Everybody else has ruled them in, and their main suspect just conveniently died on them. Making him an even more perfect fall guy. Now he can't answer any of the charges."

They had reached Jackson's statue, rising above the hilltop where he had held the line that won the First Battle of Manassas-Bull Run for the Confederacy and earned himself the name Stonewall. Hunter walked past Stonewall Jackson and sat down on one of the Civil War gun carriages behind him. He looked up at Ryan.

"Okay, now that you know my thinking, are you going to help?"

"I've got my work to do for the committee, Simon. Senator Harding's running it now and he's not taking kindly to any suggestions about pursuing the Reinbold-Shevlin enquiry an inch further. He's keeping me pretty busy digging up information about every one of the Cuban exile groups, militant or not."

"That might help you get information out of some of them about the date when Torriente and Lugo left the States. As for the rest, you'll just have to do a lot of overtime work. For free. For me. In or out, George?"

Ryan sighed and looked up at the statue on top of Henry Hill, as though seeking inspiration from it. "I ever tell you one of my ancestors rode with old Stonewall?"

"One of mine," Hunter told him, "rode with Sherman."

"Bully for you and the winner's side." Ryan looked to Bauer. "You a Civil War buff, Klaus? I understand a lot of Germans are."

Bauer smiled. "Of course. And being romantics we naturally favor your side, the South."

"Yeah, you dig losing causes." Ryan met Hunter's waiting stare again. "Okay. I'm in."

It was the answer that Hunter had been expecting. "The first thing I'll want from you is all the information your people gathered on Reinbold and MARS Limited—and Paul Shevlin. Everything. I also want the senator's appointment book, and any lists you've got of everybody he had appointments with, or just happened to see, or who wanted to see him, or who was asking about him in the two months before we left for Europe. Plus what you and the rest of DeLucca's inner circle were doing during that time, and who you were all seeing."

Ryan looked dubious. "That's a ton of material, and one hell of a lot of people. Take weeks to pull all that together, and just as long for you to go through it. And a lot longer for you to make sense of it—"

"I'll get through it. With this case on me it's the only exercise I'll be getting for a while." Hunter turned to Klaus Bauer. "I've only got a very limited budget to help you in Europe. Try to make it do. For one thing I want you to check out each of the men the senator had appointments with there. *They* knew about his trip."

"But not," Bauer pointed out, "about the plan to visit the village of Rocchetta."

"That's why I'm not expecting much from your check on them. Mainly I want you to concentrate on Munich. The MARS office there and Shevlin's house outside it. I want electronic surveillance on both —taps, bugs, the works."

"It will be expensive to get people who can—"

"I've got a German cop there who'll do it for free. He owes me. Christian Froschmeier. He works for your Federal Intelligence Service, he'll get everything you need and see the job's done right. You'll only have to do the evaluation of the information his people get you."

Ryan asked Hunter, "Where will you be?"

"Dividing my time between New York and Europe. In New York there are a couple of guys—one with the FBI there, the other with the vice squad—that I'm going to turn loose on the backgrounds of Torriente and Lugo. In Europe you can always leave a message for me at my father-in-law's house. If he's not in, my wife will be. And I'll be there at least enough to let Odile and our baby know I exist."

"And the rest of the time?"

"Keeping track of the Munich operation Klaus and Christian Froschmeier will be organizing. Checking on Diego Bandini's progress down in Italy. And setting up another operation . . . I'm gonna wire Shevlin's villa outside Monaco and Reinbold Enterprises inside it."

Bauer shook his head. "Impossible. Shevlin's place, yes—it is in France. But Reinbold Enterprises, no. You cannot establish electronic surveillance inside Monaco. Nobody can."

"The Monaco police and SBM's Monte Carlo security force can," Hunter told him. "And they will, if the French police ask for it. They'll always cooperate with a police request from France. Once, some years ago, they didn't cooperate. The French just cut off Monaco's water supply. They never refused again."

"How do you persuade the French police to make such a request?"

"My father-in-law is a retired police commissioner. In France, once a commissioner always a commissioner. He'll talk to some of his friends in the French police. They'll talk to their friends in Monaco. Nothing official, just cop to cop. Favors owed for favors given. In France it's called System D—it means finding ways to get around laws that cause unreasonable problems for reasonable people."

Bauer was looking at Hunter with a trace of awe. "I said before that we could have used a man like you for the senator's investigation. Now I am certain. It is like Bonaparte returning from Elba, you seem to have an army waiting to join you in battle."

"At least a battalion."

"And we keep mixing different wars," Ryan grumbled. "And don't forget, men, Bonaparte got clobbered at Waterloo and Stonewall got himself killed at Chancellorsville."

Hunter turned to him. "One point, George. Keep the details of what we're going to do as close to your vest as you can. I don't intend to tell even Chavez any more than I absolutely have to. And not *until* I have to. Especially, there are two things I don't want *anybody* told . . . that we're using Klaus and my father-in-law, and that we're going to bug MARS Limited and Reinbold Enterprises. We've got to keep as tight a lid on that aspect as we can. Whoever we're after has already proved his ability to pry open boxes that were supposed to stay locked. And if it *is* Paul Shevlin, he's got an old-boy network that's even better than mine."

Ryan nodded.

Hunter braced his left hand on the worn metal of the old cannon next to him and shoved to his feet. "Then let's get to work."

IN MOSCOW IT was already cold early that September. Mikhail Talgorny's study was warmed by a fire crackling in an old-fashioned cast-iron stove. The study door was made of heavy oak, and with it closed, General Hájek could hear no sound from the other end of the large apartment where Talgorny's servants were preparing lunch for the two of them.

That Talgorny had called him from Prague for this private interview confirmed what the chief of Czech Intelligence had suspected: if anyone outside the Politburo knew the Kremlin was laying plans for a takeover in Turkey, it did not include anyone below the topmost level in the KGB.

"All of the investigations into the attack on Senator DeLucca continue to pursue their enquiries in harmless directions," Hájek said. "The only exception is the one being conducted by the man who was in charge of the senator's security. And that seems to be making no progress that needs worry us."

"I have already been informed of these matters," Talgorny said. "I have also just been informed that the second operation has been performed on Senator DeLucca, and has been declared a success. You are aware of this, I am sure."

"When the surgeons who performed the operation call it a success, Comrade Talgorny, they mean that the fragments of bone and bullet splinter were removed from his brain, and that he survived the removal. He remains in a coma, kept alive only by the uninterrupted use of oxygen and intravenous nourishment. Not one of the doctors is willing to predict whether he will eventually recover. All of them still agree that if he does it will probably take as long as two years before he could recuperate sufficiently to resume an active life—"

"That is why I summoned you for this talk, Comrade General. Whether DeLucca will eventually recover his faculties is of course of interest to you. And to our friends of the KGB. But for the purpose of Gallia's risk assessment, the senator is no longer a problem. Do you agree with me on this point?"

"I do . . ." General Hájek hesitated, then added guardedly, "It is Gallia's feeling that to assemble all of the pieces of information necessary for him to make the assessment you ask for will require a great deal of time, but I am sure he can complete it well before Senator DeLucca could possibly interfere with his work again."

"How long does Gallia estimate?"

"Perhaps as long as a year."

"Very well. That is acceptable." Talgorny fixed his cold, pale eyes on Hájek and spoke again in that neutral tone that always unnerved the general. "You fully understand how important, and how delicate, this matter is?"

Of course General Hájek did understand. The move being contemplated by the Politburo could even be the beginning of another war. But he merely nodded and said, "Gallia will be informed that he may now proceed."

TWENTY-TWO

CÔTE D'AZUR, LONDON, CÔTE D'AZUR, HAMBURG

THE CAST had been removed and replaced by a smaller one. Hunter's broken shoulder was healing but ached constantly. His right arm was in a sling to inhibit sudden movements. The therapist had given him a sponge-rubber ball to be used as the first stage of restoring the use of hand and arm. The exercise sent twinges of pain through the length of the arm, but it was becoming automatic.

He held the ball in his right hand now and continued to squeeze it every few seconds as he sat in Olivier Lamarck's living room and read through the last of the mass of committee documentation Ryan had forwarded from Washington. His conclusion was the same as Ryan's —there was nothing in any of it that shed new light on the attack on Senator DeLucca.

Hunter turned to stare out the window, down past the slopes of palms and fruit trees to the placid blue of the Mediterranean Sea. The house was built into a slope below the Col de Villefranche. Hunter had joined Odile and the baby here after a frustrating two weeks in New York. Today Odile had gone off after lunch to do her food shopping. Her father had driven away earlier to check on the wiremen he had doing surveillance on Reinbold Enterprises, leaving Hunter to baby-sit with his daughter—asleep in the guest bedroom—and to brood on his stalled investigation.

He turned from the window to look at four file cards he had taped to a shelf of Lamarck's bookcase. On each he had written one bit of information:

The last date when anyone had seen Torriente and Lugo around New York.

The date, sixteen days later, of the attack on DeLucca in Italy.

A statement from a pretty Puerto Rican girl who had been dating Torriente in the Bronx. According to her, Torriente had been full of excitement the last time she'd seen him, bragging that he was soon going to become a very important man in the Cuban exile movement. He hadn't explained why.

A message passed on to Hunter's FBI friend in New York from a police official that somebody had been looking for Lugo in the South Bronx about a week before Lugo and Torriente disappeared from New York. The police official refused to divulge how he knew this, and said he had no idea who the searcher had been.

And that was *all* Hunter had.

The electronic surveillance in Munich and Monaco, and on Paul Shevlin's homes outside both places, had turned up oddments of information that would have been interesting to the committee when it was run by DeLucca—but nothing relating to the attack on him.

In Washington, Ryan had failed to turn up anything new.

In New York, Hunter had people continuing to dig into the backgrounds of Torriente and Lugo, but they still didn't find what he needed: new contacts the dead Cubans had made before leaving for Italy.

In Italy, Diego Bandini had failed to discover the movements and/or associations of Torriente and Lugo prior to the hit. He was now pursuing another possibility suggested by Hunter. Every international air terminal was loaded with closed-circuit video cameras. With the cooperation of Italian airport police Bandini was going through all the tapes over the sixteen days between the time the Cubans had left New York and the date of the attack. If they showed up on one of these tapes, so might someone accompanying or meeting them.

But so far, Bandini had not reported any results.

Hunter got up and went to check on his daughter. She was still sleeping peacefully in the guest room. He envied her. Climbing the outside steps to the road above the house, Hunter took a walk. Maybe it would help clear his mind, maybe he would come up with a fresh approach. . . .

When he returned there was a thick envelope addressed to him stuck in Lamarck's mailbox. It was from Ryan and had been delivered by State Department courier. Hunter took it down the steps, looked in the guest room and saw that Sivane was still asleep. Going back to the living room he opened the envelope.

A covering letter explained the rest of the pages: the last batch of information that Klaus Bauer had sent in just before the DeLucca attack—a new list of news media firms which Bauer had reason to believe were owned or controlled by Reinbold Enterprises. Since it had arrived after the committee had dropped that line of investigation, the list had been filed and forgotten. Ryan had just come on it. Though he found nothing in it of use to them, Hunter *had* asked to see everything.

He read through the pages and had to agree with Ryan. They listed a weekly magazine in Ireland, a literary journal in Italy, a Canadian daily, a news agency in Hamburg, two local TV stations in DeLucca's home state, a new financial journal in Switzerland. Nothing.

As he tossed it aside on the living room table the phone rang. It was Bandini calling from Rome. The first thing he told Hunter was, "Plug in your scrambler."

Lamarck had this house and phone line fumigated regularly against electronic eavesdroppers. But long-distance calls could be monitored without splicing into any line; they could be picked up from the airwaves they traveled over. Against this Hunter had installed a small portable scrambler. Each of his main contacts had another keyed to his.

Hunter plugged the phone into his scrambler unit. At the other end Bandini did the same. Now they could still hear each other but the only thing anyone else could hear anywhere between the two ends of the conversation would be garbled noise.

Bandini had more bad news—on a line of enquiry that Hunter didn't want the opposition to be aware of. He had finished going over all the video tapes from every major airport in Italy for the sixteen days before the attack on DeLucca. Torriente and Lugo did not appear on any of them . . . "They must have flown from America to some other part of

Europe," Bandini said, "and then come the rest of the way to Italy by car or train."

"Yeah. Thanks for the try, Diego." Hunter hung up the phone and resumed working the rubber ball in his right hand. His fingers were tiring from it, and the pains through the arm were getting stronger. He forced it—squeeze and relax, squeeze and relax . . .

He brooded about the airports of Europe, any one of which might have been the one Torriente and Lugo had come into from the States. He could turn the problem over to Interpol but was reluctant to chance it. That method was too open to too many cops, any of whom could be moonlighting for MARS. He sure as hell didn't want Shevlin tipped off to this line of enquiry.

Hunter decided, finally, that he'd have to turn the job over to his father-in-law. Lamarck would enjoy taking on both the work and the travel: he hated being retired. It would be much slower, though. Well . . . Lamarck could start with countries closest to Italy—France, Switzerland . . .

Odile came in carrying two string bags filled with groceries. She looked at her husband's brooding expression and sighed. Without a word she turned and walked toward the kitchen with her purchases.

Hunter looked after her, and some of his brooding was displaced. She had her normal figure back, exactly as it had been when he had first seen her sunbathing on the patio outside, and had had to restrain his instant desire to reach out and touch. Odile had never been thin; she was all ripe, firm curves and a pleasure to look at, front, side, or rear.

When she returned from the kitchen, she noted the change in his expression. Smiling to herself, she went to feed the baby and take a quick shower. Then, wrapped in a towel, she carried Sivane outside in her wicker crib to sleep on a shaded part of the patio. Coming back inside, Odile took the ball out of Hunter's right hand and put it on the papers on the table.

"You can stop squeezing inanimate objects for a while," she told him. "I'm here."

He grinned and reached out with his good hand, stripping away her towel. Almost ritually, Odile truned slowly for him, giving him time to study all of her. He stopped her when her back was to him. Bending, he gently bit one of her superb buttocks.

She looked over her shoulder at him, her breath quickening. "You are a sinful man, Simon Hunter."

He got to his feet and put his left arm around her nakedness, cupping a full breast as he took her into the guest room. "Some sense of sinfulness is necessary for good lovemaking."

"*I* taught you that . . ." Odile's fingers made quick work of unbuttoning his shirt. Carefully she stripped it off him, then pushed him to a sitting position on the bed. Kneeling beside the bed, she was less gentle about tugging the sandals off his bare feet, then pulled off his slacks and undershorts.

She looked with satisfaction at his response to her, then leaned forward and took him into her mouth. He made a groaning sound and fell back across the bed. Odile continued what she was doing for a time, then climbed onto the bed over him. She knelt astride his face, lowering herself to his lips and tongue. Until it was she who was moaning.

She moved down his body, still straddling him, until she felt his hard maleness against her pubis. Slowly, she lowered herself, until he was deep inside her . . .

Later, she slept deeply. Hunter sprawled on his back beside her, his hand between her thighs, drifting lazily in and out of sleep. All of him was relaxed at last; his mind was entirely cleared—

And a small piece of data clicked in place. Hunter's eyes snapped open, drowsiness abruptly gone.

He got off the bed without waking Odile and padded naked into the living room. Going to the table, he leafed through the list of Reinbold-controlled firms that had arrived that day from Ryan. He found the one he wanted, the news agency in Hamburg:

"Vita Bureau."

Hunter stood for a moment looking at the name. Then he was sure.

Leaving the room, he went down a short flight of steps to the floor below. It contained Lamarck's own bedroom. Outside it was a covered patio. Against its wall were stacked labeled cardboard file boxes containing all the committee's dossiers and reports. Hunter opened the box labeled "Requests for Appointments." He took out one of the folders marked "Journalist requests for Interviews." Leafing through, he found it:

A request for an interview with Senator DeLucca, from a European journalist named Sabina Remsberg. She had gotten only as far as DeLucca's secretary, Ruth McCormick. Her request had been turned down.

She had been from the Vita Bureau in Hamburg.

Hunter went back into Lamarck's bedroom and looked at the alarm clock on his side table. In Virginia it would be a few minutes past seven in the morning. He put through an overseas call.

A sleepy-sounding Mrs. Ryan got her even sleepier husband to the phone.

"George. I've got something." Hunter waited until they were both on scramblers, then told Ryan about Sabina Remsberg . . . who represented the Vita Bureau . . . which probably belonged to Reinbold Enterprises . . .

Ryan took a moment. When he spoke again he sounded less sleepy but far from convinced. "Most of the reporters from that agency would be legit, no matter who it belongs to."

"Check her out anyway. Let's at least make sure. Talk to Ruth McCormick and see what she can remember about this Sabina Remsberg."

"Okay, I'll get back to you later today. It'll be night, your time. How late can I call?"

"Anytime. As soon as you have something. Even if it's negative." Hunter rang off, then placed a call to Klaus Bauer in Munich. When they were both switched into their scrambler untis he told what he had.

Unlike Ryan, Bauer got excited. "I can get a plane to Hamburg this evening."

"Take your scrambler along. Call and give me your number as soon as you're checked into a hotel there." Hunter gave Bauer the name and number of a Hamburg police detective. "Tell him you're from me. He can check me at this number if he wants confirmation. He'll be able to get you access to the Vita records and files without alerting anybody there about the reason. I want everything they've got on this Sabina Remsberg, and I don't want them to know it's her we're interested in."

THAT AFTERNOON THE Medusa left her London apartment wearing a leotard under her coat, just as she had on many days recently, and walked three blocks to the Dance Centre on Floral Street near the Covent Garden Market.

She began with a one-hour stretch and limbering class: floor and isolation exercises, falls and recovery, jumps and turns, followed by two hours of modern and jazz dance classes, finished off with a half-hour swim in the Centre pool.

Her leotard was still wet with perspiration when she got back into it. She put the coat on over it, checked her watch, waited six more minutes, then made her exit from the building. She's timed it exactly right.

The jazz dance teacher, Jonathan Gregory, was at the Centre entrance, preparing to leave at the same time. He was in his early thirties, good looking but beginning to bald. She said good-night to him and he nodded in response. But all his attention was focused on a beautiful boy of nineteen who was leaving at the same time. Gregory watched the boy get into a Jaguar driven by a distinguished, beautifully dressed man with gray hair.

The Medusa walked off without looking back. She knew the love-sick agony with which Gregory would watch the Jaguar pull away with the boy. She'd observed it on previous evenings.

She walked the three blocks to her apartment. Of all the places she kept for herself in different countries, this was the one she had had the longest. Five years. After a long shower she got into an old shirt, jeans and sneakers. Checking the time again, she ate a dinner of salads she'd brought at the vegetable shop next to the underground station a block away. When she finished she washed and stacked the dishes, put on a silk-lined leather jacket and went out.

She strolled to the Covent Garden Market, now converted into glass-roofed arcades of chic shops and restaurants. Entering the Punch and Judy pub, she climbed to the second floor, bought a gin-and-lime, carried it out onto the balcony. The seat she took was at one end looking down on the portico of St. Paul's Cathedral, where Eliza Doolittle met Henry Higgins. It always made her think of herself and Shevlin. She had told him that once. He had shrugged it off. "I didn't create you. You were ready-made when we met."

Jonathan Gregory, her jazz-dance teacher, came out onto the pub's balcony some fifteen minutes later with his own drink, as she'd expected. He seemed to live his life as he conducted his classes: adhering to a strict timing and rhythm. Unaware of her presence, he took a seat nearby. He stared absently into space, his face miserable.

She got up and carried her drink to his table. "Well, hello . . . may I join you?"

Gregory looked up at her, startled. His face swiftly rearranged itself into a bland lack of emotion. "Yes, well of course, do sit down."

She settled into a chair across the table from him, took a sip from her glass and gazed across the square at the church, making no effort to start conversation. Gregory frowned at her profile, annoyed at the intrusion into his solitude. But there was nothing in her manner on which his annoyance could feed. It was the same at the Centre. He'd caught her a couple times observing the way he looked at Stephen Cort, the boy who always went off with that despicable barrister in the Jaguar. But there was never anything amused or challenging in her expression, more an odd kind of quiet understanding.

Finally Gregory felt compelled to make the polite effort. "I've been meaning to talk to you at the Centre."

"Oh?"

"It's time we transferred you out of the nonprofessional classes into the intermediate group. Of course you didn't start young enough to ever go into ballet, but you are extraordinarily supple and strong—and driven, if I may say so. You don't belong with those people who only come to tone up their figures. You *could* possibly become a show or cabaret dancer, if that interests you."

"I'm afraid it doesn't. I really only go to classes for the exercise."

That wasn't quite true. She also went because Gregory taught there.

He said, "Three uninterrupted hours is a bit much for only exercise."

"I have a great deal of energy, and boredom, to work out of my system."

"Ah?"

She didn't explain, but it was true enough. She was bored, and when that happened her energy level threatened to choke her. There was nothing challenging enough in what she was doing in London. And there was too little risk from any direction to give any of it real meaning for her.

None of the investigations was leading in her direction—including Simon Hunter's. Shevlin's information was that Hunter had gotten nothing about her activities in Washington and New York; and nothing about Torriente and Lugo from the time of her contact with them until the attack in Italy. "You did your job well," Shevlin had told her. It made what she was doing too easy. Including this, with Gregory . . . shooting fish in a barrel, as Shevlin would have put it.

She looked at the wide leather straps Gregory always wore around both wrists. Reaching across the table, she touched scar tissue that showed at the edge of the strap on the inside of his left wrist. "Love isn't worth doing that to yourself."

He jerked his arm away. "You're quite observant. And impertinent."

It didn't faze her. She looked at him steadily. "I notice something like that when I see it. My brother did the same. But perhaps he cut deeper. He has been dead for three years."

It shocked Gregory. He took a moment to adjust. When he spoke again his tone was softer. "I'm sorry."

"Be sorry for yourself," she said. "There aren't that many intelligent faces in the world that I'd care to see another one lost over something so stupid."

"Why . . ." Gregory hesitated, but was encouraged by the complicity that now existed between them. "Why did your brother do it?"

"Probably for the same reason that you tried. Because of an idiot of a pretty boy." She gestured at his wrists. "Am I right? Was that for love too?"

"As a matter of fact, yes."

"And now you're getting into a state of depression over an entirely new love. You *are* a fool."

He smiled at her. "You're quite right, I am." He looked at the leather straps around his wrists. "As another matter of fact, I did cut deeply enough. I'd be dead too—if my mother hadn't walked in on me immediately after I did it. A forceful woman, my mother. She had tourniquets on both my arms and was driving me to her clinic within minutes."

"Her clinic?"

"My mother is a nursing supervisor at the Howe Clinic. You probably read about Howe in the papers. That's where they have the American senator who was shot in the head in Italy."

The Medusa shook her head. "I never read the papers. Too depressing."

"It was on the telly too."

"I don't have a television set either. For the same reason."

Gregory dropped it, not, of course, realizing that the Medusa had scored.

IT WAS SHORTLY after ten that night, French time, when Ryan phoned Hunter from Washington. Odile was downstairs with her father, helping him pack. Lamarck had a reservation to Paris for the following day to check out the stored video tapes with the airport police at the Roissy and Orly terminals. Hunter was alone in the living room when he took the call and switched on the scrambler.

"Ruth McCormick is pretty shook up, Simon. You may have something, after all."

"Tell me."

"The first time I asked her about Sabina Remsberg she took it calmly enough. Remembered the girl, said there was nothing about her outside of what we've already got on record. The Remsberg girl came in and asked for an interview with the senator. Ruth told her DeLucca's schedule was too crowded for that to be possible. The girl left. That's it. Nothing. And as Ruth pointed out, the senator wasn't even scheduled to go to Europe yet, on that date."

"That's true."

"Yeah, but Ruth acted a little disturbed when I finally told her about the Vita Bureau belonging to Reinbold. Almost guilty about something. Plus, she remembered this Sabina Remsberg as soon as I mentioned the name. Which struck me as strange, considering the hundreds of people coming around the senator's offices in those days. So I went down to storage and had a look through the videocassettes recording visitors to DeLucca's suite. Figured I could at least get you a picture of Sabina Remsberg. Turns out, the cassette for the day she came is missing."

"Nice . . ."

"Not necessarily. There's another cassette missing, from a different day when this girl *wasn't* there. So it could be just carelessness during transfer. Still, it's odd."

Hunter gripped the phone hard, waiting.

Ryan went on. "So I went and had another talk with Ruth. A hard one, this time. At her home. And she suddenly broke down. Said she and this Sabina met a few nights later, by accident. Both of them just happening to be at the same movie. They had drinks together, got friendly. Saw each other the next few nights running. Ruth took the girl home . . . her last night in America according to Ruth . . . for a late dinner. I get the feeling they had a little lezzie affair going, short but sweet. *But*—the girl couldn't have gotten DeLucca's European schedule from her then either. It still hadn't been set yet, and Ruth swears she never saw the girl again after it was set. And I'm inclined to believe that. Still . . ."

"Yeah," Hunter said. "*Still.* What does this girl look like?"

Ryan gave him Ruth McCormick's detailed description of Sabina Remsberg. "Tomorrow I'll get Ruth together with a police artist and try to come up with a likeness of the girl. But you know how those drawings usually turn out—they can fit a thousand different people. Anyway, Simon, all of this could still be nothing more than coincidence."

"It could," Hunter agreed. "I'm checking out Sabina Remsberg from another direction. Just keep this quiet while I do."

KLAUS BAUER WAS having a last drink in the bar of his hotel with Hunter's police contact in Hamburg, Franz Dietrich, when he was paged to the phone. It was a call from Hunter. Bauer said he'd phone back and took Dietrich up to his room. He placed the call, got the scrambler out of its case and plugged into it.

He told Hunter that Dietrich was with him. "We had a very pleasant dinner together. He is being most cooperative. Tomorrow morning he will arrange with the tax office to get authorization to check all of the Vita Bureau's records. A fairly routine procedure that should not alert them to what we are actually seeking—"

"Tomorrow's not soon enough," Hunter said. "And that method could take days. Put Franz on."

When he had Franz Dietrich on the line Hunter told him, "Something's come up. I need the information on the girl faster than I thought when I sent Klaus up there. Could you get him into this Vita Bureau so he can go through their records *tonight?*"

"Are you asking me to do an illegal break-in, Simon?"

"I'll appreciate it, Franz."

"That is a flagrant abuse of police powers, you know."

Hunter repeated, "I'll appreciate it."

AT TWO O CLOCK in the morning, the door to the guest room where Odile and the baby slept was closed, and her father was asleep in his own room on the lower level.

Hunter sat beside the phone in the living room, working the rubber ball in his right hand, forcing himself to keep up a steady rhythm.

He snatched the phone off the hook in the middle of the first ring.

It was Klaus Bauer. "Breaking in was pretty easy. Your friend Dietrich brought along a police locksmith. He had us inside the Vita Bureau offices in less than a minute."

"What have you got on Sabina Remsberg?"

"Not so much. All of the other journalists working through the agency have extensive dossiers which include their photographs. There is none on Sabina Remsberg. And apparently she has never visited the agency in person. She began mailing in unsolicited articles four years ago, shortly after the agency's former owner died. She hasn't sent in many, but most of those she did have been sold. According to the agency's financial records, payment is mailed to Sabina Remsberg at an address in London. It is the only address they seem to have for her."

"Is there a phone number that goes with it?"

"No. Just the address. If you've a pencil ready I'll give it to you."

Hunter wrote down Sabina Remsberg's London address, still awkward with his left hand. After hanging up he called the information desk at the Côte d'Azur Airport.

The first plane he could get to London was a British Airways flight leaving a few minutes before eleven in the morning.

Hunter recognized an old, familiar feeling, coming on strong: if you put on enough pressure, from enough different directions, something finally had to break.

"Sabina Remsberg" could be it.

TWENTY-THREE

LONDON, WASHINGTON, D.C. LONDON, ANKARA, PARIS, LONDON

AT NOON the next day Paul Shevlin and the Medusa met again inside the Britannia Saloon Bar.

"Hunter's investigators still aren't coming up with anything to worry about," Shevlin told her. He looked a bit troubled, though. "That's according to the information Borg's been passing along to Hallberg. But I'm getting the feeling Hunter isn't telling Chavez everything. It may be time for me to do some harder digging into what his people are really up to."

"My latest information is that DeLucca is showing signs of coming out of coma," the Medusa said. "That was two days ago. But even so, it will be a long time before anyone can tell whether his mind will come back to normal. And even longer before it is known if he'll be able to resume an active life."

"I agree. But just in case he surprises everybody, we have to be ready to finish him off. *Will* we be ready?"

"If it becomes necessary." She told him about Jonathan Gregory and about Gregory's mother who was a nursing supervisor at the clinic. "Gregory and I have become quite friendly. He even told his mother he has been going out with a *girl* lately, and was amused by how excited she got. She's beginning to hope he is changing his tastes. She wants to meet me."

"Be careful about that. The security around that clinic—"

"I am being careful," she said coolly. "So careful that it is becoming very dull."

"Simmer down. It's necessary. Can we get to his mother—the way we may have to?"

The Medusa nodded. "Her son is the key. He's the most important thing in her life. She feels responsible for him—and guilty about him. He's illegitimate, never knew his father. She raised him by herself and blames herself for his being gay."

Shevlin thought about Andrau's DISIP contact in Venezuela. Gregory could probably be persuaded to go to Venezuela . . . a fake dance contract with a large advance payment would do it. Once there, DISIP could be signaled to arrest him, hold a threat of torture and death over him.

"Do you figure his mother would do what we need, if she knew it was the only way to save her son's life?"

"Yes." The Medusa studied him. "I don't too much like any of this, Shevlin. Do you?"

Shevlin did not. Not this time. He blamed that on what had begun worrying him lately—aging, and a related loss of the predatory edge. But he did not say this to the Medusa. What he did say might have been addressed to himself as much as to her:

"Don't get stupid on me, kid. In this business when you go soft, you're dead."

IT WAS A few minutes before two in the afternoon when Hunter arrived at the London address that the Vita Bureau sent Sabina Remsberg's checks to. The building was behind High Street Kensington. The apartment number turned out to be a one-room office with open mailboxes covering two walls. One box for each letter of the alphabet.

It was a convenience address for people who did not have their own office or lacked a permanent address. Also for people who did not want their wives, husbands or business associates to know about certain mail they received. Or for those who, like "Sabina Remsberg," simply did not want those who sent them mail to know their real addresses.

The entire staff consisted of a cheerful middle-aged woman named Mrs. Simak. "I'm sorry," she told Hunter, "but I do not discuss my clients. That is one aspect of the service I supply and they pay for. Privacy."

The man who had come to the office with Hunter was a plainsclothes police driver supplied by a friend at Special Branch. He took out his credentials and showed them to Mrs. Simak.

"That, of course, changes the situation," she said immediately. "With a police request, my conscience is clear." She took a folder from a file-cabinet and opened it on her desk. "Here we are. Sabina Remsberg. She has been using my service for a little over four years. She doesn't often get mail, as you can see here. Most of it seems to come from Germany. She pays a yearly fee in cash. Most unusual. Clients generally pay me monthly. Some by the week."

"Do you have an address?" Hunter asked. "Or a phone number?"

"Many clients give me one or the other, so I can forward their mail or notify them if some has come in. For Miss Remsberg I have neither. You see here? It would be marked at the top of the page. No address, no phone. She drops in from time to time. There have been occasions when a letter would come in for her and as much as a few months might go by before she came to pick it up." Mrs. Simak pointed to the mailbox marked "R." "She stopped in earlier this week for her last letter."

The plainclothesman looked at Hunter. "Bad luck."

Hunter nodded. He asked the woman to describe Sabina Remsberg. Her description tallied with the one Ruth McCormick had given Ryan. But other than that she had nothing further to tell Hunter.

Dead end.

THE CONVENIENCE ADDRESS proved to be only the first dead end. The search for Sabina Remsberg kept running into more of them.

The fact that all her Vita Bureau checks were sent to London had to mean that either she lived there or came fairly often. But there was no address or phone number listed for her anywhere in Great Britain —and no bank account—under that name.

But she had to have a way to cash the checks. Bauer and Dietrich conducted a more detailed study of the Vita Bureau's financial records, this time making use of tax office authorization. And this time they found it—all of the checks made out to Sabina Remsberg had been cashed by her person at Vita's bank in Hamburg, sometimes months after they had been issued. She used a Dutch passport and driver's license as her ID in cashing the checks. It took Holland three days to wire Hunter the next dead end—both documents were false.

Every dead end that had been set up to block a trace on Sabina Remsberg made Hunter more stubbornly convinced that she was the vital lead he needed. The bank manager in Hamburg agreed to notify Dietrich if and when the girl came to cash the last check; and to try to delay her until Dietrich got there. Somewhere, sometime, the girl was going to surface again. But the waiting became increasingly frustrating.

THERE WAS ONE day, however, that made all of Hunter's stay in London worthwhile. Frank DeLucca had come out of his coma. Hunter went to see for himself.

At the Howe Clinic the security around DeLucca was properly tight, but the man in charge of it had gotten a call from the embassy to pass Hunter through after examining his credentials.

DeLucca looked pitifully small and shriveled in the hospital bed. Except for his head, swollen by a hive of bandages. He was no longer on oxygen, but there were IV tubes stuck in both of his arms. A nurse was taking his temperature when Hunter came in. Hunter walked to the other side of the bed and saw that DeLucca's eyes were open.

Hunter looked down at him. "Hello, senator."

The nurse shook her head. "He hasn't regained any speech as yet. He is conscious but that's all one can be certain of at this point."

Hunter sat down on a chair beside the bed. It seemed to him that DeLucca's eyes followed him, and that they were aware. He leaned closer, trying to see if he was right. "Remember me, senator? Simon Hunter. I'm the guy who was supposed to save you from all this."

"He probably can't understand you," the nurse said. "It's not sure if he even knows who he is, or what's happened to him."

On impulse, Hunter reached out his left hand and grasped DeLucca's. After a moment, one of DeLucca's fingers moved. It tapped against Hunter's palm. Twice. Contact.

DURING THAT MONTH of September three conferences which seemed to have no connection between them took place in different parts of the Western world. From each William Reinbold extracted information he needed for the risk assessment that Mikhail Talgorny had ordered through Kopacka.

The first was in Washington, D.C. At one of the weekly meetings of the National Security Council in the Cabinet Room at the White House the subject of U.S. commitment to Turkey's future political stability and military strength was raised. One of the members of the council was Treasury Secretary Boyce. He had achieved his position as a reward for financial contributions to the President's election campaigns, contributions drawn from his wealth as one of the largest landowners in the state of Idaho. Over the past six years one of Boyce's closest business friends had become the director of Consolidated Resources, a mining corporation engaged in extensive digging in Idaho. Several days after the NSC meeting in the White House Boyce had dinner with the mining company's director, who expressed worry about the future security of his firm's lead and copper mines in Turkey. Boyce told him about the decisions reached by the Security Council. Since Consolidated Resources belonged to Reinbold Enterprises, William Reinbold had the information before the week was out.

The second meeting took place in London between the head of ALCON, Ltd., and representatives from the U.S. Office of Science and Technology. ALCON was a Reinbold-controlled research firm specializing in optical-magnetic electronics. It was one of many companies bidding for a U.S. contract to develop an electromagnetic cannon as part of a new American program to catch up with Soviet research into high energy particle-beam space weapons which threatened to render ICBMs obsolete. ALCON failed to win the contract, but during the bidding it had access to the program's cost and time factors, which enabled Reinbold to make an estimate of that aspect of America's future capability if the Soviet's Turkish move should trigger an open conflict.

William Reinbold personally attended the third conference, in the Turkish capital. The men he met with were the Turkish premier, his interior minister, the chairman of the Tourism Bank of Turkey and the head of the State Planning Organization. Reinbold proposed to make a massive investment in the development of tourist resorts along both the Mediterranean and Black Sea coasts of Turkey, but he wanted assurances that these investments would not become valueless because of future developments. Especially, he worried about a possible threat from Russia.

The Turks reminded him of their country's long-standing ties with the United States and that they had the biggest army of all America's NATO allies. They also explained certain countermeasures recently taken to deal with such a future threat.

The data Reinbold gleaned from these three conferences formed the starting point for the risk assessment. He would need a great deal more before it could be completed. In the days that followed, he planned the methods through which he intended to acquire the rest of it.

OLIVER LAMARCK SAID, "Stop!"

He had shrunk with the years. His clothes hung loosely on what had been a powerful figure. His face was deeply seamed and at times his fingers trembled uncontrollably, but when he spoke the sound of accustomed authority was still strong.

The airport cop immediately hit the button that stopped the turning of the videocassette. Lamarck pushed his steel-rimmed spectacles higher on the bridge of his nose and leaned forward. The frozen frame on the cassette player's screen showed two young men—one tall and slim, the other stocky—going through passport control at the Charles de Gaulle air terminal.

Lamarck switched his scrutiny to a pair of photographs on the desk of the airport security office beside him: Hernan Lugo and Ricardo Torriente. Again Lamarck looked at the images on the TV screen. The two young men at passport control wore heavy sunglasses. But they were, unquestionably, Lugo and Torriente.

Lamarck leaned back in his chair, told the security man to continue.

After the cassette had finished, six more were run for the former police commissioner. They were from different video cameras scattered throughout the terminal, but all of them recorded on the same day as the first one.

Torriente and Lugo showed up on two other cassettes.

Lamarck had the last one replayed, and frozen on a frame that showed the two leaving the baggage area, each carrying a suitcase. He asked for a magnifying glass with which he examined the frame. He then phoned Hunter, plugged into his own scrambler, and told him, "We're in luck. I'm still in Paris and I've got them. Both of them. They entered Europe together via Charles de Gaulle. Twelve days before the attack in Italy."

There was a sound like a sigh at the other end of the line. Hunter asked his father-in-law, "Is anybody *with* them?"

"If you mean holding their hands, no. There are passengers coming through ahead of them and behind them, any of whom *might* be accompanying them. But if so it is not obvious. At least it is not to me."

Hunter cursed softly. "Then it won't be to me either."

"Our luck may not be quite over," Lamarck told him. "I was able to make out their baggage tags on one frame. They came in on an Air France flight—from Montreal, Canada. If you were to have a look at the videotapes recorded at the airport of Montreal on the day that flight took off, you may be able to spot them there. And *there,* you might be able to detect someone accompanying them—or seeing them off."

A moment's silence at the other end, then Hunter said, "Have the tapes you've got of Torriente and Lugo cut out and spliced together. I'll stop off in Paris on my way to Montreal and pick it up from you."

A FEW HOURS later the phone rang in the Medusa's London apartment.

"Yes?"

"Meet me." It was Shevlin's voice. "Same place. Now."

Dial tone. The Medusa stood for a moment holding the phone. Whatever had brought him back to London so quickly, he had sounded tense. She put down the phone and went out. . . .

She found him waiting for her in the Britannia. He looked the way he had sounded, worried. As soon as she was seated beside him he told her about it: "Hunter is trying to locate Sabina Remsberg."

She straightened. "How did he pick up on that?"

"I don't know. What I do know comes from two sources. A guy from the State Department told me Hunter was using the London embassy to look for an address, phone or bank account listed under your Remsberg name. Naturally they didn't find any. But a couple of nights before, Klaus Bauer and a cop friend of Hunter's broke into the Vita

Bureau's offices and went through their records. The locksmith they used to get in told a cop I know in Hamburg. There's only one thing they could have been after in those Vita records."

The Medusa nodded. "Sabina Remsberg. Me."

"There's no connection between you and that name—just as long as you don't go near that convenience address of yours, and don't try to cash that last check from Vita. But I want you to lie low for a while. Keep away from the clinic, and those dance classes. Stick pretty much to your apartment. That's safe. There's nothing about the Remsberg name to lead them there."

She looked at Shevlin with a faint smile. "At least now you're not the only one who has made a mistake in this operation. Somewhere along the line I did—or they would not be after Sabina Remsberg."

"It's not necessarily *your* error."

But she knew it was, and who it was. Ruth . . . "Does Reinbold know about this?"

"I had to alert him. The error could have been made somewhere in his own setup."

She asked quietly, "What did he say?"

"He agreed with what *I* told him. Just lie low here until this blows over—"

"And if it doesn't?"

"It will."

"You sound very sure of that."

Shevlin nodded. "I am. I've just been to Washington to make sure. I tipped Borg about Hunter using German police to do an illegal search of private property for him. Borg passed it on to Defense and State. Both departments are furious and by now they'll be putting pressure on Chavez to stop his man Hunter from using foreign cops for illegal work that could hurt our relations with other countries, and to stop Hunter from keeping what he's up to secret from his own boss."

"Will they stop Hunter's investigation?"

"Either that or Hunter will have to clear *everything* he intends to do with Chavez from now on. And Chavez will have to clear it with Defense and State. Which means that Borg'll know too, and fast. Hallberg's keeping in close touch with Borg. I've told them to notify me immediately if Hunter turns up anything more connected with the

Sabina Remsberg name. So we'll know in plenty of time if he does start getting closer to you."

"And if he does?"

"We'll just get you out of London."

She was watching his eyes. "How far?"

Shevlin made his eyes meet hers. It was not easy. The two of them knew each other too well for comfort. "We'll figure that one out if and when it comes to it. But it won't."

She smiled at him.

Like a jungle animal accustomed to being both hunter and hunted, she scented danger . . . and not only from Simon Hunter. So what was more natural than that after leaving Shevlin she went off to take certain actions to save her own hide . . .

TWENTY-FOUR

MONTREAL,
WASHINGTON, D.C.
MONACO, SORBIO, LONDON

SIMON HUNTER sat in the security office at Montreal's Dorval International air terminal, intent on the screen of the videoplayer as the last of five cassettes was run through for him. Torriente and Lugo had appeared on two of the previous ones. They turned up briefly on this one too in a line of passengers passing through the boarding area for the Air France flight to Paris.

But, again, it was not apparent that anyone else around the two Cubans was actually *with* them.

When the last cassette ended, Hunter stared thoughtfully at the blank screen. He squeezed the rubber ball in his right hand as hard as he could, and held it that way, tightly compressed inside his large fist.

The chief of the airport security took in Hunter's expression. "Nothing, eh?"

"I'd like to see that last cassette again."

Hunter waited until Torriente and Lugo appeared, going through the boarding area. A few frames after they moved on out of camera range he had the cassette stopped. What showed on the screen now were people going through boarding immediately after the two Cubans.

Just behind them were a middle-aged couple who didn't interest

Hunter. But behind the couple there was another passenger who did. A tall, attractive young woman.

Hunter studied her image until he was sure of it. Then he took out the cassette Lamarck had given him in Paris. "Will you run this one for me?" he asked the security man.

He was right. The same young woman appeared twice on the Paris cassette. Each time in the same position—a few people behind Torriente and Lugo.

But in none of the tapes—from Paris or Montreal—could he detect any sign of contact between her and the two Cubans.

He had the cassette stopped on one of the frames in which she appeared.

It might be a coincidence.

There was only one thing that indicated it might not be. She *could* fit the description both Mrs. Simak and Ruth McCormick had given of Sabina Remsberg.

The phone on the desk rang. The airport security chief picked it up, listened and passed the phone over to Hunter. "It's for you, from Washington."

It was Chavez. His voice was cold as ice. "Hunter, you are not going to ask me how I knew where you are. And I am not going to ask you why I had to check with other people to find out—not until you get your ass down here. I want you in my office before this day is out."

"I'll be there," Hunter told him. He didn't ask what had Chavez in such an uproar. That didn't take much of a guess.

When he hung up the phone he turned back to the security chief as though nothing unusual had happened. "Can you turn that cassette a little further for me? Slowly, frame by frame."

He had stopped again on a frame in which the young woman's face showed most clearly. Leaning forward, Hunter touched the screen with a blunt fingernail. "How long would it take to get a photograph of just this portion . . . her face?"

"When do you need it?"

"Now."

"Give me an hour."

While the security chief arranged for it Hunter used the phone to reserve a seat on a flight to Washington leaving in an hour and a half. Then he placed a long-distance call to George Ryan.

WHEN HE LANDED at Dulles International he was carrying four copies of the photograph of the young woman's face. Ryan was waiting for him with a car. As he drove toward Washington Ryan glanced uneasily at Hunter. "I had to tell Chavez where to find you. He's boiling."

"Have you located DeLucca's secretary?"

Ryan nodded. "Ruth is waiting for us. But I better take you to the Pentagon first. Chavez—"

"No. *First,* Ruth McCormick."

She was waiting at her home. She did not sit down, nor invite Hunter and Ryan to do so when she let them in. Her slim figure was rigid. Her face was composed but drawn so tight that the bone structure showed sharply.

Hunter showed her one of the photographs. "Is this Sabina Remsberg?"

Ruth looked at the girl's picture. Her voice was so low that Hunter could barely hear what she said. "Yes . . . that's her . . ."

CHAVEZ MADE A point of turning up the recorder on his desk. "This conversation is for the record. All of it, Hunter."

Hunter sat perfectly still across the desk from him and said nothing. Chavez wasn't acting angry. His voice was quiet, very calm. With Chavez, that was the worst possible sign.

"I'm getting fragged by everybody in State and Defense," Chavez went on. "You persuaded a German police officer to break at least three different German laws for you in the name of the United States government."

"No, I didn't invoke the name of the government. It was strictly a friend-to-friend favor. And it's done all the time so what the hell are you acting so shocked about? Sir?"

"It isn't supposed to be done without authorization. I never authorized you to do it. You went sneaking around behind my back and got it done and never bothered to inform me about it." Chavez glanced at the recorder as though to assure himself that it was still taking down everything he said, looked back across the desk at Hunter. "I had to find out about what you're doing from other people. I had to sit there looking stupid and surprised—and admit one of my own men doesn't have enough respect for me to check his operations with me before going ahead with them."

"It wasn't a matter of respect, sir."

"I don't care what you call it, Hunter. As of now your investigation is terminated. Try going on with it and your job will be terminated. Along with your ability to use any branch of government in the future. Is *that* clear enough?"

Hunter took out a photograph of "Sabina Remsberg" and placed it on Chavez's desk. He explained who she was, that she had been nosing around Senator DeLucca's staff, and that she had been with Torriente and Lugo in America and in Europe prior to their being killed during the attack on DeLucca.

Chavez looked at the picture. He did not touch it, but his expression betrayed a hint of new interest. "So?"

Hunter told him about the complicated measures that had been taken to block anyone attempting to trace the girl. "To me that means she has to be a key person in the attack on DeLucca. Maybe *the* key. I suspect if we can find her we'll maybe find out who planned the attack. I don't think you're angry enough at me to ignore that possibility."

Chavez placed a forefinger on the photograph and pulled it closer. He looked down at the face. He was tempted, and it showed. He'd been made to look foolish for allowing one of his men to run an operation on his own in his own way. But if his having done so resulted in breaking the case wide open, he would come out smelling very sweet indeed.

He looked at Hunter again. "*If* I were to consider letting you run with it—just a bit longer—how do you intend to proceed from here? In *detail.*"

"I intend," Hunter told him in a level, formal tone of voice, "to make copies of this picture of Sabina Remsberg. A lot of them. Wherever she's operated, wherever she is now, people are bound to have seen her. Given time, there has to be some lead to her—and to those behind her. I intend to circulate the pictures of her here in Washington, then in New York and then in Europe—in Italy and London, especially around the Howe Clinic."

"I hear the senator's coming out of it better than the doctors anticipated."

Hunter nodded. "He's a tough little guy. And that's bound to be worrying the people who tried to kill him. They may be nosing around the clinic, looking for a way to finish what they missed the first time. This girl, who called herself Sabina Remsberg when she was nosing around Washington, may be the one doing it for them *there* too."

Chavez was silent for some time. He looked at the recorder, at the photograph of the girl, at Hunter. "If I let you follow this lead a while I have to keep State and Defense informed of what you're doing. *Everything* you're doing. That means you have to keep *me* informed, every step you take. No more holding back on me."

"I understand that."

"Don't understand, *follow orders.*"

"Yes, sir."

But what it meant, Hunter knew as he descended to the Pentagon photography lab to make copies of the girl's picture, was that whatever he did from this point on was going to have to be accomplished the day before yesterday. His time was running out fast.

EVEN BEFORE HUNTER left the Pentagon, Chavez had informed his superiors of his decision to let his man run with the investigation just a little while longer. He explained why.

Within an hour Borg knew about it and passed the word to Shevlin's partner, Nat Hallberg.

Which presented Hallberg with a problem. Shevlin's instructions were to notify him *immedately* if the name Sabina Remsberg came up again. Now it had. But Hallberg didn't know how to reach Shevlin at this moment. His latest information was that Shevlin had gone off to meet with William Reinbold. Hallberg had never been informed where those meetings took place.

Finally, he did the only thing he could come up with under the circumstances . . . he encoded the information and sent it to the Munich office of MARS Limited, to be given to Shevlin whenever he made contact. He sent an identical encoded message to the Reinbold Enterprises headquarters in Monaco, addressed to William Reinbold and to be passed on to Shevlin.

Hunter's electronic surveillance teams recorded the message at both places, but since no one had as yet been able to break the MARS code system, they did not know what the message was about.

Nobody at the Reinbold communications center in Monaco understood the code either. But since the message was marked urgent and addressed to William Reinbold, it was sent on to him by shortwave radio.

The Monaco surveillance team picked that up too, though there was no way to determine the location of the radio over which Reinbold received the message.

IN THE SORBIO tower Paul Shevlin finished decoding the message. Reinbold caught the brief spasm of panic in his expression. It was gone when Shevlin turned from the radio table.

"Hunter has photographs of the Medusa," he told Reinbold heavily. "He's making copies for circulation in America and Europe."

Not a ripple disturbed the placidity of Reinbold's pudgy face. "I told you," he said calmly. "A week ago when we learned he had begun digging into her Sabina Remsberg name. Now you will have to admit I was right. She has become too dangerous. She has to be disposed of. And quickly."

Part of Shevlin knew that Reinbold was right. But another part of him refused to accept it. "It's not necessary, I'll get her out of London. Take her to the Far East . . . I know places there where nobody would find her."

Reinbold regarded him coldly. "She is the only direct link between the DeLucca attack and us. Now they have her picture. Sooner or later someone will recognize her. In a year, or five years. From now on your Medusa will always be a ticking time bomb. Are *you* willing to lose everything you have spent the better part of your life building for yourself? *Everything?*"

Shevlin's face got stubborn. "No more than you are. But her appearance can be changed. Plastic surgery . . ."

"And the people involved in performing this change? You would have to eliminate them. And others. You want to make this too complicated. Which means increasing the risks surrounding her. Make it simple. Kill her."

Shevlin said flatly, "I have to try it my way first."

Reinbold just looked at him for a time. His original decision, he saw, had been the correct one. And he had been right to notify Kopacka of it, well in advance.

"Very well," he told Shevlin, "*try* it your way. Get her away from London. Take care of it now. Our other business will have to wait."

It took Shevlin by surprise. He had not expected that Reinbold would give in so quickly.

It continued to bother him when he left the tower and went through the Sorbio ruins toward the waiting helicopter. Reinbold had let him off the hook much too easily. Part of him knew what that could mean, but another part was strangely reluctant to deal with it.

INSIDE THE TOWER Colonel Kopacka came down from his listening post and joined Reinbold. They watched the helicopter lift off and fly north toward the airfield where Shevlin had chartered it. St. Étienne.

"Your estimate of men's emotional responses remains quite accurate," Kopacka said. "He could *not* be trusted to do it, finally."

"At least not soon enough to eliminate further risk. The two men you had Prague send—they are in London by now?"

"They have been for two days." Kopacka watched the helicopter disappear over the mountains. "Shevlin will have to wait at St. Étienne for a flight to Paris. And there he will have to wait for a flight to London. Impossible for him to arrive there before tomorrow morning. By then she will be dead."

He gave Reinbold a slip of paper. On it was a London telephone number and three words.

Reinbold contacted his Monaco headquarters by radio. He told the communications center to call the London number at once and give anyone who answered the message: "Peter is waiting."

When he turned from the radio Kopacka said, "Shevlin has a peculiar attachment to the Medusa. How do you estimate his reaction to learning she has been eliminated?"

"Once it's done he will accept it. Because there will be nothing further he can do about it, and because he *knows* it is necessary but cannot face being responsible for it. The decision will have been taken out of his hands. That is what he truly wants—in his stomach if not in his brain."

HUNTER ENTERED THE office of Special Branch Inspector Ivor Klar, a compact man with a rugged, sleepy-eyed face. Dropping wearily into a chair next to Klar's desk he told him, "Contact. I've just finished showing the girl's pictures to everyone who works at the Howe Clinic. Three of them are quite sure they've seen her in a nearby pub. At different times. Two of them remember mentioning the senator's condition to her."

"That does it then." Klar opened a drawer and took out a copy of the Sabina Remsberg photo Hunter had given him earlier that day. "In that case we're justified in—"

He was interrupted by the ringing of his phone. Klar picked it up, spoke into it, shifted in mid-sentence to passable French and then handed the phone to Hunter. "Your father-in-law, calling from the Riviera. Lucky man."

Over the long-distance connection Lamarck's voice sounded thin and wavery. "You have been difficult to track down, Simon."

"What have you got?"

"A strange phone call from Reinbold headquarters to a number in London. The man who answered did not identify himself. He only asked, what? The caller from Monaco told him: Peter is waiting. That's all. The man in London hung up. End of call. You agree? Strange?"

Hunter jammed the phone into place between his raised left shoulder and his ear and reached for a pencil with his good hand. "Give me the London number." When he had it he said, "Thank you, Olivier. Keep it up." Replacing the phone in its cradle he showed the number to Inspector Klar and told him about the three-word message.

Twenty minutes later Klar had an address to go with the number. It took another half hour for Hunter and Klar to get there—an old brick house in Chelsea two blocks from the King's Road that rented rooms by the week.

"Two foreign gentlemen had the room with that phone," the landlady told them. "Finnish, I believe. Quiet, well behaved. Checked in two days ago, paid for the week, but checked out almost two hours ago."

"Did they *make* any phone calls?" Klar asked her.

"Couldn't. I have a lock on the dial. Too much trouble to keep track of outgoing calls and charge guests for them. Incoming calls don't cost me, of course, so they can get as many as they like and I wouldn't know about it."

"Was there anything about these two foreign gentlemen that struck you as in any way unusual?"

"No. Well, wait . . . yes, there was *one* thing." She paused.

Inspector Klar waited with iron patience.

"They never went out together," the landlady said. "Not even for meals. They went out separately. One of them always stayed in their room."

As soon as they had left the house Hunter said, "So one would always be there to get the phone message."

"Splendid," Klar said. "Now all we have to do is put that together with the message, Peter is waiting. And where do we go from there?"

"I," Hunter told him, "am going back to my hotel, have an early dinner and get enough sleep for a change. I hope you are going to be doing something with that picture of Sabina Remsberg."

Inspector Klar nodded. "She's good-looking enough for some of the tabloids to run it. But not before tomorrow."

AT THAT MOMENT the two "foreign gentlemen" were inside the Medusa's apartment near Covent Garden.

They had phoned first to make certain she was not in. One of them was the STB's most talented locksmith. But the locks on her door were specials, and it had taken him some twenty minutes to open them all without leaving marks. He had also searched carefully before opening the door, and found a bit of transparent tape fastened between the top of the door and the wall above. This he had removed very carefully before they went in.

The other did the interior work while the locksmith stood on lookout at one of the windows, in case the Medusa returned before the job was finished. She did not. The second Czech finally screwed the earpiece of the phone back on and tapped the arm of the locksmith. Neither had said a word since entering the building.

They left the apartment, relocked the door from the outside and stuck the transparent tape back in place. Then they went out of the building, walked to a cab rank and were taken to a small hotel at which they had made a reservation.

Each had two airline tickets. One was for a flight late that night to Amsterdam. The other was for the following morning to Brussels. The one they took would depend on how long it took the Medusa to die. Whichever flight they took, the next stage of their trip would return them to Prague.

Once each hour one of them left the hotel, walked to a public phone and dialed the number at the Medusa's apartment.

Sometime that evening or night she was bound to return, and to pick up the phone when it rang.

The timer was set for a two-second delay. That insured that she would be holding the phone to her ear when the nitro charge inside it exploded.

TWENTY-FIVE

LONDON, NORMANDY, LONDON

WHEN THE Medusa woke it was night and a cold draft blew through the open windows. When she had gone to sleep that afternoon it had been warm and stuffy inside. She had covered herself only with a sheet and had pushed that away sometime while she had slept. She felt chilled now, her bare skin pebbled with gooseflesh.

Swinging herself off the bed, she went to the windows, closed them and pulled down the shades. Then she moved through the dark room and turned on a small bedside lamp, looked at her watch beside it. Still plenty of time.

Going to the small kitchenette she lit a burner under a pot of water, then went into the bathroom and took a hot shower, scrubbing herself all over until the chill was gone from her flesh. After drying herself thoroughly she put on a bathrobe and returned to the kitchenette. The water was boiling. She made herself coffee and a breakfast of ham, eggs and toast. When she was finished she got dressed and prepared to go out to her apartment near Covent Garden.

Since Shevlin had warned her that Hunter's investigation had focused on her Sabina Remsberg name, she had taken a number of precautionary measures—not only against Hunter.

Like Shevlin she had emergency bank accounts in several countries under a variety of names—along with safe-deposit boxes containing cash, false papers and other items she might need. Some Shevlin knew; others he did not. From Shevlin she had also learned to keep emergency bolt-holes ready in areas where she spent a great deal of time. This one-room apartment in the Golders Green neighborhood of London was one such bolt-hole which she had divulged to no one. Her regular apartment near Covent Garden was owned under the name Sharon Horn—the same one she used in Ireland. The Golders Green place she rented on a yearly basis, paying for it by check from an account she kept in the name of Victoria Lear.

Here she had been spending most of each day, much of it sleeping. Nights she would drive out of the city and work off steam hiking and running through the countryside. But twice each day, and once each night, she checked her Covent Garden apartment. Whenever Shevlin could not reach her there by phone, or when he did not wish to use phone communication, he would send a telegram there, or leave some other form of message in her mailbox.

Carrying her shoulder bag she went out to the car she had leased using a credit card made out to the Victoria Lear name. In the locked trunk of the car she kept an overnight bag that contained the essentials she would need if an emergency situation prevented her from returning to either apartment. Getting in behind the wheel, she drove toward Covent Garden.

A few blocks from her apartment there she glanced at her watch, then pulled over to the curb and parked. If there was a message for her, she wanted to be close enough to pick it up quickly. But she still had five minutes to go. She sat in the car and waited.

MAURICE THOMSON HAD retired four years ago after a career with the Metropolitan Police. He had soon found both the inactivity and the low retirement pay galling. Thomson had solved both problems through a connection with a small London private detective agency that farmed out small jobs to him in return for a percentage of his fees.

At precisely ten o'clock that night he climbed out of the Covent Garden underground station and walked toward the girl's apartment. This was one of his simpler jobs. Each morning at eleven o'clock, each afternoon at five, and each night at ten he went there to see if there was any mail or message, then conducted a short routine check of the apartment itself. The girl who owned the apartment, Sharon Horn, was being pestered by an American boyfriend she said she no longer cared to see. She was staying with friends until the man got tired of trying and went back to America.

She had given Thomson copies of all her keys. In the entry of the building he used one of the keys to open Sharon Horn's mailbox. It was empty. Thomson mounted the stairs to her apartment. He examined her door locks with a magnifier. There were no marks of forced entry. The bit of transparent tape was firmly in place where he had left it. Thomson removed it and rolled it into a tight ball that he put in his pocket next to a roll of fresh tape. He then unlocked the door and went inside the apartment, switching on the lights.

He went through the entire apartment. Nothing had been disturbed. The windows were all locked and the bits of tape he'd fastened at their sides were still in place. He had swept the apartment for room bugs and phone tapping that morning; the girl had said once a day was enough, considering the cost of renting the electronic detection equipment. Having completed his job, Thomson sat down in an easy chair to wait for the girl's phone call.

The phone rang an instant later. Thomson frowned at his watch. There was still three minutes to go, and Sharon Horn always called right on the dot. Still . . .

He got out of the chair and went to the phone. Picking it up, he put it to his ear and waited for the caller to speak first—

The sound of the explosion could not be heard three blocks away through the noises of London's night traffic. The Medusa looked at her watch and waited two more minutes. The she got out of the car and walked to a public phone booth. Entering it to make sure nobody else would be using it when she wanted to make her call, she waited another minute, then took the phone and dialed her apartment number.

She got a busy signal. A small line deepened between her eyebrows. Hanging up, she waited a full minute, then dialed her number again. Another busy signal.

Leaving the booth, she strolled in the direction of the apartment, her gaze ranging over the people ahead and buildings on both sides. A police car sped past her and turned into the street where her apartment was located. She hesitated, then walked on, turning into her block.

A crowd was gathering in front of her building, around the parked police car. One of the cops remained beside it. His partner had already gone inside the building. The Medusa drifted closer and looked up at her apartment. All of its windowpanes facing this street had been blown out.

The cop who had gone inside leaned out one of the broken windows and called down to his partner. "Man's been killed by the explosion in here." The one at the car got on the police radio to call it in. The Medusa turned and walked back to her car.

She did not think about what had happened, or even why. Thinking was for later. Now only movement mattered—following the flight plan she had prepared and putting distance between herself and London.

She drove out of London and sped southeast through Kent, toward Dymchurch on the Channel coast. Her precautionary measures had included leasing a 60-foot cabin cruiser in the Victoria Lear name. The boat had twin engines, its fuel tanks were full. She had also topped off its spare tank. More than enough to get her across the Dover Strait.

LATE THE NEXT morning Paul Shevlin finished having a coffee with his contact from the Metropolitan Police and told him he could be reached at the Savoy Hotel if anything further developed concerning the explosion. In the cab taking him to the Savoy, Shevlin wondered where she was: far from London, of that he was certain.

The man killed by the explosion at her apartment had been a private detective hired to protect "Sharon Horn" from an annoying suitor.

Part of Shevlin was proud of her—her sensitivity to nuances was as keen as ever. He had warned her about Hunter, but she had read more in his warning than that—perhaps from his tone of voice, or in his eyes. Perhaps he had even *wanted* to warn her.

He had known, even then, that it could come to this. Reinbold had let him off the hook and hired somebody else to kill her.

To *try.*

Reinbold knew she was formidable, but couldn't grasp *how* formidable. So they had missed.

And now she would be figuring that the attempt had been planned by *him.* And there was absolutely no way he could locate her to persuade her that it wasn't true. Even if he could have gotten in touch with her now, Shevlin realized, she would almost certainly not believe him. And he could hardly blame her.

He hadn't actually done it, but it was too close to truth for comfort. Sensing the possibility, he could have *prevented* it.

How? he challenged himself. By tying up Reinbold and smashing his radio? That picture was farcical . . . he wouldn't have done it, wouldn't have ruined everything he'd built out of his life by doing it just on the chance that that nagging little suspicion had been correct.

He could have warned her of the possibility—on time—by phone or telegram. Or the last time he'd been with her.

But he hadn't. Maybe—face it—he hadn't wanted to.

He had told Reinbold that killing her wasn't necessary. But he wasn't sure that was true. If it *were* necessary, would he have done it? He wasn't sure.

But Shevlin was sure of *some* things now . . . with those photos of the Medusa circulating around London, Hunter and his inspector friend would soon know the apartment belonged to Sabina Remsberg, alias Sharon Horn. They'd have plenty of leads to follow—neighbors around the apartment, people at the Dance Centre, at the Howe Clinic. That was okay, it would keep them busy in London—and wouldn't lead them to the Medusa . . .

Wherever she was by now, Shevlin knew, *he* didn't have to search for her. When she was ready she'd find *him.* And he had better be ready for her when she did.

BY THEN THE Medusa was off the Normandy coast of France, anchoring the cruiser close to the shore between Cap Griz Nez and Wissant.

She had changed to jeans, shirt, rubber-soled boots and a loose-fitting boating jacket. She got the black wig from her overnight bag and put it on, making sure none of her natural hair showed. She put on sunglasses, tied the yellow scarf over her head and under her chin.

From the bag she next took an American passport and credit cards, a French residency permit and bank book, and an international driver's license—all in the same name. Closing the overnight bag, she put it with her shoulder bag in the cruiser's dinghy and rowed to a small, empty pebble beach.

It took her an hour to walk to the town of Wissant. From there she got a bus to Calais, where in a subbranch of the Crédit Lyonnais bank she kept a safe-deposit box under the name of the documentation she was now using. From this she took a large amount of cash in French francs and two envelopes containing documents for her under different names. She then went to an Avis office four blocks away, rented a Mercedes sedan and drove through Calais to a large news kiosk that carried foreign newspapers. As she had expected, that morning's British papers had already arrived via hovercraft from Dover. Buying up all of them, she drove south out of the town. When she was well below it she turned into a country road, pulled over to the side and stopped. There she went through the newspapers to see if there was any mention of the explosion in her apartment.

There was not. But there was something else—one of the papers carried a picture of her. The headline above the photo read: "HAVE YOU SEEN THIS WOMAN?" Under it was printed: "Going by the name of Sabina Remsberg, this young woman of unknown nationality is urgently wanted for questioning in regard to a crime. She is believed to be somewhere around the London area. If you have seen her the police ask that you contact them immediately."

The Medusa pulled down the sun visor of the Mercedes and looked at her reflection in its mirror. It was all right. The wig, sunglasses and scarf altered the shape of her face. Anyone searching for her and looking at her directly might spot her, but nobody who happened to have seen the newspaper picture and who glanced at her in passing was going to recognize her. Even that danger would end once she left the Channel towns behind, and if she avoided large cities. Few towns in the French interior got British papers, and no French papers were likely to carry the picture.

Making sure no one was in sight, the Medusa climbed out of the Mercedes and stuffed the newspapers deep into the mud of a drainage ditch. She got back in the car, drove to the N1 Highway and drove south, keeping just below the speed limit.

She understood the reason for the attempt to kill her. Her picture in the British paper only explained the timing of the attempt. That had made it imperative that it be done immediately. Her existence had become too much of a danger to William Reinbold—and to Paul Shevlin.

But the reason was of no importance. Not to her. Not now.

Shevlin had tried to kill her.

It was possible that he had not actually set it up himself. If he had, it would have been arranged more carefully and she would probably be dead. But he had surely *known* that someone would try it. That made it the same.

Briefly, she argued with herself: Paul Shevlin would never have done that—not to her. Then she reminded herself of what he had said . . . "Don't get stupid. In this business, if you go soft you're dead."

He had tried to kill her.

She felt something inside her that she had never felt before in her life, and she could not identify it. It was as though *Arakel* had betrayed her.

What she felt was neither shock nor hate. It was something that remained lodged in her, like the broken point of an arrow caught between her ribs. It hurt each time she took a deep breath.

The Medusa swung around the outskirts of Paris and took the Autoroute du Soleil, racing south toward the Riviera coast of France.

Her expression became fixed, like frozen lava. Somber, cold, purposeful.

SIMON HUNTER RETURNED to his London hotel the next afternoon after a long morning of following up leads with Inspector Klar. There was no shortage of leads now. Several people around London had recognized the picture of the girl, though none of them knew her as Sabina Remsberg.

At the place where she had taken dance and exercise classes she was known as Sharon Horn. All her fellow students recognized the picture. So did a dance instructor who had gotten friendly with her—and who happened to be the son of a nursing supervisor at the Howe Clinic.

Sharon Horn was also recognized by neighbors as the owner of an apartment where a mysterious explosion had killed a private detective. If the explosion was an attempt to kill *her,* who had set it? And why?

It left Hunter with nothing but loose ends. He still had more digging to do.

There was a message waiting for him with his room key in the hotel lobby. It was from his father-in-law. Hunter went up to his room and placed a call to him in the south of France.

"Another strange occurrence," Lamarck told him. "Last night Shevlin's villa in the hills above Monaco was burned out. Completely destroyed. Shevlin had a man on guard there. He was found by the firemen lying unconscious on the patio behind the burning building. He says somebody he didn't see or hear knocked him out. An official at Reinbold headquarters in Monaco phoned Shevlin and gave him the news a few hours ago. He's at the Savoy in London, in case you didn't know."

"I do know. How did Shevlin take the news?"

"Quietly. Didn't say anything at all for a few seconds. Then he just thanked the man for calling him and hung up."

Hunter chewed on it for a few moments. Somebody had tried to kill Sabina Remsberg-Sharon Horn in London. Now somebody had burned down Paul Shevlin's villa on the Riviera. There were ways the two could be tied together, but he was not sure which way was correct.

"Has anybody down there," he asked Lamarck, "been able to come up with anything this fire might tie into?"

"Not so far. It was definitely arson. But what that means nobody here knows."

SHEVLIN UNDERSTOOD TWO things that it meant:

The Medusa was no longer in England.

The fire destruction of his villa was her declaration of war.

Suddenly he felt very tired. Staring through a window of his Savoy suite down at the oily surface of the Thames, he thought about his house outside Munich. The first home he had ever owned. She knew how much it meant to him. It was her logical next target.

Shevlin put through a call to his Munich office and told them to place more guards around his house there: "Four of them. Day and night. I'll give them the details when I get there."

He slammed down the phone and began packing to fly to Munich.

TWENTY-SIX

SORBIO, MONACO,
CÔTE D'AZUR

THE MEDUSA lay under a screen of juniper and thornbrush, stretched flat on her stomach inside a notch in a high ridge. The mountain wind was cold. Her elbows were braced on the stony ground, her hands holding binoculars steady on the Sorbio ruins sprawling across the other ridge below her.

When a ray of the lowering sun reached through the brush and touched her face she changed her grip on the binoculars. Holding them to her eyes with one hand, she moved the other to shade its lenses so that the men in the ruins would not be alerted by any flash of sun-glint off them.

She wanted Paul Shevlin. She wanted him alone, without protection around him to complicate the encounter.

He never took anyone with him when he went to meet Reinbold . . .

It was almost two years since she had learned about Sorbio. She had been staying with him at the villa above Monaco when Shevlin had received a code message from the Reinbold Enterprises communications center. After decoding it he'd told her he had to go off to meet Reinbold. He didn't tell her where. He never told anybody where his meetings with Reinbold took place. They'd been sunbathing beside his pool when the message came. Shevlin went in to get dressed. After a moment she had gone in too to take a shower in the guest bathroom. She was passing the partially open door of his room when she heard him dialing the phone. Standing close to the door, she had heard him ask for a helicopter to be ready for him. He'd said it would be a round trip and that he would give his destination when he got there in an hour.

When he had come out of his room, dressed to drive off, she had been taking her shower.

He had returned more than four hours later, with a new assignment from Reinbold. They had gone off together to attend to it.

There were two helicopter services within an hour's drive of Shevlin's villa—one in Monaco, the other at the Côte d'Azur airport outside Nice. The Monaco one was closest. It was called Heli-Air. Several weeks later the Medusa had gone to Monaco alone, and broken into the Heli-Air office at night. It had been more than curiosity that had led her to do so. Knowing as much as possible about whatever was going on around her was one of the ways she had stayed alive. Once inside, the rest had been simple. She had found the helicopter service logbooks, looked up the day and time Shevlin had made the trip. The helicopter had gone to a place called Sorbio, half an hour's distance away. It had waited there, then brought the passenger back. The timing of the return was right too: a bit less than an hour before Shevlin had come back to his villa.

She had left the office, relocked its door and waited until the next morning to purchase survey maps of the area. She had found Sorbio on one of them up in the Maritime Alps, marked by three tiny dots to indicate a ruin.

She had tucked it away in the back of her mind, with other information stored for a time when she might need it . . .

That time was now.

The Mercedes had been left at the town of Grasse, where she had rented a camper van and stocked it with supplies to last her two weeks. She had left the van hidden in a pine forest near the point where the dirt road from St. Martin-Vésubie to Sorbio had been cut long ago by the landslide. The rest of the way she had hiked, carrying a sleeping bag and a knapsack filled with enough supplies to last her five days.

If the waiting stretched longer than that she would go back to the hidden van for more supplies. She did not think it would stretch too long. The failure to kill her, or find her, would be worrying Reinbold more with each passing day. Before long he would want to confer with Shevlin again.

Stretched out in her observation post, she waited without impatience. She had, after all, been there for two days.

The men in Sorbio were Asians. Two of them, with a look of hard competence to them. Their movements and weapons advertised their occupation. Guards. Both wore pistols. One usually carried a pump-action shotgun; the other an automatic rifle. On the first day the one with the shotgun had gone off to hunt and come back with some birds and a fox. This morning he had gone out again and bagged three rabbits. They lived and ate in the lower part of one of the two squat Sorbio towers. By day they made occasional patrols around the perimeter of Sorbio. Sometimes one would mount to the top of their tower and scan the area through binoculars. After they had bedded down for the night there were several times before dawn when one or another of them would come out of the tower and take a turn through the ruins.

Now they were both inside their tower, perhaps taking a nap after their lunch. Once more the Medusa studied each of the routes by which she could reach Sorbio: the ones for a night approach, and the single alternative she had decided on if it had to be done by day. Then, yet again, she took an unhurried, detailed survey of the ruins themselves, committing each part of them to memory.

The options open to her would be different by day than by night. Everything depended on *when* Reinbold would come.

Once he was here, Paul Shevlin would come. She had incorporated the method for insuring that into her calculations.

He would come alone. And then it would be just between the two of them. The Medusa and Shevlin.

It felt right, a logical, ultimate conclusion to something they had never been able to complete in any other way, not even sexually. Something that had begun between them with that first appraising look she had given him long ago in the house of Arakel.

Perhaps it had been building in her even further back than that—since the time her father had deliberately lost her in that Malayan jungle—to survive, die or go crazy. She had never understood the odd feeling that had stopped her from killing the man then.

She waited for that feeling to come again, but it had been very many years since she had last felt anything comparable to it. It did not come to her now.

The Medusa watched and waited.

Just before sunset the Asian guards made a final daylight turn around the ruined village, diverging to follow separate routes. One of them stopped outside Sorbio, raised binoculars and scanned the higher slopes where the Medusa was hidden.

She lowered her own binoculars from her eyes and made her mind utterly blank—so that it would transmit nothing that might cause a warning tingle in the man's nervous system. His survey swept on beyond her position. Minutes later he joined his partner, and they went inside their tower.

As it became dark a light appeared in the lowest window opening of that tower. It was their suppertime. More than an hour later, with a half moon riding over the mountain tops, they came out of the tower for another patrol of the village. When they returned, the lamp continued to burn in their tower for about half an hour. Then it was put out for the night.

With night the mountain wind had become frigid. The Medusa ate a cold meal, then slid backward under the bushes to her hidden sleeping bag.

It was still dark when she woke, an hour to go before dawn. Shivering once she was out of the sleeping bag, she put on a heavy wool jacket and ate a cold breakfast, then crawled back to the observation point.

The first streaks of predawn light were fingering the sky when the two guards emerged from the tower for their first morning patrol.

IT WAS MIDAFTERNOON three days later when a helicopter flew in from the west. The Medusa trained her binoculars on it as it put down on the crest outside of Sorbio. But the man who climbed out was not William Reinbold.

The helicopter lifted off and turned back in the direction from which it had come. Colonel Vasil Kopacka reached the ruins and entered them. The guards emerged from cover and greeted him. He briefly spoke to them, then walked on. The Medusa's binoculars followed

Kopacka as he went past the tower where the guards lived to the other tower. He disappeared inside it.

She had no idea who he was. His identity did not matter to her. It was Reinbold she waited for.

AN HOUR BEFORE sunset, another helicopter appeared, this one coming down from the north. It was much larger than the one which had brought Kopacka. When it landed two men climbed out carrying submachine pistols. They stood slightly apart, scanning the ruins and the surround terrain. Reinbold climbed down between them.

The two Asian guards remained inside Sorbio. Kopacka strode out to greet Reinbold. When Reinbold saw him he spoke to his bodyguards. One climbed back into the helicopter and handed two briefcases down to the other. The second bodyguard set them on the ground beside Reinbold and joined his partner inside the helicopter. Kopacka picked up the briefcases and carried them for Reinbold, leading him back into Sorbio.

The helicopter flew off to the north, to wait at the airfield outside Grenoble until whenever Reinbold radioed for it to return and pick him up.

Reinbold and the STB agent entered Kopacka's tower and mounted the steps to the main room, where they settled down to discuss the most recent information gathered by Reinbold for Talgorny's risk assessment—and the dangerous problem posed by the disappearance of the Medusa . . .

From her observation post she glanced toward the lowering sun, just dipping behind one of the higher mountain peaks. She looked down on Sorbio again, waiting.

Gradually dusk settled in. The two guards began their last daylight patrol. A lamp was lit in the upper tower room where Reinbold and Kopacka were conferring.

The Medusa let herself relax a notch. No helicopter could risk landing in this terrain after dark. Reinbold was here for the rest of the night.

It was possible that the first part of what had to be done could be accomplished the simplest way.

It was almost fully dark when the guards returned to their own tower. Soon a lamp was lit inside their window.

She got up from her observation post and made her way down through cover toward Sorbio. There was on need to think out the route as she descended, every step of the way she had chosen was imprinted on her mind. All her senses could be concentrated on listening for sounds from the village, and on making none herself.

The half moon cast a graveyard glow across the Sorbio ruins by the time she got there, deepening the shadows among the crushed and broken houses. She moved through these shadows as surely as though she could see clearly. The light still showed from the lower window of the guards' tower. Silently, she approached until she could see inside.

The guards sat at a wooden table, finishing their supper. The shotgun and automatic rifle leaned against their chairs. She drifted sideways a bit, studying more of the interior. It was a large single room with two bunks in one corner, a gun rack against one wall with boxes of ammunition and more weapons: a machine pistol, another shotgun and two Winchester lever-action carbines.

One guard got up and began stacking the dishes and cutlery in a large tin basin. The other went to a sideboard and uncorked a fresh bottle of wine that he put on the table with their two glasses and picked up the shotgun. The other came to get his automatic rifle.

The Medusa melted back into the darkness. Behind her a section of wall jutted out from a pile of boulders that had rolled from the mountainside across the village and buried the houses in their path. She lowered herself to the ground where it was darkest, in the tight angle where the house wall joined the largest boulders.

A moment later the tower door opened and the guards came out to make their last joint turn around the village before settling down for the night. They shut the door and walked past the Medusa. She waited until she could no longer hear their footsteps.

Getting up from the ground, she went to the tower door, opened it, stepped in swiftly and shut it behind her. Some ten seconds later she came out, returning to the dark angle. She sat down with one shoulder against the wall and the other against a boulder.

The guards returned, passing her hiding place again, and entered their tower . . .

An hour later the lamp inside their room was still burning. The

Medusa got up and moved close enough to the window to look in. After a moment she moved closer, stood there and observed the two guards. Then she walked around to the door and went inside.

IN THE MAIN room of Kopacka's tower William Reinbold sat behind the desk engaged in a rare argument with the STB officer. His control.

"His usefulness is not quite ended yet," he stated sharply.

Kopacka, seated in a chair to one side of the desk, shook his head. "*Another* like him can be found. And we can always create another firm like his—what Senator DeLucca liked to call a Frankenstein Cell. But at this moment Shevlin is becoming almost as much of a problem as his Medusa. When the investigators tire of searching for her, they will concentrate on him again. And if he does not lead them to you, he *may* eventually lead them to her."

"That is precisely why we still need him. Are you unable to grasp that? Shevlin remains our best chance of finding the girl and eliminating her. *After* he has done so, we can discuss again the question of eliminating him . . ."

Kopacka started to repeat himself. "The danger—" He stopped. Reinbold was staring at something behind him. Kopacka twisted around in his chair.

She stood there, holding the shotgun she had taken from the guards' room in one hand. Her finger was against the trigger.

Both men realized who she was, instantly. Kopacka came to his feet.

She told him: "Do not move again."

Kopacka glanced at Reinbold, who had not moved in his chair. He was sitting there, his mouth hanging open. Kopacka didn't blame him —this wasn't anything he was accustomed to or trained for. There was a gun in the top desk drawer, but getting at it was going to be up to Kopacka. He *had* been trained for this.

He edged closer to the desk.

"I told you not to move," she told him quietly. The mouth of the shotgun tilted slightly, covering him.

Kopacka snapped at her coldly: "Put that down and we will discuss this sensibly. Put it *down.*" He knew how to use the tone of absolute authority when necessary. Invariably it froze the men it was used on. He lunged then for the desk drawer—

The shotgun sounded like a cannon in the confines of the room. The concentrated blast of shot struck Kopacka in the face, nearly tearing his head from his shoulders. The force of it did lift his body and hurl him against the wall. He bounced away from it loosely and toppled to the floor.

William Reinbold stared down at the blood, shredded flesh and fragments of bone that had once been the face of Kopacka, and experienced something that had never happened to him before. His whole body began shaking, and there was nothing he could do to stop it.

THE NIGHT STAFF of the communications center at Reinbold headquarters in Monaco received an encoded message from him by radio shortly after midnight. The message was passed on to Paul Shevlin by phone at his home outside Munich.

The message was picked up by Hunter's surveillance teams at both Monaco and Munich; but the code words meant nothing to them.

It meant something to Shevlin. But by that time it was too late to get a flight out of Munich. He had to wait until morning.

At eight o'clock in the morning Klaus Bauer put through a call from Munich to Simon Hunter in London. "There was another one of those code messages last night from Reinbold Enterprises to Shevlin's home here. Shevlin just made a reservation on a plane to the airport at Nice. Flight Number 315. It takes off in half an hour and is due to land at twenty past ten this morning. I cannot tell if this information is useful, but perhaps it will mean something to you."

Hunter put down the phone and thought for a time on what it *could* mean. Nothing concrete, but it was another bit that might be made to tie together with certain previous ones: Someone had tried to kill Sabina Remsberg-Sharon Horn—just before her pictures went into circulation in London. Two nights later someone had set fire to Shevlin's villa in the south of France. Now Shevlin had gotten a code message from the south of France and taken the first flight he could out of there.

Hunter looked at the girls' photograph on his hotel room table, phoned Heathrow Airport, then Oliver Lamarck's home.

Odile answered, told him her father was just sitting down to breakfast and started to ask how London was turning out. Hunter cut her short and told her to get her father to the phone. Having grown up the daughter of a cop before marrying one, Odile managed not to sound hurt or angry as she got Lamarck from the breakfast table.

Hunter told him about Shevlin. "The next flight out of London won't get me down there until a couple hours after he does. I'd appreciate it if you could be there when he lands. Just watch him and see where he goes."

WHEN PAUL SHEVLIN came off the flight from Munich, Lamarck was at an upper window of the Côte d'Azur terminal building, from which he could watch through binoculars without being observed. He had an airport cop inside the lower floor to keep track of Shevlin there. They both saw him transfer to the airport's helicopter service. Twenty minutes later they watched a chopper fly off with Shevlin, heading for the mountains of the interior.

TWENTY-SEVEN

SORBIO, CÔTE D'AZUR,
SORBIO

THE CODE message had instructed him to send the helicopter off as soon as he landed. It was already in the air, flying back toward the coast, by the time Paul Shevlin entered the ruined village of Sorbio—and realized that something was very wrong.

The two Cambodian guards should have showed themselves by now. Neither was in sight.

With no change of pace Shevlin went on into the ruins as through he had noticed nothing. But he shifted slightly to the left with each step as he approached the nearest tower—the one the Cambodians used, putting its bulk between him and the other tower, giving him a few moments during which he was hidden from most of the village. He used those few moments for a burst of speed that put him against the tower wall beside its partially opened door.

He reached under his jacket behind him and drew a Beretta pistol from the holster clipped to his belt at the small of his back. Thumbing off the safety, he spun toward the door, kicking it open and going in with the gun in his fist leading the way, ready to fire at anything that moved.

Nothing inside the room was moving. He took a fast sidestep that placed his back against the wall between door and window, where nobody could see him from outside.

The Cambodians were sprawled across the floor on either side of the table. One of them had a leg tangled in the legs of the chair that had fallen with him. Near the other lay a broken drinking glass. Another glass was overturned on the table next to an opened bottle of wine.

In the center of the table stood a small medicine bottle—the one Shevlin had given the Medusa in London containing the poison for DeLucca.

It was empty now.

Which took care of any small, lingering doubt about whom he was dealing with. She wanted him to know.

His body responses satisfied him that the reflexes he needed were still operating at peak, or near it. Each of his senses had abruptly become sharpened. His mind had automatically stripped itself of every extraneous thought and emotion, focusing swiftly, coolly on the immediate alternatives.

He looked at the gun rack. There were no weapons left in it; and none anywhere else in sight. Outside, he would have no chance with a handgun against a rifle. He could be cut down before getting within effective pistol range of his adversary. But as long as she stayed inside confined spaces the Beretta would be better than a larger weapon. Its line of aim could be shifted faster.

She might be any place in Sorbio, or around it. But she surely would have been where she could watch him walk into the village. She knew where he was. She might not know about the underground passages to the cistern . . .

Crouching below the window level, Shevlin swiftly crossed the room and opened a trapdoor in the floor. A ladder led down into the gloom below, but he did not intend to use it. He shut his eyes for three seconds, then opened them and jumped. He bent his knees as he landed at the bottom, going down into a low crouch and holding the Beretta at arm's length in front of him, his finger poised to squeeze the trigger.

No shot was fired at him. He listened as he gave his vision a few moments more to adjust to the gloom. There was only a heavy silence. The tunnel ahead of him was short and narrow, lit dimly at intervals where there were breaks in its stone vaulting. Shevlin straightened, moved through it quietly as he could. When he reached the cistern he stopped to listen again. Still nothing. He followed another short passage, reached a ladder and climbed to a closed trapdoor at the bottom of the other tower.

Setting one foot high on a rung of the ladder, he pushed open the trapdoor and went up and out in one swift motion, landing on his back, the pistol held above him in both hands.

No one was there. He lay on the floor for several moments, listening, then got to his feet and climbed the steps. He came up into the main room with the Beretta held out steadily, chest-high.

A man with an annihilated face lay between the radio table and the desk. The radio had been smashed.

William Reinbold sagged in the armchair behind the desk, his arms dangling. His head was tilted across the top of the chairback. His tongue protruded and his bulging eyes stared sightlessly at the ceiling.

The yellow strangling-scarf was embedded deep in the soft flesh of his throat.

SHEVLIN BACKED AGAINST a wall, controlling his breathing.

Across the top of the desk lay a lever-action Winchester carbine. He almost laughed, though there was no mirth in him. She would be armed with the same weapon—of that he was certain. That was why she had left this one for him. It fitted with her character, and with what lay between them. This was the way she wanted it. Even.

He hoped it was even. That depended on whether the old reflexes were really still able to function for a sustained period.

There was one window that was dangerous. Through it the desk was in a direct line of sight with the top of the other tower. Shevlin took off his jacket and lowered himself to the floor. He stuck the Beretta back in its belt holster. Then, taking the jacket with him, he snaked across the floor. When he was below the side of the desk he stopped, looking again at the one window that mattered. He could only see sky through it from his angle on the floor. He could not see the top of the other tower, so he could not be seen from it.

Gripping a sleeve of his jacket with his left hand, he whipped the jacket above him, slapping it down on the desk and pulling it back to him. He repeated that. Each time he did, the carbine was dragged a bit closer to the edge of the desk. The fourth time he tried, the carbine fell.

He caught it with his right hand before it hit the floor. Dropping the jacket, he levered the carbine to get the first cartridge ready to fire, then scuttled across the floor and went swiftly back down the steps.

He did not waste time checking out the Winchester to make sure it was fully loaded and operational. He could read her mind better than that. She had left the weapon as a challenge, not a trap.

From the top of the other tower the Medusa saw the carbine pulled off the desk and disappear below her line of vision.

Now it could begin . . .

Carrying her own carbine, she climbed down an interior ladder, and then down another. She did not descend into the lowest room. Just above its ceiling there was a gaping hole in the tower wall. She climbed into the opening and positioned herself, looking down. Below was a mound of stone rubble. Holding the carbine with one hand, she jumped.

She landed just right, feet first with her legs spread for balance. But as it took her weight some of the rubble shifted. She twisted to keep herself from falling.

The unexpected movement saved her.

A shot rang out from a caved-in house near the tower. The bullet burned across her hip and slapped off the tower behind her. She let herself fall, rolling down the side of the rubble pile and then instantly rolling away from it toward the corner of a broken length of wall. Another shot. Splinters of stone were knocked off the corner inches above her head just as she rolled behind it, getting the wall between her and the source of the shots.

She sat up with her back to the wall, holding the carbine ready in both hands. Rising just enough to get her feet under her, she slid along the wall, changed direction and went around a boulder, shifted direction again, entered one side of a shattered house and went out the other. When she reached a protected corner she settled to the ground again and examined the wound.

It was not deep, but blood trickled from it, straining her jeans around the bullet rip.

She reminded herself that she deserved it. He had *known* where she was, had used the underground passage, sprinting through it to get there before she could come all the way down. Paul Shevlin was still the best she had ever met. She would not have to remind herself of that again.

From her pocket she got a handkerchief and stuffed it into the bullet rip, packing it against the wound under her jeans to stop the bleeding. Then she again hefted the carbine in both hands and stayed put . . . no point in circling to get at the place he'd fired from, he'd no longer be there. Deliberately, she thought herself into his head, groping for what he would decide to do next.

Nowhere, she was certain, were there two people who knew each other so intimately as she and this man . . .

SHEVLIN HAD REACHED a break in what had once been the main defense wall of the Sorbio fortress. He crouched low inside the break, breathing hard. He had moved very fast to put distance between himself and the point from which he'd tried to finish her and had missed. She was too quick, even when caught by surprise.

Now she would be stalking him. She knew he would no longer be where he had fired from. Her best tactic would be a wide circling movement around it, checking each possible exist route for tracks. She was good at that; and he was bound to have left some, moving that fast.

But he was where he wanted to be. Below him, outside the wall, a deep dry gully cut away from Sorbio between rugged slopes studded with boulders and scrub pine. Using that gully he could get outside the ruined village and come back into it from a different direction.

Gong to the ground, Shevlin crawled down into the gully. He looked back. As he had thought, the remnants of the defense wall above hid his movement from any point in the village. Keeping low, he went along the gully until he reached the point he wanted, where the gully passed a cluster of high bushes that would screen his swing back up other slopes to Sorbio.

He raised himself slightly and looked back again. All of the village was still hidden except the very tops of the two towers. She would not go up there again . . . that, she would know, would put her in a trap if he were anywhere close to them. He pulled himself out of the gully to move into the bushes—

There was the sharp, flat report of a carbine shot. His cheek was torn as he flung himself into the bushes and dragged himself forward under them. The next shot missed, shredding foliage to his right as he snaked behind the cover of a boulder. There he stopped. Drops of blood ran down the side of his face. He cursed softly, almost gently.

She *had* gone back to the top of a tower, taking a chance that he wasn't near enough to trap her there. Guessing that he wasn't, or just sensing it—or reading his mind. And from down here he was too far to get back in time. She would already be on her way down out of the tower.

But that also meant she could no longer spot the route he took from this point to get back inside Sorbio. And there were several to choose from.

For a long moment Shevlin leaned against the boulder and looked further down the slope in the other direction. He *could* go down there —away from Sorbio, and just keep going.

He could but he wouldn't. He had no intention of spending his life hunting her, or waiting for her to come after him. Let it finish here and now. Either way.

He considered the various routes he could use to get back into Sorbio, then stopped himself. She had read his mind before. He believed that. He chose a route at random, without thought. And he followed it swiftly before she could reach another position that overlooked these slopes. But when he came up just under the village he shifted direction and made the final approach with great caution, using the cover of rockslides and stands of pine to reach another opening in the outer defense wall.

He stepped into the opening, stopped there, listening, then he edged out of it among the ruins. When he was against the side of a collapsing house he stopped again, standing still and listening once more.

She was less than two hundred yards away. Also standing motionless and listening.

Neither could hear the other. But as though sensing each other, they began to move again at the same time, stalking each other through the ruins—their minds and nerves and skills narrowed down to that and nothing else.

BY THE TIME Simon Hunter met his father-in-law at the Côte d'Azur Airport the helicopter pilot had returned from taking Shevlin to Sorbio and Lamarck had talked to him.

"The pilot does not know Shevlin by his real name," Lamarck told Hunter. "But he had flown him to and from Sorbio before. So have other pilots here, a number of times. They have also taken another man there at different times. A Dutchman—or so he claims."

"Have they ever flown a young woman there or back?"

"No. I have already showed them the girl's photographs. No one recalls having ever seen her, in any capacity."

"What's up there? Other than this ruined village?"

"Nothing. Which is of course what makes these flights so curious. It made *me* curious enough to phone Heli-Air in Monaco. They, too, have made quite a number of flights to and from Sorbio."

"Carrying Shevlin?" Hunter asked Lamarck. "Or this Dutchman? Or somebody else?"

"The Dutchman and a man who might be Shevlin. Nobody else."

"How long have these Sorbio flights been going on?"

"Over the past three years, it seems. The pilots say two of the Sorbio towers appear to have been restored somewhat. But that is all—not enough to warrant so many visits, one would think. I was about to phone to some of the other helicopter firms in the general area to find out—"

Hunter interrupted. "I want to go up there and have a look."

"I thought you might. I have had two highly recommended young cops standing by to go with you." Lamarck tapped Hunter's shoulder cast. "Healthy ones. Just in case you happen to need them."

IT WAS SOME years since Shevlin had been in a situation requiring this kind of sustained tension over so long a time. The knowledge was still there, but some of the energy was fading. Fatigue was the most insidious danger in a protracted stalk. It caused careless moves. He could not afford another one.

Not with the Medusa.

He had to get her before his physical resources ebbed below that danger line. Above all, before his nerves frayed and his senses dulled.

A wisp of dust drifted upward some hundred yards ahead of him.

The mountain wind caught it and then it was gone. Swiftly, silently he sidestepped into the corner of what had been a small house. Now only the corner was left; and a section of roof, casting deep shade that concealed him once he was inside the corner. He stood stock-still there, his wariness honed to a renewed sharpness.

The brief drift of dust had risen out of a group of avalanche-crushed houses near the inside of the Sorbio defense wall. That point was shielded from the wind by the wall, the high piles of rock, the remnants of the houses. The only thing that could have stirred up dust in there was something moving over the dry ground.

Shevlin moved out of his corner. He did not move directly toward the point where the dust had been stirred. Instead he began a circling approach, to reach it from one side. Whenever necessary, he shifted direction to keep cover between himself and his goal. He came to an opening in the crumbling wall of a one-room house. The interior was deeply shadowed, but empty. There was a gaping window hole in a side wall, and a larger opening on the other side of the room where a door had been. The door opening could be used for his circling approach. He entered the room and started across it—

The crack of the Medusa's carbine echoed around the ruins of Sorbio. The bullet slashed through the window opening and thudded into the opposite wall, missing Shevlin by two feet.

He ran the rest of the way across the room in a crouch, dove through the doorway, fell into a dusty passageway and rolled into a ruined house on the other side of it. Coming up to his feet, he dodged out the other side of this ruin, went under a crumbling covered alleyway into a third. He stopped, squatting to look over the top of a windowsill toward the source of the shot.

It had come from an area to the right of the point where he'd seen the wisp of stirred-up dust—closer to the inside of the Sorbio defense wall. It had been almost a blind shot. At that distance, with Shevlin moving quickly through deep shadow, she could only have hit him by chance.

Shevlin did not believe it. The Medusa was too methodical a stalker, too good a marksman to waste ammunition. She had done it for a reason—to let him know where she was. Or where she had *been,* when she'd wasted that shot. To draw him into that area.

He studied the outer defense wall close to the right of that area. It was about head high there with a narrow break in it, just wide enough for someone to squeeze through—or *into.* If she were to hide herself inside that break, and wait, eventually she would get him in her sights no matter what direction he used in his approach to the area.

If he approached via the interior of Sorbio.

He surveyed other stretches of the defense wall. In places it was no higher than a man's hip; in others it had been swept entirely away by the avalanche. Not far from his own position it was about shoulder high with a wide break through it.

He backed out of his shelter and angled toward this stretch of wall, circling *away* from the point from which the Medusa's last shot had come. He took each step with ingrained professional caution . . . stirring up on dust, making no sound to give his direction away, keeping concealing cover between himself and the Medusa all the way.

When he reached the wide break in the defense wall he went to his knees and listened, then crawled into the break and stopped again. There were masses of boulders stretching in either direction close to the outside of the wall there, with gnarled scrub trees and tangles of brush growing between them, wild vines crawling over them. Shevlin eased forward, just enough to peer along the outer side of the wall toward the narrow break a hundred yards away.

He could not see her there. If his calculation was correct she was squeezed out of sight just inside that break, waiting for his approach—from *inside* the village. He rose in a tight crouch and moved out, turning in her direction, gripping the carbine.

The line of boulders continued in that direction, past the narrow break a hundred yards ahead, close to the outside of the wall. Shevlin drifted silently forward, staying near the wall, his left shoulder almost brushing against it. He did not look back. Not enough time had elapsed for her to reach the route he'd taken and come around behind him, even if she had guessed what he was doing. He kept looking from one point to another ahead of him—the boulders to his right, the wall top on his left, the narrow break in the wall as he neared it.

Most of his attention focused on that break ahead. If she guessed he might be outside, and swung out of it for a shot at him, he would have her before she could take aim.

A tiny sound among the boulders ahead to the right, across from the narrow wall opening. Shevlin froze against the wall, swinging his carbine to cover the area. A small stone had clicked against rock in there, so faint a sound that he wouldn't have heard it if his hearing hadn't been so sharply attuned.

His surprise—and fear—lasted only a moment. Then he had it under control. He looked again toward the wall-break ahead, thinking his way into the Medusa's mind.

She was too good at this to make that kind of noise by accident. What she had done was to throw a pebble to misdirect his attention—just in case he was outside. If he started into the boulders toward the source of that sound it would put his back to the break in the wall.

He did not. Instead he drew the Beretta from his holster. Holding it in his left hand and the carbine in his right, a finger across the trigger of each, he eased along the wall toward the break. One wary step at a time. When he was two feet away he paused, holding his breath.

Pointing the Beretta downward and training the carbine straight ahead at belly level, he executed a fast spin into the wall break and fired both weapons at the same time.

Even as the double blast rocked against his eardrums he knew his error. Nobody was there.

The Medusa stepped from between two boulders behind him and pressed the muzzle of her carbine against Shevlin's spine at the small of his back.

He sagged a bit, staring straight ahead into the ruins. She had out-thought him: made that small sound deliberately, knowing that he would hear it and knowing how he would interpret it.

He did not turn his head to look at her. He did not drop his weapons. Whether he held or dropped them didn't matter in this final moment.

"Last words," he said. "For the record. It wasn't me that tried to kill you."

"It's the same," she said. "You knew *he* would try. He talked to you about killing me. You could have stopped him. You didn't."

Shevlin took a deep breath of cold mountain air and tilted his head to look at the dying sun. "I warned you I was getting too old."

The carbine dug harder against his spine. Silence behind him.

When she did speak again it was a voice he had never heard from her before. It was difficult for him to identify it as hers.

She said: "Everybody gets old."

SOME TWENTY MINUTES later the helicopter carrying Simon Hunter and the two French cops landed at Sorbio. The found the dead Cambodians; and then they found Reinbold and the faceless man on the floor near him.

They did not find anybody else.

The police teams and French Alpine troopers who combed the area around Sorbio during the next weeks did not find anybody else either.

TWENTY-EIGHT

WASHINGTON, D.C.,
PRAGUE

"So you still haven't discovered who the girl was," Frank DeLucca said.

Hunter shook his head. "Not so far. And not what happened to her. Or to Paul Shevlin either."

They were in the kitchen of DeLucca's home in Georgetown. After Hunter poured them two tall glasses of cold beer Senator DeLucca operated the hand-motor of his wheelchair and scooted ahead into his game room with an angry recklessness. Hunter followed him with their beers, which he set down on the poker table.

"You drive that thing like a hot rodder," he said.

DeLucca wheeled around beside the table, glaring at him. "Driving a wheelchair is *not* what I want to be known for. I have work to do —and I want to do it on my feet." He simmered down, shrugging. "But it'll be another year before we find out if I'll ever be able to do that."

"Take it easy, senator. Reinbold's dead, Shevlin's a fugitive. Based on what's been decoded so far from those microfilms found in Sorbio, you can figure both of their companies will soon be out of business. Your enemies are finished, senator. So you can take your time about getting back into harness."

"Wrong, Hunter. There's never enough time. And there are always more enemies."

A MEETING WAS in progress in the crypt of the Monastery in Prague. Three men attended it: Mikhail Talgorny from the Kremlin, General Hájek of the STB, and a KGB supervisor.

The KGB man was not Josef Petrov. It had been necessary to place the blame for the death of Gallia, and the failure of his risk assessment, on somebody. The logical, expendable choice had been Petrov.

The purpose of the meeting was to determine how they could create another like William Reinbold, Gallia, and plant him in the West. That such an undertaking would require many years was obvious to all three of them. But, as Talgorny said, patience was a cardinal virtue, and luxury, for men who understood that time and history were on their side.